The
Belial
Library

A Belial Series Novel

R.D. Brady

"There were giants in the earth in
those days; and also after that,
when the sons of God
came in unto the daughters of men,
and they bare children to them,
the same became mighty men which
were of old, men of renown."
(Genesis 6:4)

PROLOGUE

Baltimore, Maryland
Twenty-Nine Years Ago

Six-year old Henry Chandler jarred awake, clutching his frayed bear. His breath came out in jagged bursts. He pulled his legs to his chest. Small for his age, he was dwarfed by the twin bed.

Henry's violet eyes darted around the room, straining to hear anything that told him why he'd awoken. He knew his room looked the same as it had when he went to sleep: pale blue paint on top, red on bottom. His stuffed animals, soldiers, board games, and books crammed the shelves on both sides of the door. The ceiling fan turned gently. Its air pushed the toy airplane that hung from the ceiling.

But moonlight shined through his window, casting long shadows across the floor. The shadows, misshapen, looked like monsters reaching for his bed. He clutched Huggles tighter. His mom had assured him there were no monsters under the bed, but late at night like this, it was hard to remember that.

Noises – shouts and crashes – echoed from downstairs.

Trembling, he called out quietly. "Mom?" If she

was next door, she'd hear him. She always did.

More loud bangs echoed up the stairs. He knew those sounds. Gunshots. He'd heard them on TV.

A second barrage of gunfire echoed from the first floor, throwing him into panicked motion. He struggled to free himself from his blankets. Gripping Huggles, he sprinted across the room, jumping over the toys scattered on the floor.

He peeked through the crack in the door. The lights in the foyer downstairs were on, casting the circular stairwell in a soft glow. More thumps came from downstairs, and his father screamed.

Feeling like his heart was going to gallop out of his chest, Henry ran from his room to his parent's room next door. He flung open the door. The giant bed was still made. His mom's lace pillows were perfectly positioned on the lavender quilt.

Where was his Mom? He searched the hall wildly, his heart pounding. Where was everybody?

As if on cue, footsteps pounded up the stairs behind him. He whirled around. But he knew his parents' footfalls. It wasn't them charging up the stairs. His mother's words floated through his brain. *Trust your instincts, Henry. If they tell you to run, you run.*

Without another glance, he sprinted down the hall. He rushed past door after door – the bathroom, music room, study, office, sewing room, another bathroom.

His little legs struggled to move faster. Why was this hall so long?

He kept his eyes focused on the little door two feet off the ground at the end of the hall. He jerked to a stop at the dumbwaiter, sliding the door open with a bang. Throwing Huggles on the tray inside, Henry clambered in after him.

"Hey!" A man in black charged down the hall towards Henry.

Henry slammed the door shut, locking it. His small hands curled around the thick ropes, pulling on them, lowering himself to the kitchen below. Above him, the wood splintered as bullets crashed through it. The man started kicking at the door.

"Come on, come on." Tears streaming down his cheeks, Henry's words came out in a hiccupped burst as he pleaded with the ancient pulley system to move faster. The lock above him gave way just as he reached the bottom.

Henry struggled to open the latch in front of him with his trembling hands. He yanked and yanked on the small metal handle, but it wouldn't budge. "No, no, no," he screamed.

A man's head appeared though the opening above him, two floors up. He took aim. "Gotcha, kid."

Henry covered his head with his hands just as the door next to him shot open. Two arms reached through the opening, yanking him into the dark kitchen. Henry screamed. He fell on someone as bullets slammed into the tray behind them.

Soft arms curled around him. "I've got you, baby."

Henry flung his arms around his savior. "Mom," he sobbed out.

She hugged him to her and then stood him up, firmly grasping his hand. "It'll be okay, honey."

He nodded, trying to hold back his tears. For the first time, he noticed the body stretched across the back doorway, the gun his Mom held in her other hand. "Mom?" his voice cracked.

She squeezed his hand, turning her violet eyes to him. "I won't let anyone hurt you."

He stared into her eyes, knowing she was telling the truth. "Where's Dad?"

She went still. Fear slashed across her face. "Protecting us."

Gunfire came from the front of the house and footsteps once again pounded down the stairs.

"Stay behind me," his mother ordered, releasing his hand. She gestured for him to get low behind the counter as she aimed the gun for the kitchen door. More gunfire rang out just beyond the door and a man yelled. Henry couldn't tell who it was. A body fell against the wall from the other room. Hard. Henry jumped at the sound.

Slowly, the door opened. A tall man stood silhouetted in the dim light. "Vicki?"

With a cry, Henry's mother ran across the room, catching his father as he fell. Henry ran to help. Stumbling under his father's weight, the three of them crumpled to the floor. His father gave a small cry of pain.

Henry helped his mother roll his father onto his back. Even in the dim light, Henry could make out the trauma that ravaged his father's body. Bullet wounds dotted him, blood from his chest still pumped out. His mother tried to staunch the blood with her robe.

Her father took her hands. "It's too late for that now."

"No," she argued. "I don't believe that. You can-"

He cut her off, his voice gentle. "Vic, I'm going."

Henry stared at his Dad, trying to understand what he meant.

Tears streamed down his mother's cheeks. She ran her hand along his father's face. "I love you."

His Dad held her hand to his cheek. "I owe everything good in my life to you."

"Did you take care of all of them?" His mother asked.

His Dad nodded and then grimaced. "But you'll need to find out who sent them."

"I will," she promised, clutching his hand.

His father turned his eyes to Henry. "I'm sorry for leaving you, son. I wish I could stay." He held out his other arm.

Henry felt the air leave his lungs. His father was dying. He threw himself to his father's side, sobs wracking his body. He felt his father fight to breathe. Even now, as his Dad struggled to stay with them, he felt his father's strength. How could he be dying? Who'd done this to him? Why?

As his father's heartbeat slowed, Henry gripped him tighter, as if somehow he could keep him here. As if he could give his Dad his own strength. He looked into his father's face. "No, Dad. Don't go. Don't die."

His father ran a hand through Henry's hair with a smile. "You'll be okay. Always remember how much I love you."

With his last breath, his father turned to his mother. "You must keep him safe, Victoria. Don't let anyone know who he is."

CHAPTER 1

Seven Months Ago
Las Vegas, Nevada

Sebastian Flourent tossed the handful of pills into his mouth. His shaking, liver-spotted hand reached for the glass of water. He hated taking the things, but his doctors insisted. Putting down the glass with a thud, he stood, reaching for his cane. Another indication of how far he'd fallen.

He used to be a man feared, both physically and mentally. Now only one of those was true.

He walked out of the kitchen and down the hall. A wall of windows lined the entire left side of the house. He glanced out with a grimace. Red desert rock stared back at him. He longed for the lush green fields of his family's Georgia plantation. But his doctors warned against the humidity. He'd been medically banished to this desert wasteland.

Instead of the home his family had lived in for generations, he was living his final days in a newly polished house. The architecture firm had almost swooned over the prospect of building this home into the side of Red Canyon.

At least he was able to surround himself with his things. Rembrandt, Monet, and a Picasso he'd picked up in Paris decades ago were the only souls to bear witness to his passage. He paid his staff well to keep his home immaculate and themselves out of sight.

He opened the door to his office, nodding in approval. The report he'd requested was already on his desk. The desk itself shined in the early morning rays from the windows. Crafted out of the timbers of an ancient Viking ship, he had it polished every morning. Vikings were his ancestors. He could trace his lineage back to Erik the Red and his famous offspring, Leif Ericson. Both were men of vision like him.

He took his seat behind the desk, pulling his glasses from the top drawer. Leaning back, he pulled the report closer. A grant had recently been approved to allow two archaeologists to catalogue the Crespi collection down in Ecuador.

Hmmm. This could be an opportunity. He reached over and hit a button on his phone.

A minute later, his assistant Gerard Thompson, who'd been with him for four years, appeared in the doorway. "Yes, sir?"

Jealousy flared as it always did when he saw Gerard. Only thirty years old, he was the picture of vitality. Blonde hair with brown eyes, a strong build, and military posture, he was everything Sebastian had once been.

At seventy-two, Sebastian's back had begun to curve and his once-blond hair was now perfectly white. But his blue eyes and, most important, his mind were as sharp as ever.

He gestured for Gerard to enter. "Tell me about

the two archaeologists attached to this grant."

Gerard nodded, obviously prepared for the question. "The lead archaeologist is Jennifer Witt. Age 28, single. Biological parents unknown. Adopted by the Witt family at age ten."

"Her research?"

"Interesting. Pre-diluvian civilizations. She received quite a bit of attention with a recent article on ice dams and their relationship to catastrophic flooding at the end of the last ice age."

Sebastian nodded. *Smart girl.* He remembered the article.

Gerard continued. "This is the second time she's worked with the Shuar people. By all accounts, she has quite a bond with them, particularly with their leader, Lucia Nunink."

Sebastian sat back, his hand on his chin. "And the other archaeologist? Is she the same woman from the Montana incident?"

"Yes. Dr. Delaney McPhearson. She has a Ph.D. in criminology and is finishing up her work for a second doctorate in archaeology. She has been identified as being critical in the uncovering of the Montana site."

Sebastian had to admit that the woman had shown incredible fortitude and intelligence. He'd always thought there was more to that story than had been publicly revealed, more, in fact, in line with his own quest.

And now she was in Ecuador. That couldn't be a coincidence.

Sebastian flipped through the report. The grant would begin three months from now. Maybe these archaeologists were the key to finally fulfilling his family's legacy.

"There's one other development you should be aware of, sir."

Sebastian glanced over his glasses, gesturing for Gerard to continue.

"Grevigan, the oil company, is renewing its campaign to get the Ecuadorian government to sell parts of the Amazon rain forest for oil refining. One of the areas they're interested in incorporates the Shuar land."

Sebastian sat back in his chair, stroking his chin. This development wasn't entirely unexpected. Oil companies had been trying to move into the rain forest for the last decade, but the indigenous people of the region had managed to block them at every turn. "Is there any reason to believe Grevigan will have any more luck this time?"

Gerard nodded. "They've retained new counsel, who are known for accomplishing the impossible. They're not above bribing judges to do so."

Sebastian nodded. He approved of the mindset: focused on achieving the goal no matter who or what got in the way. But in this case, it ran counter to his own plans. He couldn't have the oil companies destroying what he sought. He knew their methods would do just that. Or worse, they could stumble over the find and keep it for themselves. Neither option was acceptable.

He let out a breath. "Put the contingency plan into play. As soon as it becomes necessary, initiate it."

"Yes, sir."

Sebastian placed the report aside. "How's our

guest behaving today?"

"Still unhelpful."

Sebastian nodded. It had been a week, and still nothing. "That will be all."

Gerard gave a respectful bow before backing out of the room. Sebastian pushed away from the desk, reaching for his cane. Slowly, he made his way out of the office and down the hall.

He reached the stairs to the basement and paused to take a breath. He should have installed an elevator, but vanity had kept him from doing so. He shook his head, steeling himself for the descent.

He grasped the rail and slowly made his way down. Reaching the bottom, he paused again, his legs beginning to shake. He waited, knowing from experience that, shortly, the trembling would cease.

A minute later, pushing himself from the wall, he walked around the corner, heading for the lone door on the right-hand side of the hall. One man stood guard at its entrance. The guard opened the door for Sebastian as he drew near.

Screams assaulted Sebastian's ears: proof once again of the wisdom of adding the soundproofing.

Two guards nodded at him as he entered, but quickly returned their eyes to the captive across the room. Sebastian approved. With this enemy, no matter what state he might be in, vigilance was life and death.

He waved his hand in front of his face, trying to push away the smell of burnt flesh and rank body odor. But the repugnant smells crawled through his nose, stinging his throat. He struggled not to gag.

Across the room, a man was strapped to a metal cross, his frame gaunt, his body held up only by the binds that lashed him. An unkempt beard covered his face and he wore shredded jeans. But he had no noticeable injuries. His skin was unmarked.

Sebastian took in the state of the prisoner with a mere flick of his eyes, his attention directed instead on the man standing in front of the captive. At six-foot-five with overly-developed muscles, the man was a testament to pharmaceutical companies abilities to develop a better body. Not that Sebastian cared. What the man did with his own body was his business, so long as it never got in the way of his missions.

The behemoth's hair was cut tight to his head. A jagged scar wound its way from the corner of his left eye to the edge of his mouth. His grey t-shirt was stained with sweat and blood.

"Hugo, how's it going?" Sebastian asked.

Hugo Barton turned with a smile, his wide face looking even wider. "He's not cooperating."

Sebastian sighed with a nod. The prisoner stared insolently back at him.

Sebastian wasn't sure if it was stubbornness or a compete lack of knowledge that made the man unforthcoming. It was time to find out. He waved Hugo back and walked up to the prisoner. "Look at me."

The man met his gaze with hostility, but didn't speak. Sebastian gestured to Hugo, who took a machete and jammed it into the man's stomach. A scream tore out of the man's chest.

Hugo yanked the knife out, leaving a gaping hole.

"Can you all read the books?" Sebastian asked.

The man's eyes were wild with pain.

Sebastian nodded at Hugo.

Hugo stepped forward. "You were asked a question. Can you all read the books?"

Hugo took a serrated knife off the table next to him, plunging it into the man's side and dragging it towards the front, leaving a gaping trail.

The man screamed again. "No."

Sebastian put a hand on Hugo, who immediately stepped back. Sebastian stepped closer. "No? You can't read the books?"

The man shook his head. "No. We can't."

Sebastian turned his back to the man, his shoulders dropping. Damn. This had all been a waste of time. He needed to find another avenue.

"Sir," Hugo called after him, "what should I do with this one?"

Sebastian glanced back over his shoulder. The bound man's wounds were already beginning to heal. "He's of no use to us. Get rid of him."

CHAPTER 2

Present Day
Cuenca, Ecuador

Delaney McPhearson sank down to the cool, concrete floor of the hallway outside the vaults of the Central Bank of Ecuador. She rubbed the crick in her neck that had appeared hours ago and only gotten worse.

Her feet were no better. Days of standing had left them aching. She shook them out, trying to work out the kinks. In spite of the discomfort, she felt a sense of contentment as she stared at the wonders of the Crespi Collection in front of her.

Through the doorway of the bank vault, a three-foot statue of a golden man with four arms and four toes on each leg grinned at her from a metal shelf. Next to him lay half of a golden sphere that was two feet wide and had a three-inch lip covered in unknown symbols. On the shelf below sat a sheet of gold depicting a pyramid with snakes writhing in the sky and elephants on the ground.

The depictions of elephants alone should convince the skeptics of the ancient nature of the artifacts. Elephants had once existed in South America, but the last known elephant-like creature, the cuvieronius, had been extinct since 10,000 BC. The dawn of the last ice age had been the death knell for the entire species. That meant the artifacts in all likelihood dated from before that time period.

She sighed. If only there'd been enough carbon in the metal to date, all the skeptics could be silenced.

Laney took a sip of water, glancing around at the rest of the vault, filled to the brim with gold, silver, and other metal artifacts. She scooted a little to her right, allowing her a view of one of her favorite relics: sheets of gold covered in an undecipherable script. Some argued the artifact was final proof that the Incans had indeed had a written language, but others argued the language predated the Incans by hundreds, if not thousands, of years.

Together, the artifacts, which filled four vaults, were known as the Crespi collection: objects amassed over decades by a Roman Catholic priest in the mountains of Ecuador.

The collection had been moved to the Central Bank of Ecuador in the early 1980s after a fire had destroyed the original location and over half the treasure. The source of the artifacts remained unknown, but whoever the civilization had been, they'd been advanced. Highly advanced.

Laney took another sip of water, unable to believe how lucky she was to be part of this project.

"I see you're taking a break in your usual spot." Jen Witt smiled as she walked out of the vault two doors down.

Laney returned the smile, knowing Jen was the reason that she was here. When they'd met back in graduate school, Laney had been intimidated by her.

Standing six feet tall, with a Korean - American heritage, and an athletic build, Jen was stunning. She was also brilliant, compassionate, and committed to unearthing ancient civilizations that pre-dated known history.

Jen had contacted Laney almost nine months before about joining the expedition to Ecuador. Needing a change and some research for her dissertation, she'd leaped at the opportunity.

They were dressed almost identically: khaki shorts, tank tops, and hiking boots. In fact, since she'd arrived, that had been the entirety of Laney's wardrobe.

But their clothing was the only thing similar about their appearance. Laney was Jen's physical opposite in every way. Standing just under five-foot-four, with skin so pale it was practically translucent, a riot of red hair, and green eyes, she felt extremely average compared to Jen's more exotic looks. Luckily, Jen seemed completely oblivious to her beauty, so Laney didn't have to hate her.

Laney gestured at the gold sheets. "You can't beat this view. I still can't believe Crespi gathered all of this without any effort. It's amazing."

Jen slid down the tiled wall to sit next to her. "Well, the Shuar's thought the artifacts were fitting tributes for the priest who helped them. Still, it does boggle the mind."

Laney nodded, amazed even more now by the story as she stared at the unbelievable relics in front of her. Father Carlo Crespi had been assigned to Cuenca, Ecuador back in 1923. The indigenous people of the area, particularly the Shuar tribe, grew incredibly fond of him. In return for his kindness, they began bringing him artifacts, although they never revealed the source of their gifts. By the time of his death in 1982, he'd amassed the largest collection of metal artifacts in all of Ecuador.

The tales of the unknown source grew, though, especially the tales of the metal library. It was an incredible collection of books alleged to hold the knowledge of the ancients.

Giggles from down the hall broke into Laney's thoughts. An eight-year old girl, her dark brown pigtails and the skirt of her pale blue dress flying behind her, sprinted towards them. Hector the bank guard ran behind her, his large stomach and jowls jiggling, his face an unnatural shade of red.

Elena Nunink glanced over her shoulder with an infectious laugh, keeping just out of the poor man's reach. She stopped with a giggle next to Laney. "Lunch time?" she asked in flawless Spanish

Laney laughed but she tried to wipe the smile from her face as Hector reached them.

With one arm propped against the wall, he struggled to catch his breath. "Last warning, Elena. No running. Next time, I'll have to ban you from the bank."

The grin dropped from the little girl's face, her dark eyes now serious. She wrapped her arms around his knees. "Oh no, Hector. Please don't do that."

He patted her on the shoulder and winked at Laney. "Just no more running, okay?"

"Okay. No more running."

With a wave at Laney and Jen, he headed slowly back to the stairs. That was probably the most exercise he'd had in years.

Laney opened her arms to Elena, and she leaped into them. This time, Laney didn't hold back the laugh. No one had more joy for life than Elena. It was contagious. "So, little queen, what have you been up to today?" Laney asked in Spanish.

"I helped Nana with her vegetables. She made a basket for you. She said to pick it up when you come to dinner."

Elena was in town for a doctor's visit. Laney and Jen had agreed to bring her back to her village tonight. Elena's Nana was the unofficial leader of the Shuar tribe. Technically, the Shuar were egalitarian, but Nana, more times than not, spoke on the tribe's behalf in legal and public matters.

The Shuar had been around since before the Conquistadors, and, if the rumors were true, even back to the ice age. They had a small village a few miles outside of town. They were reputed to be the people who knew where the Crespi collection originated.

Laney and Jen had first met Elena and her Nana due to the village's connection to the Crespi artifacts. But now, there was genuine affection there. Laney still hoped they would help illuminate the origins of the collection, but even if they didn't, their kindness and joy had been a soothing balm these last few months.

Laney pushed Elena's bangs out of her eyes. "What does Nana want to speak with us about?"

Elena's face became serious. "I think Nana's worried."

Laney exchanged a look with Jen. Kids tended to pick up and share everything. If Elena said her Nana was worried, it was probably true.

"Do you know why?" Jen asked.

Elena shook her head. "No. But Manuel came yesterday."

Elena stopped talking, but Laney knew all about Manuel. Manuel Centros was the tribe's lawyer. Although the Shuar were a small indigenous group, the modern world was very interested in them, in particular, the oil companies. The tribe had been embattled in legal disputes with one oil company after the next since the 1960s. The land they'd called home for thousands of years was apparently resource-rich.

Laney gave the little girl a hug. "We'll talk to Nana tonight and see if we can help."

Elena's smile returned. She switched from Laney's lap to Jen's. "What did you find today?"

Jen pushed Elena's bangs back from her forehead. "A picture of a dinosaur. Would you like to see it?"

Elena bounced in place. "Yes, yes, yes!"

Laney smiled at Elena's exuberant response. She'd had pretty much the same reaction when she'd found the gold sheet earlier. Logically, she and Jen knew dinosaurs existed well before the age of man. Yet the sheet depicted what could only be described as an Apatosaurus, a large long necked, herbivore. How on earth had this lost civilization known what they looked like?

Jen glanced at Laney. "You coming?"

She shook her head. "'Fraid not. I have a Skype date with my uncle."

"Tell him I say hi." Jen stood with an easy grace and picked up Elena, twirling her around. Their laughter trailed behind them as they disappeared into one of the vaults.

Laney grabbed her backpack, headed down the

hall, and up the stairs. Hector buzzed her out at the top with a smile. Laney noted he didn't get up from his chair and was leaning heavily on his desk. He really needed to exercise more.

Walking through the bank, she waved at the two female tellers. She pushed open the heavy door, and the warmth of Ecuador enveloped her.

When Jen had first mentioned the expedition, Laney had pictured the Amazon rainforest - a hot, steamy jungle. She'd been happy to find that while the rainforest was part of the Ecuadorian ecosystem, it was farther east than Cuenca. Cuenca, located in the shadows of the Andes Mountains, was temperate year-round. The summers never went much hotter than eighty degrees Fahrenheit and the nights were cool. It definitely beat upstate New York's summer heat.

And with its beautiful homes with red brick roofs, it was incredibly picturesque. After her last year, she could definitely use picturesque.

She headed for the stucco fountain across from the bank. The motto of the city was engraved in its base: Primero Díos, Después Vos - *First God, Then You.* A fitting place to chat with her uncle.

Setting up her laptop in a shaded spot, she hit the power button. Waiting, she looked over at the snow-topped Andes in the distance. A chill came over her as she remembered the last time she'd been near a mountain range. She'd barely escaped with her life, her uncle as well. If not for Jake, . . .

She closed her eyes, shutting down that train of thought. For the last three months, he'd been working his way into almost every thought, and each time was a little more painful than the last.

Her computer beeped, letting her know the connection had gone through. She shook her head, trying to push the emotions away. Her feelings hadn't changed, and neither had his. Only their geography had.

"Impossible to deny and impossible to maintain," she murmured.

A man with red hair, striking blue eyes, and the white collar of a Roman Catholic priest flashed onto the screen. Father Patrick Delaney smiled, the few wrinkles he had showing at the corners of his eyes. "Hi, sweetheart." His Scottish brogue sounded more pronounced through the computer.

Laney smiled, in spite of the pang of homesickness his image elicited. "I'm good. But I miss you. And Kati and Max." *And Jake*, a voice whispered in the back of her mind.

"I just spoke with Kati a few minutes ago." Kati Simmons was Laney's best friend. Laney shared a home with Kati and her son Max. It was hard to be away from them. After a rough childhood, Laney appreciated how important it was to have people you cared about in your life.

"They're doing great, but Max keeps asking when you're coming home."

Laney smiled at the mention of her housemate's son and her heart ached just a little bit more. He was four, and growing up so fast. She hated missing any of that time.

"He keeps asking me if you've found your gold yet. He thinks you've become a pirate."

She chuckled. She'd told Max she was looking for buried treasure. And in a way, she supposed she was.

Cataloguing Crespi's artifacts was the official explanation she and Jen had put on their grant application, but they were really looking for the source of the artifacts.

"Well, we did find some incredible artifacts hidden in the back of the vault today. One depicted a dinosaur."

Her uncle's brow furrowed. "A dinosaur? How's that possible?" Her uncle was an archaeologist for the Church. She knew his brain was already trying to sort out any practical explanation for the unusual find.

"Maybe its finally proof for the Texas footprints," she joked.

While research by alternate archaeologists had convinced Laney that the date for the origins of civilization had been underestimated, she was only willing to move that date back thousands of years, not millions. Early in the twentieth century, rumors began to speculate about the existence of the fossilized footprints of man and dinosaur together along the Paluxy River in Texas. In 1968, researchers began the first of a series of investigations into the authenticity of the tracks.

By 1982, the argument that the fossils were proof that man and dinosaur had co-existed was debunked. But a few groups, mainly conservative religious groups, continued to argue that man and dinosaur roamed the earth together at some point.

"Or maybe its proof that some dinosaurs actually survived beyond the 65 million mark," Patrick mused.

Now, that argument she wasn't completely against. Some native groups even reported seeing dinosaur-like creatures in remote areas. "Are you trying to justify

16

Nessie again?"

"Well, I did race with her when I was younger. Of course, I let her win. She's an awfully sore loser."

Her uncle had raised Laney since she was eight. One of his favorite stories was about how he'd befriended the Loch Ness monster as a child. She'd believed the stories until she was a teenager.

Laney smiled. "I swear, Uncle Patrick, each day has been one amazing discovery after the next."

"Any luck finding the source?"

"No, not yet. We know the Shuar people are the ones with the most connection to it, but they haven't shared that information with us. But we've been honest about the fact that we're looking for it."

"Was that wise?"

"If you met them, you'd understand. They're good people. I have a feeling this source is their most guarded secret. The only way they'll trust us is if we're honest with them. And I wouldn't feel right getting the information any other way."

He smiled. "You're honest to a fault. It's undeniably one of your best qualities."

"Okay, you're making me sound like a saint."

"Well, you're also stubborn, single-minded, forgetful–"

"Gee, that's much better."

"Just makes you human."

His turn of phrase gave her pause. "Speaking of human, any signs of our new friends?"

Her uncle was overseeing a dig in Montana. Last year, they'd help uncover the site that pre-dated the Fertile Crescent by thousands of years. It held startling information about a group of superhumans, with incredible abilities. The two they'd run into had been hell bent on destroying the world, and one had almost succeeded.

He shook his head. "Happily, no. Although the site does have some intriguing information to provide. It looks like when they're born, the Fallen aren't necessarily aware of who they are. Awareness only dawns later."

"Huh," Laney said, digesting the new information. "That's interesting."

Patrick crooked an eyebrow. "I know that look. What are you thinking?"

"Well, it opens the door to the possibility that they're not all evil. It's the nature versus nurture debate. Hypothetically, one of them could have been born to a good family, raised with morals, a conscience. If that's the case, they might potentially not be like Gideon or Paul. They could be good."

She shook her head. "But that's only a theory. Who knows? Maybe they're all born psychopaths."

Gideon and Paul had been truly without conscience, and more powerful than anyone had a right to be. She shuddered at the memory. *Time for a change in the conversation.* "So, tell me about how your research is going. Last time we talked you were preparing to announce some of your findings."

He smiled. "We're already getting pushback from the established groups. History will have to be re-written. I'm looking forward to the coming debates." He paused. "I hear Jake's getting back from the Middle East today."

"Subtle, Uncle, real subtle."

"What? You're both good people, stubborn but

good."

She sighed. "Uncle Patrick, Jake and I are fine. We're just having some communication difficulties."

She kept her tone light. She didn't want to talk to her uncle about Jake. She and Jake were fine, sort of. They just hadn't spoken since before she'd come down here. Before she left, he'd been out of the country. Two different continents, different time zones, both enmeshed in work. Trying to cram a relationship into that kind of schedule just didn't work.

The last time they'd spoken, they'd agreed to keep their relationship light. Laney had even suggested they take a small break. She had hoped he would say he didn't want one. But instead, he agreed it was a good idea. God that had stung.

"I don't think so, Laney. I saw you two together. You don't throw that kind of thing away. It was just bad timing –"

Laney cut him off. "And now I'm in South America. So even if I was interested, the timing isn't any better."

Patrick sighed. "Fine. I'll drop it, but I still think you're being stubborn."

"Noted," Laney replied, irritation slipping into her voice.

Patrick raised his hands. "Okay, okay. Let's switch topics before you disown me. Tell me more about the Crespi collection. Is it everything you thought it would be?"

Laney took a breath, trying to tamp down her annoyance. She rarely got to speak with her uncle these days and she didn't want to ruin it. Besides, she knew he was just looking out for her.

With a deep breath, she expelled her resentment. "It's even more than I thought. Descriptions and pictures simply don't do it justice. It's impossible to look at these artifacts and not wonder at the skill of the artists. Even without the source, there's enough work with what Crespi has collected to keep us busy for a while."

Her uncle's face dropped. "A while? Are you going to extend your trip?"

"No, but I'll be coming back here sooner than I planned. I thought I might see if Kati and Max want to come. Maybe I can even talk Henry and Danny into coming down. Although we'd have to make sure there was a committed internet connection. Danny would never survive without his computer."

Henry Chandler was the CEO of the Chandler Group, an international think tank. Danny was his colleague, although considering Danny was an emancipated thirteen-year-old genius, "unofficial son" might be a better characterization.

Patrick smiled. "Maybe I could join you guys. The dig here's going well and I think I could spare the time."

The idea of her family sharing in this research would make it all perfect. "I would love it. I'll be home in two weeks. I was hoping to return here within two months. Do you think you could make that work?"

"I'll juggle a few things. It doesn't feel right for us all to be so far apart."

Laney knew what he meant. Although she'd been away before, being on a different continent made the gulf seem even wider.

"I'm going check in with Henry when we get back

from the mountain camp," Laney said. "I'll ask him about the trip then."

"The mountain camp?" The worry lines Laney knew so well appeared above her uncle's eyes. "I really don't like you staying out there."

"It'll be fine. And, heck, Jen's spent so much time in these woods, she's practically a native. Besides, we're having dinner with Nana. I think she may be ready to take us into her confidence."

"Just be careful. The mountains are no place for a girl like you."

Laney snorted. "Right. You raised me to be such a delicate flower."

Patrick's parenting skills had included the normal focuses: kindness, independence, and working hard. That upbringing, however, had also included martial arts and weapons training. Which might be surprising for a priest, but not for a priest who was also a retired Marine.

And after Montana and being shot, Laney had doubled her training efforts, even here in Ecuador. Learning there were beings sharing the world that were stronger, faster, and damn near indestructible had been an incredible motivator. Strength training, endurance runs, and even more martial arts were now a core part of her everyday life.

"I won't be able to speak with you for a few days, though. Reception isn't great where we'll be."

The worry lines reappeared. "A few days?"

She smiled. "Don't worry. I already had my brush with violence back in Montana. Statistically, the likelihood of me experiencing any more is right up there with me winning the lottery."

CHAPTER 3

Baltimore, Maryland

Jake Rogan blinked as he stepped onto the landing at the top of the stairs outside the Gulfstream 550. The twelve-hour flight from Israel had been uneventful and he'd managed to sleep for most of it. And yet somehow he still felt like road kill.

"Good to be home." Jordan Witt stopped behind Jake, slapping him on the shoulder.

"It would be better if there wasn't a little man in my head trying to pound his way out."

Jordan stepped around Jake, his blonde hair shining in the bright sunlight. "Hey, we spent a month in the Middle East. Neither of us got shot and neither did any of our crew. I think we deserved one night of heavy drinking. And it's not like we can visit hookah bars on the beach here. Come on, you have to admit, it was a good time."

"Okay. It was good. But I'm getting too old for those nights."

Jordan headed down the stairs. "Nah, you're just out of practice."

Wincing as the bright sun hit him full in the face,

Jake shook his head. He didn't care what Jordan said. He really was getting too old for this.

Walking down the short steps, he watched the rest of his group meet the important people in their lives. Sean from tech was greeted by his partner Todd. Sheila's big brood, which seemed to grow by one every time he saw them, wrapped her in hugs.

Even Jordan Witt's twin brother, Michael, had swung by to pick him up. They were identical from their pale blue eyes to their sun-bleached hair. Jake had been glad to have Jordan on this trip for some of the hairier moments. Jordan been under his command in the SEALs and when he decided to leave the military a few years after Jake had, Jake had snatched him up.

As Security Director for the Chandler Group's off-site projects, Jake had handpicked his entire security force, which was almost exclusively former military. He'd tried to recruit Mike too when he'd left the SEALs four years ago, but Mike had elected to go with the FBI instead. So he'd had to settle for Jordan – or at least that's how Jake always presented it to Jordan.

Mike gave him a sharp salute and quick smile, leaning against the Jeep's open door.

Jordan had the exact same posture on the passenger side of the car. Jake grinned. Unintentional mirror images.

Jordan yelled across the space. "Hey, you sure you don't want to join us?"

Jordan had invited him to join his family for dinner. Their parents had flown into town to see their sons. The only one missing was their sister Jen, who was off on some remote dig site.

Jake shook his head. "Nah, I'm good. Tell your

parents I said hi."

"Tomorrow, then. No excuses. You don't want to get on my Mom's bad side." Mike gave a dramatic shudder.

Jake laughed. The twins' mom was the personification of nurturing sweetness. He was pretty sure she didn't have a bad side. He nodded. "Tomorrow."

The brothers waved good-bye as they piled into Mike's black Cherokee.

His head pounding with each step, Jake headed for the waiting dark tinted Town Car, trying not to focus on the fact that he was the only one without a welcoming committee. He opened the door, sinking into the deep leather with a sigh.

"Hi, Jake."

He glanced over in surprise at the tall blonde with cornflower blue eyes beside him in the backseat. Her knockout body was straining against her low-cut, siren-red dress. A smile played on her perfectly made-up lips.

"Chelsea. Hey. I didn't know you'd be here." *Crap.*

The smile turned into a playful pout, although Jake could read the annoyance in her eyes. "Well, you haven't been returning my phone calls."

"Yeah, sorry about that. The project kept me busy."

Which was partly true. As the Chandler Groups' off-site security director, he was responsible for the safety of every Chandler project group. In more contentious areas, that generally required incredible attention to detail and occasionally gunfire. And as this last project took them to the West Bank, Israel, and even Syria, "busy" was an understatement.

But even with all the time in the world, he wouldn't have called Chelsea. They'd met through work. She was the lawyer for one of the outside design firms the Chandler Group sometimes used. She'd made her attraction known since their first meeting. Shy, she was not.

He hadn't paid her any attention at the time, too wrapped up in Laney. Then one drunken night after Laney and he'd had one incredibly polite phone call in which they decided to take a break, he'd given in. It had been stupid.

And the month afterwards had been even stupider. He'd thought he could forget Laney by losing himself in someone else. It had only made him miss her more. He finally realized he wasn't being fair to Chelsea. He'd broken it off before he left for Israel. But she hadn't seemed to understand what he'd been saying, and the month of silence hadn't clued her in either.

"Well?" Chelsea said.

He glanced over at her, tamping down his annoyance. "Look, Chelsea, we've had this conversation. We had fun, but now it's over. I don't know what it is you want from me."

She reached over and ran a hand up his arm. "You know we're good together. It doesn't have to be over."

Jake reached over and removed her hand. Her well-made up face now seemed garish to him, her clothes too tight. "Stop it, Chelsea. It's over. I'd like if we could stay civil, but this has to stop."

She tugged her hand away and flounced back in the seat, another pout on her red lips, this one real. "You don't know what you're missing, Jake."

Laney's face flashed across his mind. "Yeah. Actually, I do."

CHAPTER 4

Fifteen Miles West of Cuenca, Ecuador

Laney leaned back from the long table in the community house, patting her stomach. "Thank you for dinner, Nana. It was wonderful."

The community house was a large pavilion with a roof covering a wood floor that was filled with long tables in the center of the village. The Shuar tribe met there for all meals. It was always loud and rambunctious. Laney loved every minute of it.

Lucia Nunink, known as Nana to all, sat at the head of the table. Laney wasn't sure of her age. Her hair was long and streaked with white but her face was unlined. Laney guessed maybe her mid to late forties, as women in the tribe tended to have children young.

Nana bowed her head, her brown eyes shining. "We're always happy to feed our friends." Her eyes drifted to the one uninvited member of their group. "And others."

Although Nana preferred to speak in her native language of Shuar, she always spoke Spanish with Laney and Jen. Laney was thankful for the consideration. Both she and Jen understood enough of the Shuar language to get by, but the hard consonants and nasal vowels had proven very difficult to pronounce.

Most of the tribe had drifted off to finish their nightly activities, so now it was just Nana, Jen, Laney, and Warren Steadglow, their intern.

"Yeah, thanks," Warren pushed his food around and grimaced before finally shoving the plate away with his short, pudgy arms. Blond with pale blue eyes, his doughy body screamed spoiled and soft.

Laney struggled to keep from whacking him on the back of the head. He was the personification of the overindulged American: a twenty-six year old graduate student who'd had everything in his life handed to him, including this internship. He'd been added to their research as part of the funding agreement.

Neither Jen nor Laney could stand him. They hadn't told him about their trip to the village, but he'd shown up, uninvited and unwanted.

Jen stood, gathering the coffee mugs on the table. "Let me help clean up."

Nana nodded and turned towards the kitchen, a small building at the back of the dining hall.

Jen fixed her eyes on Laney, tilting her head towards Warren. Laney understood the message loud and clear. *Handle him.*

Laney stifled a sigh. Warren was the one part of this experience that was less than ideal. Or, put another way, a complete pain in the ass. She turned towards him. "Warren, why are you here?"

"What? I heard you say you were heading to the village. I'm part of this project, so I came."

"We're not here about the project. We're here for

dinner. You weren't invited."

Warren didn't have the common sense to be embarrassed. He waved her words away. "I don't know why you're treating them with kid gloves. We should just demand they tell us where the source of the collection is."

She stared at him in disbelief. "Demand? And then what? Break out the thumb screws? These are good people. We – and sadly that includes you – will treat them with respect. Do you understand me?"

He looked away from her gaze. "Whatever."

Laney swallowed the scream in her throat. "Well, the 'project' is done for the night. Why don't you head down to the camp and get a good night's sleep?"

He shook his head. "I think we should ask Nana about the source. We're losing time-"

She cut him off. "Let me rephrase my last statement: Go to the camp and go to sleep."

He spluttered. "You can't order me around that way."

"Actually, she can," Jen said as she walked up behind them with silent footfalls. Warren jumped about a foot. "It's in your contract. So get lost, Warren."

He stood up, glaring at Jen. "You're going to regret this."

Laney watched him stomp out of the pavilion before turning back to Jen. "Not the most diplomatic way you could have put it."

Jen shrugged. "He gets under my skin. The boy's useless."

"True. But he must have some powerful connections to have wheedled his way into this grant. Maybe we could show a little restraint."

Jen arched an eyebrow. "That was restraint. I wanted to kick his ass."

Laney laughed. "Oh, well, my mistake then. Where's Nana?"

"She went to check on Elena. She asked if we'd wait. She wants to talk to us."

"Any idea why?"

"She wouldn't say. But did you notice how distracted she was at dinner? It must be something big."

Laney nodded. "The latest oil company lawsuit?"

"Probably."

They both sat sipping their coffee, enjoying the sounds of the village winding down. The scent of lavender drifted through the air and Laney inhaled deeply. She smiled as a group of children ran past.

After a few minutes, Jen let out a big sigh.

Laney glanced over at her. "What?"

Jen blew out a breath. "If we're ever going to learn more about the source of the Crespi collection, we're going to have to lose Warren. Any goodwill we've created, he's shredding."

Laney knew how true Jen's words were. It was a testament to the Shuar's generosity that they put up with him at all. "I know. Maybe we can bury him in paperwork back at the bank while we stay here."

"Good idea. Or maybe we could just bury him."

Laney laughed. "If only. Tomorrow, though, we'll send him packing."

Nana stepped into the hut from the doorway across from Laney. "Good. You're both still here."

"Elena asleep?" Jen asked.

"Almost. But she's fighting it. She's afraid she'll

miss something." Nana took her seat back at the head of the table. "I have a problem that I believe only you two can solve."

Laney and Jen waited for Nana to explain, but Nana just glanced out of the hut, watching a family sitting together outside their home. Finally, she spoke. "The Shuar have been part of this land for thousands of years. Some argue we have been here for tens of thousands years. But recent years have seen oil companies doing what no other group has been able to. They're coming close to getting our land."

"Have they started a new lawsuit?" Jen asked.

Nana nodded. "Yes. And the judge is favoring them. I think he may be in their pocket. And if that's true, I'm not sure if anything can save our land."

Laney reached out and took Nana's hand. "How can we help, Nana?"

Nana squeezed Laney's hand. "The judge has given us one chance to protect our land. We must demonstrate why it's sacred to the Shuar."

Jen nodded. "Do you need us to write up a history?"

Nana shook her head. "I don't think that will be enough." She fell silent.

Laney glanced at Jen, who shrugged back at her.

"Nana?" Jen prodded.

Nana shook herself out of her reverie, taking a deep breath. "The tribe's still debating what to do. I am pushing them to allow you two to be taken into our confidence. But some are holding out, arguing there must be another way. I had hoped to have a decision from the tribe tonight, but some are still dragging their feet. I'll question them all again in the morning. Will you two come after breakfast?"

Jen nodded. "Of course. But can you give us a hint?"

Nana paused. "It's the reason the Shuar's guard this land so fiercely. It's the reason the oil companies can never be allowed in."

Nana wouldn't expand her cryptic statement. A few minutes later, Laney and Jen said good night and walked down the steep path back to their camp. Whenever they visited, they always set up camp away from the Shuar. It seemed important to not intrude.

When Laney was settled into her tent, she wondered what Nana had been referring to. It had to be the source of the Crespi collection. That was the only thing that made sense.

Laney pulled off her sweatshirt, taking her Glock out of the holster. Checking the magazine, she placed it on the ground next to her bed. Ever since Montana, she'd never felt safe unless she had a weapon nearby. She figured she had two options, go talk to a therapist or carry a concealed weapon. Right now, the latter was working.

Laying down, she closed her eyes, focusing on counting to one hundred. Another little habit she'd developed since Montana. If she focused on the numbers, no other thoughts were able to sift their way in.

Around seventy, she could tell it was working. But Nana's worried face slipped in. She pushed the image aside. There was nothing she could do about Nana's problem tonight. It would keep until morning.

CHAPTER 5

A few hours before dawn, an ear-piercing scream yanked Laney from her sleep. She sat straight up on her cot, her heart pounding. More screams and automatic gunfire joined a cacophony of cries.

Laney grabbed her Glock and launched herself from the tent.

People streamed down the path from the village. Behind them, an orange glow lit the night sky.

"Someone's burning the village," Jen said as she appeared out of her tent.

Laney stared up at the flames, trying to think of a reason someone would attack the village. She knew the Shuar had difficult relationships with some other indigenous tribes in the area, especially the Achura. But this kind of attack, with women and children sleeping, was cowardly. It wasn't the Achura.

Jen's ebony eyes caught Laney's, and didn't waver. She tipped her chin towards the path the villagers were streaming down. "You in?"

Gripping the gun with a nod, Laney took a step forward. A hand latched onto her arm. She glanced down at its owner in disgust. Warren.

"Where are you going?" he shrieked, his receding hairline more obvious in the fire's glow.

"To help." *You asshole.* She yanked her arm free.

He switched his grip to Jen's left arm. "You can't. We need to get out of here. You're both responsible for my safety."

Laney watched Jen's face. Her expression didn't change, except for the small tick in her cheek. *Oh, you stupid, stupid boy.*

Jen reached over with her right hand and twisted Warren's wrist until it was bent to a ninety-degree angle. With a screech, he dropped to his knees, his arm contorted in the air. She leaned down. "Help. Or. Get. Out. Of. The. Way."

Warren nodded his head so ferociously, Laney worried it would snap off his neck. "Okay, okay."

Jen released him. He stumbled to his feet and with a glare, followed after the retreating villagers.

Dismissing him, Laney turned to Jen. "Let's go."

Taking off at a run, they sprinted up the steep path. Although Jen's legs were a good few inches longer than Laney's, Laney soon outpaced her. Her smaller size made it easier for her to slip through the panicked crowd streaming down the trail.

Screams and the ring of gunfire grew louder. Smoke wafted down the path, the smell of burning wood. She could see the glow ahead where the buildings burned. Her heart sank. Everything here was made of thatch and wood. The fire would spread easily; nothing would be left.

Her thigh muscles strained, but she didn't slow. Picturing the villagers she'd come to know and care for over the last three months, she increased her pace.

Nearing the top, the crowd began to thin out. Soon, there was no one. Jen drew up beside her and they reached the top together.

Laney quickly stepped into the trees and Jen followed. A girl's scream erupted. Laney's heart pounded even harder.

"Elena," Jen whispered, her voice even, but Laney heard the emotion nonetheless.

"I know."

Silently, they made their way through the foliage. They circled the village, drawing closer to the noise.

"Who do you think it is?" Jen whispered.

Laney pushed a branch out of the way. "I'm guessing one of the cartels. A huge field was burned just over the border in Colombia two weeks ago. They're probably looking for new fields."

"But why here?"

Laney glanced over her shoulder, her eyes finding Jen's in the fire's glow. "When cartels' take over, they don't just grab the land. They also grab the people as workers. Elena's village is perfect."

"And the children?"

"The boys will be turned into workers. And the girls—" She paused, taking a breath. "The girls will be used for entertainment."

The main community hut came into view. Laney pulled Jen to the ground. Together, they stared at the destruction before them.

Armed men gathered the villagers together. Others lay where they'd been felled, pools of blood surrounding their bodies. Huts burned, and families clung together, wailing at their loss. A few hours earlier, they'd walked through this same village and it had been a place of peace and family. Now it was the scene from a nightmare.

Smoke wafted through the buildings and armed men walked in and out of the smoke like specters, dragging or shoving villagers. The violence, the weapons, it was a perfect example of a cartel taking over. And yet . . .

"Something's not right," Laney mumbled, not being able to put her finger on exactly what was bothering her.

Jen stared back at her, incredulous. "Something? Nothing here is right."

"I know. But there's something else." She stared at the men. They were all dressed in common clothes, loose cotton tops and dirty pants. The right costume for cartel men . . . Costumes? Why did she think costumes?

Laney grabbed Jen's arm. "Look at their boots."

The men were wearing the exact same black boots – military issue, if she wasn't mistaken. These weren't cartel members, although they were playing the part.

A scream pulled her attention. A young girl was being dragged into one of the huts. The large man pulling her laughed as she struggled. Finally, he grabbed her around the waist and slung her over his shoulder.

Laney felt like she'd been punched in the chest. "Elena."

CHAPTER 6

Stealth forgotten, Laney and Jen stormed through the trees on the outskirts of the village. The hut Elena had been taken to backed onto the forest. They reached the tree line closest to the hut. Thirty feet of open space separated them and their target. Two mercenaries herded a family out of hiding from the hut next to it.

Laney hefted her sidearm. She wouldn't be able to take them from here. They were too far away. She'd have to get closer. She could move along the tree line until she was right behind them, but that would take time.

She turned to Jen. "I'll take care of the guards and the family. You get our girl."

Jen rocked back on her heels. "On the count of three."

One of the gunmen roughly shoved a boy no older than seven. The father grabbed the gunman's arm and the gunman back-fisted the poor man. He crashed to the ground. The two gunmen started kicking the man with their heavy boots, the family crying.

The mother threw herself at one of the gunmen.

He backhanded her away.

Elena's scream cut through the air.

Anger and fear warred for control in Laney. She burst from the tree line, Jen at her side.

One of the mercenaries turned, his gun raised. Laney didn't even break her stride. Two shots, dead center. The other gunman dove away from his comrade.

In Spanish, Laney yelled to the family. "Run to the trees! Run!"

The family scurried out of sight as she continued to take shots at the spot where the other mercenary had found cover. Out of the corner of her eye, she saw Jen's long-legged stride eating up the distance before she disappeared into the doorway.

The second mercenary returned fire. Diving behind an empty oil drum, she waited for the pause between shots and leapt up. The man aimed for her, but she was faster. Her bullet burrowed through his forehead.

She stepped from behind the drum, her gun extended in front of her. A fist slammed down on her arm.

Pain charged through her arm and she dropped it. Shoved forward, she slammed into the drum and rolled over it, landing on the ground. Her uncle's voice rang through her head. *Always check your six.*

A mountain of a man stalked towards her. His hair was dark, his skin pock-marked. A wicked serrated knife in his hand led his way.

He loomed over her and spoke without any trace of a South American accent. In fact, he sounded like he was from Jersey. "Bitch with a gun. Let's see how you do without it."

Laney's boot slammed into side of the man's knee. He stumbled and lurched to his right to compensate. She rolled onto her right hip, kicked at his other leg. Her next kick got him in the face. He crashed to the ground.

Bringing up her left boot, she drove her heel into his chin and then changing her angle, brought it down into the middle of his face. Blood exploded from his nose.

She brought her heel down again and again and again, onto his neck, his chest and finally his groin. Rolling to her feet, she snatched his knife from where it had fallen. He lay curled in the fetal position, moaning.

She leaned down. "This bitch does just fine without a gun."

Pushing herself back from the body, she tucked his knife into her belt and grabbed her Glock. She ran for the hut, reaching it just as Jen stepped out, Elena cradled protectively in her arms.

Laney glanced back through the doorway. The man who'd grabbed Elena lay spread eagle, a knife protruding from his chest.

"Good?"

Jen nodded. "Good. The family?"

"Escaped into the woods." Laney reached out to stroke Elena's hair.

Elena looked up at her, her eyes as big as saucers. "Nana?"

"I don't know, sweetheart," Laney said. "But we'll find her."

Elena nodded before closing her eyes. Laney met Jen's eyes. They hadn't been able to tell if one of the bodies in front of the community hut had been Nana.

Laney prayed it hadn't been.

"We need to move. We're lucky my gun exchange didn't draw them," Laney said.

Jen started towards the trees. "They probably just thought it was their own men having fun."

Laney nodded, knowing she was probably right. She trailed behind Jen as they headed for the tree line, her eyes darting between the trees ahead and the village behind. She slipped into the trees behind Jen, knowing Jen was avoiding the main path. They would take a back trail that led from the village to the church.

Laney quickly overtook Jen and Elena once on the path. She'd lead the way in case any of the mercenaries had made their way into the forest.

Laney was hyper-aware now. Every snap of a twig had her imagining gunmen hidden in the trees. Who was targeting these villagers? The village was poor. They had nothing of value. Except . . . She stumbled, not noticing a root sticking out of the ground.

"Laney?" Jen asked, her voice concerned.

"I'm fine. Just tripped." She kept her voice calm.

The Shuar's connection to the source of the Crespi Collection was well known. In fact, it had been known for decades. Uncovering that source would be an absolutely priceless find. *Was that why they'd been attacked? But why now?*

A twig snapped to her right. Laney whirled around, dropping to her knee and lining up the poor Andean fox. She let out a breath, getting back to her feet as the poor thing scampered away. She glanced back at Jen. "Just a fox."

Jen nodded, clutching Elena to her.

Laney continued on the path. The violence of this

group was coordinated. It was big. That took money, lots of it.

A cold chill stole through her. And if they were after the source of Crespi's collection, the violence wasn't going to stop at the village.

CHAPTER 7

Hugo paced in front of the villagers who'd been unable to escape. Their muffled cries were the only sounds now. The forest surrounding them had gone silent, as had the gunfire.

The village had been relatively easy to subdue. He glanced at the bodies that littered the ground. Only about fifteen had been killed. An acceptable number and none of them had been their target.

He watched as his 'second in command' walked towards him, casting a dismissive eye on the bodies around him. His love handles strained against the new camos he'd put on and an M16 hung carelessly across his chest. One of his men had found him struggling up the steep path to the village.

"So where is she?" Warren stared at the scar that ran from the edge of Hugo's eyebrow to the edge of his mouth.

Most men, he'd beat to a pulp for even glancing at it too long. With this brat, he had to bite his tongue. "We haven't found her yet."

Hugo turned away from him. The kid was a joke.

He didn't know which end of a gun to shoot from. He'd been ordered to bring him along, to show him the ropes. The rest of his men had all been tested in battle. Junior here had the cockiness of someone who'd never been in a fight, but always thought he would win.

He'd even failed to complete his one job: get the two American archaeologists away from here. Hugo growled. He didn't need Americans caught in the crossfire. That would bring way too much attention.

He turned as Warren kicked the person nearest to him, a twenty-something woman holding her child. The woman cried out. The villagers leaned forward, their faces mutinous. One of Hugo's men stepped forward, warning them back.

Warren was oblivious to the reaction. "Let's just ask one of these ones where she went. I'm sure I could persuade them to answer."

Hugo latched onto Warren's arm, squeezing hard.

Warren's face paled.

Hugo spoke quietly, but with authority. "I don't care who your granddaddy is. This is my op. You will observe, but you will not touch a single person unless I tell you to." He reached down and flipped the safety on Warren's M16. "And keep the damn safety on before you blow your foot off." He flung him away.

Warren's cheeks glowed red. He opened his mouth to speak.

Hugo stared him down.

Common sense prevailed. Warren shut his mouth and took a deep breath. "Yes, sir. What can I do?"

"Now you're getting it." He nodded to the tent where his lieutenant had disappeared with the girl. "Check on Sanford. It's too quiet in there."

Warren nodded and headed off. Hugo shook his head, watching him go. His grandfather was a man to be reckoned with. But the apple had obviously fallen very far from the tree. If Warren were his progeny, Hugo would have shot him when he was a child and saved himself the embarrassment.

Turning his back on Warren, he looked over the crowd of villagers. They all looked at the ground. He pointed at them. "Eenie, meenie, minee, mo, who will tell me what they know?"

"Hugo!"

He growled at the interruption. For God's sake, the kid was worse than a two-year old. He looked over his shoulder. Warren ran towards him, his face blotchy from the exertion. "What is it?"

"It's Sanford," Warren panted out. "He's dead."

Hugo went still, his fist clenched. "What did you say?"

"Sanford. There's a knife sticking out of his chest."

Hugo's eyes narrowed to slits as he looked back at the villagers. Sanford had been his lieutenant for over five years. He wasn't easy to take down. He reached down and yanked up a girl around the age of six. He held a gun to her head while he stared at the group. "Where would they have taken her?"

"No, don't hurt her," her mother pleaded.

"This is the last time I'll ask. Where would they have taken her?" He pressed the gun harder into the little girl's temple and she cried out. "3, 2 –"

"The church." A man called out. "They would have taken her to the church."

Hugo pushed the girl back towards her mother.

She collapsed in her mother's arms sobbing. Hugo watched them for a moment. Pitiful. He raised his gun and shot the man who had spoken. He turned and walked away.

Warren had to run to keep up with him. "Why'd you shoot him? He told you what you wanted."

"But I had to ask twice." He glanced over at Warren. "Take a group to the church while I finish here. If you find the target, hold her. I'll question her when I get there."

Warren ran off towards the trucks with a nod, practically skipping in his excitement. He'd lost Sanford and now he was saddled with this man-child. Hugo beckoned his second lieutenant over. He came on a run, halting in front of him. "Yes, sir."

Hugo smiled. Now this was how a soldier should respond. "It's time to clean up the village."

His second looked at him, unblinking. "Yes, sir. What type of cleanup will this be?"

"Complete. No witnesses."

CHAPTER 8

Baltimore, Maryland

Henry Chandler, CEO of the Chandler Group, flipped through the reports on his desk. The project in Milan was on schedule and should be wrapped up shortly. Their consultation with the scientists at the Hadron collider had gone well and it looked as if a new contract would be signed soon.

Pushing the files to the right side of his desk, he pulled over a white file with a single word on it: Montana.

Leaning back in his chair, the file in his lap, he carefully flipped his purple-striped tie over his shoulder. He had a meeting with a potential client this afternoon, hence the more formal look of black slacks and crisp white shirt. He preferred jeans and a t-shirt, but he knew as the head of the Chandler Group, he needed to present a certain image.

He flipped past the opening summary and stopped on page two, assessing the latest progress on the dig. Father Patrick seemed to have the project well in hand. He'd put out a press release with some initial findings and gotten the expected pushback. He smiled thinking of his conversation with Patrick this morning. The priest was definitely enjoying being in the thick of things.

He scanned the rest of the report - nothing about the superhumans. There'd been precious little information about them on any of the monoliths in Montana. Last year, they'd learned the superhumans were actually fallen angels, and that they'd ushered in a world of violence and strife when they fell. But no new information on them had come from the ancient site.

And nothing more about you, either, a thought whispered from the back of his mind. The thoughts had been harder to shut out since Montana. He'd known what he could do since he was a teenager. But he never knew why. Was he one of them?

His parents had known. '*Don't let anyone know what he is.*' Had that been fear in his father's voice? He curled his fist, though he was careful not to slam it on his desk. He knew if he did, the desk would be damaged, if not destroyed.

Careful, always having to be so damn careful, so no one knew what he could do. Why had his parents never told him? Why leave him full of questions?

His Dad was gone, so there were no answers to be had from him. But his Mom . . . He sighed. Getting answers from her was even more complicated than getting answers from his father.

He glanced up as the door opened. A broad-shouldered man in his mid-thirties with a shock of dark brown hair walked in.

Henry shook off his thoughts, tucking them away yet again. He smiled and walked around the desk. "Jake. I thought you weren't getting in until tonight."

Jake shook Henry's hand and grinned up at him. Although Jake was six-foot-four, Henry towered over him. Standing at seven-foot-two, he towered over most people.

"Wrapped things up early," Jake replied, heading for Henry's bar. He picked up the decanter of Scotch and tilted it towards Henry.

"No, I'm good, but help yourself." Henry sat in one of leather chairs in front of his desk, surreptitiously watching Jake. Jake had never been a drinker - an occasional beer, sure, but never Scotch. And he looked like he'd lost weight. His jeans were baggier and his navy t-shirt hung a little looser.

"You okay?"

Jake took a seat across from him, his glass on the coffee table in between. "Yeah. Good. Israel wrapped up pretty easily."

Henry nodded, but didn't say anything, taking stock of his head of security. Work was fine. His health was fine. Which only left one thing that wasn't fine.

"Have you talked to her?" Henry asked, deciding to forego small talk.

Jake swirled the amber liquid in his glass with a sigh. "No. Not for about two months."

Henry sighed. He'd really been hoping these two could patch things up. If any two people deserved a little happiness, it was Laney and Jake. "Just give her some time. It's hard to downgrade from putting your lives in each other's hands to asking if she's got plans for Friday night. You both went through a lot."

Laney had been the target of a supernatural stalker. She'd borne up well and she and Jake had forged a bond through the ordeal. But reality had been tough for both of them, especially Laney. She'd lost one of her best friends to that insanity.

"Have you talked to her? How's she doing?" Jake asked, his face expressionless.

Henry read the shift in Jake's attention, though, the tautness of his shoulders. "She's good. She took a leave of absence from the University of Syracuse and started researching everything she could find on ancient civilizations."

Jake chuckled. "She started that from the hospital bed. Can't tell you how many books I lugged back from the library and bookstore for her while she was recuperating. What's she doing, going for another Ph.D.?"

"Actually, she is. With her master's classes, her doctoral work in criminology, and her work with her uncle, she was only a few credits shy. She finished them up and now she's working on the research for her dissertation."

Jake took a long drink. "Well, good for her. Where's she doing the research? Out with her uncle in Montana?"

"Umm, no. Actually, she's working with an old friend of hers, Jennifer Witt."

Jake raised his eyebrows. "Jen? Jordan and Mike's sister?"

"Yes."

Jake had been surprised when he learned that one of Laney's friends was the sister of two of his friends. He and Laney had been only one degree of separation away for years. "So, where's Jen doing her research?"

"Ecuador."

Jake grinned. "Jen always did like being off the beaten track. What are they researching?"

"The lost library of Atlantis."

The grin fell from Jake's face. "Please tell me you're kidding."

"Nope."

Jake shook his head and looked out the window. "Any sign of the superhumans?"

Jake's shoulders had tensed up again at the mention of Atlantis. Henry knew the topic was a difficult one for him. Jake was a soldier, not an academic. He didn't have the innate curiosity to seek out the secrets of the past. For him, security always came first. And God knew, the last time someone had gone searching for an Atlantis artifact, it had been brutal.

"Happily, no. For now, she seems to be spending the bulk of her time in a bank in Cuenca cataloguing artifacts."

"Good. I hope it stays that way."

"She's a pretty tough woman. I'm sure she can handle anything that comes her way."

Jake finally met his eyes. "I know. I'd just prefer if she didn't have to."

CHAPTER 9

Ten Miles from Cuenca, Ecuador

Light from the church glowed in the distance. All the lights appeared to be on and a murmur of noise crept through the air. But no gunfire. No overt indications of the mercenaries could be heard.

Laney came to a stop two hundred yards away, in a small copse of trees hidden from the path. Elena lay asleep in her arms.

Jen turned to her and whispered. "You two wait here. I'll go check it out."

Laney nodded wearily, her arms aching as Jen disappeared silently through the trees. Laney envied her ability. She still felt like an elephant crashing through the underbrush. Jen moved without sound.

Usually it took about an hour to travel from the village to the church. Their trip had taken over two. It wasn't just the dark that had slowed them down. A couple of times, they had stopped and hidden, convinced one of the mercenaries was near.

Laney's nerves were at the breaking point, as were her arms and back. She and Jen had traded off carrying Elena, even though Jen had tried to persuade Laney to let her carry her the whole time. But tough as Jen was, even she couldn't carry Elena for that distance. Especially after Elena had fallen asleep, becoming dead weight.

Laney lowered herself to the ground, her back against a polylepis tree. Its scales rustled as she settled in.

She darted a glance at Elena, who lay nestled quietly in her lap. The noise didn't seem to have woken her. Elena had only fallen asleep an hour ago. Before that, she'd bounced between trembling and quiet sobbing.

Hugging Elena to her, Laney wished she could wipe the incident from her memory. No child should have to remember a night like this.

"Are we safe?" Elena's big eyes stared up at her, although Laney could tell she was fighting sleep.

Laney smiled softly. "I thought you were sleeping, little one."

"No. I just shut my eyes. I imagined I was with Nana in the garden."

Laney ran a hand over Elena's hair. "That's a nice place to be."

"It is. Are we safe?"

"I think so. We're at the church. Jen went ahead to be sure."

Elena sat up straight, her voice full of fear. "By herself? We have to help her."

"Shh, shh. It's okay. This is Jen."

Elena still looked around wildly.

Laney hugged her to her. "It's okay. This is Jen Witt."

At Elena's dubious look, she put on her best

carnival barker voice, albeit in a whisper. "Who's the person who talked down all those men who came to your village to find Louis? Who faced that mountain lion and scared him off with only a stick? Jen Witt, that's who."

Elena's tremors seemed to calm some. "She is pretty strong."

"That she is."

"She's also as tall as a man."

"That she is."

"In fact, she might be a man."

"That she – what did you say?" Laney looked down at Elena.

Some of the sparkle was back in Elena's eyes. "Well, maybe not a man, but she's as tough as one. And Nana thinks she can be trusted. You, too. She even said you could be trusted with our secret."

"What secret?"

Elena closed her eyes with a big yawn, her voice now full of sleep. "The reason our village stays where it is. The Cave of Etsu Nantu."

Etsu Nantu. The hiding place for the lost treasure of Atlantis.

CHAPTER 10

"It's me."

Laney lowered her gun as Jen stepped out of the trees. "Sorry. Wasn't sure."

Jen smiled. "I knew we should have worked out a safety word." She leaned down to Elena, who'd opened her eyes. "Guess who I found?"

"Nana?" Elena asked, her face full of hope.

Jen nodded.

Elena launched herself at Jen, her arms encircling her neck. "Thank you, thank you, thank you!"

Relief poured through Laney. At least Elena still had her grandmother. "Everything okay at the church?"

Hefting Elena into her arms, Jen stood. "Chaotic, but no bad guys. The police were called but . . . " She shrugged.

The police might show up or they might have been paid off. It was anybody's guess. Sometimes, Laney really missed the States. "Well, I guess it's better than wandering through the mountains in the dark. We'll head back into Cuenca at first light."

Laney and Elena walked the short distance to the church. As they drew nearer, the chaos Jen mentioned became apparent. Torches lit the way, bathing the area in a wavering light.

Adults and children cried, a few wailing loudly before they were shushed. Piles of belongings with families camped around them were strewn across the courtyard.

More crying poured through the church's open door as they passed. A few priests and volunteers ran between rooms, medical supplies in their arms, their clothes stained with blood.

A tremor ran through Elena. Laney tightened her hold on the little girl's hand. "It's okay, little queen."

They followed Jen as she made her way through the crowded courtyard, heading for the back corner. Ahead, a crowd of people sat on the ground, listening with rapt attention to Nana, seated on an office chair. Her voice crackled with emotion, but also rang with authority and confidence.

"Our ancestors faced persecution and danger. They survived. It's our turn to be tested. And we'll face this challenge. We have lost those we love tonight. But we'll see them again. They'll be reborn to a new world, a better world."

Heads nodded, her audience agreeing with her. Some dabbed at their eyes as they did. Elena squirmed free from Laney and sprinted ahead. "Nana!"

Nana looked up, a smile spreading across her face, a sheen of tears in her eyes. "My child." Stick thin arms wrapped around Elena, pulling her close.

Murmurs rose from the crowd.

"Little queen."

"She is safe."

"God be praised."

Faces turned to look at Laney and Jen with nods and smiles of appreciation. Some people clapped them on the back. A few women pulled them into back-crunching hugs.

Beginning to feel uncomfortable with the attention, Laney tugged on Jen's arm. "Maybe we should give them some privacy."

"Yeah. Let's see if we can help with the wounded."

They turned to leave.

"Jen, Laney, wait."

Laney glanced back. Nana beckoned them forward. People parted in front of them as they made their way towards her. They were stopped more than once by hugs and more pats of affection.

When they reached Nana, the older woman pulled Jen into a giant hug. Elena stood just behind her, beaming. Nana then turned to Laney and engulfed her.

Nana grasped one hand of each of the women, her back to the crowd. Tears swam in her eyes and her chin trembled. "You have saved my granddaughter. For that, I am in your debt. You have given me the greatest of gifts."

She turned to face the crowd, putting her hands up for silence. The crowd went quiet. In fact, the whole courtyard seemed to have gone still.

"These two women have returned our little queen. They have been friends to our people since they first arrived. But with tonight's action they have shown that they're more than friends. They are family. They are worthy of our trust."

Nana stared at the crowd and Laney knew there was a battle of wills at hand. Nana was daring anyone to cross her. The crowd nodded as one, agreeing with her words. The tension eased from Nana's shoulder. "Thank God," she whispered.

The sound of squealing brakes drew Laney's attention to the courtyard's entryway. She craned her neck, trying to see over the crowd.

The bark of a machine gun tore through the night air. Two men by the front entrance dropped, their shirts stained red.

"Everyone down!" Laney yelled. Spinning around, she grabbed Elena, flinging her over her shoulder. She sprinted for the back of the courtyard. A stonewall ringed the courtyard but there was a door in the back corner. Jen was just a few feet behind her, pulling Nana along.

At the rusted wooden door, Laney placed Elena on the ground. *Oh God, this thing looks like it hasn't been used in years.*

"Is it the bad men, Laney?" Elena asked.

Laney wrestled with the ancient lock. "Yes, sweetie. Damn it." The lock was jammed. She took a step back and fired a sidekick at the door. The wood cracked. Jen arrived and Nana wrapped Elena in her arms.

"You got this?" Jen asked, eyeing the courtyard.

"Just a few more hits." Laney kicked the door two more times. The door flung open.

Laney grabbed Elena's hand and rushed out the doorway, Jen and Nana on their heels. They all skidded to a stop.

An old army truck stood idling, thirty feet away. A

dozen armed men stood in a semi-circle, their weapons at the ready.

CHAPTER 11

Laney grunted as she was shoved to the ground in the middle of the courtyard. Ignoring the pain in her knees, she turned to catch Elena as she was also thrown. From the corner of her eye, she saw Jen do the same for Nana.

They'd been ordered back into the courtyard at gunpoint by the men from the truck. Once again, they had wended their way through the Shuar. This time, though, everyone was kneeling, their hands resting on their heads. A few bodies lay bleeding into the dusty ground. One child, no more than two years old, lay in a pool of her own blood.

Laney jerked her eyes from the sight, her breathing becoming rapid. Flashbacks of a Montana pit filled with decomposing bodies filled her mind.

Don't think about that. Focus on now. Just get through now and then you can curl up in the fetal position for a week, she promised herself.

Laney and Jen's weapons had been confiscated when they'd been caught. Even if they hadn't, they couldn't shoot their way out of this situation. She counted at least a dozen armed men inside the courtyard and another dozen outside.

Over at the entryway, she saw a man with small eyes, a non-existent chin, and slim build. He was dressed in a safari outfit that still had pleats in it, and looked like a catalog picture of what the well-dressed man wears in the jungle, complete with a brand new pith helmet.

The man he was talking to, who wore camouflage, had his back to her, but there was something familiar about him. He turned around and pointed at Nana.

Her intern, Warren. *That little weasel.*

Warren shook hands with the man.

"I really should have kicked his ass earlier." Jen's eyes burned with anger.

"Let's make a deal. When this is over, we find Warren. Kick his ass, let him heal, then kick it all over again."

Jen nodded, a deadly glint in her eyes. "Deal."

The brown haired, Safari's-R-Us man walked towards them, Warren trailing behind him.

Laney stiffened at their approach, but Safari man paid her and Jen no attention. He only had eyes for Nana. "So, I hear you're the leader of this group," he said in English.

Nana looked at him, her face betraying nothing.

The man hesitated.

Laney restrained the urge to roll her eyes. *Try Spanish, you idiot.*

Recognizing his mistake, the man switched languages. "Do you understand Spanish?"

He said it slowly, as if Nana had the intelligence of a pet rock.

"Yes. I understand."

"Good. Are you the leader of this group?"

"The Shuar have no leader."

The man was taken aback by the answer. "But you speak for them?"

"Sometimes."

"Well, that's what I meant. Have you heard of the cave of the Etsu Nantu?"

Nana's face betrayed no inkling of concern. Laney struggled to keep her face as serene.

"Yes. But it's only a myth."

The man's polite façade disappeared into a sneer. "See, now you're just lying. I told them we could do this the easy way. I guess not."

He turned to Warren, who'd followed him over. "Your turn. Find out what I want." He headed to the entrance without a backward glance.

Warren smirked as he strode forward. He stopped in front of Jen and Laney. "Told you two you'd be sorry."

Narrowing his eyes, he turned. Pulling out his sidearm, he aimed it at Elena's head.

Nana leapt for her granddaughter. Jen jumped in front of the two of them. Simultaneously, Laney launched herself at Warren. Burying her shoulder into his hip, she tackled him to the ground.

But she wasn't fast enough. The sound of the bullet left her ears ringing. She looked over her shoulder in time to see Jen thrown back by the impact.

CHAPTER 12

Blood was splashed across Jen's arm, across her chest. The sight of it snapped something inside of Laney.

Anger like she'd never known boiled up inside of Laney and spilled out. "You bastard!"

Everything slowed down. All sights and sounds stopped, except for the sight of Warren in front of her. She waled away at him, kneeing him in the groin repeatedly. She punched him in the face so hard and so often, her knuckles split. Without pause, she switched from punches to elbows.

He tried to block her, but she wouldn't let him. Fed up with his feeble attempts, she ripped two of his fingers back, breaking them.

Howling, he screamed for help. "Get her off of me!"

She felt his cheekbone snap, his nose burst with blood. She didn't stop. Couldn't stop. Blood poured from the wounds on his face. It wasn't enough. The image of Jen falling back from the bullet's impact played over and over again in her mind, along with all the other horrific visions from tonight. The asshole needed to stop breathing.

A man grabbed her shoulder from behind. Without looking, she elbowed him in the face. He released her with a yell.

Another man tried to snake his arm around her neck. She dropped her chin, not letting him. Trapping his arm with hers, she flipped him over her shoulder with a small twist, never leaving her perch straddling Warren. The man landed on his back, staring at the sky, a stupefied expression on his face.

With a running jump, a third man tackled her. She slammed into the ground with a grunt. He kept his arms wrapped around her. She threw her head back and caught him under the chin.

He screamed with pain, but didn't let go. "Someone knock this bitch out!"

The man who'd first tried to grab her stumbled over, his eye already swelling. He slammed the butt of his rifle into the side of her head. A starburst of pain pierced her skull, before everything went black.

CHAPTER 13

Baltimore, Maryland

"So what's with the pup?" Jake asked.

He was sitting on the veranda at Chandler HQ watching Danny Wartowski throw a ball for a little black ball of fur called Moxy. The Chandler headquarters were set on a two hundred acre estate outside Baltimore. The estate had been in Henry's family for generations. When he began the Chandler Group, he'd had the main house renovated to become the company's headquarters.

Jake smiled, looking out on the rolling hills. *If you had to work, this was a nice place to do it.* The sun was beating down and he was enjoying it. The tension that always accompanied him on assignments had begun to fade.

And he'd looked into Laney's research in Ecuador. That part of the world seemed quiet right now. So he was forcing himself to stop and smell the roses.

Henry smiled over at him. "A gift from Laney. One day, she just showed up with her. Said she needed a good home and asked Danny if he could watch her for awhile."

Jake watched as Danny tried to get the dog to chase a ball. He smothered a laugh as Danny got down on all fours, his light brown hair falling in his eyes, demonstrating what the dog should do. He smiled at the childish delight Danny took in the task.

The 'boy' was technically Chandler's top analyst at the ripe old age of thirteen. His IQ was off the charts. In the four years Jake had known him, Danny had almost always had his eyes focused on some electronic device or other. He'd rarely seen him act like a child.

Henry had taken Danny in when he was only nine, acting as a surrogate father to the boy, but Danny still remained pretty closed off - an unfortunate side effect of an abusive father.

A background Jake was all too familiar with. "I never thought of Danny as a pet person."

"Me neither," Henry said. "But Laney did. Moxy – that's what she named him – has been Danny's constant companion since they met."

A shout from the lawn made Henry pause. They both turn to watch Moxy tear off with Danny's sneaker in her mouth.

Henry's face was full of wonder. "That little dog has made Danny a kid. Somehow Laney knew exactly what he needed."

"She's good at that," Jake said.

Henry turned back to Jake. "Laney sent me an email earlier, asking if Danny and I wanted to join her in Ecuador in about two months. Kati, Max and Patrick are going as well."

"The whole family together."

"She asked if you'd be on assignment around then."

Jake glanced up. "What'd you say?"

"I said I could clear your schedule so you could join us."

Jake smiled. "I just might do that."

A beeping noise sounded from somewhere around Danny. Jake didn't pay it any mind. Danny always seemed to have some electronic alarm going off signaling something or other.

Jake half listened as Henry explained about some project Danny had developed, something about nanobytes and an organic computer. He was lost after the first sentence or two. He let his mind wander and it drifted to its usual spot, Laney.

He sighed. Maybe he should just drown himself in work. When he'd been in Israel, he'd barely had time to think about her. There had to be some high-risk danger zone he could visit. Getting shot at tended to leave his mind little time to wander off into the world of 'what ifs'. Or maybe he should head down to Ecuador. Help her dig something up.

"Henry!"

Jake's head jerked up at Danny's voice. Fear laced that single word.   Danny sprinted across the lawn towards them, Moxy right behind him.

Henry knelt down so he was eye-to-eye with the boy. "What's wrong?"

Danny held up his phone. "It's Laney. I think she's in trouble."

CHAPTER 14

Northeast of Cuenca, Ecuador

When Laney came to, her first thought was that her head hurt. The second was why was the world moving?

She opened her eyes to find herself lying on her back in the old army truck. The canvas top was flapping as they bustled down the unpaved road, giving her the occasional glimpse of trees.

Her hands were bound in front of her with plastic zip ties, her head resting in someone's lap. Her hair was being gently caressed back.

She looked up into Nana's face. "Ah, you're awake. We were worried."

A wall of memories rushed her. Tears threatened to break. "Jen?"

"I'm here, Laney."

Laney's head whipped to the right. Pain lanced through her, making her groan.

Jen sat propped against the side of the truck. Elena was tucked into her side, fast asleep. The sleeve of Jen's shirt had been torn away and used to bandage her arm. A sling made from the other sleeve held it to her chest.

And apparently, the fact that she'd been shot didn't make their attackers think she was any less of a threat. Her hands were bound as well.

Laney drank in the sight of her, blinking her eyes to make sure that she was really there. "I thought you were –"

"I know. But I'm alive. He only got my arm." Jen raised her bound hands with a wince. "A little worse off, but not as bad as it could have been. Thanks to you."

Laney struggled to sit up. Nana put a surprisingly strong hand on her back and helped her. "How come we're still alive?"

Jen grimaced. "Well, you know Warren the weasel is in on whatever this is. Apparently, he was supposed to keep us out of the way. Unsurprisingly, he failed at yet another task. Killing two Americans wouldn't be as easily overlooked as killing non-Americans. They hadn't expected to find us there. They thought it would be only indigenous people. We're a little hiccup."

Jen looked at Laney, her stare conveying a wealth of information. They might have been surprised to find them there, but she was sure they were working on how to resolve that issue. And Laney was sure it didn't involve letting them go on to live a nice, long life.

"You're some fighter, my friend. You should have seen those men's faces." Nana laughed, her eyes crinkling at the corners. "They were terrified."

"I should have killed the bastards," Laney said.

"Yes. But, I'm sure you'll have the chance again." Nana nodded towards the truck behind them. "They're in that truck there."

Laney leaned against the side of the truck. Her

head pounded with every bump of the road. "Where are they taking us?"

"The cave of the Etsu Nantu," Nana said quietly.

Laney looked back at Nana, despair spreading across her chest. "Oh, Nana. You told them where it was?"

Anger flashed across Nana's face. "No. It was one of the men from my village. He's weak, always causing trouble. I should have banished him years ago."

"How does he know where it is?" Jen asked.

Nana shook her head and Laney could swear the woman wanted to spit.

"He's sneaky. He must have followed us one of the times we went to visit the Guardians. So he probably doesn't know where the actual cave is, only where the Guardians are." A troubled look crossed her face.

"The Guardians?" Laney asked.

"The other half of our tribe."

Laney stared at her, stunned. The Shuar had another half to their tribe? No one had ever mentioned them. The history books had never even whispered about them.

Nana continued. "The Guardians have been the protectors of the cave as long as we can recall. They have repelled all who have tried to seize its treasures. But this firepower..." She gestured to the front of the truck and the one that followed. "I don't think they can defeat these men. I fear many more will be killed before the day is out."

Laney nodded, knowing the natives would be no match for the armed men. And she also knew that if these men found the caves, tossing the bodies of two

American women in would ensure they'd never be found - an easy resolution to an annoying hiccup.

CHAPTER 15

Baltimore, Maryland

Jake knelt down on the grass, to make himself eye level with Danny. He tried to keep the urgency out of his tone. "What do you mean, Danny?"

Danny's face paled. "I need my computer." He turned and sprinted into the house.

"Damn it." Jake tried to grab him.

Henry grabbed his arm. "Jake, it's Danny. Kid gloves, okay?"

Jake nodded before heading into the house. He ran through the dining room and sprinted up the three stories to Henry's office, which took up a full third of the top floor of Chandler headquarters.

As Jake strode into the room, Henry right behind him, his eyes searched for Danny. Looking past the wall of windows that overlooked the back lawn and the three walls of built-in bookcases, his eyes settled on the conference table on the opposite side of the room. Danny sat at his usual spot, his fingers moving feverishly over his tablet, his eyes laser-trained on the monitor.

"Dan-" He started.

"Give him a minute," Henry interrupted from behind him.

Jake checked himself, knowing Henry was right. In a few minutes, Danny could gather more information than a room full of analysts could manage in an hour.

He crossed the room to Danny, literally counting the seconds. At three minutes, his patience boiled over. He needed to know what was going on. "Danny, how do you know Laney's in trouble?"

Danny glanced up at Jake. He quickly ducked his head back down. "When Laney went to Ecuador, I set up a program that notifies me about any trouble near her." He peeked up, looking like a dog with his tail tucked between his legs. In fact, Moxy sat next to him, with just that look.

Jake forced a smile. "You're not in trouble, Danny. I'm glad you set it up. Just tell us what you know."

Moxy leaned into him and Danny seemed to gain strength from her presence. "It just came over the wire that there was an attack on a village in the mountains outside Cuenca. It's the village Laney and Jen have been visiting."

Henry took a seat in the chair next to Danny. His tone was gentle. "But that doesn't mean they were there, Danny. They could still be in the town."

Danny shook his head, tears cresting in his eyes. "No. I checked. She was there." He began to cry and Henry pulled him into a hug.

"It's okay," Henry said, but his eyes were worried.

Jake forced himself to ratchet down his impatience. "How do you know she was there, Danny?"

Danny pushed away from Henry. He took a shuddering breath before speaking. "I put a tracker on her laptop before she left."

Shock must have crossed Jake's face, because Danny's words began to trip over themselves. "I know I shouldn't have. I just wanted to make sure she was okay. That's all."

Jake shook his head with a smile. "I mean it, Danny. You're not in trouble. In fact, I think it was pretty damn smart. I wish I'd thought of it. But even if there was trouble, it might not be that bad."

Danny put his tablet down on the table. "No. It's bad. I, um, I hacked into a satellite to get some pictures."

"You re-routed a satellite?"

Danny gave him a surprised look. "Didn't have to. It was already passing over."

Right, because re-routing would have been crazy. Thank God he's on our side.

"Here. It's a live stream." Danny turned the screen around for Jake and Henry to see.

Jake felt like the floor had dropped from underneath him. The village had been burned to the ground. The debris still smoldered and bodies littered the landscape. If Laney had been there . . .

Jake stood up. "Henry, I need to –"

Henry's voice was grim. "Whatever, you need, you have."

CHAPTER 16

Outside Cuenca, Ecuador

Laney kept her voice low to not wake Elena. "I don't understand why this all happening now."

"The Shuar's connection to the treasure has been known for decades. So, what changed?" Jen asked.

Nana sighed, not speaking right away. When she did, her voice was filled with weariness. "It's the oil companies. One of the blocs of land that they're trying to buy holds the cave. That's what I wanted to tell you last night. The court ruled that if we demonstrate the sacredness of the land, we can keep it. But to do that, we would have to reveal the cave. And it has been our tribe's job since its creation to protect it."

Laney nodded, knowing how seriously the Shuar took duty. It couldn't be easy to choose between revealing the cave or potentially seeing its destruction.

"I had wanted to ask the two of you to document the cave for the court. You are the only ones I would trust with it. But we knew as soon as I asked you, the world's knowledge of the cave would quickly follow. And some members of the tribe were hoping for another way out."

Laney thought of Henry and the resources of the Chandler Group. He would be able to help the Shuar protect it once the world became aware of its existence.

She glanced through the back of the truck. The other truck followed about twenty yards back. Of course, right now none of that mattered. They probably weren't going to live long enough to worry about the cave being uncovered.

"Can you tell us about the cave?" Jen asked.

Nana nodded, closing her eyes. "According to our history, we were entrusted with its contents by the Teachers. They weren't our people. They came from another land."

"When did they come?" Jen asked.

"Right before the great flood," Nana said.

Laney looked at Nana in shock. No. That couldn't be right. "There was a flood in Ecuador?"

Nana smiled "Not just here. Everywhere. The world flood."

A look of shock crossed Jen's face and Laney was pretty sure her face held an identical one. All cultures across the globe speak of the great flood. And they each speak of a different way in which the knowledge of the people before the flood was saved.

In Hindu mythology, the Satapatha Brahmana tells the story of Manu, the savior of mankind, and the boat he used to save knowledge, seeds, and animals. The story of Manu is almost identical to the story of Noah, which is almost identical to the story of Gilgamesh. In fact, there are over six hundred flood myths across the globe.

Despite the similarity of the tales, scientists had argued for years that there had never been a cataclysmic world flood. The closest thing would have been the melting after the last ice age, which would have been a much more gradual process.

Yet recent research had indicated that cataclysmic flooding could indeed have occurred during the melting from the last ice age due to the creation of ice dams.

"That was at least twelve thousand years ago," Jen said quietly, her voice conveying her awe.

Nana nodded, her thoughts seeming to be a million miles away. "I'm not sure of the exact time the Teachers came to us, but I do know we're responsible for keeping their knowledge safe. I have known, though, that the time would come soon when the cave would have to be introduced to the world. The world is encroaching closer and closer."

She looked back at Jen and Laney. "I'd decided you two would be the first outsiders shown the cave. I had hoped you could help us preserve what's inside."

Jen nodded. "We would have, Nana."

"I know. But it's too late for that now. I should have demanded the tribe allow me to tell you. But we have always been an equal society, even if . . ." She sighed. "We needed to all agree on the next course of action. Maybe, though, if I'd told you sooner, this could have been avoided."

Laney shook her head. "I doubt that, Nana. These men are serious. I think if you told us sooner, this would have only happened sooner."

Jen nodded. "Laney's right, Nana. The only blame here belongs to the assholes responsible for this. But now we need to deal with what's happening. Who are the Guardians you spoke of?"

"Farther back than any of us can remember, our

tribe split in two. One group would stay attached to the world, to learn if there was danger to the cave. The other would stay with the cave as its protectors. We would meet twice every year to renew our bond to each other. I fear what will happen to them. "

Nana glanced through the back of the truck, her voice gravely serious. "We're getting close. You two must stay near me and Elena when we arrive."

Minutes later, the truck slowed and came to a stop. Doors slammed.

Two men appeared at the tailgate. One raised his machine gun as the other opened it. "Out."

Elena and Jen scooted out of the truck with Nana and Laney following behind them. Laney looked around, her hopes plummeting. They were in the middle of nowhere and there were at least thirty heavily armed men. How the hell were they going to get out of this?

Warren was nowhere to be seen. No doubt he'd gone for medical attention. But the Safari's-R-Us man appeared, his khakis beginning to look limp in the heat, with sweat rings around his neck and armpits.

Laney took a perverse satisfaction in his discomfort. He looked like the type used to air-conditioned lecture halls, not the rigors of the field.

He walked up to Nana, wiping his brow with a stained handkerchief. "Now, Lucia, where are these Guardians?"

Nana looked him straight in the eye. "All around us."

The trees erupted with screams.

CHAPTER 17

Baltimore, Maryland

Jake paced along the wall of windows in Henry's office. His mind was a scramble of horrific images, with Laney center stage.

Damn it. He hated standing around twiddling his thumbs, waiting for information. He already had equipment moving into place. But before he stormed into a foreign country, doors needed to be opened.

He glared at the image of the destroyed village frozen on a computer monitor. *Little good diplomacy was going to do for those poor bastards.*

Needing a distraction, he watched Danny at the conference table. Danny's eyes were glued to his screen. His fingers flew over the keyboard. Danny had provided Laney the only protection he could, a computerized guardian angel. Jake could more than handle himself in the physical world, but Danny was the warrior in the electronic one.

Jake walked over to Henry as he disconnected his call.

Henry's face was serious. "I just spoke with the U.S. Consulate. They already knew about the attack.

An unknown group hit the village late last night and then followed the villagers to the church where the survivors had taken refuge."

"Where were Laney and Jen?" Jake asked.

"They were camping down the hill from the village. They apparently rescued a young girl from the village who was about to be -" Henry paused with a quick glance at Danny. He lowered his voice. "abused. They took out three or four armed gunmen in the attempt."

Jake felt the kernel of hope bloom. *That's my girl.* "Where did they go after that?"

Henry met his eyes. "The church."

Jake's stomach plummeted. "Are they all right?"

Henry looked away, his tone more guarded. Danny came to stand next to him. Henry reached down and pulled him close. "They tried to escape at the church, but were caught."

Henry took a deep breath. "There were reports that one of the American women was shot. I don't know which one. The eyewitness reports conflict. The two Americans were then bundled along with the village's leader and her young granddaughter into a truck, and disappeared to the north."

The memory of Laney bleeding into the ground in Montana flashed through Jake's mind. This couldn't be happening again. "What size of a force was it?"

Henry shook his head. "There aren't any reliable reports on that."

Jake nodded, knowing eye witnesses often weren't much help in these situations. "I read that the oil companies were making a play for the lands around the village. Any chance it's them?"

Henry shook his head. "I can't see how. The courts

were turning in their favor. Everybody believes it's only a matter of time before they're granted access to those lands. I think this is somebody else."

Jake stared at the satellite images Danny had enlarged on the overhead screen. The village had been annihilated. It would have been possible to do that with a small, efficient group, but his gut told him the group was probably much larger than that.

"We're going to have to go in small," he mumbled.

If it were up to him, he'd call on the entire Chandler group security force and every friend he had in the military and rain down hellfire on these assholes. But he knew they had to tread lightly. A large force would draw attention.

They needed to stay under the radar, at least until they found Laney and Jen. They didn't have time to sit in a bunch of government offices filling out forms about the intention of their visit. Besides, he was pretty sure explaining he intended to kill quite a few people while in their country wouldn't go over well.

"I agree," Henry said. "So besides the two of us, who else do you want?"

Jake looked up at Henry. He never ceased to amaze him. Brilliant, rich, and never afraid to get hands dirty when it counted. "The Witt's, of course. Yoni, and maybe one or two more. We need to be able to move quick."

Jake stood up. "When can we leave?"

"Wheels up in one hour."

"We need to call Jordan." Jake had held off calling Jen's family, hoping he'd have some good news to share. The Witt's were extremely close. This news was going to terrify them. But Jake also knew there was no way Jordan would be left behind, or Mike either, for that matter. "I'll assemble the team."

In his mind, he raced through all the operatives in the field and off-duty, making sure he hadn't overlooked anyone. A name flashed through his mind and he stilled. He looked at Henry, his voice low. "Patrick."

Henry nodded. "I'll call him."

"No. That's my responsibility." Jake turned away and headed for the empty conference room down the hall. He wanted privacy for this conversation.

He'd sat with Patrick at the hospital the last time Laney had been shot. The man's deep love and fear for his niece had been a palpable thing. He knew this news was going to devastate him.

Closing the conference room door behind him, he knew there were a thousand last minute details that needed to be addressed. But certain responsibilities took precedence. With a heavy heart, Jake pulled out his phone and dialed.

CHAPTER 18

North of Cuenca, Ecuador

The first of the arrows flew through the air.

"Get down!" Laney yelled.

Nana scrambled under the truck, Elena next to her. Laney and Jen dove in after them just as two men collapsed next to the truck, arrows in their chests.

Caught unaware, their captors lost precious seconds to inaction. Laney saw another two drop. But soon, the men who'd kidnapped them gathered themselves and returned fire.

A knife was attached to the belt of the fallen man nearest Laney. She tugged it free of its sheath.

Nana held out her hand. "Give it to me."

She handed it over. Nana made quick work of the ties that bound Laney's wrists, before doing the same to Jen's.

Laney and Jen quickly deposed the two fallen men of all of their weapons. Between them, they had one M16, a Beretta, and two knives.

Gunfire and war cries continued to erupt around them. Laney caught her first glimpse of a Guardian as he leapt from a tree. Wearing little more than a loincloth, with dyes covering most of his body and feathers piercing his nose, the Guardian buried an ax in the neck of one of the gunmen before being shot by another.

Others battled from the trees. Still more were locked in hand-to-hand combat. She noticed they used guns and rifles as well. The arrows had just been the first, silent wave of attack.

Laney's head swiveled back and forth, looking for a safe avenue of escape through the fighting. The battle raged everywhere at once.

"Jen, you see a good route out of here?"

"No. Every time a spot opens, it closes up again. I don't – what the hell?"

Laney followed Jen's gaze. A boy, no more than eleven, stood on the edge of the fight. He was dressed like a Guardian, but his skin remained smooth, unblemished. And he looked familiar.

"Eddie," Elena cried.

Laney looked at Elena and then back at the boy. It all clicked. The two groups had remained in connection through time not by yearly visits, but by family. Her eyes found Nana's. "He's your grandson, isn't he?"

Nana nodded. "This is his first year with the Guardians. He was to return to us in two months' time, at the fall solstice. Then he'll be with them every other year until he turns eighteen, when it becomes permanent."

"And he'll lead them." Jen looked back at Elena. "As Elena will one day lead your people. 'Little queen' isn't her nickname. It's her title."

Nana nodded. "Yes. To the world, we're an equal society, but there is a ruling family. For security reasons, we have never revealed that. Not to anyone. One female from the ruling family leads the people of the village while a male leads the Guardians. It's how it has always been."

Eddie motioned for them to come to him. He pointed up at the trees.

Laney saw the Guardians perched there. "I think Eddie has an escape plan. Let's move."

Her sling now lying empty, Jen picked up the Beretta with a grimace.

Laney eyes flicked to Jen's bandaged arm. "Can you shoot that thing?"

"Guess we'll find out."

"You take lead. I'll cover your run."

Jen nodded.

Laney looked at Nana and Elena. "You two follow right behind Jen. Got it?"

Both nodded, their eyes darting out into the clearing.

Laney looked at Eddie and put up three fingers.

He nodded, signaling to the men in the trees.

Laney tapped Jen on the shoulder. "On three. One, two, three. Go!"

Jen burst out from the truck, weaving past prone bodies. A gunman saw her and let out a yell.

Before he could bring his rifle around, Laney dropped him. She jumped to her feet as Nana and Elena took off at run, surprised at how fast Nana ran.

Laney took out two men as they tried to block Nana and Elena's path. She sprinted behind the other three, praying the Guardians would watch her back.

A man appeared to her right, gun raised. A bullet pierced his neck.

She smiled. *I guess they do have my back.*

A trail cut through the trees. Nana and Elena deftly maneuvered along it. Laney followed closely behind. Leaping over roots, ducking under low branches, she raced, her heart pounding.

Twenty yards in, Laney was startled by the sudden appearance of the Guardians. They materialized in the trails ahead of them, behind them, in the trees above. They formed an honor guard around them, shielding them from any danger.

The path through the forest widened. Laney didn't have to duck any longer. Without a word, the Guardians picked up the pace, racing them through the trees. Laney didn't think, didn't pause. She just ran.

The sounds of the battle receded as they travelled deeper into the forest, until finally all she could hear were the footfalls of her group as they sprinted away.

For hours, they ran through the trees, the pace grueling. At one point, Nana stumbled. Before Laney could reach her, two Guardians swooped down. Looping their arms together, they carried her, barely breaking their stride.

Ahead, another Guardian carried Elena. Occasionally, she would look over his shoulder and give Laney a wave.

Jen slipped back to run with Laney. Laney took comfort in her presence. Jen never broke her stride, never fumbled. She stared straight ahead, a determined look on her face.

The pace slowed as the sun started its slip towards the horizon. Laney's legs felt numb from the frenzied escape. She glanced over at Jen and whispered. "You think they brought sleeping bags and tents with them?"

Jen laughed quietly. "I think they can do better than that. Look up."

Laney nearly tripped as she took in the sight. A village had been built in the trees. There were over twenty huts with wood floors and thatched roofs. Each home was connected to the others by two rope bridges. Above the huts was another, smaller platform, a lookout tower.

"I've always wanted a tree house," Jen said, her eyes glowing.

Torches lit up the homes. Laney couldn't help thinking of Robin Hood and his merry men.

People had stopped to watch the group arrive. Men, women, and children looked down at them. The Guardian tribe. Their existence was unknown to the rest of the world. As far as she knew, she and Jen were the first outsiders to see them.

Laney followed the Nuninks and the Guardians up a rope ladder, stepping onto a long bridge. It swayed with her steps. She clung to the rails, butterflies dancing across her stomach. She'd never been scared of heights, but then again, most of the mountains she'd climbed stayed still as she climbed them.

Together, she and Jen followed Nana and Elena inside the largest hut. It had a wooden floor and a large fire pit in the center with a hole in the roof to allow smoke to escape. There was no furniture. It looked like it might be a giant meeting room for the group.

Eddie walked in from an entryway across from them. Elena sprinted over to him. He hugged her with a giant grin, speaking in Spanish. "Hi, little monkey."

"I've missed you."

"I've missed you too."

An older man followed Eddie in. He was more clothed than the soldiers they'd seen so far. He wore old khakis, cut off at the knees, his feet bare. His chest had the same tattoos, but he didn't have any feathers. His dark hair was dotted with only a few grays, his body still strong.

Eddie stepped away from Elena, his back going straight. He pulled Elena next to him. The two bowed their heads as the man passed.

The man stopped in front of Elena. He lifted her chin. "I have missed you, too, little queen."

Elena threw herself around the man's legs. He hugged her back with a rich laugh. He detangled Elena from his legs and tossed her in the air. She squealed with happiness as he caught her. He placed her next to her brother again, tweaked her nose, and then walked across the room to where Nana waited. Nana ran a hand through her hair as he approached.

The man stopped two feet from her. His eyes seemed to soak her in. His voice was gruff when he spoke. "Are you all right?"

Nana nodded, her eyes never leaving his. "I'm fine." She glanced over to Laney and Jen. "Thanks to these two."

The man shifted his gaze to them with a smile. "I have heard much about you two."

Nana crossed to stand next to him and his hand found hers. "Laney, Jen. I'd like to introduce you to Julian Nunink, king of the Guardians, and my husband."

CHAPTER 19

Laney lay in a hammock, watching the trees sway above her. "It's weird to watch the trees above you sway while you're in a tree house."

Jen looked over at her from her own hammock, five feet away. "Yeah. This is definitely not what I expected to be doing today." She paused. "What do you think is going to happen next?"

Laney shook her head. "I have no idea."

After they'd met with the King and recovered from learning Nana had a husband, the Guardians had begun to fill up the meeting room. Two Guardians escorted them to this hut, explaining they should wait here until the meeting was over.

"Did you see the looks we got?" Jen asked. "I don't think everyone was happy to see us."

"I overhead some of them speaking. Apparently no one outside the Guardians and the ruling family has ever been here. We're a unique case."

"I really hope this isn't one of those 'death to outsiders' group's."

Laney tried to smile, but didn't quite make it. "I

really wish you hadn't said that."

"Sorry. Let's just say, though, for arguments sake, it is a 'death to outsiders' group. Are we going to go quietly?"

This time, the grin came easily. Laney slid a gun from under her shirt. "What do you think? I managed to keep this when they took the other weapons."

Jen slid a knife out of her sling. "Great minds think alike."

Laney placed her gun back under her shirt, gesturing towards the big hut. "Looks like the meeting's breaking up." She slid out of her hammock, with all the grace of a college freshman after a few hours of drinking.

Jen leapt out of hers with the grace of a prima ballerina.

"Seriously," Laney grouched, "how do you do that? Your arm's in a sling, for God's sake."

Jen gave a little bow. "We all have our talents."

Nana appeared in the doorway, her husband at her side. Ten other tribesmen filled into the room surrounding them. "We have made our decision."

Laney took a step closer to Jen. She squeezed her hand for support.

Julian's face was a mask of severity. "No outsider has ever been allowed within our village. Any who have tried have paid the ultimate price."

Laney tensed, her hand inching towards her gun. She knew it would be suicide, but like hell she was going to stand here and be slaughtered.

Nana smiled. "So, we have decided to make you honorary members of the Guardians. You have proven that you have the heart and courage of our brothers and sisters here. You're welcomed as one of us."

Nana embraced them, kissing each of them on the cheek.

Julian did the same. When he released Laney, his eyes twinkled. "So now you don't have to hide those weapons."

CHAPTER 20

Cuenca, Ecuador

It was just before dawn and the Mariscal Lamar International airport, with its single runway, was relatively quiet.

Jake and his group had flown all night, arriving an hour ago. He'd tried to sleep on the flight, knowing he wasn't going to get much for the next few days. When he finally drifted off, though, nightmarish images with Laney center stage jerked him back to wakefulness. He hated knowing she was in trouble and not being able to get to her.

He'd decided to bring only in three extra men, plus the Witt brothers and Henry. He wanted to bring an army, but he knew they needed to move fast. Smaller meant faster.

The men were scattered around the hangar, some slept, some played cards. He'd handpicked each of them. They could all be counted on to do whatever it took.

Another flight took off on the far runway. Jake watched it go. They'd been here for an hour so far. Henry had handled customs, so they'd been left essentially alone since their arrival. Jake was glad. He was in no mood to be diplomatic with officials.

He walked outside to check the gear. They'd been able to borrow the old Bell UH-1 Iroquois, or Huey as it was more commonly known, from a mercenary group just over the border in Columbia.

The Hueys had been heavily used by the U.S. military in Vietnam, but were out of service by the time Jake had enlisted. Although the U.S. military had stopped using them in the late 1980s, this particular model had been bought from New Zealand, which still used a few today.

He pulled the clipboard from the deck of the chopper, glancing down at the gear checklist. He'd probably gone through the list about five times now. But they were waiting for one more flight and until it arrived, there was nothing to do. To keep from going insane, he was re-checking supplies. Again.

"So, I hear our girl's in trouble again."

Jake turned to see Yoni Benjamin standing behind him, sunlight glistening off his baldhead, a duffle bag almost his height hoisted with ease over his muscular shoulder. Of course, being he was only five-foot- two, it wasn't much of a feat for the duffel bag.

Jake offered his hand. Yoni crushed it in his ape-like grip. "Thanks for coming Yoni."

"Hey this is a two-for-one trip: I get to help a friend and beat up some bad guys. You couldn't keep me away."

Although Yoni's tone was light-hearted, Jake could see the anger in his eyes. Yoni was fiercely loyal and protective of his friends. And Jake knew Yoni thought of Laney as family.

On a good day, Yoni was dangerous. With incentive, he was beyond lethal.

Jordan walked up, his usually easy-going attitude replaced with a much more somber one. "Yoni. Thanks for coming."

Yoni whacked him on the back. "Don't worry, Jordan. We got this. We'll have your sister back, beating you in basketball, volleyball, and every other sport, before you know it."

The corners of Jordan's mouth lifted slightly. "You're an ass, Yoni."

"Yup." He hefted the bag above his head. "But I have excellent athletic skills, unlike some people I know. Hey, is that Mikey?"

Yoni headed across the airplane hangar, no doubt to hassle Mike with Jordan at his side. Some might think Yoni was insensitive, but Jake knew Yoni was trying to keep the men's morale up, as well as keeping them loose. If the brothers went into this mission strung out on grief, they'd get themselves killed.

"Jake."

Jake turned to find himself face to face with Patrick. He hadn't seen Laney's uncle in about four months. The priest looked good. Patrick always kept himself in shape, but Jake noticed a little extra muscle underneath his priestly black.

Jake held out his hand.

Patrick pushed it away, pulling him into a hug. "It's good to see you, son."

"You, too, Patrick." Jake drew back. "You sure you're up for this?"

Patrick smiled, although it lacked its usual warmth. "I won't get in the way. It's Laney. I'll do what needs to be done. Besides, my archaeological skills may come in handy."

"Do you really think archaeology has anything to do with this attack?"

He shrugged. "Not sure. The tribe that was attacked, the Shuar, are believed to know the location of a lost treasure of Atlantis, including an incredible library. Maybe somebody else wanted to find it first. Unless you've come up with a different reason?"

"No. This village was made up of farmers. They had nothing of value to steal. The land was fertile but small. And it wouldn't benefit the oil companies to attack them. No one seems to have uncovered any motive for the attack, especially such a brutal attack. I don't understand, though, why Laney and Jen think there are Atlantis artifacts here."

"Edgar Cayce."

Jake groaned. "Not him again."

Edgar Cayce, an early twentieth century psychic, had been world-renowned in his day for his readings. His health readings, where he diagnosed people's illnesses and provided treatment, had an incredible success record. Later on, he began to do readings on people's past lives as well. A small portion of those readings had dealt with the lives people had lived in Atlantis.

Cayce's readings on Atlantis were what had led to them uncovering the plot in Montana last year, as well as the discovery of the superhumans.

A small smile appeared on Patrick's face. "'Fraid so. According to Cayce, towards the end of Atlantis's time, three sets of emissaries were sent to three different corners of the world. Their job was to protect the knowledge of Atlantis. One of the readings suggests one of the locations was in South America."

"But why here? We're heading into the middle of nowhere."

"Have you ever heard of Father Carlo Crespi?"

Jake shook his head.

"He was sent to Ecuador by the Holy See in 1923 and stayed there until his death in 1982. In return for his kindness and services, people began bringing him incredible artifacts. Crespi maintained that all the artifacts predated the great flood. At one point, he'd had the greatest collection of gold and silver artifacts in all of Ecuador. And these artifacts weren't rudimentary tools or evidence of a simple civilization. They were evidence of a highly advanced civilization."

"What types of artifacts?"

"Incredible ones. Sheets of gold covered in symbols from an unknown language, statues, bowls, you name it. And then there are the rumors of an ancient metal library filled with the knowledge of an ancient civilization."

Jake stifled another groan. More people searching for an ancient civilization. He was beginning to think the world would be better off if the evidence of the past stayed buried. "And let me guess. Huge worldwide ramifications if the library's uncovered."

Patrick smiled. "You have to understand. If the legends are true, Atlantis was a highly advanced civilization. Their technology might rival what we have today and, in some ways, even surpass it. That knowledge could open the door to incredible advances in medicine, science, architecture, and a dozen other fields. And then there's the financial incentive. An

Atlantean collection would be truly priceless."

All the men killed in the last search for an Atlantis artifact flashed through Jake's mind. Hundreds had been killed. His brother Tom had almost been one of them, along with Laney. And if the reports on the attacks on the village and church were accurate, this search for Atlantis artifacts didn't look like it was going to have a smaller body count.

"You know, Patrick, I get the whole historical intrigue thing. But so far, all the return of Atlantis seems to be doing is getting a whole lot of people killed."

Patrick paled.

Jake cringed, realizing how harsh his words were, especially with Laney in danger. "I didn't mean . . ."

Patrick waved his words away. "I know. And you're not wrong. It seems we haven't learned the lessons of Atlantis: the quest for power will destroy everything in its path. I just pray Laney's not one of those objects in its path."

Patrick turned and walked towards the hangar, his shoulders lower than they'd been earlier.

Jake watched him go, feeling like ten different kinds of jerk. He followed behind Patrick, promising himself to do everything in his power to keep Laney from being a casualty in this latest search for the remnants of Atlantis.

CHAPTER 21

Laney opened her eyes to daylight streaming through the hut's doorway. She watched from her hammock as tribespeople went about their morning rituals. Children ran along the bridges, laughing. But the men and woman walked in groups, their steps hurried.

And there seemed to be an increase in guards watching the forest below. The whole village was on alert.

Laney looked over as Jen stirred from her sleep. "Morning. How'd you sleep?"

"Like a log. But with really rich and terrifying dreams."

"I know what you mean."

Last night, after the King and Queen's announcement, there'd been a welcoming meal. Although the Guardians tried hard to hide it, Laney could sense their deep sense of loss. Occasionally, she'd catch a tear in someone's eye or a downed face. But they were an incredibly resilient group. After the meal, they each stood and spoke the names of those they'd lost. Laney lost count at somewhere around forty-three. It had been a simple and moving tribute.

Then Julian had spoken about how their friends had gone on to join the Teachers. And that was the cue for the dance to begin. Seven tribesmen came forward and began a dance as old as the group, with only the beat of a single drum to accompany them. The dancers re-enacted the arrival of the knowledge-bringers. Elena sat in between Jen and Laney, interpreting the dancers moves.

There had been seven of them. They had arrived with giant ships filled with treasures. The dancers indicated that the greatest treasure was a set of books detailing their history and their understanding of the world.

Laney's mind whirled at the possibility of finding that library. What humanity could learn from those tomes was beyond her wildest dreams. A documentation of an incredibly ancient civilization.

As she fell into her hammock, her mind had filled with everything she'd seen. It was incredible and yet horrible at the same time: an incredible cache of ancient knowledge, and a group chasing them capable of merciless violence.

She knew she'd never fall asleep with her mind so crammed with thoughts. But she'd dropped off almost as soon as she closed her eyes, her body all but shutting down. Her subconscious, though, had continued the questions the dancers had raised. Artifacts, the Guardians, a world flood, the knowledge-bringers, death, and despair. They'd all jumbled together in a kaleidoscope of images as she slept.

Jen swung her legs over the edge of the hammock. "What's going on out there?"

"It looks like everyone's getting ready for a fight."

"Think they'll find the village?"

"I don't know. How's your arm?"

Jen looked away. "Um, fine."

"Want me to take a look at it?"

Jen stood quickly, turning her injured arm away from Laney. "No, that's okay. I changed the bandage last night."

"Good. I'm not much of a nurse anyway." Laney spied a backpack over by the doorway. She hopped out of the hammock and made her way over to it.

"What's that?" Jen asked.

Laney unzipped the pack and starting pulling out its contents - two disposable cameras, a notepad and pens, plastic bags, two flashlights. "I think these are our inventory tools."

"What? They can't expect us to still go on to the cave with all this happening, can they?"

Carefully wrapping each piece of equipment in the plastic bags, Laney loaded the equipment back into the backpack. "I don't know. But let's keep this with us until we know what the plan is. Let's go see about-"

An explosion at the base of the tree holding the big hut cut off the rest of her words. Laney dropped to the ground as the blast rocked their hut. The giant tree across from them wobbled, but stayed upright.

One tribesman wasn't so lucky. He plummeted from a rope bridge, his screams following him down.

Blasts of gunfire cut through the morning air.

Laney got to her feet and helped Jen up. Her tone was grim. "I guess they found us."

CHAPTER 22

It had taken them forty minutes to fly from the airport to the site of the attacks. Jake sat in the gunner's seat of the helo, his eyes scanning the forest below them as they flew past. He made sure to keep his mind on the mission, not letting his fear for Laney worm its way into his thoughts.

Five miles out from the village, he saw the smoke. Another minute and they were flying over the still smoldering ruins.

Not a building had been left standing, and bodies dotted the burnt landscape. A few animals scattered as they flew over, but others stayed with their meals. His gut clenched. Whoever had done this had been thorough. There was nothing left.

Jake signaled for the pilot to head to the church. A few minutes later, they were hovering above it. It was still standing, but more bodies were strewn across its grounds. A group of about ten people looked up, policemen and some volunteers, who'd been collecting bodies and digging graves.

Yoni peered out the helicopter door next to Jake. "These people never stood a chance."

"No, they didn't. So let's make sure Laney and Jen do." He attached a carabiner to a zip line and threw the rope out the open door. "You ready?"

Yoni mimicked Jake's actions on a second rope. "I'm right behind you."

Jake stepped out into the air, flying down the line. He landed lightly and disconnected himself.

Yoni dropped to the ground next to him. "I'm going to do a quick sweep."

Jake nodded, heading for the man in the dress shirt standing next to the police jeep. The shirt was stained with dirt and blood, as were his tan pants. He doubted the man even noticed. There was a horror in the man's eyes as he looked around him.

Jake held out his hand. "Mr. Carmichael? I'm Jake Rogan from the Chandler Group."

James Carmichael returned the handshake. He was a small, thin man with stringy grey hair that fell over his small blue eyes. The U.S. consulate had sent him to meet with them. "You certainly know how to make an entrance."

"Nowhere to land the helicopter, and time's critical. What can you tell us?"

Carmichael pulled out a handkerchief and wiped his brow, a tremor in his hand. "I've never seen anything like this. They killed everyone, men, women, children, old, young. It's a miracle anyone survived."

"How many survivors have you found?"

"Not enough. Maybe thirty. The priests hid some away in the cellar." Carmichael looked away, his eyes haunted. "They guarded the entrance to that hiding spot with their lives."

Now it was Jake's turn to look away, his thoughts on Patrick. More bad news to share with the priest.

Carmichael cleared his throat. "A few others were found in the woods. It's been a rough morning."

"I'm sorry. And I hate to rush you, but there are still lives at risk."

With a steadying breath, Carmichael led Jake over to a land cruiser a few feet away. He pulled a map off the driver's seat and laid it on the hood. "We're here. Your friends were put in a truck and headed northwest."

"What's up there?"

Carmichael shook his head. "Nothing. I can't figure out where they would be headed. It's almost completely undeveloped. We traced their route until here. The police refused to go further. There are reports of unfriendly indigenous people up there. If you're going to follow your friends, I would suggest you take care."

"Okay. Thanks. If you hear anything else, contact us through the Chandler Group." He turned to leave.

Carmichael grabbed Jake's arm, his eyes intense. "Mr. Rogan, I've spent my morning digging graves. These were good people. They didn't deserve this. I hope you find the monsters responsible for this and give them what they deserve."

Jake looked at the fresh graves around him, his eye focused on one that was impossibly small. He looked back at Carmichael, letting some of his anger into his voice.

"Don't worry about that. I plan on making sure they pay for what they've done here."

CHAPTER 23

Laney peered through the hut's doorway. The men who'd attacked the village and the church swarmed the grounds below them like ants.

The rope bridge in front of her swayed violently as round after round slammed into the huts. Guardians returned fire, cutting down their enemies' number, but not enough to make them turn tail and run. Two more buildings to their right erupted in flames.

Laney glanced over at Jen. "I'm open to ideas."

Jen gave her a determined smile. "I vote for escaping and taking out as many of those bastards as possible."

"Sounds good to me, although I was hoping for a more detailed plan."

Laney whirled around as flames crept over the back of their hut. She snatched the backpack from the ground and secured it to her back. Then she grabbed Jen's good arm. "Never mind. Escaping works. Let's go."

She made Jen go first on the wobbly bridge. Worried the injury to her arm was going to make the crossing difficult, she wanted to keep an eye on her. But, graceful as ever, Jen moved across the bridge without any problems.

Laney said a quick prayer of thanks for Jen's natural balance as she raced behind her. Reaching the boardwalk of the community hut, her eyes darted to a hut across from them. Icy fear raced through her. She nudged Jen's shoulder. "Over there."

One hut over, Elena and Eddie stood. Tears streamed down Elena's face. Eddie stood next to her, trying to look strong. But devastation surrounded him, and his eyes telegraphed his terror. The bridge that connected them to the community hut had been cut down. There was no way for Laney and Jen to reach them.

Julian appeared at the hut on the other side of the children. Laney released her breath. The bridge leading to the children was still attached from his side.

"Stay there. I'm coming," he yelled to the children. He took a step onto the bridge, but bullets blasted through it.

"Grandfather!" Elena cried as Julian leapt back.

In disbelief, Laney watched the ropes attaching the bridge untangle and then swing free. Her eyes flew to Julian. Even from this far, she could feel his fear for his grandchildren.

Laney's eyes darted around, looking for any way to reach them. Two ropes swung between their boardwalk and the children's, both attached to the lookout tower above. One was only a few feet from the children, too far for Laney reach. But the other was much closer to their side. "Jen? How stable does that rope look?"

Jen looked at the rope swinging ten feet away.

"You can't be serious."

"Do you see any other way to get to them?" Laney glanced into the hut behind them. There was nothing to grab the rope with.

She dropped the backpack to the boardwalk and handed Jen her gun. Taking Jen's knife from her belt, she secured it in her own. "Just try to keep anyone from shooting me, all right?'

Jen took the gun. "Damn it. Don't get yourself killed."

"Hey, I've seen Tarzan. How hard can it be?" Her tone was intentionally light, but it was an effort. Her heart hammering, she backed up to the edge of the platform. She dug her feet in like a sprinter, her eyes locked on the rope.

Don't miss. Don't miss. Don't miss. She sprinted for the edge of the platform and leaped.

She hit the rope. She was surprised by how light it was, how narrow. Her hands scrambled to hold onto it.

"Laney!" Jen screamed as she began to fall.

CHAPTER 24

Laney scrambled to get a grip on the rope. Her heart in her throat, she finally wrapped her hands around it, the coarse fibers cutting into her hands.

"I got it," she called, her voice shaking.

Jen glared down at her. "You're officially nuts."

Can't argue there. She took a second to calm down her breathing.

She had the rope, but she was too low on it. Unwrapping her hands, she began to climb. Wrapping her right foot as high as she could, she stood, pulling her hands up. Step by step, hand over hand, she climbed, ignoring the violence around her.

She saw Jen take a shooter's stance aiming for a target below her. She didn't stop to look. She couldn't do anything about the shooters below. That was Jen's job.

Finally, a little below the boardwalk, she began to swing. As she got closer, Jen extended her good arm. On the third swing, Laney grabbed her hand and Jen hauled her in.

Laney's legs felt like Jello when they touched the

solid surface. She almost collapsed to the ground. Her words came out in bursts. "See? Piece of cake."

"If we survive this, I'm dragging you to a psychologist. You literally need to have your head examined."

Laney nodded, but kept her eyes on the children across the way. Fire spread across the hut behind them. Julian was nowhere to be seen. No doubt looking for another way to get to them.

Elena's eyes locked on hers. Laney could feel the girl's trust. Laney nodded back at her. "I'm coming!"

With a deep breath, she backed up, giving herself some slack on the rope, knowing she'd need it to cover the distance.

Jen gripped the Beretta, her eyes alternating between Laney and the ground below. "Another piece of cake?"

Laney gave her a shaky grin. "Absolutely."

Exhaling a breath, she threw herself over the edge. She went weightless. Her arms and shoulder jarred as the rope went taught. She swung her legs around, aiming them straight for Elena and Eddie.

Bullets whipped through the air around her. One grazed her thigh. The sting made her flinch, but she held on.

She looked ahead. *Oh crap. I'm too low.*

Slamming into the boardwalk with a grunt, she grabbed on to the planks, sucking in a breath. *That's going to leave a mark.*

The kids ran to her. They grabbed onto her arm, trying to pull her up.

Laney shook her head. "No. Just grab the rope."

Eddie held onto the rope and Laney climbed up.

She lay down of the boardwalk, trying to get her breathing under control.

"Laney?" Elena asked from above her.

She sat up. "I'm fine, sweetheart." She took the rope from Eddie. "Thanks."

He gave her an abrupt nod.

Laney felt heat from behind her. One side of the hut was engulfed in flames and spreading quickly. She'd planned on taking them over one at a time but there wasn't going to be time for that.

Maybe I can lower them down from here. She peered over the edge. The rope fell short by about thirty feet. Too long a drop for the kids.

"Of course. Why would this be easy?" she muttered.

She pasted a smile on her face, hoping the kids couldn't see her pulse beating away like a majorette. "Okay. So, we're going to take a little swing."

"Laney?" Elena asked, her voice catching.

Laney put an arm around her. "It'll be okay." She spied the other rope, swinging only four feet away. She looked around for a pole or something to pull it in. "Eddie, do you have any kind of hook we can use to pull that rope in?"

He nodded, dashing into the hut. He returned seconds later with a boomerang.

"That'll work." She took it from him. "You two hold onto my hand, okay?"

They grabbed on and Laney leaned out, stretching the boomerang towards the rope. She hooked it on her second try.

"Pull me back," she said. They yanked on her arm. When she was steady on the boardwalk, she gripped the rope, blowing out a breath.

She tossed the boomerang back into the hut, and turned to Eddie. Spying some rope hanging from the doorway, she grabbed it, splitting it in two.

She looked at Eddie. "I 'm going to wrap this around you and you're going to swing over to Jen. Can you do that?"

He scoffed. "I am a Guardian. Of course I can."

She smiled at his bravado, but the tremor that ran through his body told her the real story. He was terrified.

She looped the rope around his shoulders, securing it in case his hands slipped. She knelt down, taking him by the shoulders, looking into his eyes. "I'll follow you with Elena. You show us how it's done. I'll count you down."

He swallowed hard but stepped to the edge.

Laney squeezed his shoulder then stepped back. "One, two, three, go!"

Eddie jumped, and Laney's stomach leaped into her throat. He sailed across the space, his body aimed right for Jen. Time seemed to slow. Finally, Jen reached out and grabbed him, the two of them falling to the planks.

Laney released her breath. *One down. One to go.* She turned to Elena. "Okay, little queen, our turn."

Her face unnaturally pale, Elena nodded but didn't say anything. Laney took the other half of the rope she'd cut and secured Elena to the rope. She glanced back at the hut. The fire crept over the wall they stood in front of.

The center of the hut groaned. Laney knew it was about to collapse, sending flaming projectiles at everything around it.

"Grab on now," she yelled, wrapping her arms around the rope.

Elena leapt on her, her legs around her waist, her arms around her neck and shoulders.

Laney stumbled under the weight. *Oh God, please help*, she prayed as she straightened.

With a deep breath, she backed up as much as she could. With a run, she plunged from their perch, driving her legs towards Jen. Elena screamed and tightened her grip.

Aiming towards the other hut, Laney strained to keep her legs up. She closed her eyes, her arms ached, her hands burned.

Her fingertips began to pull free. *No!* She screamed silently, willing herself to hold on.

It seemed like forever. She knew she couldn't last much longer.

Just as she knew they weren't going to make it, she felt hands on her calf. Her eyes flew open and she looked down into Julian's face. He was stretched out his full height, two tribesmen holding him to the platform. He reeled them in, as Jen continued to take shots at the armed men below.

Julian pulled them onto the boardwalk. Laney sagged against the hut as he pulled Elena off of her. Elena threw her arms around her grandfather, sobbing.

Laney bent her head, breathing deep, willing her legs to work, and her stomach to return to its normal position.

Jen placed her hand on her shoulder. "Tarzan's got nothing on you."

Laney knew her grin was wobbly as she tried to keep the emotions at bay. "Told you."

Jen hauled her up with her good arm. "We need to move."

"Okay. How?"

Jen pointed to a rope that had been attached to one of the railings. "Down."

"Oh good, more ropes."

Peering over the edge, the battle below glared back at her. Tribesmen and camouflaged men were locked in a deadly battle. Most were gunfights, but a few had devolved into hand-to-hand combat.

The tribesmen used the forest to their advantage. They disappeared behind trees only to reappear above an attacker, leading men towards unseen traps in the forest floor. The Shuar might be outgunned, but they were doing an amazing job in spite of those odds.

A flash of movement at the outskirts of the battle caught her attention. She squinted trying to make out the figure. "Jen, over there." She pointed.

Disgust peppered Jen's voice. "Warren."

Warren darted his head out, taking in the battle, before ducking back again. He wasn't even fighting. *Just hiding. Waiting for it to be over. Coward.*

Jen tapped her on the shoulder, drawing her attention back. "No time for him now. He'll have to wait."

Laney nodded. Jen was right. One of the tribesmen was already climbing down, Eddie on his back.

Julian gestured for Laney to go.

She shook her lead. "Elena and Jen first."

He didn't argue, just leaped onto the rope, Elena on his back. Jen followed right behind him. Jen pursed her lips as she made her way down. Laney worried her wounded arm might be too weak for the climb. But Jen made it down without a problem.

The last tribesmen tapped Laney on the shoulder, nodding towards the rope. She grabbed the equipment backpack and quickly climbed over the side. Lowering herself to the ground, her arms felt almost numb. Laney dropped the last few feet.

Jen stood hidden by some trees at the base of the rope, covering her descent. As Laney's feet hit the ground, Jen yelled out. "Laney!"

Laney whirled around in time to see a gunman line her up in his crosshairs.

CHAPTER 25

Laney went to dive out of the way, but Jen tackled her faster. The forest floor next to her was chewed up by gunfire. Jen rolled Laney away from the carnage. Laney sat up, pulling her gun as soon as they stopped.

The gunfire had cut off, at least the gunfire aimed directly at them. She followed the trail of the bullets with her eyes. A camouflaged man sat against a tree, a knife sticking from his throat.

Laney got to her feet. "Thanks."

Jen nodded, her face pale.

"Oh, no. Your arm. Are you okay?"

"I'm good."

Laney nodded, knowing Jen wasn't telling her the truth. But there wasn't much she could do about it now, anyway.

The remaining tribesman jumped to the ground next to them. Gesturing for them to follow him, he disappeared into the trees. Jen sprinted after him, Laney on her heels.

Out of the corner of Laney's eye she saw what could only be described as a behemoth. The man was over six-foot-five. He had a military haircut, and a wicked scar ran from the corner of his eye almost to the tip of his mouth. The man picked a tribesman above his head and threw him against a tree.

For just a second, her eyes met his. The violence, the predatory look on his face, set her trembling. Her legs became weak. Everything about the man screamed in charge and powerful. She struggled to shove the image of him from her mind as she ran, but he stayed, lurking at the edges.

Heart pounding, she followed Jen and the tribesman deeper into the forest. Sprinting full out, she could just make out other members of the tribe ahead of them. At one point, Laney tripped over a log and the tribesman behind her grabbed her before she could hit the ground. There was no time to do more than nod her thanks.

Hours later, Laney wasn't sure how many, they reached a river and began to follow it up stream. She was surprised by the choice. The ground was soft, their foot prints clear. In fact, they were following a trail led by other people passing this way. What was Julian's plan? They were leaving an obvious trail.

During the attack, Laney had focused on doing what needed to be done, but now the adrenaline was long gone. The horror of the last day was seeping in.

The image of the man she'd seen came back full force. He was powerful; maybe not superhuman, but powerful. And he was after them. It was easier to think they would succeed when the enemy was faceless, or better yet, Warren. But that man had been no weakling.

Jen dropped back to jog with her. "Who the hell are those guys?"

Laney shook her head, trying to clear it. "I don't

know. But they're not South American. So far, I've heard two Jersey accents and one Southern. This group's from the States."

"You know the guy in the ridiculous safari outfit?"

Laney pictured the Safari's R' Us man. He hadn't been at the battle. "Yeah. What about him?"

"There was something familiar about him, but I couldn't place him. I realized a little while ago who he is. Dr. Brandon Deveraux, III."

"Why do I know that name?"

"Probably because it's emblazoned across every introduction to archaeology text in the States."

"Holy crap!" A picture of the intro text she'd had back in undergrad slipped into her mind. "That's right. Why's he here? He's an armchair academic."

Dr. Brandon Deveraux was known for writing all his texts without leaving the comfort of his office. In fact, Laney would be shocked if he'd ever been in the field.

Jen nodded. "There've been some rumblings about how he's resistant to some of the newer discoveries. Alternate archaeologists have really been pushing hard lately to get older sites included in our understanding of civilization's development. Your uncle's work, for example, is really making people reconsider what we think we 'know' about civilization's development."

"And that means all the textbooks will have to be rewritten."

Laney knew that in academia, textbooks were where the money was made. An introductory textbook could easily cost a student $150. If a textbook was the gold standard in the field, then all intro courses would employ it, which meant the author would make millions. And once too many old copies were floating around, a new edition came out. It was an absolute gravy train.

Jen continued. "But if these new discoveries are incorporated into our history, an alternate timeline will have to be accepted. And Deveraux won't be writing those texts."

"I get that. But it still doesn't explain why he's here. What does he hope to accomplish?"

Jen dropped her voice. "The cave of Etsu Nantu. If it's what we think it is, it's the complete history of a technologically advanced pre-historic civilization. And if he gets there first, he gets to write that history. He'll be in high demand everywhere."

Laney looked at Elena sleeping in the arms of her grandfather ahead of them, as a chill stole over her. "Or he and his friends can keep that information from ever being released. Maybe even destroyed. But I don't understand who the men with him are. Deveraux doesn't have access to this kind of fire power."

"Whoever they are, they seem committed to finding the cave, no matter who gets in their way."

Laney swallowed. "And to them, we're all just another obstacle to be removed."

CHAPTER 26

About an hour upriver, Julian put up a hand to stop the group at a rock outcropping. Nana appeared from the cave a few feet up and ran down towards them. Laney smiled as she wrapped Elena and Eddie in her arms.

Julian walked up to the threesome, completing the hug. Pulling back, he spoke with Nana. Although Laney was too far away to make out the words, she saw Julian gesture towards her.

Nana nodded before walking over. "So I hear we have you to thank once again."

"It was a team effort."

Nana raised an eyebrow. "So you didn't fly across open air, in the middle of a gunfight, on a flaming rope, to save my grandchildren?"

"Flaming? The rope wasn't on fire." Laney looked at Jen, who didn't meet her eyes. "Jen?"

"Actually, it was."

Laney stared at her in shock.

Jen shrugged. "It was at the top. You were already with the kids when I noticed it. There didn't seem to be any point in telling you. I knew what you were going to do. So I-"

Laney held up a hand. "Hold on. Let me get my breath back. I'm flashing through images of Elena and myself plummeting to the ground."

She took a deep breath, but she knew Jen was right. Even if she'd known, she still would have taken the same action. It was the only way to save them. But it was still a shock.

She swallowed it down. She'd deal with that fright, along with all the other ones from the past twenty-four hours, later. "Okay. Now, could you tell me why we're leaving a trail a blind man could follow? Is this the cave of Etsu Nantu?"

Nana smiled. "That's what they'll think. This is the Tayos Cave."

Laney paused. "The Tayos Cave? As in Neil Armstrong?"

Nana nodded. "He was a nice man."

Laney stared at her, stunned. Back in 1976, the late astronaut, Neil Armstrong, was part of an expedition put together by Stan Hall to find the source of the Crespi collection. The Hall expedition started and ended at the Tayos cave. They explored it fully, but hadn't succeeded in finding the Atlantis artifacts.

The group had believed, however, that the tunnel system attached to the cave, if explored further, would lead them to the cave of Etsu Nantu and more importantly, the library of ancient knowledge. Other searches had been planned, but due to one reason or another, had never materialized.

Laney stared up at the cave entrance. "Is there a chance they'll find their way to the library from here?"

Nana shook her head. "No. It's too far and the way

is," she struggled to find the right word, "booby-trapped."

Jen nodded. Laney looked to her for an explanation.

"The tunnels underneath Ecuador have been known for hundreds, if not thousands, of years," Jen said. "They're believed to stretch from Peru to Ecuador and even into Chile. When the Conquistadors came, the Incans showed them storehouse after storehouse of gold. They told the Spaniards, whom they believed to be gods, the treasures were from the tunnels underneath the ground. Since that time, treasure hunters have searched through the tunnels. But very few have returned to share their tales."

Laney swallowed a lump in her throat, picturing Indian Jones-style traps. "They were all killed by the traps?"

Jen shrugged. "A large number probably were. But the tunnel system is also extensive. And from the reports of the few survivors, each tunnel looks identical to the next. It's a safe bet that many simply got lost, wandering around until their death."

Laney shivered at the image. *Okay. Note to self: stay out of the tunnels.*

Jen looked back at Nana, gesturing towards the cave. "How do you know they'll think this is the cave?"

"They'll follow our trail here. And then they'll investigate the cave. The cave itself was inhabited by people at least a thousand years ago, much later than the knowledge-bringers. Hopefully, the gunmen will waste a lot of time figuring that out. The real cave of knowledge isn't so easy to find."

Laney nodded. A red herring. It was a good idea.

It would give them time to get away and plan. "So where are we going? Back to Cuenca?"

Nana shook her head. "No. We continue to the cave."

Laney stared at her, not believing the words.

"They'll track us. We'll lead them right there," Jen argued.

Julian walked up. "We'll cover our trail. Leave Guardians to prevent them from following."

Jen shook her head. "That's a huge risk. Surely the court will understand that they need to give us more time."

Nana's voice was weary. "And if they don't? For all we know, the judge is in the oil company's pocket. They could have even orchestrated this whole thing to prevent us from getting them that report. I cannot risk our tribe's entire existence on the hope that the court will understand. They have demonstrated too many times in the past that they don't."

Laney knew that the Shuar had spent decades fighting off one corporation after another who wanted to take over their lands. And Nana was right. The courts were turning more and more in favor of the developers. Was it possible that they could lose the cave if they missed the deadline?

Nana looked Jen and then Laney in the eye. "This isn't what you signed on for. We can have members of the tribe take pictures of the site. That should be enough for documentation. There's no reason for you two to risk your lives further."

Laney glanced at Jen, who nodded back at her. She faced Nana. "We're not leaving you. And if you think the court won't understand gunplay necessitating an extension, then they certainly aren't going to be satisfied with a couple of pictures. We're in this."

Nana shook her head. "This isn't your fight. If something were to happen to-"

Jen cut her off. "And how do you think we'd feel if something happened to you or Elena or Eddie? We're in this, Nana."

Laney nodded. "Besides, we're Guardians now. And it seems we may be the only two in a position right now to help you protect our land. The only place we're going is with you."

CHAPTER 27

A warm breeze blew through the trees, ruffling Laney's hair. She closed her eyes inhaling the scents the wind brought with it. For just a moment she let herself relax, let down her guard. She tried to forget everything that had happened, and just breathe.

Jen nudged her and Laney's eyes opened. *Back to reality.*

Laney and Jen stood amongst the rest of the tribe along the shores of the Pastaza River. Ahead, Nana, Elena, Eddie and Julian stood on the rock outcropping facing the group.

Julian raised his hands and all murmuring stopped. "We have been dealt a serious blow. But we're Guardians. No one has defeated us and no one ever will. It's time to make the pilgrimage to our sacred site. Our ancestors will protect us and see us through."

Without another word, he turned. He picked up Elena, walked across the rock face and stepped into the river. One by one, the Guardians followed him. They left no trail. It looked like the Guardians' trail had ended at the Tayos Cave.

Laney stepped into the water, thankful for its warmth, even as it sloshed over her boots. She sighed. "Apparently, these boots aren't completely waterproof. And I have a feeling this is going to be a really long walk."

Jen grinned, slipping into the water next to her. "Well, it could be worse. At least it's only up to our calves."

"Your calves, Jen. It's up to my knees."

"Oh, right. Sorry."

They traveled for hours in the river, never stopping for a break. Laney marveled at the spirit of the Shuar. They'd lost at least half their numbers and yet they didn't stop to pity themselves. She glanced over at Jen. "These people are amazing."

Jen nodded. "Their loyalty to each other, their dedication to duty. They're a throwback to how people should be."

"They've lost so much and they keep moving forward. I wonder if I could be as resolute if I was in their shoes."

Jen smiled, clasping Laney's hand. "My friend, you and the Shuar are cut from the same cloth. Life hasn't always been easy for you, not when you were a kid, not a year ago, not right now. Yet here you are. Moving forward."

Laney squeezed her hand back. "Same goes for you. Maybe they weren't wrong to let us into their tribe."

Laney and Jen didn't speak again for the next few hours, both lost in their own worlds. As a group, they traipsed through the river and out again, climbed hills, clambered over downed trees, and ended up in yet another river. It was the world's longest obstacle course.

Laney's thighs were beginning to ache and her feet had gone numb. Yet the Shuar kept moving forward, and so did she.

Laney glanced over at Jen, who looked as if this trek was no more strenuous than an evening stroll around the park. "You know, if you were a good friend, you'd look a little more exhausted right now."

"I am completely exhausted."

Laney didn't believe a word of it.

"I'm just good at hiding it. Besides, my mind's racing with what we're going to see. I can't believe it. I know I should feel horror at all that has happened, and I do, but I can't help also being excited by what we might see."

"Okay, I grant you that it'll be incredible. But would a little catnap make it any less incredible?"

"Well, I think you might just get your wish." Jen nodded ahead of them where Julian was leading the group out of the water and onto the bank.

"Finally." Laney moved forward with a grateful smile. The smile quickly disappeared as Julian walked straight into the trees without stopping, the Guardians following behind.

"I'm really beginning to hate these guys," Laney grumbled.

The sun was all but gone from the sky when Laney glanced at her watch. It had been about two hours since they'd left the river. She was seriously considering throwing a tantrum like a sulky two-year old if she didn't get a small break when Guardians appeared from the trees. She couldn't be sure, but she didn't think they'd been at the village.

The tribesman in front of her halted. Exhausted, Laney nearly walked into the man. "Sorry," she muttered, shaking her head. She was practically asleep on her feet.

A group of six tribesmen separated from the group, disappearing into the darkening forest.

"Must be taking the first watch," Jen said, putting her good arm around Laney. "Look."

Laney looked ahead to where a small camp had been erected. Hammocks were strung from trees in a circle.

Laney nodded as she watched the remaining tribespeople take a hammock. She and Jen each picked one. Laney closed her eyes, dreading what dreams sleep would bring, dreading what tomorrow would bring. But too exhausted to even try to fight, she let sleep claim her. And with it came the nightmares.

CHAPTER 28

The sounds of the forest continued around them as Jake and his group made their way forward. They'd flown over the canopy of trees until they reached the site where the trucks carrying Laney and Jen had come under attack.

One of the trucks had been left behind, riddled with arrows and bullets. Bodies had been strewn through the area. Mostly men in camouflage, but a few were natives of the area, dressed in little more than loincloths, tattoos across their torsos. Patrick thought they might be members of the Shuar tribe.

A quick reconnaissance of the area didn't show any sign of Laney and Jen. Jake didn't let himself feel any relief. It was good they weren't among the dead, but until he saw her with his own eyes, he wouldn't relax. He couldn't.

They followed the trail of the other truck from the air, but soon, the trees had become too thick. They had to travel on foot. Apparently it had been too thick for the truck as well. They found it abandoned.

Jake and his group had been traveling for three

hours now, following a pretty well laid-out trail. Whoever had made it hadn't been concerned with covering their tracks. Of course, they probably figured no one would be trying to find them. And, if not for Danny placing that tracker on Laney's computer, no one would have.

But dark was beginning to descend. Jake knew they were going to have to call a halt for the night soon.

Jake paused, realizing the forest had gone silent. He signaled the group to stop, pulling his M4 to his shoulder. A scream of pain came from ahead, followed by a smattering of laughter.

Jake gestured for Yoni to check it out. Yoni slipped into the trees as Jake slowly led the group forward.

A minute later, Yoni jogged back through the trees towards Jake, his face serious. "There's trouble up ahead."

"The girls?" Jake asked.

"No sign of them. There's a village in the trees. Or at least, there used to be. It received the same treatment as the other locations. I counted four men. They're interrogating a man. And enjoying it way too much."

Jake nodded, tapping the mic on his collar. "Village ahead with hostiles. We need to take some alive."

Fifty yards later, he saw the village Yoni mentioned. But this hadn't been a fight. This had been an annihilation. None of the huts had been left untouched. Most had been burned to ash. And bodies littered the ground, both natives and intruders alike.

Jake signaled for everyone to stop when they reached a small clearing. They were still hidden by the trees. Four men in camouflage surrounded a bound

.

man on the ground. Blood poured from a wound in the man's head and his chest was a mass of red welts.

"I don't think he's going to tell us anything," one of them said, his thick Boston accent coming out clear. The man fingered his knife looking like he wanted to be tagged into the fun.

Another, the ringleader of the group with a nose that had been broken too many times, grinned back at him. "Never thought he would. These animals always stick together." He kicked the bound man in the ribs. "Now I'm just having fun."

Boston snickered. "Not that I mind, but I'm thinking one of those two bitches they carted off might be more fun, especially that tall Asian girl. I'm thinking she'd be a lot of –"

A bullet pierced the man's eye, another his neck.

Shit. Jake looked over at Jordan and Mike. Both had their weapons pulled into the shoulder.

"Move in," Jake yelled, firing at the ringleader. "We need one alive."

The firefight that ensued was short. Unprepared for the attack, three were killed. The other was injured, but his wounds weren't life threatening.

Jake moved into the clearing, his eyes peeled for any sign of movement. He signaled for Yoni and another man to make a loop and make sure there weren't any others hiding about. He knew in his gut, though, that there weren't.

"Create a perimeter," Jake barked into his throat piece. "And stay on guard." Jake moved towards the man lying on the ground.

He leaned down as the man tried to crawl away. Pulling the man back, he turned him over. "Where do you think you're going?"

The ringleader held his left hand in front of his face. His other hung uselessly at his side, blood drenching it. "Don't kill me, man. Don't kill me."

Jake snatched the front of the man's shirt. "Don't kill you? Did you give any of these people that option?"

"It wasn't my choice. I don't make the orders. I just follow them."

"You're not a soldier, asshole. Now tell me where the rest of your people went."

The man shook his head, grimacing in pain. "I can't tell you. They'll kill me."

Jake held back his anger. He gestured towards Mike and Jordan, who were standing ten feet away, their rage clear in their rigid stance. "You see those men? One of the women your friends are after is their sister. The last thing you should be worrying about is what your friends will do to you. There's a much more immediate threat you should concern yourself with."

The man stared over at the brothers. A tremor ran through him. Jake couldn't blame him. The Witt boys looked like they wanted to tear him limb from limb.

The man looked back Jake. "Look, I'm not sure where —"

Jake reached down and squeezed the man's leg where the bullet had torn through the muscle. A primal scream erupted from him.

Jake's words were furious. "I'm done playing with you. Tell me where they went. Now." Bobbing his head furiously, the mercenary said, "They headed towards the river."

Jake pulled up a mental map of the area. "The

Pastaza River?"

The man nodded.

"How far ahead of us are they?"

"A few hours. Maybe three."

Jake slammed the man back into the ground. He turned and walked away. He radioed the helicopter to pick up the wounded tribesmen and the mercenary.

Henry stood waiting for him.

"So what are we going to do with him?"

Jake looked around at the devastation the man had helped create. "I say we save the world the trouble, and put a bullet in his head. But I called the Huey. He'll pick them both up."

Henry gestured towards Patrick who was tending to the wounded tribesman a few feet away. "Probably for the best. I don't think Patrick would be up for cold-blooded murder, even against that guy."

Patrick spoke to the wounded man, clasping his hand and nodding before walking over to Jake and Henry. He gestured to the man Jake had just questioned. "What are you going to do with that one?"

"We were just discussing that," Henry said.

Patrick narrowed his eyes. "We should probably just put a bullet in his head."

Jake stared at him in shock.

Anger laced Patrick's words. "But I suppose we should let him live. I'm not helping him, though. God help me, if I go near him, I may kill him myself."

"He told us the rest of his men left about three hours ago, heading towards the river. It looks like Laney and Jen escaped with the tribesmen," Jake said.

A small smile crept across Patrick's face. "That's my girl. Let's hope they keep ahead of them until we arrive."

Jake nodded. He was thinking the same thing.

The sun was gone. What little light was left would be gone within thirty minutes. Jake wanted to keep going, but it would be suicide. They didn't know the terrain. The group ahead of them could have easily set traps to cover their trail. "The day's gone. We need to set up camp and get out at dawn."

He caught sight of Jordan and Mike walking through the rubble, checking each of the bodies. He nodded towards them. "What are they doing?"

"Looking for Jen," Henry said.

Jake inhaled sharply. *Damn.* "I'll tell them."

Henry put his hand on his arm to stop him. "Jake, they need to be sure she's not here. Let's help them."

Jake nodded, giving instructions to the rest of the team to check the bodies to make sure Jen and Laney weren't among them. He left Henry to set up camp.

Then he headed over to Jordan, placing a hand on his shoulder. "We'll find her. That guy said they left. They're not here. But we'll check, make sure."

Jordan nodded, but his eyes were haunted. He continued moving through the bodies without a word. Other members of the team spanned out to help search.

Patrick stopped next to Jake, his hands shaking. "Jake, I know we need to move quickly in the morning, but I'd like to administer the last rites to these people. And I'd like to do a quick search in the morning, make sure I didn't miss anyone."

Jake looked around. Patrick was right. They didn't have time for burials, but last rites were the least they could do. He nodded. "Okay, but at first light, we're out of here."

Henry surveyed the damage around him. "I'll stay with Patrick and we'll catch up with you. These people deserve a little peace."

"Okay," Jake agreed before re-joining in the search.

Jake worked his way through the bodies and destruction in the fading light. A few times, his gut clenched when he saw a dark-haired woman, but none had been Jen. And none of the bodies had long red hair.

Darkness fell and he stopped, surveying the sight. These attackers had been ruthless. And they were after Laney. He closed his eyes.

Hold on a little longer, Laney. I'm right behind you.

CHAPTER 29

Dawn crept through the sky when Hugo halted the men. They'd searched into the night, using night-vision goggles. It had been slow and frustrating.

The natives had been more adept than he'd expected. They'd set a number of false trails. Each mistaken path fueled his anger more. Before last night, he'd intended to kill them. But now, he was going to enjoy it.

One of his scouts came running up to him. "Sir, the trail ends just ahead at a cave entrance."

Hugo grunted. "Any sign of the natives?"

"Lots of footprints and a trail leads inside the cave. The scouts didn't hear anything inside, but we haven't done a complete search yet."

"Initiate a search and set up a perimeter. Let me know when you've found them." He dismissed the man and continued through the foliage. In another fifty yards, he stepped out of the river.

He'd checked the map earlier and knew it was the Pastaza River. Looking towards the cave entrance, he noted footsteps led straight to the rock face. No footprints led away from the spot. They disappeared right here.

He looked around, not liking it. This was simply too easy.

He shook his head. Of course, they were just a bunch of barely clothed savages. They probably didn't have the brainpower to get out of a locked room. Nonetheless, he motioned to the group of five men that stood silently behind him waiting for his orders.

A short, muscular man stepped forward. "Sir?"

"Take your men and head upstream two clicks. Make sure they didn't leave this spot. Contact tango team and have them do the same downstream."

The man gave him a crisp nod. "Yes, sir." With a sharp turn, he walked back to his men. Hugo nodded his approval. His men were well trained. They obeyed without question.

Of course, they were well compensated for that discipline. He watched as another group of ten entered the cave, their weapons held at the ready. A wise precaution.

These savages might be slow, but they'd proven to be innovative fighters. He scowled as he thought of the tree village fight. It had been a royal cluster fuck. He'd been taken unaware by the ingenuity of the tribe. The forest was their turf and they'd used it to their advantage.

Eventually he'd prevailed, but not before losing almost a quarter of his men. And not before his quarry scurried away. He wouldn't underestimate them again.

Branches broke behind him and he felt his anger rise. His scowl deepened as he turned in time to see Warren stumble from the forest, tripping over some underbrush. His face was a mass of bruises, his nose hidden by bandages, and his fingers splinted. The man was a complete embarrassment. How his family had let him live to this age was a complete mystery to Hugo. He would have strangled him in his bassinet.

He turned away, dismissing Junior from his thoughts. He raised his radio to his lips. "Alpha team report."

"Sir, we've made it through the main cavern. The space is huge. No sign of the natives."

"Keep searching. Out."

He clicked off the radio and frowned. This didn't feel right. Damn it. The area was quiet, with trees lining either side of the embankments. The cave itself was sitting high up on about twenty feet of rock face. All footprints led directly to the cave. He stepped onto the rock plateau.

He walked to the edge, staring down the river. Of course, if they'd walked in the river, there'd be no trace of them. It would only look like they'd stopped here. His radio came to life. "Alpha to base."

"Go ahead, Alpha."

"Sir, we've found, well, it seems to be a gold skeleton in a side room of the cave."

Hugo jolted at the words. Perhaps he was wrong. Perhaps this was the site they were looking for.

" Can you remove it?"

"It's in a glass case of some type. Do you want me to break it?"

He heard a gasp behind him.

Deveraux ran over to him. "No. Absolutely not."

Hugo met Deveraux's gaze as he spoke into the radio. "Yes."

"What's wrong with you?" Deveraux yelled. "That is a priceless artifact."

"Yeah, with a priceless treasure inside. But you know what? I'm betting I could find a price I'm happy to trade it for."

"You're a barbarian."

Hugo narrowed his eyes, his tone lowered. "Be careful how you speak to me, Professor. Not everybody needs to return from this trip."

Deveraux paled. His next words had a tremor in them. "It's just an unnecessary destruction. I'm sure I could find a way to open the case and retrieve the skeleton without harming it."

"Well, the next thing we find, I'll give you a crack at."

Deveraux nodded, turning away. He paused in mid-step, swinging back to Hugo. "Wait. Are you saying that's all they've found?"

Hugo nodded, eyeing the concern on the archaeologist's face. "Yes. A giant room and then an alcove off it with the gold skeleton."

"That's not right. Do you have the coordinates of where we are?"

Hugo pulled out his GPS and rattled off the location. "78' 13' degrees West and –"

"3' 6' degrees South." Deveraux finished for him.

"Correct. How did you know that?"

Deveraux closed his eyes. "We're at the wrong spot. This is the Tayos Cave."

"What the hell's the Tayos Cave?"

"Back in 1976 a man named Stan Hall led a group of explorers to try and find the Atlantis library. They never found it. They did find the Tayos Cave along with a few ancient artifacts. And, of course, they found the tunnel system that runs underneath almost all of Ecuador."

"So it could connect to the cave we're looking for?" Hugo asked.

"Yes, but it would be almost impossible to find. The tunnel system that links them has never been mapped, nor even fully explored. It's also supposed to be booby trapped by the Incans."

A panicked voice squawked out of the radio. "Sir."

"Report," Hugo barked, an uneasy feeling stealing over him.

"Sir, I have six men down."

"What the hell happened?'

"I'm not sure. We were heading through one of the tunnels when all of a sudden some sort of chemical sprayed out from the walls. Four of us were able to get clear. But the other six..."

"Yes?"

"They're dead, sir."

Hugo gripped the radio. "Clear out. Get everyone out of the tunnels."

"Sir, what about the men? Should we retrieve their bodies?"

"No. Leave them."

There was a pause over the radio. "Yes, sir."

Hugo turned to the professor. "Seems you were right, Professor. Although an earlier warning would have saved my men and some time."

Deveraux blanched. "I couldn't have known. You wouldn't give me a GPS. How was I to know where we are?"

"Out of my sight, Professor, before I decide to let

you see the Incans' work up close and in person."

Deveraux scurried away, casting a worried look over his shoulder.

More men down. He didn't mind their deaths. He did, however, mind the feeling that someone has gotten the best of him.

"Schedderton." He barked.

His second in command ran forward, stopping in front of him. "Sir."

"We're going to have to split the group. You'll lead your group downstream. I'll take the other one upstream. Bravo and tango teams are already scouting ahead. Our target has moved on. We need to run them to ground."

"Yes, sir."

"Dismissed." Hugo stalked towards the riverbank. He would track them down. And they would pay for making him search.

CHAPTER 30

Laney slept hard. When she woke, she felt like she'd aged overnight. Everything ached.

Jen let out a small groan from the hammock next to her. Laney smiled, feeling a little better that Jen was also struggling. *At least she's not a superhuman.*

Starting at the thought, Laney stared at Jen. Jen hadn't mentioned her arm since the village. Nana had given her a new shirt, which covered her wound, so Laney couldn't tell if it had healed.

Jen turned to Laney with a grimace. "I feel like crap."

Laney laughed, shaking her head to clear her thoughts as she disentangled herself from the hammock. "Same here." *Jen as a superhuman.* Hunger and exhaustion must be messing with her brain. She was Jen, not one of them.

A woman walked up and handed them each a mango and a piece of dried meat. They nodded their thanks. And then the group started moving into the forest.

Laney rubbed the back of her neck. "Here we go again."

"It can't be as long a walk as yesterday. Can it?" Jen asked.

Laney stretched out her legs before following the Shuar into the trees. "I really hope not." She looked around. "I wonder how the tribespeople they left to defend our backs are faring."

"We haven't heard any gunfire, so I'm hoping that's a good sign."

Those were the last words they spoke until the sun was high in the sky. A river could be heard up ahead.

"We must be getting close," Jen whispered.

"I was thinking the same thing," Laney said.

They stepped out of the forest and onto a rock shelf. The river spanned fifty feet across. A towering wall of rock, at least a hundred feet high, bordered the river on the opposite bank. Elena and Eddie played along the riverbank with some of the other children.

Laney looked around. "I don't understand. Where's the cave?"

Jen shrugged. "I don't see anything. Maybe we're just taking a break?"

Nana walked towards them, her eyes alight. "Are you two ready?"

Laney looked over at the rock face. It was completely sheer. If they were going to climb it, it was going to be nearly impossible. "Ready? But there's nothing here."

"You didn't think it would be easy to find, did you? How do you think we've been able to protect it all these years?"

Laney looked again at the rock wall, inspecting it

closely. She still couldn't see any openings. She glanced at the river, the water lapping against the shores and the wall of rock across from them.

She smiled. Not all cave entrances were so obvious. "I guess we're going for a little swim?"

Nana nodded.

Laney stared across the dark river. "How long a swim?"

It didn't look like the current was too strong, but she didn't know what to expect once they went under the water. Swimming in the Amazon, even just a tributary of the Maranon River in the Amazon Basin, wasn't exactly high on her list of things to do, at least not without a Hazmat suit. A myriad of horror stories about exotic parasites filled her head.

"Once you're underwater, it's about ten feet down and twenty feet across."

"Can we see under there?" Jen asked.

Julian joined them, the backpack with the camera equipment slung over his broad shoulders. "A little. It's dark. But we know the way." He held up a rope. "We've done this before."

Julian waded into the river along with another tribesman, a young, muscular man in his mid-twenties. A few feet from the shore, he dove in and swam swiftly to the other side. The other tribesman followed. They stopped at the base of the rock on the other side, treading water.

Laney looked down at Nana with a smile. "Your husband's in pretty good shape."

"Don't I know it." Nana pushed the two of them towards the river with a grin. "Now go on."

"You're not coming?" Jen asked.

Nana shook her head. "No. I've never been inside."

Laney stopped short. "What? Why not?"

"My job is to maintain contact with the outside world and monitor any threats. It's the Guardians' job to guard the cave. Only Guardians have been inside. This is a great honor you are receiving."

The gravity of the responsibility wasn't lost on Laney. She clasped Nana's hand. "Thank you for your trust."

Squeezing her hand, Nana waved the two of them towards the water. "You better go."

Laney looked at Jen and smiled. The answers to Crespi's collection, to mankind's past, maybe to its very existence, lay less than a hundred feet away. Any thoughts of rest disappeared. Excitement coursed through her. She kicked off her boots and stuffed her socks into them, seeing Jen do the same.

Jen stood. "Ready?"

Laney took a deep breath. "Absolutely."

Together, they ran to the edge of the water and dove in.

CHAPTER 31

The water was warm and Laney quickly made her way over to Julian. Jen reached him just ahead of her.

"Good. You're both strong swimmers." He handed Jen a rope. "Tie this around your waist. I'll lead you through." He turned to Laney. "George will lead you through."

George swam over to Laney, handing her a rope. She took it, tying it around her waist.

"Take a deep breath," Julian warned, before disappearing under the water.

"Good luck," Laney said.

Jen gave her a thumbs-up before following Julian down.

George held up three fingers. Laney sucked in a deep breath. When George reached one, she dove under the water with him. It was dark, but there was enough light to at least keep an eye on George as he swam ahead of her.

He angled towards the left and down. After about ten feet, he stopped. If he hadn't, she never would have seen the entrance. Tall grasses swayed in front of it, completely hiding it from view.

He disappeared through the opening. Laney followed. It was a tight tunnel. She used the sides to usher her forward.

The tunnel felt like it was growing smaller. Her breath became strained and she became desperate for air. Spots began to appear in her vision, a burning in her chest.

Just about at the end of her air supply, the tunnel ended. She popped up in a small lagoon. Greedily sucking in air, she lay on her back, floating, trying to calm her breathing. George swam for the bank, releasing his end of the rope.

Flickering light from torches on the bank gave the room a soft glow. She squinted at the ceiling. There seemed to be something carved into it. It took a moment to register what she was seeing. She gasped, causing her to go under. She came back up spluttering. "Holy crap."

The ceiling was a giant carving of the world.

"I know," Jen called from the bank. George was just climbing onto the bank.

Laney glanced over at her and started swimming. Pulling herself up to the ledge with a grin, she pulled the rope from around her waist, her eyes constantly returning to the ceiling. "Two seconds in here and I already have goose bumps."

Jen grinned back. "Tell me about it. Did you notice the extra landmass between North America and Europe?"

Laney looked back at the carving. An archipelago was dead center of the map.

"And Antarctica's not on there."

Jen grinned. "I guess Hapgood was right."

In 1953, Charles Hapgood had developed his theory of crustal displacement. He argued that the Earth had undergone multiple displacements of land as a result of the movement of a liquid core one hundred miles underneath the surface. Rather than the slow process of continental drift, which split lands apart, crustal displacement could move large bodies of land together and quickly. In line with his theory, he argued that Atlantis had never truly disappeared but just moved North, where it was renamed Antarctica.

Hapgood's theory would explain one extraordinary fact about the continent of Antarctica: evidence indicated that at one point in its history, it had a much warmer climate, free from ice. Hapgood's theory was scorned by a number of prominent scientists, but Dr. Hapgood had garnered at least one well-known supporter: Albert Einstein.

Laney wrapped her arms around herself. Were they really about to see a lost cache from Atlantis?

Jen waved towards an opening twenty feet away. "Julian said he'd go ahead and light the torches."

As if on cue, a soft glow shone through the opening. Feeling like a kid on Christmas morning, Laney got to her feet, stopping at the entrance of the tunnel next to Jen. A torch flicked on either side. The flames glowed in a holder with a lion's head on the bottom and what looked like an angel or goddess on the top. She smiled, her anticipation growing.

Laney turned to George, who stood next to the entrance, struggling to recall the correct Shuar words. Finally, she just pointed at him and the tunnel. "Are you coming?"

He shook his head, indicating he was to remain there. Laney nodded and then followed Jen into the tunnel.

Running her hand along the wall, Laney was surprised by its texture. She'd expected the walls to be rough, but they were perfectly smooth. If she didn't know any better, she'd swear they'd been smoothed by a machine. "What do you make of the walls?"

Jen stopped, running her hands over the surface. "I can't figure it out. It doesn't feel like rock. It feels almost like a piece of metal, but the texture's a little off."

"I know. I'd say it was a really strong plastic, but that's not possible, right?"

Jen glanced over at her. "A synthetic polymer mix? Is that even possible? That technology's not exactly rudimentary."

"I know. But I can't figure out what else it could be." Her mind whirled. They hadn't even entered the main cavern and already she was mystified.

Up ahead, the tunnel funneled out into a larger space, although due to the incline of the tunnel, Laney couldn't make anything out. She had to actively keep herself from sprinting forward.

Jen stepped out of the tunnel ahead of her and went completely still. Laney stepped around her and couldn't even think.

The cavern was massive, about half the size of a football field and easily eighty feet high.

Laney walked forward, her knees weak. Standing at attention at the entrance were two twenty-foot limestone statues, one man, one woman, wrapped in intricate robes, a small smile etched on each of their faces.

In fact, statues, lined the walls at twenty-foot intervals, each one at least thirty feet tall. Some bore an uncanny resemblance to early portrayals of Egyptian gods: human bodies with the heads of jackals, falcons, lions, and even a crocodile. Others were obviously fully human, complete with wrinkles and scars.

Against the wall to the right was a miniature ship made of gold. It looked almost exactly like a space shuttle. Gold spheres, small silver statues of animals, intricate boxes, and chests were spread out across the space.

And the walls. The walls were lined in sheets of gold, covered in carvings, just like the ones in Crespi's collection. It was overwhelming.

Laney looked at Julian, who stood next to one of the giant limestone statues. He smiled at her. "Go on."

Her knees weak, Laney didn't know where to start. Shaking her head, she finally just turned to her right, starting with a metal scroll on the wall. Awe filled her.

"Jen, come look at this."

Jen stepped over to her, grabbing onto Laney's arm. "It's the Vimanas."

Laney nodded. The Vimanas were ancient flying machines described in Sanskrit epics. The information from those ancient texts was astonishing in its detail. Drawings done based on the descriptions resembled current space shuttles.

But on this metal scroll in front of them, there weren't reading about an ancient space shuttle. They were seeing the actual picture of one.

Alternative archaeologists claimed that the machines described in the epics weren't mythological, but actual machines used in antiquity. Of course, no credible archaeologist believed they were blueprints for spaceships, despite the descriptions of aerial battles that littered a number of ancient texts, including the Bible.

A few feet from the blueprint was a miniature model of a space shuttle. Laney traced its outline. Fuselage, two wings, even thrusters at the back. She glanced back at the drawing a few feet way. She struggled to come up with some other interpretation for the object, but her mind couldn't conjure one. *My God, were we capable of flight thousands of years ago?*

Jen headed across the room but Laney walked along the perimeter of the room to the right. A miniature ancient city was painstakingly crafted in one spot, with an organized city grid and something that looked like a type of monorail.

Laney was starting to feel lightheaded. It was incredible. It was proof that humanity wasn't at the pinnacle of its evolution. If anything, humanity was only getting back to where it once was.

She looked around and saw Jen standing in the middle of the room, next to a large rectangular table. Laney made her way over. It looked like an ornate conference table. She ran her hand over it. It was made of the same material as the walls in the tunnel. Seven chairs were placed carefully around it. She lifted one. It was unbelievably light. Yet she could tell it was incredibly sturdy. "What is this material?"

Laney glanced over at Jen when her question was greeted with only silence.

Jen was staring, mesmerized by the seven chairs surrounding the table. Each one had a different design etched into every inch.

One had the signs of the zodiac, another long forgotten animals from the sea. A third had human/animal hybrids. A fourth had what looked like airplanes and hot air balloons. The fifth had an array of land-dwelling animals, many Laney had never seen or heard of before. The sixth had what looked like constellations and the seventh was covered in pictures of humans engaged in different tasks.

"There's seven," Jen whispered, her voice reverent. "Seven."

Laney looked back at her, not sure what she meant, until it hit her. Once again, she felt the ground beneath her shift. Throughout ancient tales, seven had always been a critical number. There were seven gods in Greek mythology. In India, seven helpers. The advanced peoples of a myriad of myths and legends always seemed to come in the number seven.

Could there have been seven teachers? Were the gods, the helpers, and the teachers related? Could they have been the same people?

Laney turned to say something to Jen, but now it was her turn to be without words. She stood up from her inspection of the chairs, her body on automatic pilot.

Across from the table, in an alcove twenty feet away, stood shelves lined with metal folios. A metal library filled with the knowledge of an ancient civilization.

Laney stepped into the alcove. Reaching out with a trembling hand, she touched the book in front of her. It was about eighteen by twelve inches and made completely of silver. She tried to pull it out, but it was too heavy. Instead, she ran her trembling hand along the spine. Unknown symbols were etched there. The folio next to it was covered in different symbols and made of gold leaf.

She looked to her right and left. Row upon row was filled with the books. "There must be dozens of these," she murmured.

"Not dozens," Jen said, coming to stand behind her. "Hundreds."

Jen was staring up.

Laney followed her eyes. This time her legs did go weak. She reached out a hand to steady herself. The rows of books continued up for another twenty feet.

Jen pulled Laney into a hug. "All this knowledge."

Laney wrapped her arms around her. And then they were jumping up and down, laughing and crying at the same time.

Laney wiped her eyes. "It's beyond amazing."

"It's unbelievable. We really need to get shots of this."

The comment brought reality crashing back. This wasn't a well-planned expedition into an ancient site. This was a desperate trip forced by gunmen.

Laney took a deep breath, a little kernel of excitement still bouncing around in the back of her mind. But she needed to focus. "Okay. We need to grid the cavern off and start documenting it. And we need to do it quickly."

"I wonder if we should also take one artifact as proof for the court?"

Laney tried lift one of the books. "Well, we're certainly not getting one of these out. They weigh a ton. I wonder how they got them in here."

"Well, that was easier."

At Laney's questioning glance, Jen said, "This whole area was above sea level before the last ice age. If these date before that, they would have simply walked them in."

"That would explain the stairs in the lagoon."

Jen's eyes were wide. "Are we really talking about an incredibly advanced civilization from at least twelve thousand years ago?"

Laney glanced back up at the portfolios, a huge smile on her face. "I guess we are."

CHAPTER 32

Laney and Jen explored the rest of the main room. They photographed everything they could and jotted down notes of observations not captured by the film.

They tried to keep their excitement at bay and be objective observers.   At times, though, it was impossible

Discoveries that flew in the face of history were strewn throughout the room. Laney could barely take it all in. Every time she tried to focus on one artifact, her eyes would catch sight of another.   She had the attention span of a sugar-filled four-year old.

Finally, though, she and Jen made their way to the back of the cave. There were three huge doorways. Each was fitted with a ten-foot tall stone door engraved with intricate carvings.

Laney peered at the doors, running her hand along the seam. A perfect fit. The skill of the artisans had been way beyond rudimentary stone tools. This was machine precision.

Laney looked over her shoulder at Julian, who'd come to stand next to her.   He had been quietly allowing them investigate the cavern. "Where do they lead?"

He shook his head. "I don't know. I haven't explored them. Our job is to guard the site, not wander through it. We don't come this far in."

Laney stared at the three entryways. "I'm betting one leads towards the coast. We're what, maybe three, four miles from it?"

Jen nodded. "That sounds about right. But which one?"

Laney leaned close, placing her ear on the door in the middle. She waved Jen over. "Listen."

Jen leaned her ear against the door. "Is that water?"

Laney nodded. "I think so." She leaned into the door on the right. "I don't hear it here. How about that one?"

Jen put her ear against the door on the left. "More water."

Laney stood back and looked at the doors. "So one's an escape and two are what?"

"Booby traps," Jen said.

Laney glanced over at her, nodding. "Maybe a safety measure to keep the treasure from falling in the wrong hands. If the wrong people found the cave, it could be flooded."

It made sense. She turned, and then her attention was diverted from the doors by an eleven-foot-long sarcophagus. And that's how it went. Every time she saw one amazing artifact, another would distract her.

Despite all the incredible sights, though, it was the metal folios that kept pulling her back.

Last year, she had learned that Atlantis had been populated by two groups of people, the Children of the

Law of One and the Sons of Belial. The Sons of Belial had only been interested in garnering power. But the Children had been good people, pacifists, knowledge gatherers.

According to Edgar Cayce, as the end of Atlantis had approached, the Children had sent out three sets of emissaries, carrying the knowledge of Atlantis with them. Had the Children written these tomes? Was she looking at that lost knowledge?

Her hands and eyes roamed the books hungrily. *All that knowledge*. And some of the symbols looked familiar. But she couldn't quite place them.

She called over to Julian. "Julian, can you help me get this book out?"

He came over and helped her lift the gold leaf book from the second shelf. They placed it reverently on a small stone table just inside the alcove. Jen walked up to join them.

"Why this one?" Jen asked, peering at it curiously.

Laney pointed at a symbol on the spine. "I think this is written in Enochian."

Enochian, the language of the angels, was an incredibly controversial language. In the sixteenth century, John Dee and Edward Kelley had discovered it. They maintained it had been revealed to them by angels.

Laney stared at the other tomes. Were they all written in Enochian?

"Are you sure?" Jen asked.

"No. But see this symbol? That looks like the Enochian symbol for time."

Laney flipped to the next page and her heart seemed to slam to a stop.

"Laney?" Jen asked.

Laney traced one of the words on the page. She swallowed, trying to find her voice. "This word. It's also Enochian. I know it."

Jen stared at the symbols. "What does it spell?"

"Azazyel." Spots began to appear around her vision. Azazyel, the most dangerous of the fallen angels. The angel who'd taught mankind how to fashion and wield weapons. And the one who'd tried to end the world only a few short months ago.

Jen grabbed her arm. "Laney? You okay?"

Laney stared at her, not comprehending the words right away. She hadn't expected to see his name here. She didn't want him or his kind to be related to this cave. Fear charged through her and she had to talk herself down. *He's dead. He's dead.*

She closed the book, her hands trembling. She didn't know why his name was here and she didn't have time to figure it out. Right now, they needed to figure out how to protect the cave and its contents.

Shaking off the fear, Laney glanced at her watch. "We've been in here for almost two hours. We need to get back out and figure out our next step."

Jen nodded. "You're right. We need a plan."

Laney turned to Julian. "I think we have all we'll need for the court. Jen and I can write this up tonight and get it to the court tomorrow." She let out a breath. *If, that is, we don't get killed before then.*

She thought of Henry and the Chandler Group. She knew he could help.

"And I have a friend who'll help us protect it."

Julian looked around the cave, his expression fierce. "I don't want outsiders near our cave."

Laney knew how hard this must for him. "I know. But the world's coming. And my friend's very good at operating in that world. He'll help you keep all of this safe."

Jen nodded. "I think you need to look at this next step as the way to protect it. The world has changed and now the way you protect it needs to change as well."

Julian nodded, although Laney could tell he wasn't fully convinced. He took the camera from her and placed it back in the plastic bag and then into the backpack. He slung the pack over his shoulder. "Let's get outside and we'll take you to Machala. You can make the necessary arrangements from there."

Laney followed Julian back through the tunnel and to the lagoon. George was in the same spot, patiently waiting for them.

Before tying the rope George handed her, Laney stood next to Jen, staring up at the map of the world. The same tingle of excitement she'd felt when she'd first seen it coursed through her.

This whole cave system was filled with the relics of an ancient civilization that predated all known civilizations by thousands of years. And she was one of the few people in the world, heck, in the history of the world, who'd seen it.

Jen touched her shoulder as she stepped to the edge. "See you topside." She disappeared under the water attached to Julian.

Laney took one last look at the ceiling before tying the rope around herself and diving under the water with George.

She swam along the tunnel, trying to imagine how

the world would react to this finding. There would undeniably be some who would deny its authenticity or try to find a way to fit it into a pre-conceived notion of development.

That map, though, made it all but impossible. While it didn't date the site, it did indicate that the people who created it had the capability to capture aerial views of landmasses.

The implications were truly mind-boggling. And then there was Atlantis, prominently displayed on the carving, right where Plato said it would be.

Light pierced through the dark water ahead. Laney's eyes drifted towards the surface. When they popped up, everything was going to change. She smiled as she burst out of the water.

She turned toward the shore. The smile dropped from her face.

The tribe was surrounded by armed men. Laney's eyes searched the crowd before falling on Nana, who had her arms wrapped protectively around both Elena and Eddie. A bright red mark stood out on her cheek.

Julian was being held face down on the sandy beach. Jen struggled as two large men pinned her arms behind her back.

"Dr. McPhearson," Brandon Deveraux called, his clothes now a mass of wrinkles. "I believe we have a lot to discuss."

CHAPTER 33

The second set of divers dove into the water and disappeared. On the bank, equipment had been brought from a clearing not too far away. Giant sleds had been air dropped in. More men appeared with crates that they were busy unpacking.

Laney sat next to Jen on the bank watching all the activity with a heavy heart. The rest of the Shuar tribe surrounded them, all bound. No one in the group spoke.

Laney couldn't imagine what was going through their minds. They'd already lost almost half their members and now the very reason for their existence was about to be stripped away from them.

She pictured the tribesmen who'd stayed behind to cover their escape. Were they all dead as well?

When these men found the entrance, they would loot the entire site. There would be nothing left. This group, whoever they were, had come prepared. Air drops of equipment had begun even before they'd left the cave. In no time, they'd have a full-scale excavation in progress. At least, as soon as they found the entrance.

The divers popped up from the river and gave a thumbs down. The man on the bank with the scar running down from his eye waved them in. He was the man Laney had seen in the battle at the tree village. Laney had heard someone call him Hugo.

Jen sat bound next to Laney, frustration punctuating her words. "When they find the cave, they'll take everything."

Laney nodded, unable to speak. She could only think of the world map and all that one piece conveyed. Her eyes raked the men, looking for Warren. He was nowhere to be seen. But Brandon Devereaux was. He stood next to the sled, instructing the men on something. She willed all her hate on him instead.

As if feeling her stare, he looked over at her. With a last comment to the man next to him, he walked over. He stopped in front of her and then kneeled down to her level. She was surprised to see what looked like remorse in his eyes. His eyes darted over his shoulder, focusing on Hugo. His back was to them as he spoke into the radio.

Deveraux's words came out hesitatingly. "Dr. McPhearson, I know your uncle. While we disagree professionally, I have always respected him."

Laney stared back at him in disbelief. "Well, while he hasn't mentioned you, I'm pretty sure hearing you had something to do with my death will sour your professional relationship."

He cringed. "It wasn't supposed to be like this. When I was first approached, I was going to be the archaeologist in charge. I wasn't told about the rest of this."

"Did you even ask?" Jen asked.

He looked away. "No. They offered a lot of money and to be honest, I need it. Plus, if I could get ahead with the new research . . ." His voice trailed off.

Disgust laced Jen's words. "You could retain your position in the field."

"I know what you think. I'm not a bad man. But you need to be careful. These men are ruthless. Whatever they want, give it to them."

He stood and walked back to a group of men latching cables to a sled. Hugo's narrowed eyes followed Deveraux's retreating form.

Laney didn't need Deveraux's warning about the ruthlessness of these men. She'd seen it first-hand. And the man walking towards them was the personification of it.

Hugo stopped in front of the two of them. He didn't bother to bend down. He just stood there, towering over them.

Laney craned her neck to look up at him. She glanced over her shoulder, realizing two men had walked up behind them. One of the men reached down, yanking her up. Jen received the same treatment next to her.

Laney held in the yelp that wanted to escape her lips, her stomach bottoming out. Whatever Hugo wanted them for, it couldn't be good.

The man holding her cut through the ties that bound her hands. The other man did the same to Jen's. Confused, Laney rubbed her wrists, looking back at Hugo. What game was this?

Hugo stared down at her. "We need you to show us the entrance to the cave."

"Why us?" Laney asked, inwardly knowing it would be a cold day in hell before she helped these bastards.

He waved towards the rest of the hostages. "I don't want any problems in translation. And I also don't want to play any games."

The two men who had untied them pulled Elena and Eddie from Nana. The children screamed and tried to break away, but the men held them securely.

Nana ran after them. Another man blocked her way, punching her in the stomach. She dropped to the ground, the air knocked from her.

With a roar of fury, Julian leaped to his feet. He sprang at the man who'd struck Nana. The man pulled his sidearm and shot him point blank. Julian crashed to the ground, blood pouring from the wound in his chest.

A wail erupted from Nana as she crawled for him. She put her hands on his wound, trying to stop the bleeding. Tears streamed down her cheeks. Blood ran through her hands, dripping to the ground below.

Shocked by the swiftness of the violence, Laney turned to Hugo. Anger boiled through her. "What is wrong with you?"

He smiled. "I'm just very goal orientated. Now, I need you two to show us where the entrance is."

In response, Laney glared back at him.

Jen nudged her. "Laney, Elena and Eddie."

Two divers stood at the edge of the bank, ready to dive. Elena and Eddie had each been latched to them. But unlike Hugo's men, the children had no gear. They stood on the edge of the river, terror spreading across their faces.

Laney pulled her eyes from them to Hugo's face.

"Like I said, you'll show us where the entrance is." He waved his arm and the divers dove into the water, dragging Elena and Eddie with them.

CHAPTER 34

The children didn't even have a chance to scream before they disappeared below the water's dark surface.

"No," Laney yelled, sprinting for the water. Jen beat her to the water's edge and dove in. Laney followed, her arms and legs churning frantically under the murky water.

The divers were treading water fifty feet in. Eddie and Elena thrashed in the water next to them but the divers held the rope taut, not allowing them to reach the surface.

Jen's height gave her an advantage and she outpaced Laney. She swam right by the two divers, heading straight for the cave. Laney approved. Jen didn't waste any precious time making sure they followed. She knew they would.

Jen disappeared through the tunnel entrance. The first diver followed her, Eddie being dragged in his wake.

Laney reached the second diver just as he entered the cramped space. She rushed in behind him. Pushing him forward, she tried to protect Elena's head from being slammed into the walls of the tight space.

As the diver emerged into the pool, Laney shoved Elena's head up towards the air before she surfaced.

Gasping, she looked at Elena. She was turning blue, not breathing. Shaking, Laney yanked the rope off Elena's still form and pulled her towards the bank, not even looking at the bastard diver. Jen was already at the bank, hauling up a spluttering Eddie.

The first diver walked off, talking into his radio, not sparing them a glance.

"Jen, grab her," Laney yelled.

Eyes wide, Jen grabbed Elena, pulling her up. "No."

Laney hauled herself out. Jen was already breathing into Elena's mouth. Laney scrambled over to them.

As soon as Jen stopped her breaths, Laney began to pump her chest. "Come on, little queen. Stay with us."

Jen began her breaths again. Laney prayed as she watched, her whole body going numb. *Please don't be dead.*

Eddie pulled himself to Elena's other side, taking her hand. "No, sister, no."

Laney began chest compressions again when Elena coughed. She quickly turned her onto her side, patting her back. "It's okay, sweetheart. Let it out."

Elena coughed for a few minutes, water running from her mouth and nose. Finally, she stopped and lay curled around herself. "I want Nana," she cried.

Jen pulled Elena into her arms, rocking back and forth. "I know, honey. We'll get you back to her."

Laney pulled Eddie into her arms. He didn't resist as his tears fell along with his sister's.

Up ahead, the second diver blocked the entrance to the cave, a nine millimeter in his hands. Jen's words were meant to calm Elena, but Laney knew the likelihood of them keeping that promise was all but nonexistent.

CHAPTER 35

It had been hours since they'd entered the cave. Laney wasn't sure of the exact time, as neither she nor Jen had a working watch. Her watch had been smashed during the furious swim in. She'd ask one of the men surrounding them, but they all seemed too busy looting priceless artifacts to answer a simple question.

Deveraux had at least done a good job of making sure all of the artifacts were protected. The whole cave had been recorded and photographed. Then each artifact was carefully wrapped and placed in a water-tight container. The artifacts would survive, but it killed Laney to watch everything slowly disappear.

Behind Laney and Jen, Eddie and Elena lay curled around each other, fast asleep. For the first hour or so, they'd been terrified, but exhaustion had finally won out and they'd fallen into a fitful sleep.

Laney reached over and pushed back Elena's hair, then Eddie's. "I hate that they're in the middle of this."

"I know. These men are inhuman." Jen watched the last of the folios get loaded in their crate and sealed. "Nothing seems off limits to them."

Laney leaned back against the cave wall. "Okay, my friend, what's our plan?   They're about finished emptying this place and I'm pretty sure we're not going to last much longer past that."

Jen held up her wrists. "At least, they didn't lock us up this time."

Laney looked at all the firepower in the room. "I'm guessing that has to do with the fact that we're grossly outnumbered and outgunned.   I may be fast, but not faster than a speeding bullet."

Jen's eyes narrowed.   She motioned towards the entry. "Speaking of bullets, isn't that Warren?"

Laney glanced over at the entrance.   Warren stood in dive gear.   With his hood down, the massive bruises that dotted his face stood out.   Laney took satisfaction in the bandages covering his nose and the splints on his fingers.   He looked over at the two of them.

"Bastard," Laney whispered.

Warren   started   walking   towards   them,   his pronounced swagger still there.   A larger man followed behind him.

"Oh look, he's made a friend," Laney said.

Warren stopped in front of them, the same, familiar smirk on his face.   "Well, seems like you two got your comeuppance."

"Us?   Have you looked in a mirror lately?" Laney asked.

Warren narrowed his eyes, gesturing at the two sleeping children.   "Maybe I should let some of the men have fun with these two.   Some of them like the more tender flesh.   Like my friend here."   He jerked his hand over his shoulder at the hulk standing behind him.

"Any of you touch them, and you're dead," Jen

said.

He laughed. "And who's going to do that? You? Maybe you don't understand exactly who's running things around here."

Laney looked over at Jen. "Tough talk from a boy who needs a bodyguard to talk to two helpless woman."

Jen shrugged. "You know what they say, all talk, no penis."

Warren's face grew red. "You'll regret that, bitch." He reached down to grab Elena.

Laney sprang to her feet, her right uppercut landing just under his jaw, followed by a left cross and then a right hook. He dropped to the ground.

Jen dropped to her back and up-kicked his partner as he leaned down to grab her. The man flew back, crashing into a sharp rock behind him. He didn't get up.

Laney stomped on Warren's groin. She grabbed the front of his shirt, pulling him up. "Next time you antagonize someone who just kicked your ass, make sure they're not in the position to do it again."

"I think that's enough."

Laney looked back at Hugo, who stood behind her with three other men only a few feet away. She backed away, her hands up.

Hugo gestured for two of the men to help their fallen comrades. Laney looked over at Jen, regretting baiting the worthless man. She glanced down at Elena and Eddie. *Please don't let them pay for my actions.*

Hugo glared down at them, his arms crossed over his large chest. "I know I should be ticked off at you for taking down two of my men, though, to be honest, they weren't really worth much to begin with. But, an example must be made. Bind them up."

Two men placed zip ties round their wrists, pushing them to the ground. They did the same to the children, who screamed in fear when they woke. Laney and Jen scooted next to Eddie and Elena, keeping them between them.

Laney closed her eyes. *Just let it be quick.* A minute passed and no shots rang out. She opened her eyes.

Hugo smirked at her from above. "Oh, you thought I was going to shoot you? Now what kind of example would that be? I'm just waiting for something."

Beyond Hugo, a man made his way quickly towards them, a rectangular box in his hand, two lanterns tucked under his arms.

Hugo gestured to the large stone doors behind them. "Place it over there."

The man placed the two lanterns at the base of the doors. Between them, he placed the container and then hit a button. A clock face glowed red.

"Do you know that drowning is supposed to be the worst way to die? But don't worry, you may be crushed to death before that ever happens." Hugo turned and jogged towards the entrance. The three men with him followed him out.

The cave was now empty of everyone and everything except for Laney, Jen, the kids, and Hugo's going-away present.

Laney stared at the clock face and the dull, grey, clay-like substance that could be seen beyond it. C4. Thirty minutes and this place was going to blow.

CHAPTER 36

Laney watched the timer count down in disbelief. This couldn't really be happening, could it? "Why are they blowing this place? Why not just leave it?"

Jen shook her head. "They need to remove all traces. I'm betting they're trying to collapse the rock face."

Laney felt hollow. "Right on top of us."

A small explosion from outside the cave shook the roof and small bits of rocks were torn from the ceiling. Smoke and debris blew back through the entry tunnel. Instinctively, Laney and Jen shielded the children.

"What was that?" Elena cried.

Laney stared at the entrance in horror. "They destroyed the lagoon." She looked across the children's heads at Jen. "They wanted to make sure we couldn't escape."

"Not happening." Jen squirmed in her seated position.

"What are you doing?"

"Hold on. Almost there." Jen continued her shaking and then held up her unbound hands.

"How did you do that?" Laney asked.

Jen moved to Laney's back. "There was a rip in my ties. I just gave them a little help to finish the tear."

Laney could feel Jen sawing through the binds. But then she could swear she felt Jen just pull them apart. Laney held up her hands, rolling her wrists to restore the circulation.

Jen had already moved onto Eddie's bindings. With quick movements, she had them off him and moved onto Elena. "I've been thinking about how to get out of here. I think the stone doors are the answer. We open the middle one, we escape."

Jen freed Elena with a final tug. After a quick hug for the terrified girl, she moved towards the large doors.

Laney looked after Jen in shock as she moved towards the stone doors. What the hell was going on? How had Jen released them all so quickly?

"Laney?" Elena asked.

Laney shook her head, pulling herself back. She walked over to the kids and gave them both hugs. "Come on." She ushered the two children to the doors. And the bomb. The kids stared at the clock, seemingly unable to tear their eyes from the countdown. Twenty-three and a half minutes to go.

"You two stay here for a minute." She turned to follow Jen.

Eddie latched onto her hand. "Are we going to die?"

Laney stared down into his face. His bottom lip trembled even though she knew he was trying to be brave. She couldn't lie to him. He deserved the truth. "We're going to do everything we can to keep that from happening."

Elena wrapped her arm around her big brother. "Don't worry, Eddie. Laney and Jen won't let anything happen to us."

Laney nodded, turning away, not sure what to say to the conviction in Elena's voice. She walked over to Jen and kept her voice low. "Any thoughts?"

Jen glanced over at her. "Are you familiar with Derinkuyu, in Turkey?"

She struggled to place the name. Then it hit her. Derinkuyu was an underground city in the Cappadocia region of Turkey. It was one of over two hundred cities that had been uncovered. They were believed to have been created to protect citizens from marauding armies. Some of the cities could hold up to 50,000 people.

"What does that have to . . ." Laney's voice drifted off as she stared at the door in front of her. "The doors. They built giant rock doors into the cave entrances to protect them from invaders."

Jen nodded. She turned, inspecting the walls nearest the doors. "When invaders arrived, they'd lock the doors. And the same mechanism could be used to open them." Jen's eyes raked the cave near the doors. "There."

Laney followed Jen to a small alcove in the wall. At the bottom of the alcove, were three stone levers.

Laney stood next to her, looking down at them. She prayed they still worked. "Which one opens the safe door?"

Jen shrugged, her voice quiet. "I'm not sure. Probably the one on the right." She went silent and Laney met her eyes. "But if not . . ."

Laney's stomach bottomed out. "We drown."

Jen nodded.

Laney looked back at the countdown clock. "Just over twenty minutes left. We need to make a choice."

Jen's hand raised above the levers and stilled. "What if we choose wrong?"

Laney took her hand. "If we do nothing, then we die for sure. But if we choose right, we live. So, let's at least give living a shot, okay?"

Jen nodded. Taking a breath, she pulled the lever.

CHAPTER 37

Jake peered out of the trees at the scene along the river. A group of indigenous people huddled together, covered by two guards. A few minutes ago, they'd heard an explosion and made their way to the riverbank.

The helicopters had led them here. They'd seen one flying towards the river and then away again with its package. The helos weren't going very far. They returned after about twenty minutes. They must be storing the cargo nearby. Maybe they even found a clearing where a cargo plane could land and take off.

The explosion had clued them to the exact location, but it had taken them hours to get here from the tree village. They'd found the Tayos cave and then wasted time breaking into two groups looking for the trail up and down the river.

His group had come across another bloody skirmish. More natives lay dead, a few camouflaged men as well. He shook his head. This group didn't even collect their own dead, just left them to rot.

He'd thought about radioing the helicopter to speed up the search but he hadn't wanted to let anyone know they were in the area. Instead, they'd double-timed it. And so far, it looked like no one was the wiser.

Up ahead, two guards pulled a sled into the trees from the water. They were emptying something out.

"Must be the cave Laney and Jen were looking for," Yoni whispered as he sidled up next to Jake.

Jake nodded. "Looks like these guys are prepared. This is a high-end operation."

"Must be waiting for another helicopter," Yoni said. "Any word from Henry or Patrick?"

"They're only a few minutes behind us." Jake and the rest of the group had taken off just before dawn. Patrick had stayed behind, doing a final search when light had dawned for any more bodies at the tree village. Unfortunately, he'd found some.

"Any sign of the girls?" Jordan asked.

Jake glanced over at Jordan, whose face was tight with emotion. "No. There are a bunch of tribespeople on the bank being held at gunpoint, but I don't see any sign of Laney or Jen."

The sled was almost at the tree line and no more appeared from the river. The two men on the shore guarding the tribespeople glanced over at the retreating sled.

Jake shook his head. "I don't like this. I think we're showing up at the end of the party."

"Okay. So what's the plan?" Jordan asked.

One of the guard's radios squawked to life, interrupting Jake's reply. "That's the last sled. The boss said to wrap it up." One of the men on the shore asked. "Clean up time?"

"Affirmative," came the radioed reply.

The man nodded. He and his partner walked

towards the bound group on the ground. They raised their weapons.

Jake was faster. His first bullet caught one of the men in the chest, his second in the neck. He collapsed back into the river. Jordan's gun took down the second guard.

A barrage of gunfire from the direction of the retreating sleds targeted Jake's position. *Shit. There must be more men just inside the tree line.*

Jake scuttled across the ground on his stomach, reaching a giant tree. From the corner of his eye, he saw Jordan do the same across from him. Jake sat up, his back firm against its trunk. He looked around. Mike and Yoni had taken up similar positions, returning fire. The other three members of their team were pinned down.

The last sled was still being dragged into the trees. Jake fired on it, taking out one of the men. Over the gunfire, he could hear the approach of the helicopter. He looked up and saw it coming in from the west, a long cable dangling from it. "They're trying to link it up. Aim for the chopper."

The words were barely out of his mouth before machine gun fire raked the ground around him. With a yell, he dove for cover next to Yoni, driven back by the sniper. "Where the hell's that coming from?"

Yoni peeked out from behind his tree. A bullet nearly took off his head. He pulled back. "Not sure. I think the trees somewhere to our right."

Jake glanced out, but the shooter forced him back again. "Shit."

He could hear the helo getting closer. It was hovering just above the tree line. *They must be linking up the last sled.*

He struggled to form a plan. There wasn't one. Until that sniper was taken out or ran out of ammo, they were sitting ducks.

A shot from a rifle cut through the air and the blasts from the sniper stopped. Jake glanced out. Henry stepped into the clearing, firing at the helicopter. It was already pulling away, its payload swinging underneath.

Jake stood, lining the pilot up in his sights. He squeezed the trigger just as the pilot veered to the right. The shot went wide. He fired off five more shots in rapid succession. They hit the body of the chopper, but none did enough damage to down it. It flew off, its cargo swinging beneath.

"Damn it." Jake yanked his radio from his belt. "Foxtrot Charlie, we need a ride now." He rattled off their location.

"Ten minutes," came the reply over the radio.

"I'll check and make sure we don't have any stragglers." Yoni disappeared into the woods, three men joining him.

Henry came to stand next to him.

Jake tipped his head towards where the sniper had been. "That your shot?"

Henry shook his head. "Nope. Father Patrick's. Did you know he was a sharp shooter back in the day?"

"At this point, nothing that man can do surprises me."

Jake glanced over to where Patrick was speaking with some of the native people. Pulling out a first aid kit from his pack, he knelt next to a man lying on the ground. Placing pressure bandages on the man's chest, Patrick kept up a rapid conversation with a woman with long white hair. Tears streamed down her face. She gestured towards the rock face across the river.

A feeling of dread began to well up in the pit of Jake's stomach. He started towards Patrick.

"Jake?" Henry called out.

Jake didn't answer. He couldn't. A rumble started under his feet. He stared across the river. The giant rock face seemed to quiver. Then, with a tumbling roar, it caved in on itself, sending rocks, water, and dust flying in every direction.

Jake dropped as the ground shook with the force of an earthquake. After a few seconds, the trembling stopped and everything went quiet. He stared with stunned disbelief at the pile of rocks across from him. "They blew the whole thing up."

Henry leaned down and offered his hand. "They must have gotten everything they needed from it."

Jake grasped it, pulling himself up. Dusting himself off, he walked towards Patrick who sat on the ground, staring across the water. Cries of grief rose from the group on the riverbank.

A look of pain was frozen on Patrick's face. Tears tracked their way through the dust covering the priest's face.

Jake leaned down and put his hand on Patrick's shoulder. "Patrick?"

Grief-stricken eyes focused in on Jake. "They're gone, Jake. They're gone."

"What are you talking about?"

With a shaking finger, Patrick pointed to the rubble. "Laney and Jen. They're under there. We're too late."

CHAPTER 38

Jake sprinted for the water. "Laney!"

He was about to jump in, when Henry wrapped his arms around him, holding him back. "No, Jake. You can't help her this way."

"Let me go. She could be under there. She could still be alive."

Henry's hold didn't break. "You saw what happened. No one could survive that. A mountain of rock just collapsed on itself. She's gone, Jake. She's gone."

Jake pulled himself free, glaring at Henry. "She's not. You know her. She wouldn't go down without a fight. If there was a way to survive, she'd find it."

"I know that. But Jake, even if she did, without the right equipment, we'll never be able to reach her in time. Or Jen." Henry's voice broke on Jen's name.

Jake jerked his head up and looked at Henry. He saw the anguish etched into his friend's face. He knew that if there was a chance they could save them, Henry would be leading the charge.

Seeing Henry's pain hammered home the loss.

Tears sprang to his eyes. He sank to the ground. Desperate loss clawed at his chest. He pictured Laney struggling to breathe, unable to escape, her lifeless body crushed beneath the rocks.

He remembered the last time he'd seen her: She'd been laughing, making cupcakes with Max and Danny. She'd pulled him into the kitchen, forcing him into an apron and handed him a mixing bowl. Her eyes had sparkled the whole time.

They were too late. She was gone. And there was nothing he could do.

"No!"

Jake's head whipped around at Jordan's yell. Jordan and Mike sprinted for the river and dove in.

"I'll get them," Henry said, running after them. Yoni dove in behind him.

Jake watched as the brothers' dove under, again and again. Each time they popped back up, the hole in his chest grew larger. Finally, whatever Yoni and Henry were saying to them, got through. They let themselves be dragged back to shore.

Yoni, his clothes dripping, walked up to Jake, his eyes red, his signature bounce absent. "Jake?"

Jake wiped his eyes and stood to face him.

Yoni glanced up at him. Looking away, he cleared his throat, a slight quiver in his voice. "The helo's approaching. What do you want us to do?"

Jake stared back at the rocks, desperately wishing he could turn back time. If they'd only gotten here a few minutes sooner. *I'm sorry, Laney. I'm so damn sorry.*

Forcing himself to focus on the task at hand, he knew he needed to do one last thing for her. Or die trying.

There was no tremor in Jake's voice when he spoke, only conviction. "Laney and Jen died for what they stole. We're going to get it back."

CHAPTER 39

Laney pulled Eddie up, dusting some of the debris off of him. "Everybody okay?"

Jen had picked the right lever. When the middle door had opened, Laney and Jen had sprinted through with the children.

Luckily, there was an identical door mechanism on the other side, allowing them to close the door behind them. Then they'd gone on a mad sprint through the dark tunnel.

When the bomb had gone off, Laney had thrown herself on Eddie and Jen had done the same for Elena. The explosion had shook the tunnel, and rocks rained down on them. Besides some bumps and scrapes, though, they were good.

"I'm okay," Elena said, her hand firmly grasped in Jen's.

"Eddie?" Laney asked.

"Okay."

"Well, I don't hear the rush of water, so the doors seem to be holding," Jen said.

"Good thing we moved the bomb," Laney said.

Before escaping through the tunnel, Laney had moved the bomb over to the other side of the cave. Easily the most nerve-wracking walk of her life.

Laney breathed a sigh of relief that the doors seemed to have held. She looked around the tunnel, grabbing one of the lanterns that had been left behind by the mercenaries. "Okay, let's get moving."

Jen grabbed onto her hand. "Hold on a sec. We need to go carefully."

Laney stared at her, not understanding, when Jen's warning about the tunnels came back to her. Her stomach dropped. Booby traps. They were lucky their panicked run or the explosion hadn't set any off already.

She stifled the urge to scream in frustration. They just couldn't catch a break. Avoid a bomb, end up in a tunnel system filled with booby traps.

With a nod to Jen, Laney turned to Elena and Eddie. She spoke with her most sing-song voice. "Okay kids, you two walk behind us and if we say to do something like, duck or run, don't hesitate, just do it. Okay?"

"Because of the booby traps?" Elena asked.

Eddie nodded next to her.

Jen smothered a laugh.

Laney glared at her. *So much for keeping the danger from the kids.* "Yes. Because of the booby traps."

They trudged down the tunnel, making their way slowly through the dim light. After about thirty minutes, the tunnel began to angle up.

Elena tugged on Laney's hand. "Laney? Is it going to be okay?"

"Well, we're heading up now, which is good. It means we're heading towards the surface. I bet we find an exit real soon."

"But what about Grandpa? He was shot," Eddie said.

"I know, sweetheart. But I have to tell you, your Grandpa's one tough man. I think it might take more than a bullet to keep him down."

Eddie nodded his agreement, but Laney's heart felt heavy. She didn't think Julian could survive that hit, not without immediate medical attention. And there was no chance of him getting it way out here. She just couldn't bring herself to say that to the kids.

They walked on for another few minutes in silence, each lost in their own thoughts. Laney's mind drifted to her family and how they would cope if she didn't come back from this. Her Uncle Patrick had been there for every moment since she was eight, always supporting her unconditionally. Kati and Max. She wouldn't get to wake up to the sound of Max running through the house, or share a glass of wine with Kati at the end of the day.

The faces of her friends whipped through her mind. Danny, Henry, Rocky. Her throat felt thick and tears burned her eyes. She loved them all so much. She knew her death was going to hit them hard. And the idea of not seeing them again was wrenching.

A picture of Jake came center-stage in her mind. She'd been trying to keep him out of her thoughts. It was too painful. But even his image was stubborn. She felt a stab of longing. She wanted to see him one more time, even without things being settled between them. She didn't know what she would say, but it didn't matter. She just needed to see him.

She took a shaky breath. And then she heard a

click.

"Stop!" Laney yelled. Everyone froze in place.

"Laney?" Jen called out, her voice small.

"Yeah?"

"I think I just stepped on a booby trap."

CHAPTER 40

Jake's chopper chased the other helo through the air. They were about two miles behind and gaining.

"Come on, come on," Jake urged. The other helo was a speck in the distance, but it looked like it might be landing.

He tapped his mic. "Drop us a quarter mile from the spot." He knew if they went any closer, there was a good chance their chopper would be blown from the sky.

Two minutes later, the helicopter was setting down in a clearing. Jake was out of it before it had fully landed, Jordan and Mike on his heels. He sprinted for the woods, heading for the drop zone. A glance back at the brothers showed their determination. Their resolve to make these bastards pay outdistanced even his own.

The sounds of men wafted through the air. Jake picked up his pace, but Jordan and Mike flew past him. They burst from the trees. The twins set off round after round, mowing down every man in their path.

Jake veered away from the brothers, heading for the cargo plane that seemed like it was about to take off.

One last crate was being loaded by two men. He took out one of the men, but the other managed to shove the last pallet into the cargo hold. The door began to close.

Jake sprinted towards the plane, but he knew he wouldn't be able to do anything to keep it from taking off. To his right, he saw a large man who'd been giving the orders head for the last remaining helicopter. Jake changed direction, sprinting for him.

Jake crashed through the trees, laser-focused on reaching his target. The man was tall, at least six-foot-five, and had an overly muscular build.

Something about him was familiar, but Jake couldn't place him. *Doesn't matter who he is. He killed Laney. He's going down.*

The man reached the helicopter, jumping into the open door way. He circled his hand in the air. The chopper rose.

Jake dropped to his knees, lining up his shot. He looked through the scope, the man's face situated perfectly in the center.

Shock jolted through his system. His finger paused over the trigger. Stunned, he watched the helo lift off and fly out of range.

Henry and Yoni burst through the trees behind him. They raked the air with gunfire, although it was futile.

Jake stood, staring after the disappearing craft, unable to believe what he'd just seen.

"Jake?" Henry asked, his tone concerned.

Jake looked at him blankly.

Yoni slapped him on the shoulder. "What the hell happened? Why didn't you take the shot?"

Jake shook his head. "I froze."

"Froze?" Disbelief laced Yoni's words. "I've seen

you in every kind of firefight and I've never seen you lock up. What was different about this one?"

"I knew the guy."

"Who is he?" Henry asked, his voice solemn, his eyes serious.

Jake looked back at him, feeling completely cut off from reality. "It was Derek Collins."

Yoni went still, his face a mask of shock. "Jake, it can't be Derek. He's dead."

CHAPTER 41

Kneeling on the tunnel floor, Laney examined the plate Jen had stepped on. "It's some sort of ancient pressure plate."

"Kind of figured that. Any idea what it connects to?"

"Well, nothing's moving yet, so I'm guessing it doesn't go into effect until you step off." Laney raised her lantern to examine the ceiling. Nothing. It all looked smooth and polished.

"Over here," Eddie called, standing along the wall.

Laney's heart skipped a beat. "I thought I told you guys to stay back."

Elena stood next to her brother. "We wanted to help. And I think we found the trap."

Laney swallowed the yell in her throat. She'd ordered them back down the tunnel. But here they were, in harm's way. She illuminated the wall behind them as she walked towards it. "I don't see anything."

"Put your hands here." Eddie took Laney's hand and pressed it against the wall.

Small indentations covered the wall. She shone her

light on one and realized that the small hole was filled with a spike of some sort, the same finish as the wall. It was almost impossible to see. She ran her hands over the wall. There were tons of the things.

She quickly crossed to the other side of the cave. More indentations. She looked back at where Jen stood. Right in the cross hairs.

"I'm guessing some sort of flying projectile?" Jen asked, her voice tight.

"Looks like."

Laney saw the tremble in Jen's hands. The same tremor worked its way into her own. She didn't know what to do. She couldn't see any way to shield Jen from the onslaught and no one was fast enough to get out of the way.

Except . . .

Her head jerked up. She looked at Jen's arm. She thought about how easily Jen had trekked through the forest, the grace with which she moved, how easily she'd gotten out of the bindings. "How's your arm, Jen?"

"What? My arm? Who cares how my arm is?"

Laney walked over to her, and stared into her eyes. "It's healed, hasn't it?"

Jen looked back at her, terror in her eyes. Laney couldn't tell if it was from the situation, the question, or both.

Jen nodded.

"I'm guessing you generally heal pretty fast? Run pretty fast?"

Jen nodded, tears in her eyes. Her voice was quiet, almost a whisper. "Yes. I always have. I don't know why. I keep it hidden. People haven't always been kind about my abilities."

Swallowing the lump of fear in her throat, Laney backed away, fear shooting through her. Enhanced physical and healing abilities, just like Paul, just like Gideon. Her breath picked up. It felt like the walls were closing in. Jen was one of them. She was a Fallen.

Laney gasped when a hand slipped into hers. She looked down into Elena's face. "We need to help her."

"Elena, you don't understand. There's more at stake here than-"

Elena cut her off, sounding older than her years. "No. I do understand. I know Jen. I know who she is. She's good. She's your friend. You need to help her."

Laney breathed deep, looking back at Jen, who had tears running down her cheeks. *What am I doing?* she thought with dismay. This was Jen. They'd been friends for over ten years. She'd never had any reason to do anything but trust her.

Squeezing Elena's hand, she stepped back towards Jen and took a deep breath. "Well, right now, I think those abilities just may save your life."

Laney turned to Elena and Eddie. "Okay guys, I need you to go back down the tunnel the way we came."

Elena glanced down and shook her head. "It's too dark."

Laney walked over and handed her one of the lanterns. "Take this. Keep walking until I tell you to stop."

Elena shook her head. "Laney, can't we-"

Laney's voice was firm. "No. Eddie, take Elena down the tunnel. Wait until I tell you to stop."

Eddie nodded, looking every bit the child warrior. He pulled Elena behind him.

When they were fifty feet away she called out for them to stop. "Just stay there until I tell you to come back."

Laney followed Jen's light back to her. "Jen, shine the light at the ground again."

She did, and Laney found the edge of the plate. Careful not to step on it, she positioned herself right in front of Jen.

"That was good thinking," Jen said, her voice low.

"What?"

"Making sure the kids wouldn't be able to see."

Laney sighed. "I was hoping you didn't pick up on that."

Jen handed Laney her lantern and then clutched her hand. "If this doesn't work, promise me you'll go see my family and tell them how much I love them. Tell them they were the perfect family and that I know it wasn't easy taking me in and –"

Laney looped the lantern's handle over her arm and squeezed Jen's hand. "Shh, shh. It's going to be okay. You can do this. And you can tell them all that yourself. Now here's what you're going to do: You're closer to the back of the plate than the front. So, very slowly, keeping the same pressure, I'm going to help you turn around until your facing down the tunnel, the way we came."

"Laney, you need to back away. If this thing feels a shift-"

"I don't think it's that sensitive. I think it's more of a pressure/no pressure kind of sensor. So I'm going to help you turn, so you end up facing the right direction, and not a wall."

Jen took a shuddering breath.

"Okay. You ready?" Laney asked.

"Yes."

Slowly, with Laney bracing her, Jen began to turn clockwise.

Laney moved with her, her eyes on the ground tracing the outline of the plate. Breath held, Jen finally faced back down the tunnel, the front of her boots touching the edge of the plate.

"See? Piece of cake," Laney said, feeling a cold bead of sweat roll down her back.

Jen let out a shaky laugh. "You really need to stop saying that. Now, what's the next part?"

Laney forced some levity into her voice. "Well, that part's easy. You're going to dive off the platform and avoid all the darts."

"Oh, good.   I was afraid it was going to be something difficult."

Laney gripped her hands. "Jen, you have this in you. It's part of who you are. I'm going to walk down the tunnel. I'll keep the lantern on. You're going to aim for me, okay?"

Jen jerked her head, a tremor in her voice. "Okay."

Laney backed up fifteen feet. She'd seen what Paul and Gideon could do. This would be child's play for them.   But Jen had been hiding this ability for her whole life. Laney prayed she could tap into it now.

"Just aim for me," Laney said. "Don't hold back. You leap with everything in you. Got it?"

"Got it."

Laney placed the lantern on the floor next to her, a beacon for Jen to focus on. "Count of three?"

Jen paused. Laney could feel the terror coming off of her.

"Count of three," Jen finally called.

"Okay. Here we go." Laney took a deep breath. "One, two, three."

CHAPTER 42

Jen moved so fast Laney didn't see her, didn't hear her. But she felt her. Jen plowed into her with the force of a train.

Laney's head whipped back. She crashed towards the floor. Jen's hand slipped between Laney's head and the ground just before they met.

Jen sat up quickly, pulling Laney into a sitting position with her. "I can't believe that worked."

Laney gulped. Neither could she. She flashed the light up ahead to where Jen had stood. Dozens of arrows pierced the walls on either side.

The kids sprinted down the tunnel towards them. Eddie stood grinning at them. Elena flung herself at Jen. "You made it."

"Sure did, kiddo." Jen hugged her back, her breathing still a little uneven.

Laney straightened up from the floor, stifling a groan. Her butt was going to be one massive bruise.

"You okay, Laney?" Eddie asked.

"I'm good. Just whacked into the floor a little

hard."

"Sorry about that," Jen said.

Laney grinned. "That's okay. You just don't know your own strength."

"No," Jen said quietly. "I really don't."

Laney clapped her hands. "Well, I think we've had enough excitement for today. How about we find the exit to this place?"

"Yes," Eddie said. "I want to go home."

Laney ruffled his hair. "Me, too. You two, stay behind us, okay?"

The kids nodded.

Laney and Jen led the way down the tunnel. The soft light of the lanterns speared the darkness ahead of them, shifting between the floors, the walls and the tunnel ahead.

About thirty minutes later, the children trailed behind them, their steps tired, but moving forward. Jen spoke quietly. "I knew I was different when I was eight. One of my foster brothers pushed me out of a tree. I managed to flip and land on my feet. I couldn't believe it. When I was falling, time seemed to slow, and I knew just what to do."

Jen glanced over at her. Laney knew she was checking her expression, and any disapproval or shock would close her off. She kept her face neutral. "Must have scared the hell out of you."

Jen smiled tentatively. "A little. But it thrilled me, too. I couldn't seem to get hurt." Her face darkened. "But my foster brother and his friends realized I was different. They increased their attacks, always trying to get to me, to make me cry, to hurt me. It was too much. I ran away a year later, lived on the streets for a while."

Laney's heart went out to her. "You were only nine."

"Nine, but pretty good at taking care of myself. Eventually, though, DCF caught me." She smiled. "And I was sent to live with the Witts."

"They don't know about your abilities?"

Jen shook her head. "No. I never wanted to risk it. I loved them too much. It would have killed me if they turned their back on me because I was different."

Laney thought about Jen's family. They'd been there for every special event, sending her care packages at school, showing up one weekend a month to visit in college, calling every night. Their bond was incredibly strong. "You know they would never turn their back on you, right?"

"My head knows it. But my heart? It's too scared to take the chance. So I've never told anyone. Not until you."

"How have you been able to keep it a secret? Don't you just occasionally slip up? Run too fast? Jump too high?"

Jen shook her head. "No. I've trained myself not to use those abilities. I was so scared of what would happen since I was a kid, I'm always on guard against using them. Now, it's second nature to hold back."

"The wounds of childhood run deep." Laney thought of her own childhood trauma. Maybe that was why she pushed Jake away. She loved her parents and they died. She trusted her aunt and her other uncle and they hurt her. It was twenty years later and she still felt the effects of those wounds.

Jen nodded her agreement. "I thought I needed to keep it hidden, to keep from being a target."

"Do you still think that?"

"I don't know."

"Well, your secret's safe with me."

Jen gave Laney's hand a small squeeze. "Thanks. But I don't understand how you knew. How did you figure it out?"

"Let's just say, I've met people like you before."

Even in the dim light, Laney could see Jen's eyes light up. "You have? Where? What are they like?"

Laney struggled to find the right words. 'Deranged, psychopathic killers' would probably not be very comforting.

Jen read her face. "I'm guessing not good."

Laney gave her a small smile. "Well, I've only met two." Her head jerked up with a start when she realized that wasn't true. Including Jen, she'd now met four. Henry was one as well. At least, she thought he was. He had the strength, the speed, but she'd never lumped him in with Paul or Gideon. Henry was simply too good to associate with those two.

So now she had even numbers. Two good, two evil. What did that say about their nature? Or were Jen and Henry a different breed of superhumans?

Laney was about to speak when Jen put up her hand. "Listen."

Laney paused, struggling to hear anything in the silence. It all sounded quiet, almost muffled. In fact, it sounded like a white noise machine, although it seemed to be getting louder with each passing second.

Panic flooded her system. She pictured the doors back in the main hall, the ones holding back tons of water. "The doors burst."

"Run," Jen yelled.

Laney reached back for Eddie's hand. Jen did the same for Elena. Together, they sprinted through the tunnel blindly, a wall of water chasing them in the dark.

CHAPTER 43

Laney ran with her arm along the wall, moving too fast for the dim light of the lantern. She prayed they didn't run into anther booby trap. Up ahead, she saw a small shaft of light.

"Jen," she called.

"I see it," Jen yelled back.

As they grew closer to the light, Laney could make out the hole where the light shone through. But the rest of the space was packed with rocks.

"Damn it," Laney screamed, stumbling to a stop.

Jen didn't say a word, just started tearing the rocks away from the exit. Laney leaped in and helped. But part of her reeled at the size of rocks Jen was throwing as if they weighed no more than tennis balls.

The sound of water grew closer. Laney pulled back a large rock and daylight burst through. Frantic, she and Jen pulled and yanked rocks out of the way until there was hole big enough to squeeze through.

Jen peeked her head through and then ducked back inside. "There's a small ledge on each side." She grabbed Elena and started to push her through. "Climb through and go to your right."

Elena nimbly climbed over the rocks and disappeared through the hole.

Jen pulled Eddie to the opening. "Eddie, climb through, but stay to your left."

"But Elena . . ."

Hand on his back, Jen gave him a little push. "There's not enough room. You need to trust us."

He nodded and scampered through. Jen looked back at Laney.

"Go," Laney yelled, the sound of the onrush of water almost deafening.

Jen jumped through the hole and to her right.

Laney clamored through the opening after her. She couldn't help looking behind her, though she wished she hadn't. Even in the dim light, she could see the wall of water twenty feet away and moving fast.

CHAPTER 44

Laney scrambled through the opening in the rocks and to the left just as the water burst through behind her. Eddie latched onto her arm as the water pushed against her leg, threatening to take her over the edge.

Grabbing onto the rocks and Eddie's hand, she pulled herself onto the ledge, panting. "Thank you."

"You're welcome."

The ledge was small, only about three feet deep and five feet long. She looked down and her stomach dove for her feet. They were on a sheer cliff face, twenty feet above the ocean. She looked up. The side of the cliff looked like it had been sheered off, starting at the top. A rockslide must have created the opening.

Her eyes found Jen across from them. Her ledge was a little wider, but not any longer. "You two okay?"

Jen nodded. "For now."

The smaller rocks on the ledge next to Laney began to shake. She looked closer at her ledge and the cliff face behind it. Her stomach bottomed out again. The ledge wasn't part of the cliff face. It was part of the pile of rocks blocking the exit.

The water was building behind it right now. The only reason it hadn't exploded out was because of the hole they'd created. But when enough pressure built, it would burst outward, sending them crashing for the water below in a storm of rocks.

She looked over at Jen's ledge and saw she was in the same situation. "Jen, the ledge."

Jen stared at her. Then looked down at her ledge. When her face paled, Laney knew she understood what she meant.

Jen knelt down to speak with Elena.

Laney turned to Eddie. "Eddie, can you swim?"

He nodded.

"Good. Because we're going to have to jump."

Eddie's eyes darted to the long drop next to them. He started to breathe rapidly.

Laney knelt down, taking him by the shoulders. "Eddie, look at me. You can do this. We can do this." She took his hand, clasping it in her own. "You're going to hold onto my hand and you're not going to let go. Do you hear me? You don't let go."

He nodded, but his eyes were filled with fear. Rocks began to skitter off the ledge and drop to the water below.

Laney stood up and yelled to Jen. "Count of three?"

Jen nodded, Elena's legs wrapped around her waist. Jen's arms held her tightly to her chest.

Swallowing the lump of fear in her throat, Laney clasped Eddie's hand even tighter. "One, two." Deep breath. "Three."

She and Eddie jumped out from the cliff. From the corner of her eye, she saw Jen do the same with Elena.

They dropped fast. But not so fast that Laney couldn't hear and see the water break through above them, a cascade of rocks and water racing after them.

CHAPTER 45

Laney plunged into the cold water feet first, her hand tightly clasped in Eddie's. Rocks pierced the water around them like bullets. The water swirled, tossing them around like driftwood. A rock slammed into the side of her head, another slammed into her ribs.

Eddie's grip went slack. Laney grasped him even tighter until the tumult stopped. Opening her eyes, she struggled to find the surface. Spying sunlight below her, she righted herself. Hauling Eddie behind her, she kicked for the light.

She burst through the surface and sucked in a lungful of air. She pulled Eddie up and saw he'd been hit in the arm and head. He coughed out some water and then went quiet. She grabbed him and pulled him close, listening to his chest. His heart beat strong.

She released a breath, tears welling in her eyes. "Thank you. Thank you," she mumbled.

"Laney!" Elena yelled.

Jen waved from thirty feet away, Elena wrapped around her neck. Other than a few cuts, they both looked fine. Laney waved back. Jen started to swim over, towing Elena with her.

Laney waited until Jen pulled to stop next to her. "Well, that was fun."

A short laugh burst forth from Jen. "Seriously, when we hit dry land, I am dragging you to the nearest shrink."

"Is Eddie okay?" Elena asked.

Laney nodded. "He'll be okay. He just took a little knock to the head."

Jen gestured farther down the coast. "I think there's a beach about a mile down that way."

Laney looked in the direction Jen had pointed with a sigh. Right now, one mile might as well be a thousand. She felt tired just thinking about the swim. "Okay. Let's get going before we run into some sharks."

"Sharks?" Elena's voice came out as a squeak. She tightened her hold on Jen's neck.

Jen glared at Laney.

Laney grimaced. "Sorry. That was just a joke. I'm sure there are no sharks near here." *Although with our luck*, she thought looking around, *I wouldn't be all that surprised to see a fin cutting through the water*.

Shaking her head, Jen turned and began swimming towards the coast, Elena riding on her back. Laney flipped onto her back. Pulling Eddie's torso onto her own and trapping him with her legs, she began a slow backstroke following in their wake. She knew she should be thrilled they'd made it. And she was. It was truly a miracle.

But those mercenaries had done everything in their power to try and kill them. What was going to happen when they realized they'd failed?

CHAPTER 46

Jake watched the canopy of trees fly by beneath him. He'd always loved flying in helos. There was something incredibly freeing about it. But right now, he felt like he was encased in a layer of lead. It was hard to breathe. His limbs each felt like they'd gained ten pounds.

Jake and his group spent the better part of the afternoon helping the Shuar at the riverbank and dealing with red tape. The U.S. Consulate and the Ecuadorian government had been called.

Getting the tribespeople to trust the military had taken some time. Patrick had finally managed to broker a tentative peace. Apparently, Laney had spoken with the tribe's leader about him. Trust in Laney is what had sealed the deal.

The U.S. Consulate was working on smoothing the waters with the Ecuadorian government. They hadn't been thrilled when they learned about Jake's group's actions. Of course, they'd been less thrilled to hear about the looting of a priceless ancient site and the killing of Ecuadorian citizens by a group of mercenaries. Finally, the government men had thrown up their hands and ordered Jake's group out of the country.

Wind blew through the open doorway of the chopper and Jake closed his eyes. Laney was gone. It didn't seem real. She was so full of life. She couldn't just be gone.

He used to hate when people said death had them all ripped up inside. It sounded so melodramatic. But now he got it. His chest felt empty, and yet, at the same time, it felt like something was trying to claw its way out.

He crushed his fist in his hand. And somehow Derek Collins was the reason. He couldn't wrap his mind around it. Derek had been a member of his platoon in Afghanistan. He'd been a SEAL. And he was supposed to have died seven years ago when his Humvee hit an IED. They'd never found the body, but they'd found his dog tags and part of his uniform. How could it have been Derek?

He closed his eyes, picturing Derek when they'd started SEAL training together. They'd bonded, been good friends. Took leave together. He and Yoni had even gone home with Derek a couple of times to stay with Derek's family for holidays.

Of course, everything had changed after Derek had been wounded in Iraq. It was a massive concussion. Derek's whole personality shifted overnight. He became cruel, violent. Jake knew Derek had been a breath away from being kicked out of the military, if not locked up, right before he died. Had he faked his own death to avoid it?

His chest thudded painfully. And now, Derek was

responsible for Laney's death.

He turned from the door and watched Patrick in the back of the chopper. Laney's uncle sat with his head leaning against the bulkhead, his eyes closed. An occasional tear would slip from underneath his lids and strike the floor. Patrick didn't wipe them away.

Jordan and Mike sat on the other side of the helo, their shoulders touching, but each lost in their own world of grief. They'd always looked out for Jen, their little sis. Jake knew how close the Witt family was. He couldn't imagine how they were going to get through this.

Henry sat stone-faced in the helo's other door, glaring at the ground below them. Even Yoni sat lost in grief, with none of his usual jokes.

Jake turned away as the airport came into view. He knew the Ecuadorian government was searching their plane. When they were satisfied that they weren't trying to sneak anything out of the country, they'd be allowed to leave. Actually, forced to leave.

He hated leaving without Laney's . . . He stumbled over the word, even in his mind. Without Laney's body.

The Huey touched down with a little bump. Jake jumped out. He turned to help Patrick down. The priest seemed to have caved in on himself. Jake wasn't sure if he would stay upright.

Yoni slipped an arm around Patrick's waist. "I've got you, Padre."

Jake nodded his thanks as Yoni walked Patrick towards the hangar. He grabbed his gear from the open doorway.

Jordan and Mike walked towards the hangar, their

arms slung around each other. Jake wanted to say something to them, but what the hell could he say?

Henry walked over to him. "What do you need, Jake?"

Jake shook his head, tears gathering in his throat. He swallowed them down. "Nothing, Henry. Nothing."

Henry clapped him on the shoulder and stood with him, giving him his strength. Taking a deep breath, Jake turned towards the hangar.

"I wonder what's happening over there," Henry mumbled.

Jake glanced up, noticing for the first time the commotion on the far side of the runway. An ambulance was waiting on the tarmac next to a few other cars. A rescue helicopter landed. Paramedics rushed to open the doors of the chopper.

"Any idea what's going on over there?" Henry asked the pilot as he came to join them.

"There was a sea rescue not too far from where you were."

Jake's head jolted up. "Who was rescued?"

"Two women and two children."

Jake went still. He met Henry's eyes. Without a word, the two started running for the ambulance.

Jake slowed as they neared. Two children, a boy and a girl, were carried from the helicopter and placed into the waiting ambulance. A tall, dark haired woman appeared next, her warm skin tone unnaturally pale. And then behind her, looking even smaller wrapped in a large coast guard blanket, a pale woman with a riot of red hair stepped onto the tarmac.

Jake's heart slammed to a stop in his chest, his

knees almost giving out.

She looked up and her piercing green eyes met his. Shock crossed her face, before a smile appeared.

Jake bulldozed past the startled paramedics and wrapped her in his arms, pulling her off her feet. He breathed her in.

"Laney."

CHAPTER 47

The blood pressure cuff woke Laney. Her eyes flew open, her hands rolled into fists. The nurse jumped back from the bed.

Laney shook her head. "Sorry."

The nurse smiled as she unwound the cuff, patting Laney's arm, before leaving the room. Laney rubbed her eyes, a thin film of sleep covering them.

"You're awake," her uncle said from the chair next to the hospital bed. From his red eyes and rumpled clothes, he'd obviously slept there.

"I'm awake," she agreed with a small smile. They'd all been taken to the hospital after touching down at the airport. Laney had fought against being kept overnight but her uncle had insisted. One look at his pained face and she'd given in. If it gave him peace, she'd stay in the damn hospital.

She glanced at the window. It looked like dawn had broken a few hours ago. "What time is it?"

Patrick glanced at his watch. "Just after nine. You slept for over fifteen hours."

Laney looked at Jen, who sat on Patrick's other

side. "Where'd your armed guard go?"

Jen smiled. Her brothers had refused to leave her side since they'd found her. "I convinced them to go get something to eat." She nodded towards the other bed in the room. "But they stood next to my bed last night while I slept. They should be wolfing something down right now and sprinting back up stairs to join me in about thirty seconds."

Although her tone was sarcastic, Laney could tell she was comforted by her brothers' concern. She glanced through the doorway, trying to keep her look casual.

"He stayed here last night, as well." Jen said quietly.

Laney nodded, a small comfort taking root in her stomach. She fell back on the pillows, her body aching. No particular pain stood out, just an overall ache. "How's everyone else?"

Patrick stood. "The kids are asleep in the room next door. Eddie woke up some time last night. Jen, here, has already checked herself out."

"What about Julian?"

"Back in surgery this morning."

Laney glanced over sharply.

Patrick put up his hands. "Not an emergency. They knew they'd need to do a follow-up surgery on him. He was stable enough that they were able to do it this morning."

She nodded, closing her eyes. She supposed that was the best they could hope for. "What about the Shuar's court case? Did they get an extension?"

"Yes." Jen said. "But only a few days. And now writing up our description of the cave and documenting their claim is more important that ever."

"The pictures from the site actually survived," Patrick said. "Henry's having them developed. And I told Jen I would be happy to help write the report for court."

Laney knew how important that report was going to be. Without it, the Shuar would never be able to prove the contents of the cave belonged to them. That was, if the contents were ever found.

Patrick leaned over and kissed her on the forehead. "I'm going to call the diocese. There's much work that needs to be done. Arrangements need to made."

Laney took his hand. "You're going to stay down here a little while, aren't you?"

He nodded. "It wouldn't be right for me to leave. I've seen the devastation here. I can't turn my back on it. I have to go make some calls. I'll be back in a little bit."

Laney watched her uncle leave. She sat up with a groan. "I don't suppose you feel as lousy as I do?"

Jen gave her a little smile. "One of the small benefits of being whatever it is I am."

Laney stretched her back and rolled her neck. Not too bad. "A hot shower and I'll be good as new."

"Well, I already had one and I think lukewarm is the best you can hope for."

Laney laughed, and looked up when Jen didn't join her.

Jen's eyes were worried. She leaned forward resting her arms on Laney's bed. "I wanted to ask you a favor."

Reaching over, she gave Jen's hand a squeeze. "You don't have to ask. Like I said, your secret's safe with me. But I think you should tell your brothers."

Jen sighed. "Maybe one day."

"Am I interrupting?" Henry asked from the doorway.

Laney started, hoping he hadn't heard their conversation. "No, you're good."

Henry stepped into the room.

Laney looked over at Jen who was staring at Henry, a look of shock on her face. Laney smiled. Henry's gigantic stature often had that affect on people. "Jen, this is Henry Chandler."

Henry walked over to Jen, clasping her hand in his. "Your brothers have spoken very highly of you. I'm glad to finally put a face to the stories."

"Um, it's good to meet you," Jen stammered.

Now it was Laney's turn to be shocked. In all the time she'd known Jen, she'd never seen her lose her cool. Amazing. Someone had actually broken down Jen's indestructible façade.

Laney cleared her throat. Henry dropped Jen's hand like it was on fire. *Even more interesting.* "Any word on who that group was or where the artifacts were taken?"

Henry shook his head. "No. I'm pulling as many strings as I can to find out. We think they're heading for North America. We're checking along the way to the States, assuming that's their destination. But they could really be anywhere."

"We have to be able to find a trace of them. That operation was too well coordinated. Have you tracked down Deveraux?" Laney asked.

"I've got people at his university, his home, and all his haunts. No one had any indication where he'd gone.

He took a leave of absence and didn't leave any contact information. According to his financials, he's up to his ears in debt: his credit cards are maxed, he's upside down on his mortgage, and to top it off, he seems to have a gambling problem."

"I guess he did need the money," Jen said.

"What about that behemoth that ran the group?" Laney asked. "They called him Hugo. A monster like that has to have a colorful background."

Henry opened his mouth to say something, before glancing over his shoulder at Jake down the hall. He stepped closer to Laney, lowering his voice. "That guy we know. Or at least, Jake and Yoni do. He's a former Navy SEAL, but he was supposed to have died seven years ago."

Laney stared at him for a moment and then shook her head with a shrug. "You know, not the strangest thing I've heard recently." She glanced through the door at Jake, who was talking into his cellphone. "Who's Jake speaking with now?"

"He's helping make arrangements for the Shuar tribe to get them protection, and aid. I've also begun preparations for helping them rebuild."

Laney smiled. "I'm surrounded by good men."

Henry blushed, making Laney smile even more. He glanced at Jen. "I thought you might be a good point person for the reconstruction efforts. That is, if you're staying for a little while."

Jen nodded. "I am."

"I'm staying too," Laney said.

"No."

All eyes turned to the doorway. Nana stood there, her shirt still stained with Julian's blood. Her back was straight, but her eyes held a world of grief.

Jen stood. "Nana?"

Nana grasped Jen's hand. "He's gone. My husband is dead."

Laney felt like the air had been sucked out of the room. She scampered off the bed. "What can we do?"

Nana nodded at Henry before turning to Laney. "Do what Julian would want. Jen will help us rebuild. But it's your duty to track down the men responsible for this."

Laney was floored by the task. How on earth was she going to accomplish that? "I'll try, Nana."

"No," Nana's voice lashed out. "You will not try. You will do it." Her voice softened. "You're a warrior, Delaney McPhearson. I have known that since I met you. You're capable of this task. And you have resources we do not." She nodded at Henry.

Henry returned the gesture. "Anything you need. The Chandler Group is at your service."

Nana turned back to Laney. "You are one of us now. I think you and Jen were sent to us for a reason. Jen will help us rebuild here. You will return what has been taken from us."

Laney thought of Julian, his love for his family, his tribe. She thought of all that the Shuar had been through, all the members they'd lost, all the destruction they'd experienced. The men who'd attacked them had been without mercy.

Laney walked over to Nana, who had tears streaming down her cheeks. Laney pulled her into a hug. "Yes, Nana."

CHAPTER 48

The next morning, Laney stepped out of the passenger seat of the old Range Rover at the airport. The Chandler Group jet stood fifty feet away, its engine running.

She'd spent most of yesterday and last night working on the report for the court. Except for two hours at sunset. Then she'd gone to be with the Shuar. They held a memorial for Julian and all the others they had lost. The grief had been palpable. Laney's chest constricted just thinking about it.

But that was all the time she'd had to grieve. Right after the ceremony, Laney, Jen, and her uncle had continued their work on the report. The report was good, but it would still need a little more editing. She was going to have to leave that for her uncle and Jen. She'd been voted off the island.

Laney walked around the truck as Nana climbed out of the driver seat. "Nana, I can stay."

Laney liked to think that Nana was here to wish her well. But she knew Nana was making sure she got on that plane.

Nana hugged her and then pulled back, still holding Laney's arms. "Good luck, Laney."

Laney nodded, feeling the pressure of Nana's request. She'd do everything in her power to help the Shuar retrieve what they'd lost and get justice. She just wasn't sure it was within her power to accomplish this particular task. "I hate leaving you guys right now."

"I know. But you'll help us better from afar."

Laney pulled Nana in for one last hug and whispered in her ear, "I'll miss you."

Nana smiled, but Laney saw the tears in her eyes. "And we'll miss you."

Laney turned and walked up the four steps into the plane with a deep breath. She'd only met these people a few months ago and yet she felt like she'd known them her whole life. Leaving right now, with everything they were going through, was killing her.

Jake glanced up from his seat against the wall on the left. "You okay?"

"Yeah. I'm good." It was only the two of them on the plane, besides the pilot. Henry had already returned to the States with Yoni. Her uncle, Jen, and Jen's brothers were staying behind.

"I'll go tell the pilot we're ready." Jake got up, pulling the door to the plane closed and locking it before disappearing into the cockpit.

Laney took a seat across from where he'd sat. She glanced out the window. Nana was already driving away. A lump in her throat, she let out her breath slowly trying to keep the tears at bay. Leaning her head back against the seat, she closed her eyes.

The plane began to taxi. She glanced out again as the landscape flew past and then they were up in the air.

She glanced over at Jake's still empty seat. Maybe he was going to sit with the pilot for the flight. She shook her head. She couldn't blame him. Everything was so stiff between them now. Neither of them seemed to know what to say to each other. She wanted to go back to when it was easy between them.

Sadness weighed her down, opening the door to all the other emotions she'd been holding back. Since the attack at the Shuar village, she'd been constantly on the move and when she'd lain down to sleep, she'd been too exhausted to think. But she'd known it was only a matter of time before everything that happened caught up with her.

Unwanted, the images flowed through her mind, a wave she couldn't hold back. The attacks at the villages, the sight of Eddie and Elena disappearing under the water, Julian being shot, the wall of water rushing after them. One terrifying scene after another crashed through her mind.

"Laney?"

She looked up at Jake who'd silently slipped into the seat next to her. He reached up his hand and wiped the tears from her cheek. She didn't even realize she'd been crying.

"Jake, I-"

He put a finger to her lips. "Laney, look. I know we have a lot unsaid between us. And we'll get to that. But right now, you look like you need somebody. And I'm right here." He held out his arms. "Two arms, no waiting, no strings."

Laney stared at him, debating what to do. Her stubborn side told her, not to look weak.

You need to talk things through first.

The rest of her though told her to take comfort. *He loves you. Whatever else has happened, he loves you. And right now, you need to lean on someone.* And, lord knew, Jake was strong enough.

Laney told her stubborn side to shut up. She let Jake pull her into his lap. Putting her arms around his neck, she let herself feel all the emotions she had shoved down for the last few days. She cried for the Shuar, for Nana, for Julian, for Elena and for Eddie. She cried for Jen and the secret she'd had to keep. And she cried for herself. For all the fear she'd refused to let herself feel over the last few days.

The harder she cried, the stronger Jake's arms felt around her. He leaned down, whispering in her ear. "I've got you, Lanes. I've got you."

CHAPTER 49

Las Vegas, Nevada

Sebastian sat in his office, watching a red-tailed hawk soar through the air. Majestic, strong. A predator of the skies.

He turned from the window. *Where was Gerard? Why was there no word yet?*

If he'd the strength, he would be pacing along the floors. Who was he kidding? If he had the strength, he'd be down in Ecuador. Instead, he had to sit and wait for news. It galled him.

"Sir?" Gerard appeared at the door behind him.

Sebastian turned quickly, grabbing onto the back of the chair next to him. "Have they succeeded?"

Gerard nodded. "They just entered American airspace."

Sebastian released a breath. Finally. "Is everything ready for their arrival?

"Yes sir." Gerard crossed the room, hitting the remote on Sebastian's desk. The television, hidden within the buffet, rose. Gerard opened the cabinet doors underneath, placing a DVD in the player. "But there's news."

"What?"

"The two archaeologists, McPhearson and Witt. They survived the cave."

Sebastian sat back in surprise. How on earth were they still alive? Hugo was a brute, but he was an incredibly talented brute when it came to death. His mind raced. Delaney McPhearson seemed to be developing quite the track record of escaping death. Maybe she required more attention.

Sebastian's eyes narrowed as the screen flickered to life. "What's this?"

"It's the security tape from the Ecuadorian airport."

On the screen, the focus was on the rescue helicopter. Two children were taken from it, followed by an Asian woman, and then a red-headed woman. But Sebastian's attention wasn't on the individuals departing the chopper. He was focused on one man at the edge of the screen. The man was tall, easily over seven feet.

He felt a chill. "Who is that man? The tall one?"

Gerard looked at the screen. "Henry Chandler from the Chandler Group. I'm surprised we got this picture. As far as I know, he's never been photographed."

"Chandler. His company's now overseeing the dig out in Montana, correct?"

"Yes, sir."

Sebastian went silent, taking in the tall man. Like McPhearson, Chandler had been involved in the Montana situation, and here he was again. And he was tall. Extremely tall.

"This was back in the days when there were giants in the land," Sebastian mumbled.

"Excuse me, sir?"

Sebastian ignored him, a flash of memory pulling his attention. His father had been talking on the phone a few days day before he died. He'd mentioned a Chandler. Hope began to bloom. *Could it be?*

He turned to Gerard, a renewed energy giving his words extra force. "I want everything you have on Henry Chandler. And I mean everything – school records, medical records, family history. Everything. And I want it yesterday."

"Yes, sir."

"And then I want you to go to the basement. My father's old files are in storage room B. Look for any reference to the name Chandler."

"Yes, sir. Can I ask why?"

Sebastian looked back at the screen and smiled. "Because Henry Chandler may be the answer to our prayers."

CHAPTER 50

Baltimore, Maryland

Laney stepped out of the Navigator in front of the three-story estate house that was the Chandler Group's headquarters. The building, modeled after Jefferson's Monticello, had two long wings on either side of the front entryway. Black shutters contrasted sharply against the red brick. Four white columns held up the circular roof above the entry.

Dating back to the latter half of the nineteenth century, the building looked as it probably had when first constructed. Henry had taken pains to restore his family's ancestral home to its original glory, both inside and out.

In spite of the building's enormity, Laney felt relief at the sight of it. While she lived in upstate New York, she couldn't deny that over the last year, Henry's estate had become her home away from home.

"Laney!" Danny tore down the marble front steps. He threw his arms around her waist, nearly knocking her over.

She hugged him back with the same enthusiasm. "There's my hero."

Danny pulled back so he could look her in the face, keeping his arms wrapped around her. "You okay?"

She ruffled his hair. "I'm fine. Thanks for sending the cavalry after me. You saved a lot of lives."

"Me? I didn't do anything."

Laney hugged him to her again. "You got the ball rolling. Without you, none of the rest would have happened."

"She's right." Jake walked up behind them. "You did good, kid."

Laney smiled back at Jake, but didn't know what else to say. She'd cried herself to sleep on the plane and he'd held her the whole time. She'd only awoken when the pilot had come on to tell them they were landing. Jake had smiled at her and she'd smiled back. Then they'd studiously avoided any serious conversations.

Right now, they were keeping everything light. She weighed each word she spoke carefully to avoid any possible double meanings. It was exhausting.

Danny looked back at the car. "Where's Patrick? I thought he'd come back with you."

"He decided to stay and help Jen with the reconstruction effort. It's going to be extensive. Henry made sure, though, they have everything they need." She glanced around. "Where is he, anyway?"

"He's on the phone with the head of the FAA. Trying to track down the plane."

Taking hold of Danny's hand, she walked up the steps. "Any trace of them yet?"

Danny shook his head. "No, nothing. I haven't even been able to figure out who they were. Everything about them was fake: the name they used when they filed their papers with the Ecuadorian government, the plane registration numbers, the flight plan. Absolutely nothing was real. They could be anybody and anywhere."

Jake walked up. "Don't worry. We'll track them down,"

Laney met Jake's eyes as the images from Ecuador ran through her mind. He nodded at her. And she felt the promise. They'd find those responsible. Whatever the cost, they'd find them.

CHAPTER 51

Las Vegas, Nevada

Sebastian leaned back in his desk chair, paging through Devereaux's preliminary notes on the Shuar collection. He shook his head, unable to believe the riches and knowledge that had been hidden away in a cave for thousands of years. *I did it, Father. After all these years, it's ours.*

He flipped to the next page. Deveraux estimated that there were three hundred folios. The archaeologist hadn't had a chance to unpack them yet, but he knew those were the priority. Sebastian smiled, thinking of the knowledge they held. And what that knowledge would earn him.

Sebastian looked up as Gerard knocked at his door. "What have you found?"

Gerard walked over, standing in front of Sebastian's desk, a small notebook in his hand. "I've got the background on Henry Chandler."

"And my father's files? Have you found anything in them?"

"Not yet. I've been through about a third of them. Your father was a very detailed man."

"Yes, he was."

"Sir, most of the notes refer to Council work." Gerard paused. "Is it all right for me to be reading them?"

Sebastian fixed Gerard with a stare. For the first time he could remember, he saw fear in Gerard. Which, given the topic, was perfectly understandable. The Council was little-known, but the whispers of its activities were terrifying.

Sebastian's family had been members of the Council since its inception. In fact, his family was rumored to be its founders. His thoughts darkened when he remembered how his own membership had been denied after his father's death.

The Council had been tracking down the relics from Atlantis since the eleventh century. As far as he could remember his family's mission had always been to acquire one of the famed city's legendary libraries. *And now I have succeeded.*

His smile dimmed as he thought of the Council's current leadership. *Cowards.* Secrecy had become their highest priority, even at the cost of its other goals.

A necessary precaution, he admitted, although the current leadership took it to extremes, making their actions timid. Perhaps his being denied membership was actually a blessing. The Council never would have taken the necessary steps down in Ecuador, which meant they never would have acquired the library.

Sebastian inspected Gerard, enjoying the unease on the man's face. "You weren't planning on sharing the information with anyone else, were you?"

"Of course not."

"Then you should be fine."

"Of course, sir. And I would never betray your trust."

Sebastian's eyes drew to a squint. Was there a hint of sarcasm in Gerard's response?

His aide looked back at him, his face innocent.

Sebastian shook off the suspicion, but tucked it away in the back of his mind. Gerard might require a little extra supervision. He waved to the papers in Gerard's hand. "Tell me what you've found on Chandler."

"Well, I assume you know his recent history. Age thirty-five, head of a well-respected global think tank. His personal net worth comes in just below a billion dollars."

Sebastian rolled his hand. "Yes, yes. Titan of information. Philanthropist, pseudo-father to a super-genius. I need his more distant history."

"Yes, sir. Henry Chandler was the only child of James and Victoria Chandler. His medical records indicate nothing of interest. In fact, he appears to have never been sick or broken a bone. At least, he's never been treated by a doctor for anything other than yearly check-ups, which have all been normal."

Sebastian nodded.

"The only note is of his rapid growth when he turned twelve. As of his last recorded doctor visit, he was seven feet, two inches."

"What did you find out about his parents?"

"Both are deceased. His father was killed in a home invasion when Henry was six. Henry grew up with his mother and later inherited the family estate. He converted it into the main headquarters for the Chandler Group."

Sebastian stirred at the mention of his James Chandler's violent death. "The father. How was he killed?"

Gerard paused to flip through his notes. "He was shot through the heart. Multiple times. The M.E. made a note that there were multiple gunshot wounds to other parts of his body but they were older, already healing. But there was never a police report on the earlier gunshot wounds. And there was no record of him ever having been treated for them. In fact, the ME said the wounds indicated he'd been attacked multiple times over the previous weeks, if not months."

Excitement began to course through Sebastian. *Multiple wounds over multiple time periods. Or multiple wounds that healed quickly, during the same attack. James Chandler was a Fallen.* Sebastian could feel it in his bones.

Gerard pulled out a photo and handed it across the desk.

Sebastian's weathered hand reached for it. A handsome family. The father was of average height and Henry was still a child in the shot. He glanced at the mother and the hair rose on the back of his neck. He leaned back in his chair, staring at the woman. He knew that face.

"The mother," he croaked. He took a steadying breath. "What do you know of the mother?"

Gerard looked abashed. "Actually, she's been difficult to find any information on. According to her marriage license, she was Victoria Smith before she married Chandler at the age of twenty-one. But I can't find any information on her before that point. She died when Henry was eighteen."

231

Sebastian pierced him with his eyes. "How did she die?"

"Her car ran off a bridge during a storm."

"Was the body recovered?"

Surprise flitted across Gerard's face. "No, actually, it wasn't."

"We need to learn more about the Chandler family. Going through my father's notes is your priority."

"Yes, sir." Gerard bowed his head and turned. The door closed softly behind him.

Sebastian pushed back from his desk. He shuffled over to his bookcases, his mind moving much faster than his aged limbs. His eyes scanned the shelves, searching for the binder. *There.*

He moved to the right hand side of the shelf, annoyed that he now had to stretch to reach the top shelf. A few years ago, he would have been able to reach it with ease. He pulled down the binder, annoyed again that it felt heavy in his hands.

The Council had added to the binders over the decades. Some of the information dated back hundreds of years. They had rules about it being locked away. He smiled. Another benefit of no longer being associated with them.

Shuffling back to the desk, he placed the old album in the center of the blotter, pushing his other papers aside. He reached for the Chandler family photo. He flipped through the binder with his right hand, clenching the picture in his left.

He grunted as he turned page after page. *Where is it?* Finally, his hand stilled.

He stared at the woman on the page. Long, wavy hair, intelligent eyes, and a feminine grace came through clearly in the sketch. The documentation attached mentioned her startling eyes, a deep violet, and her red hair. It was the first sketch he'd ever seen in the binders. The image had stayed with him through the years. He'd even dreamed of her as a child.

He looked from the sketch to the picture in his hand. It was the same woman. They were identical.

His mind reeled at the possibility. His eyes darted between the two women. In the sketch she was identified as Lily Adams. But unless the artist had taken some dramatic license, it was undeniably the same woman – Victoria Chandler.

He looked at the date etched in the bottom-right corner of the sketch and his heart seemed to skip a beat: 1732. *Who is this woman?*

CHAPTER 52

Baltimore, Maryland

The next morning, Laney sat in Henry's office, which had turned into command headquarters in the search for the Ecuadorian group. A dozen analysts were scattered throughout the room, and more worked down the hall and on other floors.

The project was getting the full court press. Not, however, that it seemed to be helping.

Laney had been in this room since she'd arrived yesterday, only stopping long enough for a catnap on the couch in the corner. The hour she slept hadn't made a dent in her exhaustion, and she was now running on caffeine. She rubbed her eyes and ran her hands over her face. "Damn it."

Jake glanced up from across the table where he was reviewing air traffic reports from Central America. "What?"

"How can an operation this big not leave a trace? What were they, ghosts?"

Jake smiled. "Actually, I checked with some friends in the CIA. It wasn't them."

She rolled her eyes. "That's not what I meant."

"I guess you're not having any luck tracking down Warren?"

"Not a drop. Apparently, he doesn't exist, either. There is no Warren Steadglow. All the background information he provided to get on our grant is fake. A really good fake, but fake nonetheless."

"That takes money."

"Yup. And from his attitude, it was clear he had that in spades. But damn it, I was hoping it was a way to track down this group. But it's just another dead end."

"Do you have any photos of him? You could run them through facial rec."

"No. I didn't exactly go out of my way to document his part of the project. If anything, Jen and I were trying to keep him out. I've gone through all my shots and I don't have any of him."

"What about Jen? Does she have any?"

Laney stood up and stretched. "I doubt it, but I'm going to give her a call. I want to check in, see how everyone's doing. Be back in a little bit."

Laney walked out of Henry's office and down the three-story spiral staircase. Most days, she imagined she was in a giant hoop skirt, and holding a fan as she descended; it was that kind of staircase. But today, she was too frustrated to let her imagine run wild with her.

Warren, that little scum. He'd used Jen and her for information. And he was right in the heart of whatever this was, she knew it. All the other men who'd been involved were trained operatives. No way they'd let someone like Warren tag along unless he was connected to the money.

She crossed the black and white tiled foyer and

made her way through the dining room with the blue and white toile wallpaper. Wending her way around the mahogany table that could seat eighteen, she threw open one of the French doors that lined the entire back of the house.

She stepped out onto the veranda with a sigh. Green hills spread as far as she could see. Hummingbirds and butterflies flitted around the line of flowers that bordered the space. A giant magnolia tree stood off in the distance, just coming into bloom. She closed her eyes and breathed deep, willing herself to calm down.

Opening her eyes, she walked over to one of the loungers and took a seat. She pulled out her cell, dialed Jen, and stretched out her legs.

Jen answered almost immediately. "Hey, Laney."

"Hey. How are you doing? How's the rebuilding?"

"The physical rebuilding's moving quickly, thanks to Henry. But the psychological rebuilding? That's going to take a lot longer, if ever. Your uncle's been great, though. He's in the thick of things. Always there with a shoulder to cry on or a hammer to nail something. He's been incredible."

"I talked to him this morning. Being able to help is why he went into the priesthood. But I can feel his heartbreak for the Shuar people. In one fell swoop, they lost the reason for their existence and almost all of their people. I don't know how they'll rebound from that." Laney paused. "How's Nana?"

The sigh came across loud and clear. "She's struggling. I mean, she's strong and doing what needs to be done. But every once in a while, I catch a look on her face and it breaks my heart all over again."

Laney remembered Julian's face as he tossed a

squealing Elena in the air. He had been a good man, a good leader. He didn't deserve what had happened to him. "It's not right, Jen."

"No, it's not." The shared grief stretched between them before Jen spoke. "Any luck tracking down the monsters responsible for all this?"

"No. Not a trace. It's like these guys dropped from the sky and disappeared right back into it again."

"You sound tired."

Laney stifled a yawn. "A little. Until these guys are caught, though, I don't think I'll be able to close my eyes without seeing the horrors they created."

"Yeah. I can't say my dreams have been all that easy, either."

Laney gave herself a mental shake. "Speaking of horror shows, I'm having trouble tracking down Warren. Everything on his application was fake."

Jen's voice burst through the phone. "That son of a bitch! I swear, Laney, if I ever see that cockroach again, I'll end him."

"Not if I see him first. But right now, we just need to find him. And I'm not having any luck. I was hoping to track him down through a picture. But, believe it or not, I don't have any."

Jen snorted. "Well I never took any of him intentionally. He's so damn pasty, he'd ruin my shots."

"Hey, careful with the pale jokes," Laney joked.

"Your pale's beautiful, his is unhealthy. There's no comparison. I'm guessing you want me to look and see if I have any photos of him?"

"Yeah, and the faster the better."

"Well, I guess I better get on it then. The sooner you track down the asshole, the sooner we get someone to pay for what they did. And the sooner we can get the Shuar's treasure back to them."

"Give Nana my love and giant hugs to Elena and Eddie for me."

Jen laughed. "I forgot to tell you what those two have been up to. They've decided that you and I are THE guardians of the tribe. They've created a whole series of stories about us and are teaching them to all the little kids. We're being portrayed as a cross between superheroes and gods."

Laney smiled. "I miss them."

"They miss you, too. Just find that asshole and come see them."

"I will. Take care."

"You, too."

An hour later, Jen sent Laney an email with a single word in the subject line: CREEP. Laney smiled as she clicked it open. Sure enough, there was the creep in all his glory. He hadn't been the subject of the shot, just caught in the background. Luckily, he'd turned towards the camera just as Jen had clicked the shutter.

Laney quickly cropped the photo, isolating Warren's face, and submitted it to the facial recognition program. After hitting enter, she leaned back taking a sip of coffee. *Now what?* She couldn't think of another approach, at least not one that someone else wasn't currently covering.

Drumming her fingers on the table, she looked around the room. Half a dozen analysts had their attention firmly directed on their monitors. Another half dozen were on the phones. Jake had left to find a private spot to speak with some of his military contacts.

Her eyes fell on the giant white boards that had

been pulled in front of Henry's walls of books. Pictures from Ecuador covered them, along with a list of all leads that were currently being chased or had already been ruled out.

Pushing back from the table, she walked over. Her eyes scanned the lists. FAA, money trails, covert ops, artifact experts. The leads already investigated went on and on, with absolutely nothing to show for it. Somehow, though, they'd forgotten to investigate Warren until now.

Laney shook her head. She must be more exhausted than she realized. They should have checked into him much earlier. But kicking herself wasn't going to help. She just needed to hope she found something on him that would lead back to the rest of the group.

Her eyes flicked to the entry on the bottom of the second column of leads. Secret societies. Last night, Laney had researched any organization, past or present, that might be interested in the Ecuador find. She's discovered a ton of them, even a few secret societies buried in the past. Until they had more to go on, though, there was absolutely nothing to suggest they were related to what was going on.

She scanned the lists again. *What are we missing?*

"Hey Laney, your monitor just beeped," an analyst called out.

Surprised, she walked back to it. *That was fast.* She pulled out her chair, her eyes already glued to the screen. Over two thousand hits.

She clicked on the first. "What the hell?"

A newspaper article from seven years ago appeared. The picture was of two young men with their arms wrapped around two gorgeous young women. She recognized the young man on the left. Steve Lucentia, son of two-time Academy Award winner Matthew Lucentia. He was Hollywood royalty. And next to him was Warren.

Dragging her jaw off the floor, she scrolled through the other pages. More shots of Warren carousing with the children of the rich and famous. Apparently, though, he wasn't famous himself. In the pictures where he was identified, it was with the ubiquitous title of "friend".

She continued flipping through the pages, hoping maybe somewhere a name was attached. As she scanned the articles, she couldn't help but be shocked by his life. She knew he was wealthy. His attitude screamed it. But this life she was looking at was beyond that. Yachts, luxury cars, exclusive clubs. This was Gatsby wealthy.

Finally, a senior class picture popped up from Beverly Hills High School. Warren Friendenburg. She grinned. *Found you.*

She typed in his name, looking for a birth announcement. Sure enough, twenty-three years ago Warren Friedenburg had been born in Las Vegas, Nevada to Michelle Friedenburg. No father was listed. She ran a search on his mother. She was listed on a bunch of uppity social groups and charities. Digging deeper, though, she found the old life: a former Las Vegas showgirl. No marriages on record.

Laney drummed her fingers on the table. How did the son of a Vegas dancer go from Caesar's Palace to Beverly Hills? Sugar daddy?

She needed more information. And she knew just who could find it for her. Pulling out her cell, she dialed.

Yoni's voice bounced through the line. "My favorite redhead. What are you up to?"

She grinned. "Hey Yoni. I'm good. But I was wondering, how would you like to take an all expenses paid trip to Vegas?"

CHAPTER 53

Las Vegas, Nevada

Sebastian shuffled into his bedroom. Heavy velvet drapes were already drawn across the large windows. The light by his bed was lit, casting a soft glow on the king-size bed in its four-poster cherry wood frame. The navy blue comforter was pulled back, the white sheets crisp and inviting.

He headed to his walk-in closet, complete with an island of accessories, a wall for shoes, and more suits than he could ever possibly wear. He'd just stepped in when there was a knock at his bedroom door. Annoyed, he turned around. "Who is it?"

Gerard's voice was apologetic through the door. "Excuse the interruption, sir. But there's some information you need to see."

My father's files. He must have found something. Excitement bloomed in Sebastian's chest. He walked over to one of the two deep navy wingback chairs positioned next to the fireplace. Once seated, he called out. "Come in."

"My apologies, sir. But I thought you would want to see this."

With an impatient gesture, he beckoned Gerard forward, careful to keep the excitement from his face. Gerard placed the folder in his outstretched hand. Pulling his reading glasses from his jacket pocket, he began to read.

It was a memo from his father to the Council. He believed that he'd found a possible location for one of the Fallen. He flipped to the next page. The Council was dismissive in their response. He glowered at the censure in the correspondence:

We are unconvinced in the validity of your source. At this time, we recommend no action be taken. Further, you should be aware your role in the Council is currently under investigation due to previous actions not fitting with the Council's agenda.

"This is why you woke me?"

Gerard gently took the folder. "If I might, sir?"

He nodded.

Gerard flipped through the papers, pulling out two. He handed the first report to Sebastian. "This one is the report on the mission at the Chandler house."

Sebastian nodded, his eyes scanning the document. "Yes, yes. I know all of this."

Gerard handed him the second page. "This appears to be a handwritten note by your father about the mission. The passage I think you'll be most interested in is at the bottom."

The date made him jolt. It was the day his father died of a heart attack.

The edge of the paper had been nibbled at. He glared at it. His father's wife had wasted no time in removing all traces of him from her life. She'd ordered all his papers and possessions into the basement the day of his death. It was the first stop before she had them tossed. They'd been crammed down there, without any concern for their organization or the mice that had made a meal of a man's lifetime of work.

He remembered his anger when he'd seen his father's treasured files crammed into the damp basement corner. No order, just piled on top of one another. He'd had his crew in and out in two hours, removing every last shred of paper. Then he'd waited for his stepmother to return home. He smiled. A shame dear old stepmom couldn't outrun the flames.

Sebastian scanned the shortly worded note. It detailed the last mission his father had ordered. But as he read the notes, he realized his father had never informed the Council of his actions.

He skimmed the rest of the note. His father's last sentence made Sebastian catch his breath. Now he knew why his father had kept the identity of the target secret and who his father suspected James Chandler actually was.

Sebastian's eyes sprang back to Gerard, his words urgent. "Test Chandler now. If he passes, take him immediately."

"If he doesn't?"

Sebastian glanced back down at his father's note. *Could it be?* "Take him anyway."

244

CHAPTER 54

Baltimore, Maryland

*F*rustration. *That is my perpetual state,* Laney thought as she walked down the stairs of her cottage. She'd spent the night in her cottage down on Sharecroppers' Lane.

Like other estates from the nineteenth century, Henry's estate had at one point had a row of two dozen sharecropper homes. During Henry's renovation, he'd turned them into cottages for guests and extra offices. It was like a little country village tucked into Henry's big rolling estate. Henry had even installed old-fashioned streetlights.

Laney's cottage sat at the end of Sharecroppers' Lane. Inside, the walls were covered in a buttery yellow with blue and white accents, overstuffed furniture, and a constant supply of fresh flowers. Since she'd been spending so much time down there, she'd brought down a bunch of her pictures which now covered the walls, along with her throws. The cottage was small, but beautiful. She absolutely loved it.

But her love for the little cottage hadn't helped her sleep last night. She'd tossed and turned, trying in vain to come up with another avenue of investigation and to keep the horror of the last few days from her mind. At 4:30, she'd finally given up and gone for a run, followed by a heavy bag workout.

How had the group covered their tracks so well? She felt the weight of Nana's decree on her shoulders. She couldn't let her down.

"Assholes," she muttered as the group from Ecuador slipped into her brain, yet again. Tightening her laces, she thought about all the damage they'd done. She still couldn't get over how ruthless they'd been.

The lack of progress in finding them was maddening. If she was being honest, though, finding those responsible wasn't her only source of frustration. She also wasn't sure how to deal with Jake. They were working together and pretty well, but there was so much unsaid between the two of them.

She couldn't deny the joy, though, that had shot through her when she'd seen him in Ecuador and felt his arms around her. She'd known she was safe then.

But then again, feelings had never been their problem. Reality was. He had a job that took him all over the world. She had one that required periods of intense focus. And when she needed to focus, he was free. When she was free, he was overseas. And after everything that happened last year, she'd just needed some time to think things through. And, of course, he'd taken up with the first warm body he'd found.

She leaned her back against the wall. Relationships really sucked sometimes. She blew out a breath, pushing herself off the wall. *All right, enough with the pity party.*

She stretched her arms above her head, trying to

work out the kinks in her shoulders. Even with the workout this morning and the boiling shower, she hadn't gotten rid of all the aches. Well, it was going to have to wait. There was work to be done, information to find.

Of course, she didn't have any ideas of where to start searching. *Let's hope inspiration strikes on the walk over.* She crossed to the front door and pulled it open.

"Morning." Jake stood on her doorstep with a smile.

Laney jumped back. "Um, morning. What are you doing here?" Butterflies danced through her stomach.

Jake held up a cooler with a blanket thrown over it and a thermos tucked under his arm. "I thought maybe you'd be up for a picnic breakfast."

Laney's heart melted a little bit. But then she thought of all that she needed to do, all they needed to find out. "I'd love to, but we don't have any leads yet. Maybe after-"

"Laney, no one's currently in mortal danger. The Shuar's legacy is already gone, and people are working on the problem around the clock. They've all taken time off to sleep and eat. You can, too."

She knew he was right. She'd barely spent any time away from the investigation. Running herself ragged was getting her nowhere. Maybe taking her mind off the issue for a little while would let her look at it fresh.

And the idea of spending time alone with Jake and maybe getting rid of this uncomfortable wall between them was too tempting to resist.

She took the thermos from him. "All right. I'm in."

Together, they walked around the side of the

cottage. Jake held out his hand and Laney clasped it as they walked up the small hill. Up ahead, a path cut through the trees.

They walked for a few minutes in silence. Laney looked around. "I've never been to this part of the estate. What's over here?"

Jake glanced down at her. "A surprise. Close your eyes."

She looked at him, her eyebrow raised.

He nudged her. "Come on. Trust me."

With a sigh, she closed her eyes, letting Jake lead her. She could tell they were heading up a hill. After a few minutes, he stopped. "Okay. Open them."

She did and gasped. A giant field of mammoth sunflowers stood at attention at the bottom of the hill. Each of the stalks was over ten feet tall. He grinned, tugging her down the hill towards them.

Laney felt she'd arrived in a different world as she walked between the towering stalks. In the middle of the field was a square clearing, ringed by the sunflowers. It was incredible.

Jake laid out the checkered blanket while Laney inspected the flowers more closely. They were amazing. There must have been hundreds of them. She felt like a Lilliputian.

"Breakfast is served."

Laney turned. Jake had spread the blanket, laying out pastries, eggs, and fruit.

She sank to the ground across from him, the unease she felt around him slipping away. "This is perfect."

Jake leaned forward placing a kiss lightly on her lips. "Now it's perfect."

They ate breakfast and talked, really talked, for over

two hours. They shared everything that had happened in the time they'd been apart. The connection they'd had almost since the moment they met began to strengthen.

Laney felt content in a way she hadn't for months. She lay on her back staring at the clouds drifting by above them.

Jake lay next to her. Slowly, he began to talk about Hugo when he'd been Derek Collins. "It's hard to explain. One day he was this incredible guy, practically a brother, and then he was a stranger. One I wouldn't turn my back to. In Iraq, I should have reported him, but I kept thinking he would snap out of it. That he'd be Derek again." Jake shook his head. "So stupid."

Laney rolled on her stomach to look him in the eye. "Not stupid. Hopeful."

Jake reached up and pushed a stray hair behind her ear. "One day, we got a report that a family had been attacked. The mother and daughter had been raped. The whole family shot point blank. Neighbors said it was a U.S. soldier. I knew in my gut it was Derek. The next day, he died in a roadside bomb. Or so we thought."

Laney lay her head on his chest. "I'm sorry, Jake."

"I spoke with some Navy doctors and they mentioned frontal lobe trauma sometimes results in massive personality transformation."

Laney nodded. "He was a pseudo-psychopath."

"A what?"

"Think of it as adult onset psychopathy."

"I thought psychopaths were born psychopaths."

It was a common assumption. True psychopaths were born that way, a fact that had always bothered

Laney. It meant there were two-year old psychopaths running around right now, who had no chance of becoming good people. They would grow up to prey on others.

"Generally, that's true. But it's not the only way. In 1975, the term was coined for individuals who first demonstrated psychopathic traits later in life, generally after frontal lobe trauma."

Jake looked up. "Like Derek."

"No. Derek's gone. He's Hugo now."

Jake stroked her hair. She rolled over, facing the sky again. "Any idea about how to find him?"

"I've been thinking about that. I have one lead I'm going to run down but it'll have to be in person. It's not an over-the-phone kind of conversation."

"When will you go?"

"Probably tomorrow." Jake went quiet and Laney just lay listening to his heartbeat. She knew how hard it had to be knowing a former friend was responsible for of all this violence.

After a few minutes, Jake seemed to shake himself from the past. "So tell me about the cave. What was it like?"

She smiled, picturing the Shuar's secret. "It was unbelievable. It still seems like a dream. When I first got in there, there was this world map on the ceiling of the lagoon, including Atlantis."

"Accurate?"

"As far as I could tell. There were a million discoveries, each one more amazing than the next. But it was the library that kept pulling me back. Have you seen the sheets of symbols in the Crespi collection?"

"Yeah. Your uncle showed me some pictures. He

said no one could make out what the symbols were. He said most people believe they're an unknown Incan language."

"That's the common belief. In the cave, there were hundreds of folios on shelves in an alcove. Each folio was filled with similar sheets in different metals - silver, gold, some I couldn't identify. And the alcove itself was covered in sheets of metal imprinted with symbols."

"The same writing?"

"Not all of it, no. But I did recognize some of it."

"What language was it?"

"Enochian. I couldn't read much though. But I did make out some words."

"From your face, I can tell those words weren't joy or something equally uplifting."

"No. It was a name. Azazyel."

Jake started. "Are you sure?"

She nodded. "After Montana, I looked into Enochian. I'm not great with languages, but I learned some. Azazyel was actually one of the first words I learned."

Jake raised an eyebrow.

She shrugged. "A fallen angel tries to kill you, you tend to want to figure out as much of his backstory as you can manage. Anyway, his name was on one of the books, but I didn't have time to translate the rest of it."

"Were any of the men at the site Fallen?"

An image of Jen flashed through her mind. "No. Just regular scumbag humans. But can you imagine what those books could hold? I think, if anything, it's a history of the world, of the Fallen, of things we can't even begin to comprehend."

Jake's voice was thoughtful. "It might even be more than that."

Laney looked up at him. "What do you mean?"

"It may be an explanation about how to defeat them. A description of some form of angelic kryptonite."

"Do you think there is such a thing?"

It was Jake's turn to shrug. "I don't know. But I'm guessing we think the authors are the Children of the Law of One, right?"

They knew the Montana find was one of the locations for one of the Atlantis libraries hidden away by the Children of the Law of One. A second library was rumored to be in a secret cavern underneath the left paw of the Sphinx in Egypt. And it looked as if Ecuador was the third.

Laney nodded. "Yes. They're the most likely authors."

"Well, they knew their world was coming to an end. And they were trying to protect the knowledge they'd gathered for future generations. I'm betting part of that knowledge included the weaknesses of the Fallen."

"Now that would be great." The smile dropped from her face. "Of course, we have to get the artifacts back first to see if that is in fact true."

"Don't worry. We will."

She found herself staring at him, unable to look away. God, she'd missed him. His deep brown eyes, the sexy timbre to his voice, the feel of his hands on her skin. Why had she ever let him go?

She sighed. "I suppose we should get back and help with the search."

"I suppose we should." She caught the flash of disappointment on his face. Jake's hand cupped her

252

face. "I've missed you, Laney."

The butterflies in her stomach began their mad dance again. She hesitated, feeling the pull of work. But all that had happened between her and Jake last year and everything that had happened down in Ecuador a few days ago flashed through her mind. Life was too short to push aside these moments and hope they happened again later. She leaned up, her lips touching his.

That was all the invitation he needed. He rolled her over, pinning her to the ground, his kiss urgent.

She wrapped her arms around him. Work could wait.

CHAPTER 55

Laney rushed up the stairs of the Chandler headquarters. She and Jake had stayed in the field most of the morning. At one point, she'd even fallen asleep. She'd woken up when Jake had kissed her. A thrill shot through her when she thought of his lips on hers. She didn't know exactly what their status was, but right now she didn't care. She was happy.

Pulling out her phone, she quickly scanned her emails. No message from Yoni. She was hoping he'd have found something on Warren by now. She shoved the phone back in her pocket. She'd call him later.

Opening the door to Henry's office, she gave Henry a smile as she made her way to her desk. She flipped on her screen. Henry walked over behind her, placing his hand on her shoulder he leaned down and whispered, "About time you two made up."

Laney struggled not to blush. She turned but Henry was already heading back to his desk. Shaking her head, she dove back into work. The rest of the day was a never ending stream of dead ends. Every time she thought maybe, just maybe, she found a lead on Warren or Hugo, she ended up disappointed.

By that evening, all she had to show for her efforts was a screaming headache. Just after ten, Jake fetched her.

"Time to get some sleep, Lanes."

She shook her head. "I just need to do a few more-"

He pulled her out of her chair. "It'll keep until tomorrow. You need to get some sleep. You can barely keep your eyes open."

He did have a point. She'd read and re-read the article on her monitor four times and she still wouldn't be able to tell anyone what it said. A little rest was probably a good idea.

Jake took her hand, walked her down the stairs, and out to his golf cart. That was all she remembered. She must have fallen asleep as soon as she sat down. She woke up briefly as they reached her cottage to make her way inside.

Too tired to change, she fell on the bed. Jake curled up next to her. She'd slept better than she had in months.

When she awoke, he was gone. She leaned over to the other side of his bed and his scent was still there. She smiled. She hadn't imagined him.

Hugging herself, she got out of bed. Fifteen minutes later, she was making her way to the main house, disappointed she hadn't seen Jake. Stifling a yawn, she walked into Henry's office.

Henry looked up from his desk, a tired smile on his face. "Morning, Laney."

She smiled as she walked over to him, slinking into one of the three leather wing chairs in front of his desk. "Morning. Did you get any sleep last night?"

"A little."

She looked at him, not believing a word. "I'm guessing a very little. Where is everybody?" Henry's office was strangely silent.

"I sent the analysts to the lab down on the second floor. They've set up a command center down there."

"Any luck?"

Henry blew out a breath. "No. More walls. But Danny slipped into his lab early this morning. He mentioned something about a new angle. Maybe he'll come up with something."

She nodded and, trying to keep her voice casual, asked. "And Jake?"

"He took off this morning." He glanced over at her, eyebrow raised. "I'm guessing you knew he was going?"

Laney looked out the window, her mind trailing back to their picnic. And his arms around her last night. She felt the blush creep over he cheeks. "I knew he was, just not when. How do you think he's doing with all of that?"

Henry sighed. "I don't know. He's playing it pretty close to the vest. But he's mentioned Derek before. They'd been pretty close before his personality shifted. Derek even saved his life a few times."

A knock sounded at Henry's door. Danny stood poised in the doorway, Moxy next to him. That was odd. She'd never known Danny to knock. Henry's office was basically Danny's office.

"Hey Danny," Laney called.

Danny looked at her, but didn't say anything. He walked slowly into the room, his head bowed low. He stopped at the edge of Laney's chair.

Laney reached out to take him gently by the arm. "Danny? Is everything all right?"

He looked up, his face stricken. "It's my fault, Laney. I'm the reason they attacked that village and all those people died."

CHAPTER 56

Las Vegas, Nevada

Rifling through the photos of the artifacts that sat on top of his desk, Sebastian smiled. He hadn't felt this good in years. It was as if the find had rejuvenating properties to it.

A knock sounded at the door only a second before it was pushed open. His grandson Warren shuffled in, his face still bearing the hallmarks of the violence from Ecuador.

"It is customary to wait until someone tells you to enter," Sebastian instructed.

"Yeah, sorry," Warren mumbled heading for the wet bar built into the back corner of the office.

Sebastian shook his head, his eyes following his grandson, his heir, as he poured two fingers of whiskey into a crystal tumbler. He'd hoped the trip would mature him, make him a man. But that hadn't happened. He was still the same overgrown child he'd been when he left.

He blamed the boy's mother for that. She'd always been a stupid girl. He'd met her a few times when his son had brought her around. But when she'd gotten pregnant, he'd told his son under no circumstances would he allow him to marry her.

The mother had taken the boy away and been paid very well to look after him. He always figured his son would provide him with a legitimate heir. By the time his son died five years ago, though, that hadn't happened.

Warren's mother had overindulged him, never made him work. He had no discipline. Apparently, Sebastian was going to have to finish the child-rearing himself.

Sebastian looked at the dark contents of Warren's glass. "It's not even noon."

Warren took a long drink. "It's five o'clock somewhere."

Sebastian pushed back from the desk with a sigh. He walked over to the two wingback chairs by the window, gesturing for Warren to join him. Once seated, his grandfather examined Warren's face closely. "Your bruises seem to be healing nicely."

Warren glowered, his voice stiff. "They're fine."

"So, the trip was a success. You brought back the artifacts. That is quite an accomplishment."

Warren stayed silent, looking bored.

"Do you realize what this means? Our family has been searching for this for lifetimes. And finally we have realized our goal." He looked at Warren expectantly.

Warren shrugged.

Anger spiked through Sebastian. He grabbed Warren's arm, squeezing his forearm.

"Hey let go," Warren yelled, trying to pull his arm away.

Sebastian pulled him closer. "You listen to me.

You come from a long line of powerful men. You need to respect that. You need to respect me. If not, everything you have, the money, the cars, the women, they'll all disappear. Do you understand me?"

Warren nodded, his face pale. "Yes, Grandfather."

Sebastian released his arm. It was a start.

CHAPTER 57

Baltimore, Maryland

Laney pulled Danny over to the couch in Henry's office. She and Henry bookended him between them. Danny looked like he was on the verge of tears. "Danny, honey, tell us what you found."

Danny's voice was so quiet, Laney had to lean forward to hear him. "It was the tracker I put on your computer. I wasn't getting anywhere with tracking the group down. Sometimes it helps if I focus on something else. I realized I'd left the tracker on your laptop. So this morning, I went to my lab to remove it."

Henry rested his hand on Danny's back. "And what did you find?"

"Someone had piggybacked my signal. There was someone else hearing and seeing everything I was."

Laney sat back, shocked. Someone else had been listening in on her conversations? The sense of violation was overwhelming.

Danny glanced up at Laney, his voice pleading. "Not that I was looking. I had a program set up so it kept track of your movements and cross-referenced them with any dangerous activities. I wasn't spying. I swear."

"I'm not mad, Danny. Not at you, at least. I'm just a little, well, a little shocked."

Henry looked over at her. "Laney, did you say anything that would lead someone to think you were close to finding the source of the Crespi collection?"

It felt like a lifetime had passed since she'd last been on her laptop. She struggled to recall the last conversation she'd had on it. "I don't know. I mean, I think the last time I was on was . . . oh my God."

"Laney?" Henry prodded.

"Last time was right before I went to the Shuar village. I was talking to my uncle. I told him I thought Nana was going to reveal the origin of the collection."

Tears streamed down Danny's face. "I'm so sorry, Laney. I was trying to protect you. And I put you in danger."

Laney pulled him into a hug. "No, honey. It's not your fault. None of this is your fault." She looked over his head at Henry, pleading him with her eyes to help soothe the boy.

Kneeling down in front of him to look him in the eye, Henry gently pulled Danny from Laney's embrace, "Laney's right, Danny. This isn't your fault. Think about it. This operation was huge and well-organized. This wasn't something pulled together at the last minute."

Laney nodded. "And they already had Warren the weasel embedded with us. They probably had other ears we don't even know about yet. In fact, your tracker's what saved a lot of lives."

Danny looked at her, his eyes wide and confused. "What? How?"

"You knew almost immediately that I was in trouble. And you managed to get help down there faster than anyone else could have. If you hadn't put that tracker on, you guys would probably just be finding out about the attack now. And you would have been too late to help me or any of the Shuar."

Laney could see the logic getting though to him. Danny, though still a child, was at his heart logical.

Henry nodded. "In fact, now that you've found this second signal, you can hopefully trace it back to its source. This could be the break we've been waiting for."

Danny nodded. "You're right. I should have thought about that."

Giving him a hug, she said, "Well, even geniuses have an off day."

When he pulled back, a smile was back on his face. "I'm going to get back to my lab. I'll find the source."

"We know you will," Henry said.

Together, they watched him leave, Moxy once again trailing behind him.

Laney looked over at Henry, the anger she'd kept a lid on for Danny's sake, boiled up. "We need to get these assholes."

Henry nodded, his face tight. "Agreed."

CHAPTER 58

Forest Hills, NY

Jake walked down the block in Forest Hills, Queens. The houses were all train car style with narrow alleys between them. He hadn't been here in years. The last time, he and Yoni had come home with Derek for Thanksgiving.

He stopped at the chain-link gate in front of the yellow and brown two-story house. Plastic flowers sat by the front door and metal gates covered the windows. A butt-ugly pelican stood in the middle of the postage-stamp-sized yard.

Opening the gate, he walked up to the front door. He rang the bell, but it didn't seem to work. He rapped on the door three times.

"I'm coming. Keep your pants on," came the male voice from inside.

A shuffling walk told Jake the speaker was older. There was a pause before the deadbolt pulled back.

A weathered face, with sharp blue eyes, peered out at him through the opening of the chained door. "What do you want?"

"Mr. Collins? It's Jake Rogan. I'm not sure if-"

"Jake Rogan? Well, shit." The door slammed shut. The chain rattled. Hal Collins threw the door open. "How the hell are you? Come in, come in."

Hal backed out of the way, ushering Jake into the dimly lit house. Jake was surprised by the welcome and by how neat the house was. He could see the track lines of the vacuum in the old blue carpet. The wood paneling of the hall was crowded with pictures of family.

"Come on through to the kitchen. I just made some coffee." Hal shuffled ahead of him, his hunched shoulders making him appear shorter than he'd been years ago.

He was only sixty-five but a life of manual labor had left him looking older. His hair was completely white, his back bent, and he was awfully skinny. His suspenders seemed to be the only thing holding up his pants.

Jake followed him into a small, clean kitchen. The white linoleum floor was worn but sparkled. The white counters glistened and a small bouquet of daisies sat in a vase on the old wood table.

Hal grabbed two mugs from the cupboard. "Have a seat. How do you take it?"

"Black's fine."

Hal nodded, pouring coffee into each mug and setting one in front of Jake. Reaching over and grabbing the sugar shaker, Hal poured a small mountain of sugar into his own. He took a sip with a smile. "Damn. Jake Rogan. I read about you and that whole Montana mess. I told my wife, 'See that boy? Told you he'd make something of himself.'"

"It wasn't just me. Yoni was there, too."

Hal slapped the table. "Always liked that boy. He gotten any taller?"

"Afraid not. He did, however, get married, and even has a son. Thank goodness the baby looks like his mother."

Hal laughed, taking a sip. Silence descended and Jake tried to figure out a way to broach the topic at hand. How does one ask a father if he'd seen his violent, allegedly dead, son recently?

Luckily, Hal seemed to know why Jake was here. "I guess you're looking for Derek."

Jake nodded. "You knew he was alive?"

"Not right away. Wasn't until about three years after the military told us he died that he showed up. My wife and I about collapsed."

"How did he seem?"

"Just as he was the last time we saw him before he 'died.' In other words, nothing like my son." Hal's hands shook. He clasped them together. "Derek was never the same after that accident. Our boy was a good boy, always helping out, doing the right thing. The man we met after that accident, he wasn't our son."

"Why did he come back to see you?"

A look disgust crossed Hal's face. "To gloat. Show us what a big shot he'd become."

Jake nodded. That was the Hugo he remembered.

"You were always good to him," Hal said, "even when he didn't deserve it. That business in Montana? Derek never would have done what you did."

"Years ago, he would have."

Hal nodded, conceding the point. "But that Derek's gone. Tell me, what has he done now? Has anyone been hurt?"

266

Jake looked at the shell of a man before him. He couldn't add any more heartache to the man's life. He opened up his mouth to speak when Hal put up a hand.

"Actually, don't tell me. I think I'd rather not know."

"When Derek came here, did he say where he was going? Who he was working for?"

Hal sat back thinking. "Some company recruited him. Not one of those mercenary for hire outfits, a private company. He was real proud. Puffed up. To be honest, I spent most of the visit trying to get him to leave."

"Do you know the name of the company?"

"Um, I think it was some Italian outfit. Bellissimo. Corromo. Something like that."

Jake nodded. He handed Hal his card. "You hear anything, you call me."

Hal took the card and nodded, his face dropping. "Yeah, sure, kid."

Jake stood to leave, taking in the still house. He knew Derek's only sister lived down in Virginia. Pictures of grandkids who probably rarely visited were on the fridge. Hal had been forced to retire early due to a bad back. His days must be pretty quiet, maybe even lonely.

Jake sat back down again. "Don't think I ever thanked you for taking me and Yoni in all those holidays. It was a real treat to have a home cooked meal."

Hal waved the compliment away. "Anybody would have done it."

"No, they wouldn't have. Thank you." Jake spied a covered dish on the counter. "Any chance that's pie?"

Hal smiled. "Yup. Apple. Wife made it yesterday. Want a slice?"

"I'd love some."

Hal stood, and then stopped, looking down at Jake. "Jake, Derek ain't a good man, not anymore. When you find him, don't go giving him the benefit of the doubt. Any kindness in him was killed off by that roadside bomb."

Jake nodded and watched Hal shuffle off to get the pie. Hal didn't have to worry. Hugo had gotten his one and only break from him. The next time he saw Hugo, he was going to kill him.

CHAPTER 59

Baltimore, Maryland

Later that afternoon, Laney sat in one of the conference chairs in Henry's office, twirling a pencil in her fingers while staring at the ceiling. "My head hurts."

Henry chuckled. "I think everyone's head hurts. We're getting nowhere with this."

Henry was right. They still didn't have a clue on who the group was, where they'd gone, or how they knew about the library. Danny wasn't having any luck tracking the signal from her computer. It was being bounced through servers across the globe.

This had been a well-oiled operation. Anything they thought was a lead dried up almost immediately. Dr. Devereaux had essentially disappeared and they'd found nothing on Hugo or Warren. And they had no idea who was footing the bill.

Laney sat up. "Okay. That's enough."

Danny looked up from his monitor over at Henry's conference table. "What?"

"We need a break. This approach is getting us nowhere. We need to step away and then come back fresh."

Henry smiled. "What did you have in mind?"

"Well, I do believe it's Tuesday, which is usually bookstore day."

Danny looked at her with a grin. Laney knew Henry and Danny headed to the big bookstore in the Inner Harbor every Tuesday for at least a few hours. It was their weekly ritual. And when she was in town, she usually tagged along.

Laney smiled back at him. "Well, I think we need to keep that tradition alive. I was thinking maybe you two could go ahead to the bookstore. Jake should be back in a little bit. When he arrives, we'll meet you there and then go get a burger at that hamburger place that opened up near the bookstore. What do you think?"

Henry nodded. "I'm all for it."

Danny turned off his tablet. "I'm ready."

CHAPTER 60

Henry pulled his Suburban through the gates of the estate, waving at security as he drove past. The country road was quiet, the sun shining up ahead, a few clouds dotting the sky. The perfect day to take a little break.

Henry smiled over at Danny, who sat in the passenger seat, practically bouncing in place. A trip to the bookstore. For Danny, it was the equivalent of being let loose in a candy shop. Henry knew the feeling. There was something about new books that were full of possibility.

"Do you think they'll have De Grasse Tyson's new book?" Danny asked.

"I don't know. We'll have to see."

"And what about the Marvel Encyclopedia of Superheroes? The new edition was supposed to come out today. Do you think they'll have some in stock?"

"I'm sure they will."

Danny chattered away happily next to him. Henry was glad he'd taken the time. Laney was right. Time away was good. And hopefully, it would allow them to look at the problem from a fresh angle.

He glanced down at Danny, who grinned in response. They needed this step back. It reminded him there were other important things in life.

"Do you think we could stop for milkshakes before the bookstore?" Danny asked.

Henry gave a little laugh. "I think-"

A prickling sensation rolled down Henry's neck. He whipped his head to the left.

A black pickup burst from behind the trees at the side of the road. It broadsided their SUV, flipping them over and over again.

CHAPTER 61

Henry shook his head, trying to stop the ringing in his ears. He pushed the air bags out of his way. The SUV was on its roof, the windshield a spider web of cracks.

Suspended upside down, blood rushed to his head. He pulled out his cell phone, but there was no signal. He wasn't surprised. This part of the road was notorious for spotty cell capability.

He looked over at Danny, who was looking dazed. "Danny?"

Danny grimaced, a cut on the side of his forehead. "I'm okay. What happened?"

The squealing of brakes cut off his reply. Through the windshield, Henry saw two trucks idling, four men exiting them. Twisting his neck to look behind them, he saw another two men getting out of a truck behind them.

"Henry?" Danny asked, fear in his voice.

"Stay here." Henry punched at his seatbelt, releasing himself. He pulled on the handle, but the door was jammed. Throwing his shoulder into it, it flung open.

Henry stumbled out, quickly righting himself.

Four men stood looking at him, another two held back at the pickup behind him. They didn't speak. All wore baseball caps, flannel jackets and were, in a word, non-descript. Medium height, medium build, unremarkable features.

"Now," ordered one of the men.

A man in a Red Sox cap ran at him, throwing a front kick. Henry blocked the kick, jabbed the man in the face, followed by a cross to the stomach. He grabbed the man by the throat and threw him towards the ground. As the man hit the ground, another kicked at Henry's back legs.

Henry leaped out of the way, snaking his arm around the second man's neck, pulling him into a chokehold. "What do you want?"

The man didn't respond.

"Henry!" Danny yelled.

Henry whipped around. Two men dragged Danny from the car. With a roar, Henry flung the man he was holding away.

Seeing Danny in danger unleashed something inside of Henry that he'd kept carefully locked away for years. The need to protect Danny overrode any other thought, any other emotion. Logic was gone. He was in pure predator mode. He leapt over the car, ten feet in the air and eight feet across.

The men holding Danny stopped to gape at his actions. Without hesitation, Henry aimed a front kick into one of the men's chest, sending him flying. A crack told him at least one of the man's ribs had broken, if not his sternum. Wrapping his hand around the other man's throat, he swung him like a rag doll before throwing him across the road.

Danny stared at Henry, his mouth hanging open.

Henry leaned down, grabbing Danny's arms. "Danny, you need to run."

"No. I'm not leaving you."

Henry could hear the men coming up behind them. "Now, Danny, run. Get help." He turned Danny around, pushing him towards the woods.

Danny stumbled. Then, with one last look, he disappeared into the trees.

Henry turned just as a man pulled out a Taser. He leapt to the side, barely missing the prongs as they sprung towards him.

He swept the man's legs from him and landed a punch to his face. The man's head snapped back, his eyes rolling back into his head.

"Get the boy," one of them yelled. Two men sprinted towards the trees.

Anger surged through Henry. "No!"

Leaping towards one of the men, he tackled him to the ground. With satisfaction, Henry felt and heard the bones in his face crunch. He slammed the man's head into the ground for good measure. The man screamed, clutching at his ruined face.

With a short burst of speed, he tackled the other man around the knees, dropping him to the ground. Kneeing the man in the middle of the back, Henry grabbed him by the hair, slamming his face into the ground three times.

Visions of the man hurting Danny raced through Henry's mind. "You don't get to touch him," he growled, slamming the man's head into the ground one last time and releasing him.

He turned to face the other men. A sting in his side sent pain shooting through him. He crashed to his knees. Reaching down, he yanked the prongs from the Taser out. The pain disappeared almost immediately. He stood, turning to the four men lined up behind him.

One pulled out a gun, but another yelled at him. "No guns. We need him unharmed."

The men moved forward, slowly circling towards him. One shot a dart at him. Henry ducked out of the way at the last moment, avoiding it. But he walked right into another one. He pulled it out, but he could already feel the effects. His movements were growing sluggish, his thinking muddied.

He stumbled towards the men. *I have to protect Danny.* Another dart pierced his side.

He crashed to his knees and fell forward. He couldn't move, couldn't think.

"Okay men, let's load him up," was the last thing he heard before unconsciousness claimed him.

CHAPTER 62

Laney jogged down the main drive of the Chandler Estate, before turning onto the country road. Jake had just arrived back. He had a few leads he wanted to run down before they met up with Henry and Danny. It should give Laney just enough time for a quick run and shower.

She ran at her regular pace for two miles. She glanced at her watch and picked up the speed.

Five-minute mile, here I come, she challenged herself.

She flew down the road, focusing on her breathing, the cadence of her step. Up ahead, she saw the mile marker and managed to coax just a little more speed out of her body. A blur of dust trailed behind her.

She crossed the mile marker and glanced at her watch. Four minutes, fifty-seven seconds.

"Yes!" She threw her hands up in the air and did a little victory dance, with lots of deep breaths and a couple of bends at the waist. She might not be superhuman fast, but she was pretty damn fast. She sucked in a lungful of air. *As long as I don't have to run that fast for long.*

Her breathing back under control, she turned around and headed back to the estate. In the back of her mind, all the Ecuador facts and mysteries swirled. She paid them no attention. She needed to ignore them for a little while. Right now, they were all jumbled together.

The estate appeared in the distance and she smiled, thinking of the afternoon to come. It would be nice to take a break from everything to spend time with her boys.

Movement in the field to her right had her turning her head. A small figure ran out of the woods towards the road.

She paused, putting her hand up to shield her eyes from the sun and squinted. Her heart hammered in her chest. *Oh my God. Danny.*

She sprinted across the road, vaulted over the divider, and into the field. Her legs pounded down the earth as she flew towards him. The closer she got, the more she could feel Danny's fear.

Her eyes scanned the field behind him. *Henry. Where was Henry?*

She put on a burst of speed to reach him. She dropped to the ground in front him, grabbing his arms. "Danny? What's happened?"

Tears coursed down his cheeks, a small cut bled down the side of his face. His chest heaved. He struggled to get the words out, his sobs making him impossible to understand.

Finally, he took a breath. The words tumbled out, full of terror. "They took Henry."

CHAPTER 63

Laney called security from the field. She grabbed Danny's hand, running with him towards the road. Two security cars shot out from the estate. One raced ahead to the sight of the ambush. The other halted at the guardrail near them. A guard leaped over the rail, sprinting towards them.

When the security guard reached them, he grabbed Danny in his arms, and raced back to the car. Laney ran behind him, her mind a kaleidoscope of fear and questions. Who'd taken Henry? Why? How had Danny escaped?

The guard all but threw Danny in the back of the car. Laney leaped in the front.

"Has Jake been told?" she asked as the guard pulled the jeep into a U-turn.

"Yeah. He's assembling a team for a search and rescue and taking point on the operation."

She nodded, glancing into the back of the car. Danny's tears had dried, but he continued to shake as he stared out the window.

Laney turned back to the guard. "Do you have a tablet in here?"

"In the glove compartment."

She opened it up and pulled out the tablet. Reaching over the seat, she handed it to Danny. He glanced up at her, his eyes wide. "See what you can find, Danny."

He nodded, grabbing the computer. His fingers flew over the device as they sped along the drive.

Pulling to a sharp stop at the front of the main building, Laney and Danny leaped from the car. Danny sprinted up the stairs. Laney was right behind him, taking them two at a time.

Danny raced ahead of her, throwing open the doors to Henry's office. He threw himself into a chair at the conference table, his eyes never leaving the screen of the tablet.

Laney stopped in the doorway. Jake was on the phone behind Henry's desk. She caught his eyes. He shook his head and her heart dropped.

Danny pulled up to one of the monitors, still not talking. He even ignored Moxy, who'd placed her head in his lap.

Jake hung up the phone and walked over to her. With a glance to make sure Danny couldn't overhear, he spoke low. "We've tracked the trucks by street cams. But when our security reached them, they'd already been abandoned." He lowered his voice with a quick glance at Danny. "These guys were professionals."

A shiver ran though her. She reached for Jake's hand. "And Henry could be anywhere."

He squeezed her hand. "We'll get him back, Laney."

She nodded, but she couldn't help think of the similarity to the Ecuador group. Both were professional jobs, leaving little to no trace. "Jake, do you think there's any chance this is related to what happened in Ecuador?"

Jake turned to her and Laney knew he'd had the same thought. "I don't know, Laney. I really don't."

"I've got something," Danny called from the table.

The screen above the conference table flickered to life and showed the road where Henry had been taken. She walked quickly over, Jake beside her.

"Is this happening right now?" Jake asked.

Danny shook his head. "No. It's a recording."

"There's a security cam out there?" Laney asked.

Danny nodded. "I developed a new type of camera. I had prototypes strung along that street, to test how they worked in real world conditions. You would never know they were there unless you looked for them."

His bottom lip trembled. He took a deep breath, steadying himself. The move pierced Laney's heart.

On the screen, Danny scrolled back, the images too blurry to make out. He stopped the tape twenty-five minutes before and let it play.

Two minutes later, Henry's SUV entered the screen. She flinched as it was broadsided by the pickup, flipping it multiple times until it came to rest on its roof. Two other pickups pulled into view in front of the upended car. The one that had rammed them pulled in behind it.

She watched Henry shove open his door with such force it was ripped from its hinges.

Seconds later, Henry took out the first two men who moved on him with efficient moves. And then the fight changed. Two of the men grabbed Danny, pulling him from the car. Laney wanted to leap into the screen and kill them for touching him.

But she wasn't needed, she realized with shock as Henry leaped over the car. Not over the hood, but the base. He must have jumped at least seven feet in the air and ten feet in distance. Laney felt her jaw drop. She couldn't find any words.

"I thought I'd imagined that," Danny whispered.

Laney looked at Jake who was staring at the screen with the same dumbfounded expression. On the screen, Henry moved with lightning-fast reflexes, taking out the two men who'd touched Danny. He moved equally fast taking down the men who tried to follow Danny as he ran for the woods. Finally, the men tranq'd Henry and he fell.

Laney's heart ached at the image. It took four of the attackers to lift Henry into the pickup. Gathering up two of their own men who weren't moving, they sped out of sight.

Laney grabbed onto the back of the chair. She turned it so she could sit before she collapsed. "Did that really just happen?"

She wasn't sure if she was asking about Henry's abduction or his skills. She knew about Henry's abilities. She'd seen them first hand in Montana, but seeing it again brought it all back. Henry was skilled beyond reason, beyond humanity. If she saw anyone else with those skills, she would be terrified.

But it was Henry. He was practically her brother and that was the most important, the most defining quality about him. But now all those memories came crashing back along with all the questions she still harbored. Who was Henry really? Was he a fallen angel? Was he something else?

"I don't understand how he did that." Danny's brow furrowed.

Laney knew he was trying to figure out a rational explanation for what he'd seen. She and Jake had never mentioned Henry's abilities to Danny and neither, apparently, had Henry.

A nagging thought stayed just out of her reach. "Danny, can you back up the recording? Slowly?"

He did and Laney stared at the screen, ignoring the fight. She focused on the periphery of the action. "There. Danny, can you focus in on that one guy over by the red pick up?"

Danny zoomed in and the man became clear. A baseball hat and sunglasses hid most of his face. He was dressed the same as his partners, but he had one extra accessory. "Is he holding a camera?"

Jake stepped closer. "Yeah. He's taping the whole scene."

Laney felt cold. "Somebody wanted to see that fight."

CHAPTER 64

The next two hours were a whirlwind of activity. Jake and the Chandler estate's security were on the phone pinning down operative locations, trying to firm up the search and rescue team.

They'd debated whether or not to call in law enforcement. Right now, they were holding off. Fact of the matter was, the feds had no legal grounds to get involved, and the Chandler Group had more extensive resources than the local police. So for now, it was just them.

"And if we need to go in and get him?" Laney had asked.

"I'll ask for forgiveness from the feds later if I need to, but I won't ask permission to save Henry," Jake said

Laney knew what he meant. Law enforcement wasn't going to be allowed in on this search. Not if Jake could avoid it.

Danny was locked in his office, creating algorithms to break the signal on Laney's laptop. He was convinced Henry's abduction was related to Ecuador.

Laney stayed in Henry's office, out of everyone's

way. She had no role to play in this search. She felt useless. She paced along the windows that lined the back of the room. Jake and everybody else of importance was down at security, looking for any trace of Henry. So she was here alone, left with only her uncomfortable thoughts.

She stared out the back lawn. Henry's abduction had to be related to the Shuar's treasure. There couldn't be two incredible incidents, could there? Or was it just a huge coincidence?

But if it was related, why take Henry? He'd never seen the treasure.

She sat down, closing her eyes, picturing the treasure. The map in the lagoon, the tunnel, the treasure space. The statues standing at attention along the walls, the sculptures, the books.

Shoving her awe aside, she focused on the find with objective eyes. *Okay, okay. What does the collection tell us?*

The find was proof of a highly advanced pre-diluvian society. They had a group of seven individuals who saved the knowledge of the society. They were capable of flight, maybe even space flight. They were educated. They had a written language.

What the hell did any of that have to do with Henry? Why would they need the head of a think tank? Did they need his resources?

She shook her head. No, whoever this group was, they had tons of resources. Besides, no ransom call had come so far.

And why had they recorded the abduction? Someone who couldn't be there must have wanted to see it. *But why?* Laney pictured the truck slamming into Henry's SUV, it flipping. Henry fighting the men off and then . . .

And then when the men went after Danny, Henry revealed what he could do. *Was that the point? To get Henry to reveal his abilities?*

She moved over to Henry's desk, sitting in his large chair, twirling herself back and forth as she tried to piece together the puzzles. "Okay, the Crespi collection and a superhuman. What do they have in common?"

Her phone interrupted her musing. She pulled it out. Yoni. "Hey Yoni."

Yoni's voice bounced through the line. "How's my favorite redhead?"

Laney's heart clenched. He didn't know. She took a breath. "Not so good." She explained about the attack on Henry and Danny.

"Son of a bitch. Who's leading the search?"

"Jake and Kevin."

"Good. They'll find him, Laney."

"I know," she said, even though she had no confidence in the words. She cleared her throat. "Are you calling about Warren? Did you find anything?"

"Yeah. I found your boy's daddy."

Laney grabbed a pen and legal pad, pulling them into her lap. Thank God. A break. "Who was he?"

"Antonio Flourent."

Laney scribbled down the name. "That name sounds familiar."

"It should. He was the heir to his daddy's company; Flourent, Inc."

Laney sat straight up. "Holy crap."

Flourent, Inc. was a worldwide corporation that dabbled in a bit of everything. The name was splashed across billboards, boats, race cars. She pushed her pad aside and googled the net worth. Her eyes grew wide at the amount of zeros on the screen. She let out a low whistle. "Wow. Now that's rich."

"Well, apparently daddy didn't approve of his only son shacking up with a Las Vegas dancer. He refused to let them marry. Threatened to disown him. So, the son set the girl up and made sure little Warren never wanted for anything."

"Except a father."

"Yes. Except that."

Laney was surprised to feel a stirring of pity towards Warren. She told herself she was feeling pity only for the boy he'd been, not the man he was now. "Where's his Dad now?"

"Dead. About five years ago in a boating accident."

"Any other kids?"

"Nope. Warren is the one and only."

"Grandpa still alive?"

"Sebastian Flourent. And yup. But according to my source – her name's Bubbles, by the way – Grandpa never met the boy and never wanted to."

"Does Bubbles still speak with the mom?"

"No. Not since they moved to Beverly Hills."

Laney sat back. "Okay. So Warren has an uber-rich grandpa. Did the old man have a change of heart as he got older? Did he reach out to his only grandchild?"

"I don't know. And I gotta go. I'm going to get the next flight out to you guys."

"Okay, Yoni. We'll see you soon."

She disconnected the call and googled Sebastian Flourent. Recluse, believed to be living somewhere in the Southwest. Hadn't been seen much in public for about fifteen years. Used to be a man of industry. Rumors about an illness around ten years ago. His father died of a heart attack thirty years ago, leaving him Flourent Inc.

That name. Something about the word was stirring a thought. She sat back, staring out the window. Flourent. She knew she'd seen it somewhere else. She was sure she'd read it somewhere in the last few days. Glancing around the office, she struggled to remember, but she'd read so much it was impossible to pinpoint.

She ran her hands through her hair and then stared up at the ceiling. "God, if you're listening, we could really use a break right now."

CHAPTER 65

Washington, DC

Abigail Dresden sat in one of the private dining rooms of La Chaumiere. Quiet, out of the way, it was the location for some of DC's biggest deals. With her immaculately-tailored, deep-magenta suit and perfectly coiffed brown chignon, she fit in with all the power brokers.

Of course, nothing about her appearance was real. Padding filled out her figure, adding pounds to her lithe frame. Heavy make-up took years off her fifty-seven, and the wig completed the look of a young Washington power broker. Her 'Abigail Dresden' persona. Of course, Abigail was only one of a legion of personas she used. But precautions must be taken. Precautions were life.

Her menu sat untouched in front of her. Ralph Gregor, her bodyguard, glanced in. Thick dark hair sat upon a perfect face that time had aged well. Although her age, his shoulders were still as wide as when he'd been a star linebacker in college.

He'd been with her for over thirty years. They knew each other so well, words were almost unnecessary. With a subtle nod, Ralph intercepted the waiter about to walk in and closed the door.

Abigail pinned the man across from her with her violet eyes. "I'm waiting, Senator."

Former Senator Paul Glancy wiped his forehead with his linen napkin. A not so thin line of perspiration had worked its way there almost as soon as he sat down. Sweat rings had bled onto the collar of his white shirt, leaving a sodden stain. His yellow-and-white striped tie hung loosely from his thick neck.

"Ms. Dresden, you have to understand. These people are brutal. If they knew I was talking to you-"

She raised a single finger. He went silent. Her voice was whisper soft. "The information. Now."

He nodded, a stammer in his voice. "It was, it was seven months ago. That's the last report we have on him. He disappeared."

She let the silence draw out between the two of them, knowing silence was often a much more effective interrogation technique than words.

A minute passed before Glancy spoke. His words jumbled together, trying to fill the void. "The Council has used every resource, but we haven't found a trace of him."

"And the others?"

"Others?"

Abigail let out a sigh. "I'm getting annoyed, Senator."

"The others, right. We currently have seventeen verifieds under surveillance."

"Unverifieds?"

"Around twenty." He paused. "And there's something else. It's in the report, but you should know, we have indications that they're grouping together."

"Grouping? How many?"

"At first, two. The biggest group was ten."

Only years of practice allowed her to keep the fear from her face. If they were grouping, that could mean only one thing. *I'm not ready. She's not ready. We need more time.*

She handed him a business card. "You'll forward all the information you have on them to this email address."

He took the card with only two fingertips, staring at it like it was poisonous snake. "But, but, they'll trace it to me. They'll trace it to you."

"They won't trace it to me. You, however—" She shrugged. "Consider taking a long vacation."

"But –"

The door slid open. Ralph stepped in. "A situation has arisen."

Abigail's chest grew tight and fear spiked through her. There was only one reason Ralph was ever allowed to interrupt one of her meetings. "Leave," she ordered Glancy.

"Ms. Dresden, there must be another –"

The anger she'd leashed for the meeting slipped a notch. "Leave. Now."

Glancy knocked over his chair in his haste to escape. Ralph stepped aside at the door, then closed it after Glancy, who ran down the narrow, heavily carpeted hall to the front doors.

Abigail was on her feet, grabbing her bag. Her eyes searched Ralph's face for a sign of the news. Concern. She could see concern in his brown eyes. That scared her more than his words. "What's happened?"

"It's Henry. He's been abducted."

CHAPTER 66

Las Vegas, NV

Pain roared through Henry's chest, jerking him into consciousness. His eyes flew open and his arms wrenched upward, only to meet resistance. He panted, his heart feeling like it was going to explode out of his chest.

As the pain passed, he realized he was strapped to a metal cross. His shirt was gone, his wrists and ankles secured by chains. The room had sheer metal walls, no windows. There was no way to tell where he was or even what time of day it was.

"Good. You're awake."

His eyes focused on Hugo Barton who stood ten feet away. Henry stared at the syringe in his hands. "What did you inject in me?"

Hugo dropped the syringe onto the table next to an assortment of knives, scalpels, and other sharp instruments. "Adrenaline. You were taking too long to come around."

"You could have killed me."

Hugo's eyes narrowed. "Now see, that just isn't true, is it?"

Henry stared at him, not certain what the man was suggesting. He stayed silent.

Hugo picked up a scalpel and walked over to him. "My employer has some questions for you." Without warning, he slashed Henry across the chest.

Henry gasped at the pain, gritting his teeth. When it passed, he snarled. "Shouldn't you at least ask me a question first?"

"I think we both know you wouldn't just start answering. So I thought we'd skip the pleasantries and get right to the pain."

Henry yanked on his restraints, but they were too strong.

"Tsk, tsk. Those'll keep you there. But just in case, I have a backup plan."

Hugo walked over to the table next to the door with all of his tools. There was a small remote on it.

Henry hadn't noticed before. His attention too focused on all the sharp, shiny instruments.

Hugo picked up the remote and pushed a button.

The metal behind Henry began to grow warm and then hot. Henry arched his back, trying to keep it from pressing against the metal, but there wasn't enough give in the restraints. His skin began to sizzle as the metal burned through it. He bit his lip, not wanting to give the man the satisfaction of a response, but soon a scream erupted from his lips.

Hugo smiled, pressing another button and the metal began to cool.

Henry's skin had now melted to the beams. He blew air from his mouth, trying to manage the pain.

Hugo walked up to him, a serrated knife in his hand. With the tip, he traced the spot where he'd slashed

Henry before. Only a faint red mark was there now.

Hugo looked up into Henry's eyes. "Let's not waste time on denials when the proof's right here. My boss tells me that you're not really human, that you have special abilities. And right now, he needs one of those skills. He's asked me to persuade you to cooperate."

Henry stared at the man. All he saw in him was cruelty. And this man had the gall to accuse him of not being human. There was no morality in this man, only evil. "You and your boss can go to hell."

Hugo smiled. "I was hoping you'd say that."

CHAPTER 67

Baltimore, MD

Laney paced Henry's office, struggling to come up with some string she could follow to help find Henry. For all she knew whoever had grabbed Henry was gathering up as many superhumans as they could find. She stilled. *Oh no.*

Trembling, she pulled out her cellphone and dialed. "Please answer," she mumbled as the phone rang out over and over again.

"Hello?"

Laney released her breath and sagged against the wall. "Jen. Are you all right?"

"I'm fine. Why? What's happened?"

Laney quickly told her what had happened to Henry and why they thought he was targeted. "If they're grabbing people with powers, you need to be careful. Really careful."

"I will. Trust me. Besides, I'm not exactly a showboat when it comes to those abilities."

"Have you told your brothers?"

"No. I haven't figured out a way to work 'Hey, I've had superpowers since I was a kid' into the conversation."

Laney gave a small laugh. "I could see why that would be a little bit difficult. But you need to let them know. You could be in danger and they need to be ready for that threat."

Laney could hear the sigh through the phone, and the fear. Jen's voice was small when she spoke. "What if they can't handle it?"

"Jen, your brothers flew half way around the world to save you. They're both former Navy SEALs. I'm pretty sure they can handle it. It might rattle them for a second, but they love you. You know that."

"I know."

"Good." Laney paused. Although she did want to warn Jen, she thought the chances of her being targeted were pretty low. There was another reason she needed to speak with her. "Can I ask you a question?"

Jen paused before answering, probably recognizing the seriousness in Laney's tone. "Okay."

"When you met Henry, you seemed rattled. I thought it might be due to his size, because I've seen people react like that to him. But now I'm thinking your reaction was based on something else."

Laney waited as the silence on the phone grew. Finally, Jen spoke. "I don't know how to explain it. I mean, yes, I was surprised by his size. But it was more than that. I felt an automatic connection to him."

"You mean an attraction?"

"No, not exactly. It was stronger than that. It was a connection and a knowledge."

Laney leaned back against the wall. She knew the answer to the question but she asked it anyway. "Because you knew he was like you?"

"Yes," Jen said simply. "I knew he had the same abilities I did. I don't know how, but I knew."

Laney nodded. "And you've never felt that connection with anyone else?"

"No. Just Henry."

Laney's mind whirled with the possibilities. It didn't help her find Henry, but it was damned intriguing.

Jen cut into her thoughts. "What are you going to do about Henry?"

Laney thought of all Henry had done for Danny, her, her uncle, Jake, Jen, the Shuar. And the list went on. "We're getting him back, Jen. I'll call you when I hear something." She disconnected the call, staring out the window.

"Laney, I need to speak with you."

Laney turned around. A man with a wild halo of grey hair and thick glasses stood in the doorway. His hands moved quickly, his eyes darting around the room. His nervousness was palpable.

Laney crossed the room towards him. "Dom? Are you all right?"

Dom was Dr. Dominique Radcliffe, a world-renowned physicist and agoraphobe. Laney had never seen him out of the bomb shelter he used for his residence and lab. Whatever had ushered him out must be important.

Dom bounced in place. "I know who's behind the Ecuador attack."

CHAPTER 68

Laney sat Dom down at the conference table but his nervous energy had him leaping from the chair almost immediately to pace the room.

"I've never been in Henry's office before. He's invited me, of course. But I'm more comfortable in my lab. Henry's always come there."

Laney nodded, feeling the fear coming off Dom. Henry was his friend and Dom was terrified. "We'll get him back, Dom. Jake has everybody working on his abduction."

Dom stopped pacing for a moment, but then continued on. His words came out even faster. "When I realized the connection, I knew I needed to speak with you right away. But I didn't want to leave the lab. But it was important. It was for Henry."

Dom kept talking, his words coming out like a flood. Laney struggled to figure out a way to calm him down enough to find out what he had to tell her.

The door opened and Jake walked in carrying a tray. *Oh thank God.*

Laney smiled, spying the chocolate chip cookies on

the tray. She'd texted Jake to let him know Dom was here. And obviously, Jake was hoping Dom's favorite treat might calm him a little.

Jake placed the tray on the table, ignoring Dom's incessant talking. He spoke over the agitated genius. "Hey Dom. Laney said you might have some information on the group behind the Ecuador attack." Jake placed a pile of cookies on a plate next to a giant glass of milk.

Like a moth drawn to a flame, Dom sat down and picked up a cookie. "Yes. I'm pretty sure I know." He took a bite of the cookie, gulped down some milk and stared off into space.

Laney breathed a sigh of relief. At least, he'd stopped talking. She waited and Dom stayed silent, contentedly chewing on his cookie. Of course, a little talking would be helpful. "Dom?"

He looked up as if surprised to see her there. "Oh, right. It's the Council." He grabbed a handful of the cookies and stood as if he was about to leave.

Jake put up a hand. "The Council? Who are they?"

Dom sat back down. "Only one of the longest running secret societies ever. Their goals are to track down Atlantean artifacts and use them for their own monetary benefit. Of course, the Council is their modern name."

"Modern name?" Jake asked.

Dom nodded. "Sure. Their other name was way too obvious." Dom ate another cookie.

"The Imiatores Belials," Laney said, remembering the name from her research.

Dom nodded. "Yup."

"Who?" Jake asked.

Laney tore her eyes from Dom to look at Jake. "It's one of the secret societies I looked up. They were obsessed with finding artifacts from Atlantis. They began in the eleventh century and allegedly disbanded in the nineteenth."

Dom shook his head. "Not disbanded. Went underground."

Jake leaned forward. "Dom, is there any reason to think the Council might be behind Henry's kidnapping?"

Dom stared at his plate, which was now empty. Laney quickly filled it with more cookies. Dom munched on one while talking. "Only if they thought he was a Fallen."

Laney sat back, thinking about the man taping Henry's abduction. Henry moved just like a Fallen.

"Of course," Dom continued, "Henry's not a Fallen."

Laney and Jake exchanged a glance. Laney spoke slowly. "Of course he's not."

Dom nodded. "But his dad was."

CHAPTER 69

Laney and Jake stared at Dom in disbelief. Did Dom know about Henry's abilities?

Dom must have felt their stares. He stopped eating and looked up. "What?"

"What did you mean about Henry's father being a Fallen?" Jake asked.

Dom looked between the two of them, confused. "You two didn't know? He's listed in that file I gave you last year."

Last year, in the search for those behind the kidnapping of Jake's brother, Dom had given them a list of people he'd identified as fallen angels. It had led them to Azazyel. But after identifying him, Laney hadn't looked at it again. And she wasn't sure Jake had ever even seen it.

Laney and Jake both shook their heads.

Dom sighed. "Well, it's obvious. Have you heard about how Henry's dad died?"

"It was a home invasion," Laney said.

"True," agreed Dom. "But the coroner's report indicated that James Chandler had been shot multiple

302

times over the course of a couple of weeks. The wounds were all at a different stage of healing – some almost completely, some just starting, some halfway there, etc. And there was never a report of the earlier attacks."

Laney looked at Jake, who shook his head. He'd never heard any of this either.

Dom continued. "Anyway, he was obviously shot at that one incident, but his wounds healed almost as soon as he was injured. Except for of course, the last few, which were point blank in his heart."

Laney tried to take in what Dom was saying, but her head was swimming. "So you're saying Henry's a nephilim?"

Dom nodded. "Yup. That was the point of the test. To see what Henry could do."

"You've seen the footage?"

"Of course." Dom took a long drink. Apparently discovering his friend and boss was the offspring of a fallen angel wasn't exactly rocking Dom's world.

"But why would the Council want Henry or any other Fallen?" Jake asked.

"Do you remember when we talked about the Fallen? I explained how each of them had different abilities that they brought with them. Well, for some of them, it involves reading Enochian." He looked at them expectantly.

"I don't get it," Jake replied.

The truth crashed through Laney. "The books from Ecuador. Some were written in Enochian. They need someone to translate them."

"So they just grabbed Henry, hoping he could read them?" Jake asked.

Dom nodded. "Of course, Henry wasn't the first.

You know I like to keep track of the Fallen? Well over the last few years, some have been disappearing. I thought someone might be gathering them up. I just didn't know why. I'm guessing it's the Council, trying to see if they can read the books."

"As a nephilim, will Henry be able to read them?" Laney asked.

Dom looked up slowly. "I don't think so. I don't know as much about nephilims, they're harder to track. But in the cases I do know of, the offspring only have some of their parents' gifts. . ." His voice trailed off.

"And Henry already has the physical abilities," Jake said, "meaning it's unlikely he'll have any of the cognitive ones."

Dom nodded.

"Which Fallen was Henry's father?" Laney asked.

Dom's face scrunched up. "That's the funny thing. In almost every case where I've identified a Fallen, I've been able to figure out the original identity."

"But in Henry's case?" Laney prompted.

"I've never been able to. I have no idea which one Henry's father was."

CHAPTER 70

Jake had helped Dom back to his lab after he'd finished his cookies. Laney spent some time just trying to wrap her mind around what Dom had told them. The Council had been looking for Atlantean artifacts since the eleventh century. It made sense they'd be behind the Ecuador attack.

From what she'd read, the group was full of aristocrats, the wealthy, the power players. They'd definitely have the ability to put together the Ecuador attack. But the method of attack was very unlike them. They liked to go under the radar. The Ecuador attack seemed to go against their centuries-long need for secrecy.

She shook her head. But Dom was a genius. If he thought it was them, it probably was.

Speaking of geniuses, she hadn't seen Danny since right after they got back. She knew he hadn't slept last night. He was probably still in his lab. She walked out of Henry's office and down the hall.

The door to his office was open. The carpet muffled her footsteps as she walked towards it, stopping just outside. Danny was sitting at his desk, although desk was probably too simple a term for his setup. Twelve monitors were lined up in front of him. Computers and technology Laney couldn't even guess at surrounded him.

Danny sat hunched over a few keyboards and a wireless mouse, his fingers flying. His big blue t-shirt, rolled up at the sleeves and grey sweatpants, seemed to swallow him up, making him look even younger and smaller.

Occasionally, he would grimace and look up, touching the screen of one of the monitors and, with a flip of his finger, send a program into the trash. Besides the grimaces, his face was a mask of concentration.

All the monitors displayed multiple programs, running simultaneously. It was like a physical representation of how Danny's brain worked. Data scrolled across the monitors, a kaleidoscope of numbers and letters. Laney couldn't even guess what they represented.

She bit her lip. What if they were going in the wrong direction? She knew other analysts were examining all of the Chandler Group's projects for any possible connection to Henry's abduction, but Danny was convinced it was related to Ecuador.

The longer she watched him, the more concerned she became. He was a boy obsessed. Although she tried to stay silent so as not to disturb him, the reality was that if she yelled, screamed, and set herself on fire, he probably wouldn't notice.

Moxy lay curled in her dog bed to Danny's right. Laney thought she was asleep, but as soon as Laney had moved into the doorway, her head had popped up. And if a dog could look worried, Moxy did.

Laney debated what to do. She knew Danny hadn't slept since the tracer had been found on her computer and she didn't like it. It wasn't healthy. Not for anyone, but especially not for a young boy. Granted, he wasn't exactly a normal child. But, genius or not, he was a child. Someone had to look after his health, right?

"Oh, you think that's a firewall? That's not a firewall," Danny muttered.

"Is he actually talking smack to a computer?"

Laney looked up in surprise. Jake stood next to her, his arm rubbing against hers.

She turned back to Danny. "I think technically he's talking smack to whomever created the firewall, but then again I could be wrong. Dom okay?"

"Yeah. But it took a lot of guts for him to leave his home." Jake nodded towards Danny. "How's our other genius doing?"

Laney pulled him from the doorway, keeping her voice low. "Not good. He hasn't slept since Henry was taken. And he hadn't been getting much sleep even before that. This can't be good for him. He's a thirteen-year old on the edge of a nervous breakdown."

Jake sighed, his eyes troubled. "I know, but Henry is for all intents and purposes Danny's father. He won't stop until he finds him. And to be honest, if anyone has a chance of finding him, it's Danny."

Laney blew out a frustrated breath. "I know, but I swear Jake, I am one step away from tranq'ing the kid. He's not sleeping, not eating. He's existing on junk food. He's placing a herculean burden on himself. Even a genius can't operate well under those conditions."

Jake rubbed his hands together and then cracked his knuckles. "All right. I'll put him in a full nelson and you jab him with the needle."

Laney smiled in spite of herself. "Let's call that plan B. I figure we'll start with a conversation. When that doesn't work, we wrestle him to the ground."

Jake gave a dramatic sigh. "Fine."

Laney started to head back to Danny's office when Jake pulled her to a stop. "Hold on a second."

He dropped his voice, with a quick glance to make sure Danny couldn't overhear. "I found the name of the group who hired Hugo."

"What? How?"

He grinned. "It would be nice if you didn't sound so shocked."

She cringed. "Sorry. Its just Danny couldn't find anything and I kind of think of him as the great and powerful Oz in these situations."

"Well, Oz was just a man behind the curtain. And in this case, it needed more of a human touch than a computer touch. Hugo's dad left me a message. Hugo was hired by a group known as Flourent, Inc."

Laney jolted. *Flourent, Inc. again?* "Are you sure?"

"Yeah. I'm trying to dig up what I can about them now."

He turned her to face him. She knew shock was written across her face. "What do you know?"

She opened her mouth to answer when Danny's yell interrupted her.

"Yes!"

She paused for just a second. "Not now. We need

to take care of Danny first."

Jake looked like he wanted to argue, but he nodded.

She turned and walked quickly into Danny's office, Jake right behind her. "What is it?"

Danny turned, his face triumphant, but Laney despaired at the paleness of his face, the dark circles under his eyes. "I traced the signal."

"From Laney's computer?" Jake stepped closer to the monitors.

"Yes. It leads to Nevada, somewhere around Vegas."

One of Danny's monitors beeped, drawing his attention back to it. His hands were once again a blur of motion on the keyboard. Laney had to physically bite her tongue to keep from demanding more answers.

Jake grabbed her hand and she looked up at him. "Just give him a minute."

She nodded, enjoying the warmth of his hands in hers. She let out a breath, counting to sixty in her head and then counting again.

Jake squeezed her hand with a grin. "Keep counting."

Laney looked at him, shocked.

He winked at her, whispering in her ear. "You always count when you're trying to be patient."

Danny wheeled his chair around. "I've got it locked down to a five mile area. I can fine-tune it as we get closer." He turned back to his monitors.

Laney stepped forward. "Okay, Danny, that's it. You've got fifteen minutes to set up whatever you need to set up and then you're getting some sleep."

He shook his head. "I can't. I need to-"

Raising her hand in the air, she cut him off.

"You've done the heavy lifting. Hand the rest over to some of the other analysts. You need to sleep."

"No. Henry needs-"

She cut him off, again. "What Henry needs is for you to be healthy when he returns. And if you keep this up, you won't be." She placed her hands on his shoulders, gentling her tone. "You've done the impossible, Danny. Now let the rest of us help. And we're going to need you at the top of your game when we start planning the rescue. So sleep."

Danny nodded, reluctant. "Okay, but I'm only taking a nap. And in here." He gestured to the couch in the corner. "Just in case something needs my attention."

She placed a kiss on his forehead. "I didn't expect any different. I'll be back in fifteen minutes."

Jake followed her out of the room. When they were out of earshot, he asked, "Laney? What do you know?"

She took a breath to steady herself. She felt a bit rattled. "The name. Flourent. That's Warren's father's family. I sent Yoni to get some information on them in Vegas."

"Vegas? The same place the signal was sent?"

Laney nodded.

"Looks like all roads are leading to Vegas. I'm going to start setting up for an op."

"But we don't have a target."

"No. But we're getting closer. And I need us to be ready to go as soon as we have a firm location or even a best guess." He gave her a distracted kiss before heading down the hall.

Laney leaned against a wall, needing the support.

One of her dearest friends was being held by the group who had mercilessly cut through the Shuar tribe. She knew Jake would move as soon as possible. But would they be fast enough?

She shivered. *Please don't let us be too late.*

CHAPTER 71

'Abigail' sat in the back of the Escalade. She'd removed the wig, make-up and padding. Now she looked herself. Her formerly carrot top red hair now run through with grey was cut in a no-nonsense bob that framed her gamine face. Her small figure was encased in black slacks and a deep purple cashmere sweater.

The scenery flew by as Ralph navigated the smaller country roads. It had all changed so much in twenty years, and yet at the same time there was an eternal quality to the land that never seemed to go away.

A memory of riding through these roads with Henry flitted through her mind. Back then, she'd worried that he would fall and hurt himself. She'd give anything if a scraped knee was all he had to face.

Shutting her eyes against the ache the memory caused, the same useless questions hammered at her. Had she done the right thing? Should she have told him? Warned him? Would it have prevented anything? Would it have just made things worse?

She slammed her fist into her hand. Damn it. She should know what the right thing to do was. These decisions should be easier by now. She'd been making them longer than . . .

She shied away from the thought. No point going down that old road. Now she was going to have to share that information with people other than Henry. They needed to know why he was taken. Henry would need to know why he was taken.

In the last twenty-four hours, she'd pulled all the information she could find on Henry's abduction. There was precious little. And now Laney and Jake had the information on the connection to the Flourents. But they still wouldn't have the why. Only she could provide that.

She flipped through the file in her hand on Jake Rogan and Delaney McPhearson. All the relevant background information. But she didn't need the reports, not really. Henry had told her everything about them. He considered them family. He trusted them with his life.

She shuddered, gripping the door handle. His life. She'd done everything she could to keep him safe and it hadn't been enough. Now the very information she'd kept from him could be what got him killed.

"Anything new from the estate?" She called out to the front seat.

Andrew, one of the men on her security detail and a younger version of Ralph, looked back at her. He held up one finger, jotting notes down into a pad as he listened to the phone. He closed the phone, turning to look at her.

"They've traced the signal on McPhearson's laptop. It originated in Vegas."

"Do we have an trusted operatives in Vegas?"

Andrew shook his head. "I'm sorry ma'am. We don't."

Abigail looked out the window, struggling to form a plan. There must be some way for her to help.

"Ma'am?"

She looked up at Andrew.

"Rogan has arranged for almost all security from Chandler to be flown to Vegas. Once they have the signal pinned down, they're going to go in."

Abigail nodded. "Get me a listing of all of Flourent's holdings in and around Vegas. Especially any listings they're trying to hide."

"Yes ma'am."

"What about Delaney McPhearson? Will she be going too?"

Andrew glanced back. "Yes, but she isn't part of any of the security briefings for the Vegas op. She's being sidelined. Maybe Rogan doesn't trust her abilities."

Abigail shook her head, catching Ralph's eyes in the rearview mirror. *No, he loves her.* Out loud, she said. "Have McPhearson and Rogan left the estate yet?"

"No. But they should be leaving any minute for the airfield."

She nodded, once again watching the trees go by. A memory of six-year old Henry handing her a bouquet of dandelions flitted through her mind. His smile had stretched from ear to ear. He'd hugged her, his little arms unable to reach all the way around her.

She wrapped her arms around herself, feeling the ghost of that embrace. Her chest tightened. "Intercept them."

CHAPTER 72

Jake gripped the steering wheel, staring at Laney's little cottage. Flowers crept up the lattice on the side, spilling over the porch roof. The bloom of colors contrasted brightly against the pale brown stone façade and black shutters.

He wanted to turn his truck around and drive to the airport without her. He knew, though, that she'd never forgive him. But he hated the idea of her being put in harm's way again. It was like a knife to his chest. In fact, he'd rather be stabbed than let her get hurt.

With a muttered curse, he pushed open his door and stomped up the three steps to her door. He was about to knock when the door flew open.

Laney stood in the doorway, her eyes wide, her face pale. "I'm ready."

He pulled her into his arms. "We'll get him back."

Laney nodded against his chest. He felt a shudder run through her. He knew how much Henry meant to her.

And the fact was, Henry meant just as much to him. Jake didn't have much of a family. He and his brother

Tom had only recently started reconnecting. For a long time, he'd been on his own. His father was gone from his life and his mom had been dead for twenty years.

Henry was alone, too. That loss had helped cement their bond. Henry was part of his family. A big part.

Laney pulled away. "Let's go find him."

Jake kissed her on the forehead. "You got it."

After tossing her suitcase in the back, he got in the driver's seat. They drove in silence for a while.

A few miles from the estate, Jake thought he should try to talk her out of coming one more time. "Laney, I know you want to help, but-"

"Jake, I'm going. And anything else you say about me staying is going to lead to a fight, so just accept it, okay?"

His eyes flicked over to her. "Okay."

She gave him a small smile, but then her eyes darted away. Alarm flashed across her face. "Jake, look out!"

Jake whipped his head around. An SUV blocked the road. He slammed on the brakes. The truck jolted to a stop.

The black Escalade idled quietly on the road, blocking the way. No one got out.

Jake glanced behind him and then looked over at Laney, pulling his Beretta from its holster. "Laney, I tell you to run, you run. No arguing, got it?"

Laney nodded, pulling her own Beretta from her bag. "Yeah, sure Jake."

Jake held in the growl. The backdoor of the passenger side opened. A tall, striking, woman with pale red hair, run through with grey, stepped out.

Jake looked down as Laney gripped his arm, her

face growing pale.

"It can't be." She scrambled for the handle of the door, her weapon left on the seat.

"Laney, no." Jake tried to grab her but she slipped out of the door.

Laney rounded the hood of the SUV as Jake leaped from his door, his gun trained on the woman. Two men stepped out of the SUVs, their weapons now aimed at Jake.

Jake swore silently. "Laney, get back in the car."

She ignored him, stopping when she was ten feet away from the woman.

Jake looked between the woman and Laney. Shock was splashed across Laney's face. *What the hell is going on?*

Laney seemed to struggle to find words. "Why are you here?"

"Henry," the woman said.

Jake stared at her. "Lady, who exactly are you?"

"Victoria Chandler. I'm Henry's mother."

CHAPTER 73

Jake followed Victoria's SUV to a little park just a quarter-mile from where Victoria intercepted them. "You recognized her from the photo in Henry's office, didn't you?"

Laney nodded. "Yeah."

Jake gripped the steering wheel. He wasn't thrilled with surprises, and Henry's mom showing up back from the dead qualified as a huge one. He glanced over at Laney sitting next to him. "I don't like this."

Laney reached out and took his hand. "I know. But we need answers and she may have them."

Pulling into the empty parking lot, he turned off the engine. The park was only about a half acre. It barely had room for a small play set and two wooden picnic tables.

Jake watched Victoria exit her SUV and make her way to one of those tables. "She's supposed to be dead."

Laney looked like she wanted to say something, but then she just shrugged and reached for the door handle.

Jake grabbed her arm. "You still have your gun?"

She nodded, pulling up her shirt to reveal it tucked into the side of her waistband.

Jake let her go, reaching for his own door handle. "Good. This time, keep it on you."

Victoria was sitting waiting for them. "Please sit."

Jake shook his head, eyeing the two men now standing next to the SUVs. "I think I'll pass."

Victoria met his eyes for a second before turning to the two men. "Gentlemen, please take a ride. Come back for me in ten minutes."

Without comment, the two men got into the SUV and took off. Victoria looked back at Jake. "Better?"

Jake nodded, but he didn't sit. His eyes darted around the park. Trees and wild growth surrounded the manicured area. Snipers could easily be in any one of those trees or lying in wait in the tall undergrowth.

His eyes flipped to Laney who sat calmly at the table across from Victoria. Her hand rested on the butt of her weapon. At least she was a little cautious.

Victoria glanced between the two of them. "I believe an explanation is in order."

"You got that right." Anger punctuated Jake's words. He knew he should calm down, but right now, he just couldn't. "Does Henry know you're alive?"

Victoria nodded. "Yes. He's always known."

Betrayal sliced through Jake. Why had Henry never told him? He distinctly remembered the conversation they'd had about the deaths of their mothers. Henry had lied to him.

Reading his feelings, Victoria leaned towards him. "Henry wanted to tell you the truth. Both of you. But there were reasons why I had to disappear and those reasons haven't changed. It's in everyone's interest if I remain dead. Coming here, I am risking your lives, and mine."

"Then why are you here?" Laney asked.

Pain crossed Victoria's face. "Henry."

Jake ignored the pang of sympathy he felt for the woman. If she'd been in hiding for almost two decades, that meant whoever was after her was serious. Perhaps serious enough to grab her son if they knew or suspected she was alive. *God damn it.* Jake's voice was harsh. "Why was Henry taken? Was it because of you?"

"No."

"So whoever's after you hasn't grabbed Henry to get to you?" Laney asked, her expression guarded, arms crossed across her chest.

Victoria shook her head. "No. I am very good at hiding. No one besides Henry, and now you two, know I am alive. Not even Danny knows. And it's important it stays that way."

Jake nodded down the road to where the Escalade had disappeared. "What about your friends?"

"Ralph knows. In fact, Henry knows Ralph. He's been with our family since Henry was a child. Andrew does not."

Jake wasn't sure he believed that. But right now, there were more pressing issues. "Look, I don't know you and I don't give a crap what you want. We already know Henry was taken because they believe he can read the books from Ecuador. What we don't know is why they think that."

Surprise flashed across Victoria face. "You've uncovered more than I realized. Do you know Henry's

320

nature?"

"He's a nephilim."

Victoria nodded. "Yes."

Jake's own father was no prize, but learning your father was a Fallen was not going to be easy for Henry. Jake didn't look forward to telling his friend. "So, Henry's father was a Fallen, right?"

Victoria shook her head. "Not exactly."

CHAPTER 74

Las Vegas, NV

Henry's arms ached. His head and chest leaned forward, his bound arms holding him upright. He'd been in this position since he'd awakened.

He thought it might be close to twenty-four hours since he'd been taken. But he didn't really know. Time seemed immeasurable when you were being tortured. It could easily be a week.

His eyelids started to close. He couldn't remember ever being this tired. *Guess I finally get to test my limits.*

Yesterday had been the 'getting to know you' stage of interrogation. Every time Hugo didn't like an answer, he sliced. And he didn't like most of Henry's answers. Half the time Henry could swear he was just making up questions to make him bleed.

Henry closed his eyes, hoping for a few minutes of sleep before the pain in his arms once again wormed its way through his subconscious. The door opened. He dragged his lids back open. Hugo entered, followed by a small, frail older man.

The older man walked over to Henry, stopping three

feet away. "Do you know who I am?"

Henry shook his head. "Not a clue."

Hugo raised his hand to strike him. The old man put up his hand. "No need. That was an honest answer. My name is Sebastian Flourent."

The man looked at him expectantly.

"Still not ringing any bells," Henry said.

Hugo punched him in the jaw. "When you speak with Mr. Flourent, it's with respect."

Henry's head swam. His legs went weak. The weakness passed quickly and Henry was just left angry.

Sebastian spoke as if the violence hadn't occurred. "Years ago, my father was interested in your family."

Henry's head jolted. "My family? Why?"

Sebastian waved the question away. "In time. For now, tell me what you know about your abilities."

Henry hesitated, debating what to say. He realized, though, the futility of lying. They'd already seen what he could do. "I have enhanced strength and speed. And I heal quickly."

Sebastian nodded impatiently. "Yes, yes. But what cognitive abilities have you retained?"

"Cognitive?" Henry asked. What on earth was he talking about?

"Come now, Mr. Chandler. I know your history. You're an intelligent man. You know what I'm asking."

Henry looked back at him, clueless. What did he think he could do?

A piercing pain in his right side shook him from his thoughts. He let out a gasp. Hugo stepped back from him, his knife slick with blood.

Henry watched as blood dribbled down his side.

Then it slowed and stopped. The wound began to knit close. Henry ground his teeth. "I don't have any extra cognitive skills, that I know of."

Sebastian shook his head, disappointment on his face. "But you see, that's not possible. Not with who your father was."

Henry stilled. "My father?"

Sebastian paused, inspecting Henry's face. A cruel smile spread across his own. "You don't know, do you?"

Henry's mind raced. His father? His father was James Chandler, a normal man. But . . .

His whole life, Henry had wondered at his father's last words: Don't let anyone know what he is. Did these monsters have the answers? Henry looked at the old man. "As far as I know, he was just a man."

Sebastian watched him for a moment. Henry sensed he was weighing the truthfulness of Henry's response. Finally, he turned. "Bring in the book," he ordered.

Two guards walked in, struggling under the weight of a silver book, one foot by two.

That must be one of the folios from the Ecuador cave, Henry thought.

Hugo carried a table from the side of the room and placed it in front of Henry. The book was laid on top.

The cover seemed to be made from silver, although Henry didn't understand why it hadn't tarnished after all its time in the cave. The pages, which were the same color, were slimmer than the cover. *Maybe made of silver leaf?* he wondered.

Symbols were engraved on the front cover. At first glanced, they appeared to be Greek. But upon closer inspection he realized that wasn't right. The book was written in Enochian. An electric tingle began to slide over his skin. The hairs on his arms stood straight up.

The symbols on the cover almost seemed to come alive. The cover read "The Alian Treaty". He didn't know how, but he knew that was what the title said.

Sebastian watched him closely. "So Mr. Chandler, can you tell us what the symbols on the front cover say?"

Henry struggled to keep his shock off his face. How was he able to read it? "Why would you think I could read them?"

Sebastian paused, picking a piece of lint from his sleeve, before looking back at Henry. "Because your father wrote it."

CHAPTER 75

Baltimore, MD

Laney's mind whirled. Henry's abilities had astounded her when she'd first witnessed them. His strength, his agility. They were otherworldly. She'd scoured countless books after the Montana incident, looking for an explanation.

At one point, she'd suspected he might be one of the Fallen and for a time she'd even wondered if he might be a nephilim, mainly because of his height. The quote from Genesis ran through her mind: "The giants came from the union of the sons of God and the daughters of men."

The more she got to know him, however, the less his status mattered. He was Henry, her friend, Danny's father. She'd put her questions to rest, knowing Henry would talk to her someday if he wanted to. And until then, she'd keep her thoughts to herself. But now Henry's mother was telling them who he was. What he was.

Jen flashed through her mind and she went still. Was it possible Jen was also a nephilim? If the Fallen could reproduce, how many nephilim could be out there?

Laney forced her mind back to the conversation as Jake spoke. "Does anyone else know what he is?"

"I don't think so. But it's not impossible. Henry's father was killed by someone who knew his nature. It's possible they could have suspected what Henry was."

"Does Henry know?"

"No."

"Would someone be able to tell the difference between one of the Fallen and a nephilim?" Laney asked.

Victoria paused, giving Laney a measured look. "A human wouldn't. But a Fallen would. From what I understand, the Fallen feel a kinship when they're near one another. They would feel a connection with a nephilim as well, but the link would be weaker."

"Do the nephilim feel the kinship with the Fallen?" Jake asked

"I don't believe so. But they do for one another."

Laney flashed on the look on Jen's face when Henry had walked into her hospital room in Ecuador. She recognized him. But was it because Jen was a nephilim or a Fallen?

"Laney?" Victoria asked.

Laney looked over sharply. Victoria was watching her again, a calculating look on her face.

Laney pulled her face into a neutral expression. She would have to watch herself with this woman. She was far too observant and right now, they didn't really know anything about her except that she'd faked her own death. They couldn't even be sure Henry knew she was alive.

"What about powers?" Jake asked. "Are their

powers any different?"

"It depends. Powers are like any genetic trait. For some, they have their parent's exact skill. For others, they have some, and for others, nothing."

Laney sat back. So Dom was right. If it were truly genetic, though, did that mean it could even skip generations and appear decades later in a family? How many exceptional athletes owed their skill to a genetic gift from a fallen angel?

"What about for Henry?" Laney asked.

"Henry has the strength and much of the speed, although I've seen some faster. He heals quickly, but not as quickly as the Fallen."

"Meaning he'd be easier to kill than they are," Jake said.

Victoria's chin trembled, but her voice remained steady. "Yes."

Silence descended as they all fell off into their own thoughts.

Jake finally broke the quiet. "Okay. Henry's a genetic freak. Good to know. But that still doesn't help us find him. And it doesn't tell us why he was grabbed."

Victoria nodded. "Because of the metal library."

Laney glanced up sharply. How did Victoria know about that?

Victoria continued on, unaware of Laney's thoughts. "Henry has always been so careful. But they threatened the most important thing in the world to him."

"Danny," Laney said softly.

Victoria nodded. "So he didn't hold back."

"But it still doesn't explain why he was targeted.

Why would they think Henry could read those books? Why would they think he had any abilities?" Jake asked.

Laney watched Victoria, a shiver of unease rolling down her back.

Jake stood up, annoyance in his voice. "We've got a lead on Henry's location. I've already begun preparations to chase it down. Henry's nature is irrelevant to that. It doesn't matter why they took him. It matters that we get him back."

Laney watched Victoria. She was afraid Jake was wrong. Dead wrong. Henry's nature did matter, very much. Whatever this woman's angle here, it was obvious she cared about Henry. And right now she was terrified. "You said Henry's father wasn't one of the Fallen. But Henry is a nephilim."

Victoria nodded. "Yes. And I think Henry's parentage is exactly why he was taken."

"Why? Who are you?"

"Just a human, no one important."

Laney glanced up sharply. There was no way someone unimportant had to fake their own death, spend twenty years in hiding, and had access to the information Victoria had. There was nothing unimportant about her.

"Then this is about Henry's father? Who was he?" Jake asked.

Victoria paused. She took a deep breath and expelled it. "What do you know about angels?"

"Quite a lot," Laney replied, thinking of all the books and articles she'd immersed herself in since last year.

Victoria shook her head. "Not the Fallen. Actual

angels."

Laney stared at her, her mind racing.

"Dom's right," Victoria said. "Most nephilim only have some of their parents' powers. But some angels are able to gift their children with multiple powers. Henry's father was just such a man."

"What powers did he have?" Jake asked.

"Henry's father was incredibly gifted with languages. All languages."

"Including Enochian?" Laney asked.

Victoria gave a little smile. "Yes, especially Enochian."

Laney struggled to recall which Fallen was adept at languages. Baraqel taught people astrology. Chazaqiel taught meteorology.

She ran through a list of names in her mind. Raduriel, Rahatiel, Machidiel. None of the skills of angels, Fallen or not, seemed to fit. The closest she could come up with was Peneume, who was supposed to have taught humans how to write.

"So who exactly was Henry's father?" Jake asked.

"This may be a bit difficult to believe," Victoria began.

Laney struggled not to laugh. A bit difficult to believe? Two of her best friends were at least part angel, she herself had helped take down two Fallen angels, one of whom had been hell bent on using an ancient weapon of mass destruction, and just last week she'd uncovered an ancient cache of knowledge hidden for thousands of year. She was pretty sure she was beyond disbelieving anything at this point.

"What do you know of Enoch?" Victoria asked.

"The guy who wrote the books about the Fallen?"

Jake asked.

Laney rattled everything she could remember. "He lived 365 years. He was Noah's great grandfather. Ascended to heaven without dying, allegedly spoke on God's behalf to Moses, has three books attributed to him, got a tour of heaven while still alive, and basically was God's most trusted."

Victoria inclined her head. "Henry was right about you."

Before Laney could ask her what she meant by that, Victoria continued. "Enoch was also an important scribe. In some cultures, he was so important he was seen as being on a level with God."

"God?" Jake asked, disbelief across his face.

Laney knew Jake struggled to believe the whole Fallen angels walking the earth bit. Asking him to believe God had a hand in all this was another leap she was sure he was going to have difficulty with.

"And Enoch never died. He just disappeared into the heavens where he became the angel Metatron," Laney said, recalling the Bible tales.

Victoria nodded. "Enoch was special. Part of that specialness is being reborn over and over again."

Laney felt her jaw drop, but she couldn't speak. Her eyes found Victoria's. Victoria nodded at her, recognizing that Laney understood.

Jake's head whipped back and forth between the two. "Someone want to clue me in?"

"James Chandler was Enoch which means . . . " Laney couldn't finish the thought. Victoria was right. It was too unbelievable.

Victoria nodded. "Yes. Henry is the son of Enoch."

CHAPTER 76

*H*enry is the son of Enoch.

The words floated through Jake's mind. What the hell was going on? This made absolutely no sense. "I don't understand. Enoch disappeared, what, before the great flood? As in Old Testament times, at least ten thousand years ago, right? And we're supposed to believe that he was reincarnated as James Chandler?"

Jake looked to Laney for an explanation. She sat staring straight ahead, her face frozen in shock. Obviously she wasn't up for explaining anything at this moment. He turned to Victoria. "Well?"

Victoria gave him a small smile. "It's true. Enoch was Noah's great grandfather. He foretold of the flood that Noah would become famous for."

Jake tamped down his impatience. "Right. Got that part. Really smart, prophetic, old guy. How does that relate to Henry?"

"One day, Enoch disappeared. He was taken to heaven, in his human form. As I said before, God enjoyed his company so much, he made him his scribe. As much as Enoch loved being with God, he also loved being human. As a gift, God allows him to visit earth from time to time."

Laney nodded. "Edgar Cayce actually mentions Enoch. He believed Enoch had lived many lives."

"And what?" Jake asked. "He shacks up?"

"Jake," Laney said, shock on her face.

Victoria's eyes went cold. "When he's here, Enoch doesn't know who he is until he's a teenager. And it's actually his job to have children."

"Why?"

Victoria's eyes dropped from Jake's. "Enoch's children are special."

Laney joined the conversation. "You mean they can read his writings."

Victoria nodded. "Sometimes. But Enoch's children always have gifts." She stared at Laney as if trying to convey something deeper to her.

"What type of gifts?" Laney asked.

Victoria shrugged. "It depends. Henry obviously has the strength, the height."

"What about Enochian? Can he read it?"

Victoria's face was tight. "Yes."

Jake felt his temper rear up. "Does Henry know who his father actually was? Who he actually is?"

Victoria shook her head. "No. His father and I agreed-"

Jake's words lashed out. "You let him walk around with a target on his back and didn't even warn him? You let him wonder who he was, what he was?"

Victoria's words were just as angry. "You don't get to judge me. You haven't lived the lives I have. You don't get to sit there thinking you know better. It was possible he would never need to know. That his life would go on unencumbered by the truth."

"You could have prepared him-"

Victoria stood up. "I did! I prepared him as best I could without having him spend his life looking over his shoulder, feeling like he had to hide away from people."

Tears shone in Victoria's eyes, but her tone was angry. "I died so he could live a normal life. What would you have had me do, Jake? Tell him he was different, that he wasn't human? Tell him people may come looking for him? Deny him any chance of having a normal life? Tell him he's the son of the most powerful angel ever? What kind of life would that give him?"

Laney grabbed Jake's hand, keeping him silent. He looked over at her and she shook her head. "Jake . . ."

He took a breath, pulling back the anger. Tears and anger flashed across Victoria's eyes. *Damn.* "Victoria, I shouldn't have said those things. Henry's like a brother to me. Him being in danger is obviously not bringing out the best in me."

Victoria nodded tersely.

Laney leaned forward. "Why are you telling us this? You died twenty years ago. And no one has any clue you exist. Why reveal yourself to us? Why reveal who Henry is to us?"

Victoria took a deep breath. "Henry was grabbed because of who his father was. Because of the gift his father gave him. If Henry reveals that gift, he can probably save himself."

Laney felt her chest tighten. But revealing that gift would mean helping the people who'd slaughtered hundreds in their quest. "Henry won't help them."

"No. He won't." Victoria said quietly. "And why

am I revealing this to you two? Because you need to
know the rest of the story. You need to know how
Flourent knew about Henry. You need to know about
the Council."

CHAPTER 77

Las Vegas, NV

Hugo went through the book, page-by-page, demanding Henry translate the symbols. Henry said nothing. And with every turn of the page, Henry tensed, knowing the pain was coming. Hugo never disappointed him.

Henry healed fast, but that didn't mean he couldn't feel pain. He could feel it. Every last inch. He glanced down to the floor, sticky with his blood. He knew he would die before telling them anything the books said. He didn't care why they wanted the knowledge. He wasn't going to help them.

He just hoped he could hold out. But it was getting harder with each slice of Hugo's knife.

The only blessing was that he had one distraction. The book. He could read every word. The tome was about a peace treaty between the Children of the Law of One and the Sons of Belial. In exchange for peace, the Children had agreed to share with the Sons what they knew of the Belial Stone.

A small note at the end indicated that, years later, the Sons killed Alian, the author of the work, when he refused to tell them how to turn the stone into a weapon.

When the final page was turned, Sebastian stood up. "You're a disappointment, Mr. Chandler." He peered into Henry's face. "But I'm not convinced yet that you're being entirely honest with us."

Sebastian sat back down, his head resting on the spires of his fingers. "Perhaps you need more incentive. It seems clear you were never told who your father was. I find that peculiar. You must have noticed something odd about him."

Henry stared at the old man. What was he expecting? An Oprah moment? Did he want Henry to break down and beg him to tell him what he knew? Not going to happen. He clamped his mouth shut.

But, he had to admit, Sebastian's words were having an effect. Why hadn't his mother ever told him who his father was? Why hadn't she warned him?

Henry struggled to remember everything he could about him. His father died when he was only six. Even now, almost thirty years later, the memory of that night was difficult.

He shied away from the emotions and focused on the details he could remember about him. His Dad was tall, but not nearly as tall as Henry. Henry remembered thinking his Dad was Batman and Superman rolled into one. But didn't every kid at that age think his Dad was a superhero?

Looking back at his father through adult eyes, though, he was just a normal dad. The only odd thing was that one world trip they'd taken the summer before his father died. They'd been gone for six months and they'd visited everywhere: Asia, Africa, South America, Europe. And everywhere they went, his father could speak the language. It didn't matter if they were in the remote regions of China or sub-Saharan Africa, whatever people they came across, his father could speak with them. But what did that mean? Who was he?

Frustration coursed through Henry. He wanted to rail, scream, throw things. But he was still bound to the damn cross. He swallowed down the emotions, tasting their bitterness. Closing his eyes, he locked his frustration away. It was a practice he was all too familiar with.

He blew out a breath. He needed to focus on now. He needed to keep up his resolve.

He opened his eyes and started. They'd all left. He must have passed out. Or maybe even fallen asleep. No matter. He was alone. He reveled in the silence.

They'd left the book propped up on the table in front of him. The electric tingle that had run over his body at the first sight of the book had turned into a warmth, as if his body was enveloped in a soft blanket.

But now a ball of cold began to form in his chest. How did he know how to read the book? He'd never in his life seen Enochian, never mind read it. Yet he'd known as soon as he'd seen it that it was the language of the angels.

A memory flashed at the back of his mind. It had something to do with his Mother.

Henry stumbled down the stairs, wiping the sleep from his eyes. He'd been up late studying for his algebra test. He stifled a yawn as he walked into the kitchen.

His mother stood at the kitchen island, red hair pulled back in a ponytail, her green robe wrapped around her, a cup of coffee in her hands. She pointed to the table. "I've put out your breakfast. Eat quick. Ralph's waiting to take you to school."

Henry slumped into his seat. Only fourteen, he was already six-foot-eight. "Can't I just take the bus?"

"We've had this conversation. I agreed you could go to public school, but Ralph drives you there and back." She glanced at the clock above the stove. "Actually, never mind breakfast. You don't have time."

Henry grabbed the bagel on his plate, dumping the eggs and bacon in between the two halves. "Breakfast to go."

Victoria smiled. "Your books are over by the door."

Henry walked over and kissed her cheek. "Love you, Mom."

"You, too, sweetie."

He held his sandwich in one hand and went to grab his books on the counter. He didn't recognize the book on the top of the pile. "Mom, this one's not mine."

She looked over. "Oh? What's the title?"

He glanced down, a warmth enveloping him. The letters seemed to swim before him. He squeezed his eyes shut and then opened them again. "The Fall of Man. It's in Greek, I think."

She nodded. "Oh. That's mine. Just leave it. Have a good day."

The cold from his chest spread throughout his body. She'd been testing him. He'd never read Greek, but he could read that book title. She wanted to see if he could read it. How had she known he had that ability?

An image of his father floated into his mind. His father was good at languages and apparently so was he.

But why? Who was his Dad?

The door opened and Hugo entered, followed by two other guards. They took their spot beside the door.

Hugo swaggered over to the table where he kept his tools. "Well, I had a great lunch. And a good lunch like that always makes me feel energized." He swiped a six-inch serrated knife from the table, turning to Henry. "Let's start back at the top, shall we?"

CHAPTER 78

Baltimore, MD

Laney was practically dizzy from all the information Victoria had shared with them. Henry was the son of Enoch and he was taken because he could read the books.

Now Laney understood Victoria's little smile when Laney had asked if Henry could read Enochian. It was a language literally named after Henry's father. But that still didn't explain how the people who'd taken Henry had known about his parentage.

The black Escalade pulled back into the parking lot. Victoria waved for the two men to stay where they were. She turned back to Laney and Jake. "Have either of you heard of the Council?"

Laney nodded, explaining what Dom had told them.

"What does this have to do with Flourent? How does he know about Henry?" Jake asked.

"The last Flourent who was a member of the Council was Sebastian's father. The Flourents believed themselves to be the true leaders of the group. They wouldn't listen to other members. Sebastian was denied membership after his father's death. Allegedly all of his father's Council notes burned in a fire at

Flourent's house."

"But you don't believe that, do you?" Jake asked.

Victoria shook her head. "It's too convenient. I believe Sebastian has all of his father's notes on the Council's activities. The reports date back centuries."

"Okay. But how does any of this relate to Henry's father?"

"Victor Flourent was the Council member who sent men to take Henry's father. They failed. And James was killed protecting us."

"They knew the identity of Henry's father?"

"Yes. But I thought that information was contained. Victor was known for keeping his secrets. He wouldn't have revealed a prize like James."

"Couldn't he have told someone after the botched attempt?"

"Unlikely. He was monitored and he didn't have time. He died the next day."

"Well, that was a stroke of luck," Jake said.

Victoria looked him straight on. "There was nothing lucky about it. I killed him."

Laney struggled to keep the shock off her face. Victoria had had Sebastian Flourent's father killed? And the way she said it. She'd admitted to murder with the same level of emotion as ordering a cup of coffee.

"I can see you're surprised," Victoria said to her.

So much for my poker face, Laney thought.

Victoria looked into Laney's eyes, not flinching. "I don't regret taking his life. He targeted my family. He killed my husband. It was only going to be a matter of time before he came for Henry. I always protect my family."

Out of the corner of her eye, Laney noticed Jake

nod. *Oh good. They've finally found something to bond over.*

But even though her thoughts were sarcastic, would she really have done any different? If someone targeted someone she loved? Weren't they rushing to save Henry right now? And the cargo compartment of the plane sure wasn't being filled with flowers.

Victoria reached down to her bag and pulled out a manila envelope. "In here is a listing of all the Flourent family's holdings. A few months ago, they purchased a warehouse in Vegas. It would be big enough to hold the Shuar collection."

Jake took the file. "How'd you find this? We have people searching for everything they can find on Flourent and no one's come up with this."

"I trade in information, Mr. Rogan. If it's out there, I can find it. My son's resources and contacts don't even come close to touching mine."

Jake looked over at Laney.

She shrugged. "It's a lead."

He nodded. "I'm going to put some people on it. You okay for a minute?"

"Yeah." Laney watched Jake walk over to his truck and pull out his phone. She turned back to Victoria, struggling with how to react to this woman. It was obvious she loved Henry, but Laney couldn't help but wonder about her sudden appearance.

"Henry spoke about you," Victoria said. "He thinks very highly of you. And your Uncle."

"We care a great deal about him as well."

"It makes me feel good to know Henry has had such people in his life."

Laney tamped down her irritation. Who the hell

was this woman? She'd disappeared from Henry's life and now she was saying she approved of the people in it? She doesn't get an opinion. Laney nodded abruptly, turning her eyes back to Jake.

"I get the feeling you're angry at me."

Laney looked up at Victoria, and Henry's eyes stared back at her. Screw being polite. "You show up after being in hiding for almost twenty years and in spite of what you say, I can't help but think that maybe your situation has something to do with Henry's abduction."

"It doesn't."

"How do you know? In fact, how did you know Henry was missing? If you haven't seen him in twenty years, how-"

Victoria put up her hands. "I never said I hadn't seen him in twenty years. I said the world was told I died. Henry has always known the truth. We talk almost every day. Seeing each other's more complicated, but we manage it a few times a year. Always different locations, different times of the year. I love my son, Laney." Victoria's voice cracked on the last sentence.

"And now what? You tell us all of this and then just leave?"

"It's a risk for me to be here. And I won't further endanger Henry's rescue by my presence. There'll be enough to worry about without what I bring."

Laney shook her head, blowing out a breath. *How much more cryptic could this woman be?*

Victoria reached out and took Laney's hand. "I know this all seems incredible, but I promise you, I have always had Henry's best interest at heart.

Whatever you think of me, please believe that any child of mine will always be my priority. I would have much rather spent my life at his side. But that was a sacrifice I had to make to keep him safe."

"I don't understand that. What were you keeping him safe from?"

Victoria sighed, releasing Laney's hand. "There were people after me. I managed to stay a step ahead of them for years, but they were getting close. I had to disappear to protect Henry. And those people are still looking for me."

"The Council?"

"Not just them. I didn't want Henry's death on my hands as well and I also wanted him to have a real life. Not one in hiding. So I died. And Henry got to live a normal life."

"But how can you be sure Henry's abduction doesn't have anything to do with you?"

"I am good at hiding. Very, very good. No one knows I'm alive. No one knows who I really am."

Laney leaned back against the counter. 'No one know who I really am.' An interesting choice of words, but Laney let it pass. There were more critical questions at the moment. "How did you know Henry was in trouble?"

Victoria smiled. "I have a bug in Henry's communications system. I had it added when Henry first set up the system. He doesn't know it's there. I was in D.C. when it alerted me to the search for Henry."

"What were you doing in D.C.?"

"I had some business to attend to. And that's all you get from me, Laney. It's safer if you don't know anything about me."

Laney struggled with the questions plaguing her. "Aren't you worried that the people looking for you will track you now that you've shown up here?"

Victoria glanced up, her voice filled with conviction. "It's worth the risk. Henry's worth any risk."

CHAPTER 79

Laney buckled her seatbelt on the Gulfstream. Her head fell back as the pilot taxied down the runway.

Victoria had left just after Jake returned from his phone call. The warehouse checked out. Jake had Yoni recon it, but it looked like that would be their destination once they hit Vegas.

Once the plane leveled off, she glanced toward the back of the plane. Jake was on the phone, coordinating for the op. The plane was filled to capacity, every seat filled. Another, larger plane had taken off earlier with more personnel.

Victoria had promised to arrange to clear their way through the airport. Jake had planned on having them all stay in a nearby warehouse, but Victoria said she'd arrange lodging.

And Laney and Jake were both sure she would come through. She might be mysterious as hell, but it was also clear getting Henry back was her priority.

Laney rested her chin on her hand, staring out the window. The visit from Victoria still seemed unreal. Who the hell was she? If she was just some 'normal' human being, she wouldn't have had to go into hiding for twenty years.

Laney didn't doubt how much Victoria loved Henry. Unless she was one heck of a good actress, those emotions were real. But was the rest? Was it possible Henry was the son of Enoch?

Laney looked down at the clouds. Was the idea of Enoch returning time and time again really so crazy? Wasn't that the essence of reincarnation? The soul returning to human form, and reliving life over and over again?

Now that she was thinking about Enoch as living multiple lives, the similarity to others became clear. The most obvious was the tale of the prophet Elijah. As in the case of Enoch, Elijah had the gift of prophesy. He also was alleged to lived an incredibly long time, and been taken up to heaven before he died. In the Bible, Elijah and Enoch were proposed as two different individuals. Was it possible that they were actually the same man?

Laney knew that a number of religions believed in reincarnation. Buddhism, Gnostic Christianity, and Jainism all did. But was it really reincarnation that Victoria was referring to? Or was it rebirth, like the Buddhists believed? In reincarnation, the individual in essence retained their identity from one life to the next. In rebirth, one's previous life determined the conditions of one's current life.

Laney rubbed her eyes. She was in no shape to parse out the intricacies of Eastern religious beliefs right now. The best she could hope to achieve was probably sleep.

She closed her eyes. The next couple of days were probably going to be brutal.

As she drifted off, though, she wondered idly what she'd done in her past lives to result in having multiple life-threatening situations placed at her doorstep in this lifetime.

Or maybe she was the reincarnation of someone. She knew that support for reincarnation often came from studies of young children who remembered their past lives in detail. Maybe she'd just forgotten who she used to be.

Turning towards the window, she pulled her blanket up to her chin. *Probably for the best. This life is tough enough without the baggage from my former lives chasing me around.*

CHAPTER 80

Las Vegas, NV

The flight to Vegas was short and, happily, uneventful. Buses took them from the airport to the Wynn. Victoria had arranged for them to have two full floors of the hotel.

She'd also had crates of weapons and gear waiting for them. They had enough firepower for a small war. Victoria had been telling the truth about one thing, at least. Her resources were extensive.

Laney dumped her bags on the king bed in the suite she was sharing with Jake. He was still at the airfield making arrangements.

She made her way back into the large living room. Off of it was a full kitchen and dining area, all done in dark woods against a plush white carpet. In fact, all the living room furniture was sleek and white. She walked to the wall of glass that overlooked the Strip. The neon of Vegas shined back at her.

The doorbell rang. Laney glanced over her shoulder in surprise. Almost everyone in the group had keys to this suite. It was going to be command central. She crossed the long suite to the door.

Glancing through the peephole, she let out a little

whoop of happiness. Flinging the door open, she crushed Jen in a giant hug, pulling her into the room. "What are you doing here?"

Jen unfolded herself from Laney with a grin. "My brothers were a little concerned for my safety when they heard about Henry's abduction, especially after we had a little chat."

Laney led her over to the couch. "How'd that go?"

"Surprisingly well. Jordan knew about the superhumans because of Montana and he'd told Mike about them. They paused after I told them and I thought for sure that was it. But then Mike gave me a hug and asked me how come he'd had to do all the heavy lifting when I moved into my apartment two years ago."

"And Jordan?"

"He claimed it was unfair not to reveal my abilities prior to our basketball games. Demands a handicap the next time we play. And he wants to know if he can tell Yoni, to get him off his back."

Laney laughed. "I've seen Yoni needle him. He might have a case."

Jen grinned, but Laney could see the relief. "It doesn't make a difference to them. All this time I've been worried and it doesn't make a difference."

Laney gave her another hug. "Your brothers are good men. You're one lucky woman."

"Don't I know it."

"Speaking of the Witt boys, where are they?"

As if on cue, the door swung open. Jordan and Mike stepped in, Yoni following behind. "So I told my wife, a Sig Sauer 9 millimeter's a perfectly appropriate anniversary gift. I even got it in pink. She said it was unromantic. What do you think?"

"I think you owe the woman flowers," Mike replied.

"A lifetime supply," Jordan added.

Yoni grunted and looked at Laney. "What do you think? Isn't a Sig a good anniversary gift?"

Laney smiled. Only Yoni would think of handguns as romantic. "Maybe flowers, jewelry, and a pink handgun."

Yoni grimaced. "Not you too."

Laney and Jen followed the men to the large dining room table next to the open kitchen. Yoni pulled up the plans to the warehouse on his tablet. He began explaining the security features of the warehouse to the Witts. They were planning on going in in just under two hours.

Laney had already reviewed the details. She headed to the kitchen to get some water. She'd just pulled a bottle out of the fridge when the suite door opened again and Jake walked in. Spying her, he changed directions to join her.

"Did everybody arrive?" Laney asked.

Jake nodded. "Yup. We should be good. And before you ask, you can't go. It's way too dangerous."

"I can hold my own."

"I know that. But you're not trained for this. These guys have been working together for years. They have their moves down."

Laney looked at him, hearing the words he was trying not to say. "And I'll just be in the way." She paused. "Is that the only reason?"

"No." Jake lowered his voice. "I know you can defend yourself, but the idea of putting you in harm's way or letting you anywhere near Hugo, it kills me. Let me protect you, just this once, okay?"

She could see the guilt that still weighed him down from the last time she'd confronted Hugo. She couldn't do that to him again. She sighed. "Just this once. But when you get back, we're going to have a long chat about the strides women have made since the 1950s."

He grinned. "Absolutely."

The smile faded from Laney's face. "Just get him back, Jake."

He traced her cheek with his finger. "I will."

She held his hand to her face. "You better."

"And when this is all over?" Jake asked her, his eyes intense. She stared at him a moment, knowing what he was asking.

She glanced over at the group. They weren't paying them any attention. She leaned up and touched her lips to his.

Jake wrapped his arms around her, pulling her into the kitchen out of view. The kiss quickly turned wild. Her hands ran up his chest and wound themselves around his neck. He crushed her to him. Laney wanted it to go on forever. What had she been thinking, saying she needed a break from this?

Reality returning, she pulled away but stayed pressed up against his chest, her heart pounding. "And when this is all over, we give ourselves a real shot."

CHAPTER 81

The warehouse was located seven miles beyond the Vegas Strip, which put it smack dab in the middle of nowhere. Desert surrounded it for miles.

Jake had his group in desert camos, helping them blend into the landscape. There were fifteen in his group, another fifteen at the back of the warehouse, and ten at the one other entrance. He was taking no chances with Henry's safety.

Jake stood next to his Jeep, surveying the warehouse. The white building was large - two stories high – and Jake knew the inside was largely open space except for a small reception area up front and an office at the back. A helicopter sat in the parking lot next to it.

"We're really using these?" Yoni asked, holding up the Taser.

Jake lowered his binoculars. Each member had been assigned Tasers along with their regular weapons. "Yeah. We're not sure this is where the Ecuador loot was brought. It could be just a regular warehouse. If that's true, it's staffed by a bunch of regular guys.

They may not have any clue what's going on. This may not even be the right place. I'm not killing a bunch of innocents."

"If they were innocent, they wouldn't be anywhere near this place," Yoni grumbled.

Jake glanced over at him. "Maybe. But we go in with caution, just in case." He tapped the mic at his throat. "Jordan? You and Mike contain the security guards at the front in thirty seconds. And everybody remember, the priority is Henry."

"And us?" Yoni asked.

Jake grinned. "We'll have the rest of the teams hold here while we check to make sure we have the right place."

The twins' SUV sped towards the gate. Jake and Yoni hopped in their own Jeep. Jake put it in gear. He sped across the empty parking lot, slamming to a stop three feet from the front door. He and Yoni leaped out of the car and sprinted for the front door. No gunfire rang out. No one tried to stop them.

Yoni opened the door, his gun sweeping inside, while Jake entered. There was a door at the back, four walls, one desk and a couple of chairs for people to wait in. The floor was covered in a navy blue commercial carpet. The walls held serviceable portraits and a sign encouraging people to ask about their monthly storage rate. Easy listening music drifted softly through the area.

Behind the desk, sat a young brunette, her eyes as big as saucers, seemingly rooted to her chair. Yoni moved to the back of the room, listening at the door.

Jake gestured for her to keep her hands up. "What's your name?"

"Um, Susie. Susie Mackelson."

"Okay, Susie, we need to know about a shipment."

"Okay," she said her voice trembling. She lowered her hands to the desk. "Um, what name-" A bullet punched through her chest.

"Yoni! What the hell?" Jake yelled. Jake reached over to feel for a pulse, although from the amount of blood sprayed across the monitor, he knew it was useless.

Yoni walked up to the desk, pulling out the Beretta that had been taped underneath the desk. "Little Susie here was reaching for this."

The door at the end of the hall flung open and armed commandos rushed through, firing unceasingly as they did. Yoni and Jake flipped the desk, to use it for cover. The computer, papers, and Susie crashed to the ground in front of it.

Jake barked into his mic. "All teams move in."

Yoni grinned. "Told you we had the right place."

CHAPTER 82

Laney walked out of her suite and down the hall. She was going crazy with nothing to do. She pulled out her key card and let herself into the second suite. "Danny?"

Danny was just coming out of the kitchen, a sandwich in his hand.

Laney smiled. "Good. You're eating. You haven't eaten enough the last couple of days."

"She insisted." He hooked a thumb at Jen, who followed behind him with a sandwich of her own.

Jen shrugged. "He's way too skinny. Besides, the way he's using up brainpower, we probably should be feeding him intravenously."

"Yeah, well, there's been a lot to do," Danny muttered into his sandwich.

"At least for you," Laney grumbled. "I've been less than useless."

Jen put an arm around Laney. "You're never useless. We just don't happen to be commandos. Right now, we're more like, um…"

"If you say cheerleaders, I swear I'll hit you."

Jen snorted. "I was going to say psychological

support."

Laney flounced down on the couch. "Sounds like a cheerleader to me."

"Well, I'm sure Jake would appreciate you in a cheerleading costume."

Laney could feel her cheeks growing warm. She quickly glanced at Danny, who was studiously avoiding her gaze. She glared at Jen and mouthed, Really?

Jen smiled. "Sorry."

Laney shook her head, but found herself smiling. "How long do you think it'll take them?"

"A couple of hours, at least," Jen said. "They'll search the whole space for Henry, even opening any crates they find. It won't be quick."

"Great. Meanwhile, we'll do what? Play 'Go Fish'?" Laney's phone beeped, letting her know she had a new text. She looked at the screen. The number was blocked. She opened it and gasped.

Henry's face was splashed across the small screen. His mouth was open, in the middle of a scream.

"Laney?" Jen asked.

A tremble in her hand, she turned the screen towards Jen.

Jen inhaled sharply. "Who sent that?"

"No idea." Laney stood and headed across the room. "Danny?"

He glanced up. "Yeah?"

"Can you trace the origin of a text message, even if the number's blocked?"

"Sure." He held out his hand for the phone.

She hesitated. "Could you just look up my phone log?"

He stopped and stared at her. "Yeah, but you have

your phone right there. Why don't you just . . ." His words cut off. "It's Henry, isn't it?"

"Yes. He's alive in the shot, but he's hurt."

He nodded, but Laney noticed the shake in his hand. She handed him the phone.

Danny's breath hitched. He turned away from her. "Give me a few minutes."

She squeezed his shoulder, then took a seat next to him. Jen leaned against the wall behind Danny. No one said a word. The only sound was Danny tapping away at his computer.

It was only five minutes later, but it seemed a lifetime before Danny spoke. "I've got the signal. The message came from another cellphone. It keeps fading in and out. It's still in the area. But there seems to be something blocking it."

Laney glanced at the brochures the hotel had left on the table. Grand Canyon tours, magic shows, all-you-can-eat buffets. "Danny? Could it be caused by a canyon?"

He looked at her. "Depends on the canyon, but yeah, it could block the signal."

"Is there a way for you to lock it down?" Jen asked.

Danny paused before answering. "If we follow the signal, I can probably give you a better idea of the phone's location."

Laney smiled. Finally, something to do. They'd track the signal, get a location, and if it proved to be anything, let the rest of the group know. "All right. Show me how to track the signal."

Danny looked up, his jaw set, his eyes stubborn. "No."

Laney raised an eyebrow. "No? What do you mean

'no'?"

"I'm going with you."

"Like hell you are."

"Like hell I'm not." The words were strong, but there was a slight tremble to his voice.

Laney knew she should be pissed. But honestly, part of her was happy that he was standing up for something. He'd spent almost the entire time she'd known him keeping to the sidelines, not making any waves. It was nice to see him with a little gumption.

Of course, she would have preferred it if he'd picked something else to be stubborn about, like maybe his bedtime.

Laney gentled her tone. "Danny, I know you want to help. And you have. But it's simply too dangerous for you to go with us."

"Really? Then how come you're going? I thought Jake said to stay here until they get back."

"Yeah, well, I'm an adult and I get to make decisions for myself," she countered.

"Yeah, well, according to the United States government, I'm an adult too."

Laney glared at him, then looked over at Jen, who was trying unsuccessfully to hold back her smile.

Jen shrugged her shoulders. "I'll go see about the supplies for our trip."

Laney watched Jen walk out of the room. *Thanks for nothing, Jen.* She turned back to Danny to try again. "Look, Danny, if anything happened to you, Henry would be inconsolable. For his sake, you need to stay here."

Danny looked at his feet, his shoulders slumping. Thank goodness. She was getting through. He looked up, his gaze steady. "I'm going."

Or not.

Danny cut her off before she could speak again. "I won't tell you how to follow the signal. I've already encoded it in my tablet. You'll never be able to break it. I'm going."

Laney couldn't believe what she was hearing. Where the hell had this come from? Frustration and fear boiled up inside her. "Why are you being so difficult about this?" she yelled.

"Because it's Henry," Danny yelled back, his voice breaking. He swatted at the tears that rolled down his cheeks. "It's Henry," he repeated, his voice sounded smaller and younger. "And I need to get him back."

Laney's heart crumbled. He'd been so brave through all of this. But he was just a scared little boy who missed his Dad. And the reality was, he'd do a better job of tracking the signal than either she or Jen ever could. Damn it.

She sighed and stared at the ceiling. What the hell was she supposed to do here? She blew out a breath. "Okay, Danny. You can come."

She put up her hand as the grin broke across his face. "But whatever I, or Jen, tell you to do, you do. No arguments."

He nodded.

"I mean it," she warned again. "I tell you to jump, run, hide, whatever. You don't hesitate, you just do it."

He wrapped his arms around her. "I will. I promise. You won't regret it."

Wrapping her own arms around him, she pulled him tight, resting her chin on the top of his head. *I hope you're right.*

CHAPTER 83

The glass behind Jake and Yoni shattered as Jake's men laser-sighted each of the security guards.

"Clear," came the calls over his earpiece.

Jake knew two other teams of his men had already entered by the warehouse's other entryways. He and Yoni jumped up, their weapons pulled into their shoulders. They stepped over each of the downed men, careful to kick their weapons away, heading for the door that led to the warehouse space.

Jake glanced in. The warehouse was massive. Crates upon crates lined the area. Jake motioned for Yoni to take a team to the left, while he took a team to the right. Mike and Jordan led their team down the middle. "Keep your shots sparing. We don't want Henry hurt in the crossfire."

As soon as the words were out of his mouth, he realized the stupidity of them. Henry wouldn't be hurt by a few stray bullets, at least not seriously. This superhuman thing was going to take a little getting used to.

A security guard peeked out from behind a crate ten yards ahead, taking a shot. Jake took him down. He kept moving forward, his eyes glued for any movement and any possible holding spot. He heard other shots across the warehouse. But no calls came over the radio. His team had been ordered to only contact him if there was a problem or they found Henry.

Slowly, they made their way through the space. Jake was surprised by how easy it was. The security was sizeable but not enough to offer much resistance. Ten minutes and they had the area cleared. Ten security guards were rounded up. But no one had seen any sign of Henry.

Jake reached the back wall and saw Jordan and Mike to his right. Mike caught his eye and nudged his chin towards a door in the back. A large window was built into the wall of the room, overlooking the warehouse floor. Jake glanced in.

A few of the crates had been taken inside and opened. A bronze folio sat on a lab table. Other instruments, brushes, a camera, and high-powered lights, gave the space a laboratory feel. In the back corner was a desk with a man cowering underneath it.

Jake flattened himself on the left hand side of the door and nodded at Jordan. Jordan grabbed the handle, flinging the door open. Jake went in high, scanning the room for any threats. None.

He glanced at Mike, who'd followed him in. Mike put up one finger. Jake nodded and called out. "You, under the desk, come out with your hands up."

Hands appeared above the desktop. "Don't shoot me. I'm unarmed."

The man stepped into view, his hands still raised.

Jake recognized him. "Dr. Devereaux. We've been looking for you."

Deveraux nodded, his eyes on the floor. "I'll cooperate."

"Good. Now tell me, where's Henry?"

Deveraux looked up, his confusion clear. "Henry? Who's Henry?"

CHAPTER 84

"Should we call the strike team?" Jen asked.

Laney shook her head, her eyes on the canyon road ahead of them. They'd followed the signal twenty minutes outside the Strip to Red Canyon. They were close, but the signal was still bouncing in and out. "No. Not until we know for sure this is worth following. We'll just take a quick peek and then call in the cavalry if we need to."

"You're going to take a right up ahead in about two hundred yards," Danny said from the backseat of the Wrangler.

Laney nodded, noting the road.

"How about calling Jake and just telling him what we're doing?" Jen pressed.

"Absolutely not," Laney said. "He'll tell us to come back. Look, we'll just check it out. Nothing dangerous."

Jen sighed, leaning back in her seat. "If there's nothing dangerous, why'd you pack the arsenal in the back?"

"Well, it never hurts to be prepared."

Jen shook her head.

Laney turned onto the road Danny indicated and they entered Red Canyon. The crimson red walls of the canyon glistened back at them. It was like driving onto Mars.

"I've got the signal!" Danny yelled from the back.

Laney hit the brakes. "Where?"

Danny pointed up and to the left. "There."

Laney stared at the rock façade, not noticing anything different about where Danny was pointing. Just more red rocks. Then slowly, the structure came into a view. It was a house, built right into the canyon walls. Its walls were the same color as the canyon. The thing was massive, easily six thousand square feet.

Most of the side was made of glass. The reflection back from the canyon made it almost impossible to see. It was like something out of Star Trek.

"Holy cow," Laney said.

"Who on earth would build a house there?" Jen asked.

"Guess we're going to find out." Laney drove carefully up the winding road that seemed to head towards the cliff house. It looked as if it was cut right out of the rock itself. She turned, incorporating both Danny and Jen in her glance. "Remember, we're just tourists looking for an interesting climbing spot, okay?"

"Yup, just tourists," Jen agreed, but her nervous tapping on the dashboard gave away her fear.

Laney glanced in the rearview mirror at Danny. "You still up for this?"

Danny's head bobbed up and down. "If it helps us get Henry, yes."

"Okay."

They drove on for another few tense minutes before

Laney pulled off to the side of the road. There was a large rock with a decent-sized pocket behind it. She pulled the Jeep into it, grabbing her bag from the backseat. "All right, everybody. Let's go for a little climb."

CHAPTER 85

The climb hadn't been as difficult as Laney had feared. Although the rock looked sheer, there'd actually been plenty of hand- and footholds. She led the climb, placing her cams and carabiners in every twenty feet or so, and looping the rope through.

After a hundred feet, she set an anchor into the rock wall. She waved down at Danny. "Okay, Danny. Come on up."

He began his climb and Laney let out a breath. He was doing great. Watching him, she said a silent 'thank you' for forcing Danny to go rock climbing with her last summer. He made the entire climb with only one fall. Then she pulled up the weapons duffel. Jen brought up the rear, carrying an extra rope and pulling out the cams and carabiners as she reached them.

Then they did it all over for the second pitch. Usually, they'd pull up the rope and remove the anchor before beginning the second pitch. But both she and Jen agreed that they should leave the rope in place, just in case they needed to make a fast getaway.

The second pitch was a little more difficult than the first. Holds were less obvious. Laney chalked each one thoroughly to make Danny's climb a little easier.

At the top of the second pitch, there was a plateau, hidden from the house by a wall of rock. Once all three of them were up, they carefully made their way around the rock. They had a perfect view of the house from here. The plateau angled up, allowing them to crawl up and lie flat. The house was a hundred yards ahead and to their right.

Laney put down her binoculars. "I don't see any movement."

"Me, neither," Danny said lowering his own. "But that's where the signal's coming from."

Jen patted him on the back. "You did good, Danny. We'll call the guys and let them know about it. But it looks like the other site is the bigger priority."

"Doesn't that look like a path?" Laney pointed to a trail that seemed to cut through the rock and towards the house.

The words were barely out of her mouth before a male voice was heard to their left.

"Never seen a guy that big. He's like NBA big."

"And did you see him take a hit? I swear I thought the boss was going to have to take out a mallet to get a reaction from the guy."

The other man laughed. "Barton's really enjoying himself."

Laney felt Danny begin to tremble next to her. She grasped his hand in hers and gave it a squeeze, hoping he stayed quiet.

The men passed only a few feet in front of them. Laney could just make out the top of their heads. Another few feet and they came into view. They were both wearing tan uniforms, guns holstered at their sides.

Security.

She couldn't tell much from the back, except they both had dark brown hair, were about five-foot-ten, and they both looked like they were in good shape. They disappeared through a door in the side of the building that she hadn't noticed.

Laney let out a breath, trying to keep her tone calm. She pulled Danny's tablet from the weapons duffel. "Danny? Can you hack into the house's security? See if you can find Henry?"

He nodded, his hands already flying across the machine. Laney caught Jen's eyes above Danny's bent head. She read the concern there.

"I'm in," Danny said.

Laney leaned into Danny, staring at the screen. Black and white images from the house flashed across the tablet. Hallways, bedrooms, kitchen, garage.

Laney fought down the urge to tell him to hurry. "Stop," she ordered.

Danny's hands stilled.

On screen, Henry stood, chained to some metal bars. His chest was bare and there were slashes across it where he'd been cut. Hugo was in the room with him, cleaning off a knife.

"Bastards," Laney murmured.

A tear fell onto the screen. Danny wiped at his eyes.

Laney wrapped her arm around Danny. Jen did the same from the other side. "We'll get him out of there, Danny. We'll get him back," Laney murmured.

"I think it's time we called in the cavalry," Jen said.

Laney nodded. "Agreed."

Just then an older man who'd been out of frame,

stepped into focus. Despite his bent shoulders, Laney had no doubt he was the man in charge. It had to be Sebastian Flourent. Sebastian shook his head, stepping towards Henry.

Trying to keep her voice calm, Laney said. "Is there audio on this thing?"

Danny nodded.

Seconds later, they could hear the man's words. "-disappointment. I'd hope you could provide us with what we need." He walked away from Henry and out of the room.

Laney's words came out rushed. "Can you follow him?"

Danny tracked Flourent from screen to screen, watching his slow progress. The man made his way down a long hallway and up a staircase. Pausing at the top of the stairs, he seemed to need to catch his breath. Then he was on the move again.

He passed through a den and down another long hallway. His steps grew closer together. Obviously, he was tiring. Finally, he walked through a doorway.

Danny flipped through camera shots, trying to find the right room.

Laney had to bite her tongue to keep from telling him to hurry.

Finally, Danny found Sebastian again. He was in an office. Hugo had joined him. Laney felt a mixture of anger and fear at the sight of him. Movement drew her attention to the other man in the room. Warren.

"Son of a bitch," Jen muttered.

At the same time, Laney said, "Audio."

On the screen, Hugo pulled out his cell, putting it to his ear as he walked out of the room. The old man sank into his seat behind the desk. "Water."

Warren moved to the bar and poured him a drink. The second man had his back to the camera. Laney felt a constriction in her chest. When he turned around and stepped closer to the desk his face became clear. Hugo.

"Has he said anything?" Warren asked.

The old man took the drink with a shaking hand and sipped. He took a minute to catch his breath before answering. "He either doesn't know anything or is unwilling to tell us."

Hugo stepped back into the room. "There's been a problem at the warehouse. A group has infiltrated it. We've lost the Ecuador find."

The old man's face was furious. "Damn it. If they tracked it there, they can track us here. We need to go."

"What about the prisoner?" Hugo asked. Even through the poor quality of the audio, Laney could hear the desire in Hugo's voice.

The old man paused, looking away. When his eyes returned to Hugo, his voice was resigned. "He's too big a risk. Get rid of him."

CHAPTER 86

Laney grabbed the duffel they'd dragged up the mountain. She pulled on a holster, placing a Beretta in its sheath. She attached magazines to the holster as well. All the while, she barked out orders.

"Danny, call Jake. Give him our coordinates. Tell him to get here now. And then you hide. No matter what you hear, what you see, you stay hidden. Your job from this point forward is to stay alive, do you understand me?"

Danny nodded, his eyes growing wide.

Laney looked over at Jen, who'd also grabbed a holster and was stuffing extra ammunition into her pockets. "Jen?"

"I'm going with you."

Laney nodded. "Thanks."

"Any ideas how we get inside?" Jen asked.

Laney pulled a sawed-off shotgun from the bag. "I brought a door opener."

The words brought a smile to Jen's face. "Piece of cake, right?"

"Absolutely." Laney turned to Danny. "Is there a

map of the house on there?"

"Hold on a sec." Danny fiddled with the tablet before turning it around.

Laney ran her finger along the hallways, retracing the old man's steps back to where Henry had been. "Okay. Henry's in the basement. I think I know how to get there." She looked at Danny. "You need to find a crevice to hide in."

Danny nodded, but hesitated. "I can open the doors for you."

"How?"

He nodded to his tablet. "The whole system's computerized. I'm already in. I can follow you like we did the old man and open the doors as you come to them. I can also disrupt the security system so they can't see you."

Laney leaned over and kissed him on the forehead. "You are one in a million. But you need to hide first. If you can't do that from your hiding spot, then you don't do it. Okay?"

Danny nodded, but his eyes shifted away from her.

Laney grabbed his arm, forcing him to meet her eyes. "I mean it, Danny. I'll smash this tablet right here if you even think of putting yourself in harm's way."

"But you're doing it."

"Yes. I'm doing it. And if something were to happen to me, Henry would be incredibly sad. But if something were to happen to you, his world would end. And it wouldn't matter if we saved him or not, he would never forgive himself. So promise me, for Henry, promise me you'll stay hidden."

Reluctantly, Danny nodded.

Laney handed him the shotgun. "Only as a last resort, okay?"

"Okay."

She gave him a hug. "I'll see you soon." She stood up and Jen stood with her.

Jen looked at the house and then back at Laney. "Into the breach once more?"

Laney nodded. "So it would seem."

CHAPTER 87

At the warehouse, Jake slammed his cell shut. He pulled a security guard from the floor, holding him up by the front of his shirt. "Where are the keys to the helicopter?"

"Wh – wh - what?" The man stammered.

Jake shook him, lifting the man onto his toes. "Keys for the chopper!"

With a shaking hand, the man pointed to a gray cabinet on the wall across the room.

Jake flung the man to the ground and sprinted for the box. "Yoni!"

Yoni came at a run. "What's happened?"

The box was locked. Jake ripped off the door. "Laney. She's found Henry."

Yoni grinned. "Great."

"And she's going to rescue him."

"Shit."

Jordan jogged up to them, overhearing their exchange. "Damn it. She's going to get herself killed."

Jake grabbed the keys for the chopper, handily labeled, and gave Jordan a baleful look. "Well, she's not alone. Apparently your sister's helping her."

Jordan paled and grabbed the keys from Jake's hand. "I'm a better pilot."

CHAPTER 88

Laney sprinted down the path, Jen behind her. The keypad next to the door ahead of them glowed red. Then with a beep, it switched to green. Laney grinned. *Danny strikes again.*

She grabbed onto the handle and glanced at Jen.

Jen nodded, her Beretta clasped in front of her. They'd agreed that the weapons were a last resort. They needed to get in quietly if they were going to free Henry.

Laney pulled open the door. Jen went in first. The hallway was lit, but there was no sign of life.

From the schematic Danny had pulled up, Henry should be to the left and one flight down. Taking the lead, Laney ran towards the end of the hall.

A door to her right opened as she reached it. A guard stepped through, shock on his face as he saw them. He started to pull his gun.

Laney elbowed him in the face, kneed him in the groin. She spun him around, wrapping one arm around his chin, placing the other in the opposite direction around his head. With a quick movement, she yanked. He slipped to the floor, his neck broken.

"You good?" Jen asked from behind her.

Laney nodded, although the ease with which she'd just ended the man's life left her a little stunned. "Let's go."

Pulling open the door, she stepped into the kitchen, Jen right behind her. "Oh, crap."

It was dinnertime. Five guards rose from the table as they caught sight of them.

Laney dove to the right and Jen dove to the left. Two guards started shooting at them while the other three sprinted across the room.

Laney returned fire, hitting one of the guards in the leg. Unfortunately, his hand seemed to be fine and he kept returning fire. She saw another guard speaking into his radio. *So much for surprise.*

A blur of motion caught her attention. Jen was now behind the guards. She took out the two shooters. The third guard paused, hearing the gunfire behind him.

Laney aimed and took out the remaining three. Keeping her gun extended in front of her, she approached the guards, kicking their weapons out of reach.

Jen joined her. "Not bad, for cheerleaders."

"Hell, that was pretty good for commandos. But one of them warned the others. We need to move faster."

Jen nodded with a grin. "Faster I can do."

Laney gestured at the door across the room. "Let's move."

They ran for the door. With a quick glance at Jen, Laney pulled it open to reveal the stairs to the basement. She started to head down when Jen grabbed her. "I'll go first."

Laney nodded and tried not to look astonished as

Jen all but disappeared as she sprinted down the stairs. Laney whirled around as the door to the kitchen flung open. Guards poured into the room.

Throwing herself through the doorway, she yanked the door closed behind her. She reached up and turned the lock, knowing it wouldn't hold them back for long.

Laney slipped down the stairs, catching herself on the banister as bullets blasted through the door behind her. She leaped down the last few steps.

Jen sprinted back down the hall to her. "What happened?"

"Reinforcements."

"Henry's down the hall to the right. There are two guards outside his door."

"What about Hugo?"

"Haven't seen him."

Ejecting the spent magazine, Laney inserted a fresh one. "Let's go."

They ran down the hall. Laney peered around the corner. "I'll go low and take the one on the right. You go high and take the one on the left. Count of three?"

Jen nodded.

Laney spoke quietly. "One, two, three."

She stepped around the corner, dropping to her knee. She pulled the trigger three times, all three shots hitting the guard in the chest. Jen's shots were just as accurate, although one went through the side of the guard's head.

Yells and the sound of pounding feet sounded behind them.

"They're through the door," Laney yelled as she sprinted down the hall towards Henry's door.

She skidded to a halt. The smell of burnt flesh

permeated the air. The metal contraption Henry was attached to was a giant burner. No wonder Henry hadn't been able to escape. He was being perpetually burned.

He was strapped to the burner, his shirt gone. Old cuts and lashes crisscrossed his chest. His head hung down, and he didn't move as they rushed in the doorway.

Laney's breath caught. *Don't be dead.* She ran across the room and pulled the plug. The contraption still emitted heat. *God damn them.*

Grabbing a stool, she dragged it over in front of Henry, and climbed up on it. "Henry! Henry!" She slapped his face.

His eyelids opened drowsily.

"Stay with me, Henry."

She reached for the shackles holding his hands in place. They were metal. She looked around. There was nothing to open them with. And he didn't look like he had the strength to break them. "Damn it. Hold on, Henry."

She ran back to the doorway.

Jen was sending off round after round at the approaching guards. She reloaded.

Laney dropped next to her, aiming down the hall. "Jen, see if you can free Henry. I'll hold these guys off."

Without a word, Jen sprinted back across the room.

A guard poked his head out from down the hall. Laney let off a shot. He ducked back before she could get him. Then a guard came flying around the corner, zigging and zagging across the hall.

"Silly boy," Laney whispered. "Zig," she said as he sprinted to the right. He changed direction. "And then zag." She let loose a barrage of shots, raking him from head to foot. He collapsed in a heap.

Behind her, she heard a shot and then the clank of metal. Laney didn't turn to look. The rest of the guards had decided to try the same kamikaze run.

Laney set off round after round. Ejecting the spent magazine, she slammed a new one in place. She didn't think, just reacted. A few seconds later, the remaining guards lay in heaps across the hallway.

Leaning back against the wall, she breathed deep. She was getting better at this, and she wasn't sure if that was a good thing or a bad one.

A grunt sounded behind her. Jen was helping Henry down.

Laney ran to help.

Throwing an arm around Henry's waist, she pulled his arm around her shoulder, staggering under his weight. "Henry? You with us?"

He gave a little groan. "Yeah. I'm here."

They led him over to a chair and tried to gently lower him into it. He grimaced as his back touched the back of the chair.

"Sorry," Laney said, pulling him forward. A scuffle of a shoe drew her attention back to the doorway.

"I got it." Jen strode across the room.

Laney held onto Henry, not sure if he could sit up on his own. He was hunched over, so Laney had a view of the burns on his back. She stared in disbelief as they began to knit together in front of her. "Henry? How are you feeling?"

He leaned up, the light coming back into his eyes. "Better."

She nodded. "Good. Can you stand? Because I

think we need to get moving."

"Yeah." He pushed off the chair, a little unsteady.

Laney helped him, but already she could see he was stronger. If they had a little more time, he'd probably be fully healed. But the room they were in was sandwiched in between two staircases. They needed to find a better spot to hole up or escape. Here, they were sitting ducks.

Laney crossed the room with Henry, trying not to wince at the sight of the bruises and cuts that marred his chest. But they already looked better than when she'd seen them through Danny's monitor. Speaking of which . . .

She looked around the room and spied the camera up to their right. She looked at it and gave a thumbs-up. "He's good, Danny."

Henry grabbed onto her shoulder. "Danny? Danny's here?"

"He's only controlling the cameras. He's not in the building."

Some of the fear dropped from Henry's face. "Thank God. I thought you meant he was nearby."

"'Course not," she lied, not able to meet his eyes. Now wasn't the time for full disclosure.

She dropped next to Jen. "Thoughts?"

Jen took a shot at someone out in the hall. "They all seem to be coming in from the left. So I think we should go right."

Laney snorted. "Excellent plan, as usual. Let's do that. Can you hold them off while I help Henry to the end of the hall?"

Jen's gaze lingered for a moment on Henry and his injuries. Laney saw the questions in that gaze, but also something else she didn't have time to think about right now. Jen's eyes returned to Laney. "Count of three?"

Laney nodded. She turned to hand Henry a weapon and stopped. He wouldn't be able to use any of them. His fingers were too large. "Sorry. I don't have a weapon for you. They're too small."

He grimaced. "Story of my life."

"Okay, you two. Time to go," Jen said.

Laney flattened herself next to the door, Henry beside her.

Jen counted down. At three, Laney burst from the doorway, her Beretta extended in front of her. She heard Henry behind her. A bullet whizzed past her shoulder and she heard the retort of Jen's weapon as she responded. She rounded the corner, followed by Henry.

The stairs were in front of them with a door at the top. And right now, it was quiet.

"Clear!" Laney yelled, aiming back down the hall to clear the way for Jen. A blur of motion, a whip of air, and Jen was beside her.

Laney grinned. "I think you're getting faster."

CHAPTER 89

"How long?" Jake demanded as they sped through the air in the borrowed EC-135.

The interior of the chopper was a mixture of handcrafted leather seats, plenty of storage space, and significant legroom. Designed by Eurocopter and Hermès, the helicopter was the ultimate in luxury, designed for the wealthiest of buyers. The four men in it right now, though, couldn't care less about the luxurious surrounding as they sped towards Red Canyon.

Mike glanced over from his position as pilot. Back at the warehouse, the twins had had a short argument over who was the better pilot. Mike won.

"Another few minutes." Mike gestured with his chin. "After that ridge, we should be able to see the house."

The sleek helicopter glided through the air. Jake had ordered half of his team to secure the warehouse and the other half to head for the house in the canyon. But there'd been only one helicopter. And it only seated four. It would take the rest of the team at least twenty minutes or so to reach the canyon.

Damn it, Laney. He'd told her to stay at the hotel. But did she listen? Of course not. Why would she do anything that didn't involve her placing herself in mortal danger?

"What's happening on site?" he barked at Yoni, who was sitting in the back with Jordan. Danny had patched through a link so they now had eyes inside the compound. Whatever Danny was watching, they could watch, too.

"They just got to Henry. And not too soon. Hugo was one his way to him. Another couple of minutes . . ." Yoni's voice dropped off.

Jake gave a curt nod. Okay. Maybe the two of them going in hadn't been such a bad idea. But his chest constricted at the thought of Laney being near Hugo again.

Yoni continued. "But they seem to be trapped in the basement. And there are more reinforcements coming down towards them. We should probably hurry."

Jake gripped the side of his chair, urging the bird to go faster. "What about Danny? Is he still safe?"

Yoni relayed the question into his phone. A few seconds later, he looked up. "Yup. Still in the same crevice. Laney made him promise to stay there or she would break his computer."

A small smile crept onto Jake's face. Well, at least she did that right.

"Oh," Yoni said.

Jake looked over his shoulder. "'Oh'? What does 'Oh' mean?"

"Um, well, it seems that Laney and Jen wanted to make sure that Danny could protect himself in their absence."

Jake stared at him. They couldn't have. They wouldn't have. "Please tell me they didn't give him a gun."

Yoni grinned. "Well, just one."

Jake groaned, dropping his head to his hands. He was going to kill all three of them when this was over. Assuming they didn't go and get themselves killed first.

"There it is," Mike yelled.

Jake looked up. The massive house was built into the side of the canyon and the brick was the same color as the canyon walls. Walls of windows added to the effect by reflecting the canyon walls. If you weren't looking for it, you'd probably never see it.

And they were storming towards it in bright daylight, without a clue what kind of security they were going against. Absolutely everything about this plan was suicidal.

Shoving those thoughts from his mind, he scanned the landscape. "Anybody see a place to land?" There was a helipad on the southeast corner of the roof, but it was already occupied with another chopper.

Jordan leaned forward from the back. "Southwest corner. The roof's flat there. We can take her down there."

Mike nodded. The helicopter shifted into a descent. A gust of wind blew hard against them.

Mike wrestled with the controls. "A little windy here."

The house was getting bigger. This thing was really was massive. Glass windows lined the wing they were racing towards. Anyone looking out would see them. But there was simply no other way to approach the place. At least not quickly.

Jake glared down at the building. He couldn't make out any people. Where was the security? How much security did they have? *God damn it.* He hated going into a place blind.

"To our left," Mike yelled.

Jake looked across him. He could just make out Danny hidden in a crevice, a hundred yards from the building. He would be invisible from the ground, but clearly visible from the air. "Yoni, tell him to stay put and contact the other team. When they get here, Danny's their priority."

Yoni nodded.

"That must have been where they went in," Jordan yelled, pointing to a door in the side of the building.

Jake nodded, a cold fear crawling over him.

"Hold on," Mike yelled as he cut back the power and increased the angle of descent. They hovered above the roof, fifteen feet, ten, and then the skids touched down with just a small bounce.

"Keep a lookout," Jake yelled as he leapt from the helicopter. Yoni and Jordan followed him as Mike shut the helo down. Wind pushed and pulled at them. They sprinted across the roof, heading for the side where Laney and Jen had entered.

Jake peered over the edge of the roof. There was a door two stories below them.

"Jake?"

Jake tapped his throat piece. "Danny? How'd you get in my ear?"

"Yoni gave me the channel. I'll guide you in. You're going in that door below you."

"Okay. Give us a second to get ready."

Yoni attached a rope to an air duct and flung it over the side. Jake stepped over and quickly lowered himself down. He took up a defensive position as Yoni and Jordan followed him down. Mike flew down the rope and landed next to him a few seconds later.

Yoni grunted. "Not bad for a fed."

"Everybody ready?" Jake asked. The three men nodded back at him.

He tapped his mic again. "Okay, Danny. Show us the way."

CHAPTER 90

Laney waited at the bottom of the stairs with Henry as Jen sprinted up them.

Jen paused at the top, inching the door open. Glancing back at them, she waved them up.

Laney turned to Henry. "Henry?"

"I'm good, Laney." And she realized he was. The bruises and cuts had all but disappeared. He was standing straight and his eyes were fully awake.

She nodded, even though she was shaken. Hopefully she'd get used to his abilities. "Let's go."

They jogged up the stairs, pausing next to Jen.

"They're coming," Henry said looking back down the stairs.

Jen pushed open the door and they spilled out into a den. They quickly made their way across the room to a hallway.

Laney recognized it. It was the one the old man had walked through. His office was at the end of it.

Laney grabbed Jen's arm. Jen looked down at her and nodded. "I know."

Gunfire erupted behind them. Henry pushed both women to the floor, covering them with his body. He grunted, his body shuddering. Laney realized he'd been hit. She and Jen rolled out from under him and returned fire, forcing the three guards back into the stairwell.

Ahead of them, the old man stepped into the hall, Hugo with him. Hugo opened fire and Laney dove down the hall, back into the den, Jen and Henry with her.

Jen returned fire with Hugo while Laney fired at the guard hidden on the basement steps.

Laney saw Henry stiffen as his gaze locked with Hugo. Henry got to his knees, a new wound in his shoulder. The bleeding, though, had already stopped.

The old man and Hugo disappeared around the corner. Henry stood. He nodded over at the giant entertainment center across the room. "Jen. Help me."

The two of them ran across the room while Laney kept the guards pinned in the stairwell. She stopped shooting only long enough to allow Henry and Jen to shove the giant entertainment center in front of the door to the basement.

Henry looked at Laney. She nodded, knowing she wouldn't be able to stop him and that she'd want the same in his situation. "Be careful."

He nodded and took off down the hall, a blur of motion.

Laney grabbed Jen's arm. "Go with Henry."

"What?" Jen asked.

"Stay with Henry. I'll be right behind you."

Laney knew Jen wanted to argue. She pushed her in the direction Henry had disappeared. "Go."

Jen disappeared after Henry. Laney sprinted down the hall after the two of them, feeling ridiculously slow.

CHAPTER 91

"Jake. He's-"

Jake's earpiece was full of static. "Yoni, can you make out anything from Danny?"

Yoni shook his head. "No. All I've got is static."

Jake ripped the earpiece from his ear. "The canyon must be interfering. Keep your eyes peeled."

Gunfire erupted from somewhere ahead of them. Jake sprinted forward. They spilled into the kitchen, their weapons trained for any movement. Five men were down. One had dragged himself to a sitting position. Blood spilled from his mouth down his chest.

"Guess our girls have been through," Yoni said, his eyes hard.

Jake just nodded, his stomach a knot.

"They went down there." Mike nodded towards a door across from them. They headed across the room. Three men burst out from the door. Jake opened fire, along with Mike and Jordan. The three men didn't even have a chance to get off a shot.

Yoni moved forward, kicking the men's weapons out of the way. Jake peeked down the stairs. It was quiet. He nodded at Mike who went down the stairs first. Jake covered him as the other two followed.

At the bottom of the stairs, they turned left and then took the first right. They came across eight more bodies. Halfway down the hall was the room where Henry had obviously been held. The scent of burnt skin lingered. A table just inside the door contained an array of sharp instruments, most of them with blood still on them.

"Bastards," Jordan muttered.

Jake moved them forward to the other stairwell. They walked up the stairs and tried to open the door. It was blocked.

"What the hell?"

More gunfire could be heard on the other side.

"Damn it." Jake yelled, sprinting back the way they'd come.

Yoni was right on his heels. "You got a plan?"

Jake didn't pause. "Yeah."

"Is it a good one?"

"No."

CHAPTER 92

Laney ran after Henry and Jen. They were quickly disappearing. She reached the end of another hallway and glanced to her left and right. Nothing. Not even a sound. "Come on guys, you could've at least left me a bread crumb."

Flipping a mental coin, she turned to her left. Gun extended in front of her, she silently made her way forward, glancing into each doorway as she passed. The place was empty.

In the third room, monitors filled the wall opposite the door, a control panel half the size of the room in front of it.

Where the hell was everybody? She cautiously moved forward glancing at the screens. A couple of cars were zooming down a road away from the building. Bodies littered the hallways and kitchen. In the top right monitor, she saw a group of at least ten guards.

She found the controls and after a minute of figuring out how they worked, zoomed in. Hugo stood out in the center of the group along with Sebastian. The phalanx of guards surrounded them. She scanned the rest of the screens. There were a few guards patrolling on their own.

On the top right, Henry and Jen sprinted towards a door. She couldn't tell how far behind Sebastian and Hugo they were. A note in the bottom right of the screen marked their location as E12.

Laney looked at the schematic of the building on the right side of the console. She'd chosen wrong. They were at the other end of the building.

She grabbed her Beretta off the console, turning towards the door. A movement in the bottom right screen caught her attention. A man was creeping along the hallway right outside the entertainment room she'd run through.

Her eyes narrowed. *Warren.*

He opened a door and disappeared. Quickly skimming the map, she found the door. It led to the basement. And the garage. Warren was trying to escape. "Oh no you don't."

CHAPTER 93

Laney traced the route from her location to Warren's and ran out of the room. Two minutes later, she was at the door Warren had disappeared through.

Laney walked quietly down the stairs, her Beretta held firmly in her hand. She hoped she wouldn't have to use it. Not because she wanted Warren to be unharmed. Quite the opposite. She wanted him to feel pain. But she also wanted him to spend a nice long life behind bars.

Mentally, she pulled up the floor plan of the basement. There was a small hallway and the door on the opposite the stairs opened to the garage. She reached the bottom of the stairs and peered around the corner. Through the crack in the door, she saw Warren struggling to get a motorcycle started.

Laney rolled her eyes. Warren on a motorcycle. She could probably just let him go and he'd accidently drive himself off a cliff.

"Why won't this start?" he muttered.

Laney crept towards the door, nudging it open with her gun. Warren had his back to her. He was jumping on the starter.

"Need some help there?" Laney asked.

Warren whirled around, reaching for the gun at his waist.

"Don't," Laney warned.

Warren's hand stilled.

She gestured with her gun. "Hands up."

Slowly, he raised his hands. "Laney. It doesn't have to be like this. I can make you rich. Really, really rich."

"You really are the dumbest man I have ever met. Do you honestly think money will erase everything you've done? All the lives you've ended?" Laney pictured the devastation at the Shuar village, the church, the Guardians' home, and Julian. She tightened her grip. She should just take him out. *It's the least he deserves for what he's done.*

Warren must have sensed his precarious situation. His hand dove for his gun, pulling it free from the holster.

Laney pulled the trigger.

Warren's left shoulder bloomed with blood. He dropped the gun. Collapsing to the floor, he screamed. "You shot me! You bitch, you shot me!"

"Of course I shot you, you asshole. You were going to shoot me."

Kicking his gun away, she reached down and pulled him to his feet by his good arm.

He screamed with agony. "But I'm the one who contacted you."

Laney stilled. "What?"

"The text message. I'm the one who sent it. I'm the one who led you here."

Laney stared at him. "Why?"

Warren just moaned. Laney shook him and he screeched. She gritted her teeth against the noise. "Oh for God's sake, grow a pair. Now answer me, why the hell did you send me that text?"

"I wanted you to catch them. To kill them."

"Who? Hugo?"

"Hugo, my grandfather, all of them."

Laney stared at him in disbelief. "You set your own grandfather up to be killed?"

"He never cared about me."

He sounded like a child. A spoiled little child.

"Oh shut up." She shoved him towards the door. "Let's go. There are some people you need to answer to."

He stumbled forward before dropping to the ground. "I can't. I've been shot."

Laney's temper was about to boil over. She crouched down until she was eye level with him. "Warren, I'm about done playing with you. You're going to walk your fat ass back up those stairs without complaint or I'm going to leave you here. Permanently." She stared into his eyes, until he looked away.

He gave a jerky nod.

"Now, move." He got to his feet and stumbled towards the door. Laney followed behind him, reconsidering her decision to let him live.

CHAPTER 94

Jake raced back up the stairs to the kitchen. Yoni and the twins sprinted after him. Jake crossed to the wall of windows looking out over the canyon, pulling his machine gun into his shoulder.

Yoni stepped up next to him, assuming the same position. "You're right. This is a lousy plan."

They opened fire, shattering the glass on the left-hand side of the room, nearest the wall. Jake ran over, grabbing a jacket from the back of one of the kitchen chairs as he passed.

Wiping away the glass from the bottom of the frame, he lay the jacket down. He leaned out, his M4 once again pulled into his shoulder. He pulled the trigger.

The windows in the next room shattered, sending glass flying. Jake ducked back in, but not before slivers of glass sliced into his forearms and cheek. A strong wind blew back in the room.

The twins had already replaced him at the window, their weapons looped across their shoulders. Mike stepped out onto the ledge. A gust of wind blew and he flattened himself against the building.

Blood seeped through his hand where Mike gripped the frame, still littered with broken glass. The gust stopped.

He made his way along the ledge, stepping through the shattered window on the other side. Jordan jumped up, nimbly walking along the ledge and jumping through the same window.

Yoni moved to the edge and peered out, but a strong gust forced him back. He looked up at Jake standing next to him. "I ever tell you how much I hate heights?"

Jake glanced down at him. The canyon floor was a sheer drop down at least four hundred feet. "You were a SEAL. You can't hate heights."

Yoni gripped the frame, pulling himself up. "I damn well can," he grumbled. "And right now, I really, really do."

Stepping out onto the ledge, another strong gust pulled at Yoni and one of his feet slipped. He let out a yell.

Jake reached out, yanking him back to the ledge. He stayed leaned across the ledge until Yoni was securely in the other window.

Taking a deep breath, Jake quickly moved across the ledge himself, not looking down. Wind tugged at him, trying to pull him off. He knew exactly what Yoni meant about heights.

He dropped into the other room, looking around. "Where are Mike and Jordan?"

Yoni shook his head. "Don't know. They were gone when I got here."

Gunfire sounded from up ahead. His earpiece crackled back to life

"- in trouble."

Jake pulled it to his ear, tapping the mic. "Say again, Danny. Who's in trouble?"

"Laney."

CHAPTER 95

Laney moved up the stairs, heading back to the main floor. Warren grumbled from in front of her. Part of her wondered what the hell she was bringing him along for. He was just going to slow her down. But she couldn't let him get away, not with all the damage he'd done.

At the top of the stairs, she cracked the door. The hallway was empty. She shoved Warren forward. He crashed onto his knees with a loud scream.

Her pulse raced, she whirled in a full circle, but his cry hadn't brought anyone. She needed to get to Jen and Henry.

With a look of disgust at Warren sniveling on the floor, she walked past him and opened the door across from her. Perfect.

She grabbed Warren by the bicep, pulling him up. "Come on, Warren."

"What are you doing?"

She shoved him forward into the closet.

He grabbed onto the doorframe. "You can't leave me here!"

Her eyes narrowed. She remembered him saying

the exact same thing the night of the attack on Nana's village. She slammed her gun into the hand nearest her. He howled with pain, pulling his broken fingers to his chest.

She slammed the door shut. Grabbing a nearby chair, she wedged it under the handle.

He kicked at the door, screaming for help. There was a chance someone would find him. But she was betting he hadn't ingratiated himself too well with his grandfather's staff. So she doubted anyone would be rushing to help him out, even if they found him.

Turning back down the hall, she re-traced her steps towards the control room, her steps cautious. She knew most of the guards were with Sebastian but she'd seen a couple of other ones. She wasn't sure where they were. Hopefully, they were leaving.

Ahead on her right was a large doorway, glass walls on either side. She glanced in. The room held a giant swimming pool with a glass roof. She'd seen it on the map. If Jen and Henry were still going in the same direction, they should be somewhere up ahead.

She glanced down the hall. Anyone would see her cut across. Her head jerked up as gunfire sounded from up ahead. She was going to have to risk being seen.

Taking a deep breath, she ran forward. Bullets shattered the glass walls surrounding the pool.

"Shit!" Laney dove for the ground, shards of glass raining down on her. Army-crawling forward until she was behind a large potted plant, she glanced around. A guard stood at the other side of the pool. She pulled her head back as he pulled the trigger, raking the pot with bullets.

Hands covering her head, Laney prayed the pot

held.

Gun blasts from her right tore through the air at the guard. Jordan and Mike stood there, firing at the gunman. She glanced back to where the gunman had stood. He wasn't standing any more. He was lying face down in the pool, quickly turning the water red.

Jordan ran over and pulled her up.

Laney pointed down the hall. "Jen. She's following Sebastian and Hugo. They're that way."

Jordan and Mike took off at a run without another word. Movement behind her made her pause. She dropped to a knee, lining up the man charging down the hall.

CHAPTER 96

Henry sprinted down the hall, Jen right behind him. Part of him reveled in finally being able to throw off the restraints he'd placed on himself his whole life. The other part was amazed that there was someone with him who shared the abilities.

Up ahead, he spied the stairs leading to the roof.

Six guards stood at the bottom of the stairs. They peppered the floor where Jen and Henry stood. Leaping back, they were pushed back behind the corner.

Henry nodded at Jen's weapon. "Anything left in there?"

She slid out the magazine. "Two rounds."

Henry looked back down the hall. He knew he could take out the guards, but not without getting shot. A lot. And he wasn't exactly sure how impenetrable he was. Or Jen, either.

A noise at the end of the hall drew his attention. Jen slammed the magazine back in, taking aim.

Jordan and Mike peeked their heads out. "Friendlies!" Mike yelled. "Don't shoot."

Jen smiled, her shoulders sagging with relief as her brothers came into view, jogging towards them. Henry moved to the side so the brothers could hug their sister.

"You okay?" Jordan asked Henry, his arm still around Jen.

Henry nodded, noting Jordan and Mike's eyes roaming his frame, looking for damages. Confusion crossed their faces for a moment when they couldn't find any. Mike looked up at Henry, the question in his eyes.

"I'll explain later," Henry said. "But right now we need a little help with those guards at the end of the hall."

Mike moved forward. "How many?

"Six."

Jordan moved next to Mike. "No problem."

With a nod, the brothers dove into the hallway, Mike going high, Jordan low. Jen tensed beside Henry, but it was over in seconds. Henry glanced down the hall. The guards all lay on the ground, still.

Henry turned to Jen. "Our turn."

Jen turned to her brothers. "Follow us."

Henry sprinted down the hall, Jen right behind him.

"They must be heading for the helipad," Henry yelled to Jen.

She nodded, her eyes focused ahead. Henry leaped up the stairs, throwing open the door to the roof. The helicopter was just taking off. He could see Hugo through the window. With a good jump, he should be able to reach it. He ran, about to leap, when Hugo dropped a grenade from the helicopter.

"No!" Jen yanked him from behind, shoving him behind an air conditioning unit. The grenade exploded on the other side, but the unit kept the blast from them.

Henry pushed himself up. The roof, miraculously

was scarred and burned, but held. It must have been fortified against a rockslide.

He glanced up. The helicopter was too far away now to reach. He clenched his fists. "Damn it!"

Jen grabbed his hand. "Henry."

He looked over, hearing the concern in her voice.

She gestured to the edge of the building. "Look."

Explosives were strung around the edge of the building. A small light blinked red.

Henry grabbed Jen, running for the stairs. The twins were just bursting through the doorway, onto the roof. Henry grabbed Jordan and turned him around.

Jen did the same for Mike. "We need to get out. The place is going to blow."

CHAPTER 97

"Don't you even think about shooting me," Jake growled as he charged down the hall toward Laney. She let her weapon fall to her side and stood with a smile.

Relief poured through Jake at the sight of her. He tried not to think how close he'd come to losing her. Again. He pulled Laney into his arms. "You're going to give me grey hairs."

She wrapped her arms around his waist, laying her head on his chest. "Don't blame me for those." Giving him a squeeze, she pulled away. "Jake, we have to help."

"We will. But are you okay?"

"I'm fine."

A yell caused Jake to glance over his shoulder. Yoni was pushing some young guy along the hall.

Yoni walked up to them, gesturing towards his prisoner with his weapon. "Found this guy in a closet."

Laney grimaced. "That's my intern Warren, the grandson of Sebastian Flourent. We need to get him out of here. Jen and Henry went after the others.

Jordan and Mike went after them."

Yoni wrapped his meaty hand around Warren's bicep. "Why don't I get rid of this for you?"

Warren tried to pull away. "No, no."

Laney rolled her eyes. "Quit teasing him, Yoni. The guy's annoying enough without that. He is, however, going to need some medical attention. Again."

"What happened to him?"

Laney shrugged. "I shot him."

Yoni grinned. "Good for you."

Jake just raised an eyebrow.

"He was going to shoot me."

Jake's eyes narrowed. The need to add some bruises to the man filled him. He took a step towards Warren.

Laney reached out a hand and placed it on his forearm. "I'm fine. He didn't even come close."

Yoni looked between the two of them. "Well, I'll take myself and the waste of sperm here back to the chopper. You two look like you have some making up to do. Jake, weren't you saying something in the chopper about killing Laney?"

Jake glowered at him. "Yoni . . ."

"Well, time to go." Yoni winked at Laney before hustling Warren back down the hall.

Laney turned to Jake. "Care to explain?"

He pulled her towards him. "Not really."

She smiled, leaning up. "Okay."

Their lips touched as Jordan's voice burst from Jake's earpiece. "Jake. The building's rigged with explosives. We need to go now!"

Laney jumped out of his arms like she'd been shot.

She paused for only a minute before sprinting away from him.

He ran after her. "Where are you going? We have a chopper on the roof."

She glanced over her shoulder at him, her eyes wide. "Danny."

CHAPTER 98

Laney sprinted down the long hallway, her mind filled with nightmarish images. *I never should have brought him. What the hell was I thinking?*

With each thought she dug deeper, willing her legs to move faster, wishing she had Henry and Jen's speed. In the kitchen, she vaulted over the bodies she and Jen had dropped without pause. She heard Jake racing behind her. He spoke into his headset, telling the group they were going for Danny and to take off without them. She'd thought about having the helicopter go for him, but if they didn't have a rope, it would take too long.

Ahead she saw the door she'd entered through. Without slowing, she barreled through it, into the bright sunlight. "Danny! Danny, run!"

She ran down the trail, vaulting up the rock to Danny's hiding place. She reached him just as he was climbing out, his face terrified. Grabbing his arm, she pulled him towards the ropes they'd climbed earlier.

She quickly attached him to the rope. "I'll take him," Jake said.

She nodded, quickly switching the rope over to Jake, thankful he'd had offered. Danny was shaking so hard, she wasn't sure he'd be able to rappel down quickly enough to get him out of range.

Jake pulled Danny onto his back.

Laney gestured down the cliff. "We pitched a second rope a hundred feet down."

Danny stared at her over Jake's shoulder. "What about you?"

"I'll be right behind you." She watched Jake expertly lower them down the rope.

Although Jake moved them down incredibly fast, she couldn't help urging him to move faster.

Finally, he reached the second anchor, dislodging himself and Danny. Laney quickly attached herself to the first rope, all but flying down. A rumble from above caused her to stop. Her eyes darted up. The rumble was followed by a series of quick explosions. She saw a helicopter fly off and she said a quick prayer that all her friends were safely on it.

She glanced down. Jake and Danny had made it to the ground. Jake was pushing Danny towards the trail, ordering him to run. But Jake was staying put. Waiting for her.

Laney reached the second anchor. Small rocks began to tumble over the cliff above. Crashes of glass and steel rang out through the canyon. The walls echoed the sounds back at her. Her hands were shaking so hard, she was having trouble attaching herself to the rope.

Finally, she snapped the carabiner in place. All but throwing herself down the rock, she still had time to look up. The rock wall above her was beginning to break apart, large rocks tumbling down its face. They were coming straight for her.

CHAPTER 99

Laney tried to move faster. The rope burned through her hands.

"Laney! Let go!" Jake yelled from below her.

She darted a glance at him twenty-five feet below. He stood there, unmoving, his gaze fixed on her. Rocks smashed to the ground around him. But he waited. For her.

She let go.

Gravity dragged her to earth. A scream escaped her lips. She slammed into Jake's chest, his arms pulling her to him. He rolled her towards the base of the cliff, into a crevice just large enough to hold the two of them. Rocks crashed to the ground behind Jake's back. Laney was crushed to his chest. She watched as the light quickly disappeared. The sound of the rocks piling up came through with thunderous crashes.

It seemed forever, but finally, everything went silent.

Laney's head was ringing and her back was jammed into the rock face. Her body was pushed as close to Jake as she could get. She wanted to look up into his face, but she couldn't move enough to do even that.

"Jake? Are you all right?"

His arms gave her a brief squeeze. "I'm okay. You?"

She gave a short laugh, followed by a few tears. "Oh sure. You know, this is just another Tuesday for me."

He rested his chin on top of her head. "That would be funny, if it weren't so close to the truth."

"I can't believe you stayed. You should have run."

Jake let out a sigh. "Don't you get it yet, Laney? You're it for me. Wherever, you go, I go. And if that means under a waterfall of rocks, then so be it."

Tears slipped their way down her cheeks and she leaned against him. "I love you, Jake."

She could hear the smile. "About damn time you realized it. I love you, too." He paused. "You know, if not for the life-threatening danger and the claustrophobia setting in, this would be a really romantic moment."

She let out a shaky laugh. "I think you and I need to take our romance where we can find it."

"Laney! Jake!" The yell came from outside the pile.

"We're here," Jake yelled back.

"Have you out in a bit," Henry yelled back. The sound of rocks being pulled away from the pile could be heard.

Jake squeezed her tight. "Ready for reality?"

She snuggled in closer. "Actually, I'm kind of good where I am."

CHAPTER 100

It had taken Henry and the rest of them an hour to extract Laney and Jake from beneath the rockslide. By then, the police and feds had shown up wanting to know what the hell was going on.

The local police had been about to drag them down to the police station, when some feds showed up, badged the local cops and sent them on their way. Laney wasn't sure what that had been all about but, honestly, she couldn't work up the energy to care right now. She'd worry about the feds tomorrow.

After a hot shower and change of clothes, Laney still felt like road kill. She pulled three plates out of the cabinet in the suite's kitchen. She gave a little grunt of pain as she placed them on the counter.

"You all right?" Jake pulled three beers from the fridge.

"Except for the bruises on my back, my front, down my legs and arms, I feel great."

Jake laughed, pulling her gently into his arms. "How about I run you a nice hot bath to work out some of those bruises?"

She wrapped her arms around his waist. "That

sounds perfect. And it would be even more perfect if I had some company in that bath." She leaned up to kiss him.

He grimaced as he leaned down.

She laughed. "Your neck?"

"Yeah."

She leaned into his chest. "Man, we're a mess."

He kissed her forehead before letting her go. "That we are."

Jake handed her a bottle of beer, beads of condensation ringing it.

Laney took a long, cool drink. Sighing, she leaned back against the cabinets. "Oh, that's good."

Jake tipped his bottle towards her. "To quiet times."

She clinked her bottle to his. "To quiet times."

The door to one of the bedrooms opened and Henry stepped out. He'd showered and changed, looking like his old self in jeans and an oxford shirt.

Jake opened the third bottle, holding it out to him. Henry crossed the room and joined them. Taking the bottle, he sat down on one of the island's stools.

"How's Danny?" Laney asked.

"Asleep."

"He worked non-stop since you were taken," Jake said.

"I hate that he went through that," Henry said.

"It all worked out in the end," Laney said. "And I think maybe it helped him grow a little. He stood up to me when I tried to make him stay behind."

"He did?"

Laney smiled. "I couldn't believe it, either. It was kind of nice to see."

Henry nodded, taking a drink, his eyes distracted.

Laney glanced over at Jake. They'd discussed how they were going to ask Henry about what had happened. They didn't want to push him, but if they were going to help him, they were going to have to get him to open up to them. They would just have to find a way to ease into it.

"Were you able to read the books?" Jake asked.

Laney glared at him. So much for easing in.

Henry's head jerked up. "How'd you know that's what they wanted?"

They'd decided on the way back from the canyon that they wouldn't keep Victoria's visit a secret. They didn't know if Victoria was planning on telling him. But they both agreed their loyalty was to Henry. They were going to tell him everything. Now that the moment had arrived, however, Laney couldn't think of a good way to start.

She took a deep breath, opting for Jake's directness. "Your mother told us."

Henry looked like he'd been slapped. "My mother? What are you talking about?"

"She came to see us after you were taken. She said she was worried, and she seemed to be."

Henry nodded, rolling his bottle in his hand. "I'm just, I'm surprised. No, shocked, actually. What did she tell you?"

"That the world thought she died twenty years ago. That she had to stay dead."

"I love my mother," Henry said simply. "I always have. But I don't understand why she does the things that she does." He looked at Jake. "I'm sorry I lied to you. But when she disappeared, I felt in many ways

418

like she had died."

Silence descended before Henry spoke again. "What does that have to do with my being taken?"

"She told us about your father. She explained where your abilities come from."

Henry looked up, a trace of fear on his face. "And?"

"You're a nephilim," Jake said.

Henry was quiet for moment. "What do you guys think about that?"

Jake shrugged. "Well, after Montana we were pretty sure something was up. We just didn't know what."

Henry let out a breath. "There's more. Sebastian and Hugo, they said …" He shook his head. "I don't know, maybe they were lying. They said my father…" His voice trailed off, leaving the sentence unfinished.

"…was Enoch." Laney said gently.

Henry looked up, shock on his face. "Enoch?"

Now it was Laney's turn to feel like she'd been hit. "You didn't know? Oh God, Henry. I'm so sorry. I thought—"

Henry took Laney's hand. "It's okay, Laney. No one told me. But I had some time to think with everything going on and he was one of the possibilities. Did my mother tell you that?"

"Yes," Jake said.

Henry sighed. "Since I was a kid, I've known I was different. The night my dad died, he warned my Mom not to let anyone know who I am."

Laney squeezed his hand. "He wanted to keep you safe. Apparently being a child of Enoch comes with some special abilities."

"But Enoch?" Henry said. "My Dad was just my Dad. And Enoch? He lived thousands of years ago. How's any of this possible?"

Laney debated how much to tell him. Henry probably wasn't up for a whole history lesson. "Apparently Enoch has lived many times. One of those times was as James Chandler."

Henry stilled, his eyes moving between Laney and Jake. "Enoch was a scribe."

Laney nodded. "And your father."

Henry's face went blank.

Jake grasped his shoulder. "Henry, you okay?"

Henry looked over at him, giving himself a shake. "Yeah, actually, I'm," he paused. "I think I'm good. I mean, if the choices are between being a Fallen or the offspring of a Fallen or the offspring of an actual angel, I'd say I made out pretty well."

Laney smiled. "Did you have any clue?"

"Since I was around twelve I knew about my abilities. But about my Dad?" He shook his head. "No, not really. The only thing that was different about him was how incredibly talented he was at languages. I guess now I know why."

Laney watched him, waiting for a stronger reaction. He seemed to be taking this all too well. But then again, he'd had a lifetime of knowing he was different. Maybe answers were what he needed, even if the answers were surreal.

Henry downed his beer and put it on the island. He stood. "Would you two mind keeping an eye on Danny? I think I'm going to take a little walk, maybe a drive."

Laney nodded. "Of course."

"You want some company?" Jake asked.

Henry shook his head. "No. I think . . . I think I need to just think some things through on my own."

Laney walked around the island and hugged Henry tight. "You know where we are if you need us.

Henry wrapped his arms around her. "I know."

Laney and Jake watched Henry walk out of the suite. Jake slipped his arms around Laney's waist.

She leaned back into him. "Do you think he'll be okay?"

"Actually, I think he'll be better than okay. Now he knows who he is. And he has people around him who know and care about him. I think he just needs a little time to sort through all of it, not to mention what happened over the last few days."

Laney nodded. "And when he's ready, we'll be here to help."

CHAPTER 101

Henry walked down the hall, his head aching but not with pain. With knowledge. How come she'd never told him? How come she didn't warn him?

He punched the button for the elevator. It arrived almost immediately. He stepped in, ignoring the obviously inebriated young couple next to him. At the casino floor, the couple stumbled out the doors, heading for the slot machines straight ahead.

Henry turned towards the back of the hotel. He walked out one of the back exits, away from the Strip. Darkness had fallen and Henry stepped into it. He liked the dark, liked feeling hidden. Since he'd started to grow at age twelve, he'd always felt conspicuous. At night, though, he could blend into the shadows. Go unnoticed.

Up ahead, a couple moved towards their car, holding hands. The man unlocked the door for the woman, a light kiss on her lips before she took her seat. Jen's face slipped into Henry's mind. He thought of finding her, telling her what he'd found out.

He shook his head, crossing the street. She'd just found out about herself. That was enough of a burden.

She didn't need any more on her shoulders.

Henry walked quickly, his long legs eating up the distance. He felt cast adrift, alone. Laney and Jake were there for him, but they weren't who he needed right now. He knew who he needed. Sometimes only one person would do.

He turned a corner, walking over to the fountain in front of a new condominium complex. It rose thirty feet in the air. Two winged angels about to take off into the air. He stopped next to it, feeling the spray in his face.

The son of an angel. And not just any angel, one of the favored angels. Was that really who he was?

His shoulders slumped. This walk wasn't helping. Walking wasn't going to ease the ache. Images from the last few days flashed through his mind. He pictured Hugo's knife plunging into his side, over and over again. He pictured the book they'd brought him. His father was the author. And he'd died to keep the Sons from using the stone as a weapon. His father seemed to have a habit of laying down his life for others.

Unsteady, he sat on the edge of the fountain. He'd always wanted answers to why he had abilities. But now that he had the answers, he wasn't sure he wanted them. His father was one of the most powerful angels. How did someone live up to that?

Pushing off of the fountain, he turned back to the hotel. He should be there if Danny woke. Re-tracing his steps, he walked back to the hotel, feeling weighed down. He was just so damn tired.

Henry reached the elevator bank and the doors popped open before he even hit the button. This time, he was alone. He hit the button for his floor and closed his eyes as it rose, letting out a breath. *Back to real life.*

The elevator dinged and he opened his eyes, stepping out of the doors. They slid closed behind him. Lost in his thoughts, it took him a moment to realize he was in the wrong place. He wasn't in the hallway leading to his suite. He was in the foyer of one of the penthouse apartments.

He shouldn't have been able to get in here without a key.

His heart gave a little leap. He walked quickly into the main living room, hope crashing through him.

She stood at the windows and turned at his entrance. The lights from the Strip reflected off her the white in her hair. She opened up her arms and he rushed over to her. He towered over her by almost two full feet, but it made no matter. He held her tight and her arms wrapped around his waist.

She rubbed his back. "It's all right, Henry. You're safe."

He let go of the fear, the terror, and let himself feel like a kid. "Mom."

CHAPTER 102

Two Days Later

Laney stood outside the warehouse in Vegas. The front windows had been boarded back up. The feds had left the day before. They'd been surprisingly understanding.

She supposed it was the goodwill they had created for the United States on the world stage. The recovery of an Ecuadorian national treasure was a political coup for the United States and the Chandler group had allowed the U.S. government to take credit for its recovery.

But the U.S. government was not being given control of the treasure. That honor belonged to someone else.

Laney stared down the road. "Where are they?"

Jake took her hand, leaning down to kiss the bridge of her nose. "They'll be here any minute. Just relax."

She leaned into him with a sigh. "I know. I'm just not good at waiting."

"So I've noticed," he mumbled.

She pulled away, playfully whacking his arm. "Are you suggesting I have flaws?"

He smiled down at her. "Would you like a list?"

She laughed.

Jake gestured down the road. "Here they come."

A black Hummer barreled down the road, raising a small sandstorm behind it. The driver slammed on the brakes, swinging the SUV to a stop only a few feet from them.

Laney waved her hand in front of her face to dispel the dust. "Whose idea was it to let Yoni drive?"

Jake moved forward to open the back door. "I'm pretty sure it was his." Before he reached it, the door swung open and a little pixie in brown pigtails and a bright pink dress burst out.

Laney opened her arms. Elena flew into them. "Laney!"

Laney hugged her tight, pulling her off the ground. "Oh, I have missed you."

Jen walked out of the warehouse behind the two of them. "Hey, any of those hugs for me?"

Elena squealed again and ran for Jen.

Laney's Uncle Patrick stepped out of the Hummer, his face pale.

Laney took his arm. "You okay?"

Patrick glared at Yoni as he leaped from the driver's seat. "I am never getting a car with that man again."

Laney tried not to smile. "Of course, Uncle."

Her uncle gave her a look, meaning she hadn't fooled him a bit with her words. He offered his hand to Nana, who stepped out of the SUV with the grace of a queen.

"It was like being on a roller coaster. Or at least, what I imagine a roller coaster would be like." She hugged Laney. "I knew you would find it."

Laney smiled. "I had a little help. I'm glad you're here."

Nana took Laney's hand. "We have some important decisions to make."

CHAPTER 103

Washington, D.C.

A week later, Laney was in a conference room, a floor down from the Smithsonian Museum of Natural History's Baird Auditorium. The violence in Ecuador had become worldwide news. Speculation and rumors were running rampant about what had been hidden in Ecuador. The Ecuadorian government had moved troops in to keep treasure seekers from running unchecked across Shuar land.

After much debate and back and forth, Nana had decided on a course of action with some help from Laney and the gang. The Chandler Group would build a repository for the Crespi Collection in the original location of the treasure. The Ecuadorian government would help with security, but the final call on all access would rest with the Shuar tribe.

Until the building was complete, though, the collection was to be housed at the Smithsonian, under constant guard. No one was admitted without permission from Nana. So far, no one had been granted permission, but Nana was beginning to consider allowing some scholars in to examine the finds.

Today, they were making the official announcement to the world press about the discovery. Nana would be there, but she didn't want to make the official announcement.

Laney had been shocked when Henry offered to do it. Henry had never been photographed, never let himself be seen by the press. But he knew his gravitas would add weight to the importance of the issue as well as highlight how secure the treasure was going to be. The Chandler Group's reputation would keep many would-be treasure thieves at bay.

But Laney knew Henry's offer was about more than that. What he'd been through at the hands of Flourent and Hugo had fundamentally changed him. Or maybe it was finding out who he really was that changed him. Probably both.

She watched him pour himself a cup of coffee across the room. There was an ease to him that had been missing before. Not having to hide who he was, having people around him who cared for him, and making it through that torture – somehow, combined, they seemed to have given him a new strength.

She glanced up as Jake walked in. Damn, he looked good. Charcoal grey suit, tailored to accentuate his broad shoulders with a pale blue shirt and navy tie, he made the banker look sexy. A brown leather messenger bag was slung over his shoulder.

Catching sight of her, Jake made his way over to her. He stopped in front of her, looking her over, from her alligator pumps to her fitted navy blue dress. He leaned forward to whisper in her ear. "Doc, you're going to make it impossible for anyone to focus on Henry's speech."

She smiled, looking up into his eyes. "You look good, too."

Patrick walked over to them. "Good to see you, Jake."

Laney took a step away, but Jake put his arm around her, pulling her into his side. He extended his hand to Patrick. "You, too, Patrick. Where are the Nuninks?"

"They should be here in a few minutes. Jen's with them. A few academics wanted to get Nana's impression of some of the exhibits. "

Jake nodded, giving Laney a squeeze before releasing her. "There's something I need everyone to see before they arrive."

He pulled a tablet out of his bag, setting it on the table. Henry walked over to join them. A video was already queued up. Jake hit play.

The screen showed the warehouse where the artifacts were stored. "When's this from?" Henry asked.

"Twenty minutes ago." Jake's tone was somber.

A feeling of dread settled in Laney's stomach. The door at the end of the warehouse flew open. A security guard sailed through it, crashing into a crate and lying still. There was a blur of motion and then a man was standing at the far side of the screen.

Laney couldn't tell much about him except that he had dark hair, mocha-colored skin, and he was in good shape. The man rifled through the open crates, before beginning to tear through the unopened ones.

His movements were incredibly fast. Her heart clenched. He was a Fallen. She glanced at Henry. Or maybe a nephilim.

Another blur entered the screen.

Startled, she looked at Jake. "There were two of them?"

Jake nodded. "They took out half the security force without raising an alarm. The other half of the force didn't realize anything was wrong until the intruders were gone."

"Are the men all right?" Henry asked.

"Yeah," Jake said. "They were all unconscious, a couple of broken ribs, bones. But all alive."

Thank God, Laney thought, her eyes still glued to the screen.

A dozen crates in, one of the thieves found what he was looking for. He pulled out a single folio. Tucking it into his side, he called to the other man and they sprinted from view.

Laney sat back, stunned. "They only took one. Why?"

Patrick leaned forward. "Jake, can you zoom in on the book?"

Jake shook his head. "No. I tried already. Picture's too blurred to make anything out. Nothing comes up. I sent it to Danny to see if he could clean up the image."

"Do we have any idea which book it was?" Henry asked.

Patrick frowned. "We can check the inventory, but I don't think it was complete. But if Danny cleans up the picture enough, maybe we can match it to one of the photographs taken at the site."

"There's something else." Jake rewound the recording, freezing it on the second intruder.

Laney stared at the face of the Fallen. The picture

was blurred, but clear enough that she could make out the strong cheekbones, the prominent chin. "He looks familiar."

"He should," Jake said. "That's Gerard Thompson, Sebastian Flourent's personal assistant."

Laney felt her jaw drop. She knew Gerard had worked for Flourent for years. His picture had been in the file they'd developed on Flourent. He'd bided his time, waiting until the library was uncovered. Just like Azazyel had done with Senator Kensington. And also like Azazyel, he was working in tandem with another superhuman.

While everyone was digesting that, Jake laid another shock before them. "And there's something else. The bodies of Sebastian Flourent and Hugo Barton were discovered in an airport parking lot in Copenhagen an hour ago."

"Any leads?" Henry asked.

"No. But they both died from broken necks. And all signs point to them being snapped by human hands."

Laney's eyes flew to Jake. "A broken neck?" She pictured Hugo's neck. It had been huge and incredibly muscular. "No human could snap Hugo's neck."

"No," Henry said quietly. "But a Fallen could."

Laney looked at the time stamp on the screen. "There's no way these two guys did that. There's a third Fallen."

"Which means we need to prepare," Jake said.

"Prepare?" Patrick asked. "For what?"

"We have a new enemy," Jake said.

Laney stared back at the screen. A chill swept through her. "More like three."

CHAPTER 104

Laney walked next to Henry down the long hall leading to the Baird Auditorium. They were at the back of the procession. Nana was first, with Jen and Patrick following behind. Jake and Elena were already seated in the auditorium.

The excited murmur of the reporters drifted down the hall towards them.

Laney placed her hand on Henry's arm. "Are you sure you want to do this?"

He looked down at her with a smile. "I've been hiding long enough, Laney. It's time to step out into the light."

"I'm proud to stand next to you."

He patted her hand. "I wouldn't have it any other way."

Together, they stepped through the curtain and walked up the three short steps to the stage. A stirring went through the crowd as they caught sight of Henry.

Laney squeezed his hand. The two of them took their spots next to the podium, Laney next to Henry, Jen next to Nana.

A dark-haired woman in her late fifties, wearing a

stylish grey pantsuit, stepped to the mic. Almost immediately, the noise in the room ceased. "Good afternoon. I am Dr. Cynthia Prodgett, Director of the National Museum of Natural History. I have the pleasure today of introducing a man who you all know, but still needs an introduction."

The crowd gave a small laugh, although Laney knew they weren't yet in on the joke. "Here today to speak on behalf of the Shuar tribe about their incredible heritage, Mr. Henry Chandler, CEO of the Chandler Group."

An audible gasp went through the audience. Cameras whirled, flashes blinded. Henry walked confidently to the podium, adjusting the mic to its tallest position, ignoring the stir his name had caused. He smiled.

"Ladies and gentlemen, I am here to speak to you about an extraordinary discovery." He glanced at Nana. "Which belongs to an incredibly brave group of people. . ."

CHAPTER 105

The press conference had gone well. Henry had spoken with confidence, emotion, and compassion. The media loved him. He answered questions for an hour before calling an end to it. Now he stood up by the stage, a group of reporters surrounding him.

Laney watched from the back of the room, leaning against a wall, next to Jake and Elena. "Am I crazy or does he seem to be enjoying this?"

Jake smiled. "I think he actually is. But I'm not so sure about Jen."

She looked at the press circle that had formed around Nana, and Jen. Jen looked like she was going to pounce on any reporter that got too close. Laney laughed. "I think Jen's more comfortable in the middle of a forest than a media frenzy."

As the words left her mouth, she watched Jen cut off all further comment, escorting Nana out the back door of the room.

Patrick walked up, nodding at Elena and Jake. "Mind if I steal my niece for a little walk?"

Jake picked up Elena. "There's some excellent cake back in the conference room. Want to try some?"

Elena grinned. "Yes, yes, yes."

Laney watched the two of them walk off. *Jake will be a good dad someday.* She stirred at the thought, but at the same time, felt contentment at it. Of course, there was no way she was going to mention that thought to him any time soon.

Laney turned to her uncle with a smile. "Where shall we go?"

"The National Gallery of Art is just down the street."

She linked arms with him. "Sounds perfect."

Escaping the zoo the National Museum of Natural History had turned into, they wandered along Constitution Avenue amidst the commuters and tourists. Traffic zipped by, but they managed to dodge across the busy thoroughfare to the National Gallery of Art. Together, they strolled along the perimeter of the building.

Laney was glad Patrick had suggested the walk. They hadn't had much time together since everything had happened, or even in the months before that. It was nice to spend some time, just the two of them. A light wind blew, gently sending the scent of his aftershave towards her. She smiled, comforted by the familiar scent.

Patrick reached over, covering his hand with hers. "Seems you've survived another adventure."

"So it seems," she agreed.

They walked on silently. Laney enjoyed the quiet, the warmth of the sun. She looked over at her uncle and realized he wasn't enjoying the peace quite as much as she was. The crinkle she knew so well had appeared between his eyes. "Uncle Patrick? What's the matter?"

He patted her hand and gestured towards a bench a few feet away. "Why don't we sit?"

Laney sat down and turned towards her uncle, waiting.

He stayed quiet for a few moments, watching the people go by, before turning towards her. Worry was stamped across his face. "Do you realize you have been in two life threatening scenarios in the last year?"

She grinned. "Well, they were rather memorable, so yes."

He gave a small laugh. "What I meant to say was, do you realize that both events seem to revolve around you? Two Atlantis-related sites were discovered on two different continents, after being hidden for thousands of years. And you're the one constant between them."

She shook her head. "That's not right. Henry, Jake, you, me, even Yoni were part of both."

He nodded, his voice patient. "Yes. But we never would have been involved in Ecuador if not for you. And Montana, you were the central fixture pulling all of us together. For some reason, these ancient sites are seeing the light of day and you seem to be the only factor in common between them."

Laney sat back in surprise. She'd never thought of it that way. In Montana, she'd been pulled in by Drew. But then she'd been the catalyst that helped find the stone. In Ecuador, with Jen's help, she'd found the library. And in both situations, she'd barely escaped death. But that had to be a coincidence, right?

Reading her face, her uncle answered her unasked question. "It can't be a coincidence. The past, for some reason, is coming to light. And you're smack-dab in the middle of it."

She took his hand. "Well, be that as it may, I'm fine. I'm here, unharmed."

He squeezed her hand, his eyes now somehow looking even more concerned. "Yes. So far you've been fine. I'm worried, though, about what comes next. Because whatever has started, I don't think it's over yet."

EPILOGUE

Victoria smiled watching the recording of the press conference from the study of her Vermont estate. Henry presented his argument rationally and without embellishment. The audience hung on his every word. Her son was an impressive man.

At the end of the conference, he stepped back. He glanced down at Laney. For a moment, they shared a smile. Victoria froze the screen. Her heart ached at the sight.

Pushing herself off the settee, she walked across the dark wood floors, before her feet sank into the deep Persian rug that covered most of the room. She pulled an old teak box from the third row of one of the bookcases built into the far wall.

Cradling the box to her chest, she walked back across the room. She paused at the large bay window, looking out at the rose garden beyond. A riot of yellow, peach, pink, red, and white petals looked back at her, all in full bloom. It always amazed her how they all seemed to bloom at the same time, coming together for a few weeks of glory.

She felt a heaviness in her chest, in spite of the magnificent sight. Other threads were coming together now as well. The libraries. The Council. The Belial treasures. And the three, Henry, Laney and Jake.

Turning from the window, she lowered herself to the settee, pulling the box into her lap. Gingerly, she opened the lid. Two baby pictures lay on top. She traced the outline of each little face before placing them aside. Gently placing two locks of hair tied with ribbon next to them, she rustled through the remaining papers. Towards the bottom, she found the old picture.

She placed the box on the side table and held the picture in her hand. Henry and Laney stared back at her, huge grins on their faces. Henry had been eight, Laney no more than three. But the affection between the two was undeniable, even through the old photo.

When she'd learned that Laney and Henry had been re-introduced, she was surprised Henry hadn't remembered. Victoria had arranged to run into Laney's family at a park. Laney and Henry had clicked right away. They'd spent hours playing together. It was undeniably one of Victoria's happiest memories.

She stared at Laney's face. Giant green eyes dominated her pale face, her red hair pulled back into two pigtails high on her head. The grin on her face was ear to ear, as she hugged Henry around the neck. She hadn't changed.

With shaking hands, Victoria placed everything back in the box. Except the picture. She propped it against the box.

Curling her feet under her, she stared through the window once again, but this time she only saw the past. She'd sacrificed so much and still more was demanded.

When would she have paid enough? When would she be freed?

She shook her head to clear the thoughts. Those thoughts wouldn't help now. She knew better than most that fate wouldn't be denied. And fate had pulled everyone and everything back together.

She'd seen the signs. She knew the time was drawing close. And now the Fallen had the book.

Her gaze fell on Laney. She'd hoped she would be spared. She'd done everything in her power to keep this burden from her. Once again, Victoria had come up short. She closed her eyes, feeling the pain of what was to come.

Now it was her time to step out of the shadows. Her eyes were drawn back to the picture that lay on top of the box. Her children were going to need her.

AUTHOR'S NOTE

Thank you for reading *The Belial Library*. I hope you enjoyed it. *The Belial Library* was a joy to write, and the follow-up, *The Belial Ring*, is just as much, if not more, fun. I'm hoping to have it out for early summer 2014. Now let me tell you a little bit about where the idea for *The Belial Library* originated.

Years ago, I heard about the tunnel system underneath Ecuador. It fascinated me. I pictured these long dark tunnels, ancient people walking through them, hiding in them, storing their treasures in them, and viewing them as pathways to the underworld.

Then one day, I saw a documentary about an Ecuadorian man who, when he was a teenager, found a cave only accessed through a river. In the cave, he saw incredible artifacts, sheets of gold engraved with symbols, and an alcove filled with metal books. Decades later, he was supposed to be part of an expedition to find the cave but he passed away before the expedition could happen.

That man's story stayed with me for close to ten years. When I started thinking about the follow up to *The Belial Stone*, I knew that the underwater cave had to be part of it. And reviewers expressed a strong interest in finding out more about Henry. Put them together, and *The Belial Library* was born.

You might also notice a few of the breadcrumbs dropped about future books in the series. Some of the future story lines have literally been in my mind for years, so I've been dropping little hints along the way. I hope they're making you curious. ☺

442

And even though I've been writing for years, I am still a new writer. As such, reviews are critical for providing me feedback about what readers like and don't and for helping other readers discover *The Belial Series*. Reviews are one of the biggest factors in determining whether or not a potential reader even glances at a book description.

So if you have the time, I would really appreciate if you could write a review for *The Belial Library*, good, bad, or somewhere in between. I read all reviews and hopefully, your review will help others decide if *The Belial Series* is right for them.

If you have any questions or would like to hear about upcoming publications, please contact me at rdbradywriter@gmail.com. I'd love to hear from you.

Thanks again for reading.

Take care,
R.D.

FACT OR FICTION?

Whenever I read a book like *The Belial Library*, I always wonder what's real and what's the product of the author's imagination. As was the case with *The Belial Stone*, the ideas for *The Belial Library* were drawn from a lot of different sources in the fields of history, religion, and archaeology. So here are some answers to what was real and what wasn't.

Edgar Cayce. All books in *The Belial Series* involve the work of Edgar Cayce. Cayce was a twentieth century psychic. He did both medical readings, where he diagnosed people's illnesses as well as past life readings. His medical readings had an 86 percent accuracy rating. Which always make me wonder, if he did such a good job with those readings, is it possible he did as good a job with his past life readings as well?

Only a small portion of Cayce's readings involved Atlantis. But the readings are completely fascinating. If you have some free time, pick up a book on him or watch one of the documentaries created about him. His abilities really make you think.

The Cave of Etsu Nantu. Is it real? Well, there is no clear answer on that. The words etsu and nantu are Shuar meaning the sun and the moon, respectively. But the name of the cave was dramatic license on my part. According to Edgar Cayce, the Atlanteans did send out three sets of knowledge across the globe to protect it. One set was supposed to have been hidden in South

America.

So is there an actual cave? According to a number of different sources, two teens did discover a cave like the one described in the book after swimming in a river in the early twentieth century. They said the cave could only be accessed from underwater. The cave held a metal library along with other artifacts from an advanced civilization. In the decades since the boys' discovery, no one has been able to find the cave. And both of the men have since passed away.

Father Carlo Crespi. Father Carlo Crespi was real, as was his collection. Google him. It's fascinating stuff. What is left of his collection is stored in the Bank of Ecuador. The collection was moved to the bank after a suspicious fire destroyed half of it at Father Carlo's church. The way in which Crespi collected his artifacts portrayed in this book is accurate: he was gifted with each of his treasures by the indigenous people he served.

The Crespi Collection. The descriptions of the Crespi collection from the bank vault are accurate descriptions of some of the artifacts from the vault (i.e., the metal sheets engraved with an unknown script, the statues, the depictions of dinosaurs and elephants, etc.)

The descriptions of the cave are taken in part from unexplained archaeological finds across the globe and from this author's imagination. For example, the Vimanas described I are real. In ancient Sanskrit text, there are descriptions of flying vehicles. The city grid with the monorail? That I made up, although there are some ancient cities that were laid out on a grid.

The Council and the Imiatores Belials. They are both fictional groups I created.

Cave Doors. The doors in the cave are real, in the sense that they are taken from the doors used Derinkuyu, an underground city in the Cappadocia region of Turkey. Although the ones in Turkey were used solely to keep invaders out.

Enoch. The stories of Enoch included in the novel, (i.e., that he was the great grandfather of Noah and that he became the scribe of God, Metatron) are true according to the Bible. Whether he has returned to earth multiple times after his ascension, well, Cayce said he did. And he was right about all those medical treatments . . .

Tunnels underneath South America. There is an extended tunnel system underneath Ecuador, spilling into Peru and Chile. The tunnels are allegedly the same ones that the Incans used to hide their gold from the Conquistadors. And people have over time tried to explore the caves . . . much to their detriment.

Crustal Displacement Theory. The idea of Antarctica actually being Atlantis is not a new idea. Dr. Charles Hapgood, the author of crustal displacement theory, did argue that large swaths of land could rapidly move from one location on the globe to another due to the movement of a liquid core one hundred miles underneath the earth's surface. And while his theory was scoffed at by a number of prominent scientists, one notable scientist of the time did agree with him: Albert Einstein.

Flood Myths. There are hundreds of global flood myths across the globe. The ones mentioned in the book (Noah, Manu, Gilgamesh) are also real and incredibly similar.

Science, however, largely disputes that there had ever been a worldwide flood. The closest science seems willing to go is ice dams. Research on ice dams, created at the end of the ice age, are theorized to be capable of creating catastrophic flooding. For more information, check Graham Hancock's Underworld: Flooded Kingdoms of the Ice Age.

The Tayos Cave and Neil Armstrong. The Tayos Cave is a real location, as are the tunnels attached to it. In 1976, Neil Armstrong was part of an expedition to Ecuador to find the metal library. They found some artifacts in the Tayos Cave, but never found the cave with the metal library. The leader of the expedition, Stan Hall, did plan later trips but for various reasons, they never materialized.

Nephilim. The Bible does speak about the offspring of angels and humans. These giants of men were allegedly incredibly powerful and usually immoral. And they were alleged to be the reason behind the global flood: to rid the world of their menace. But that never happened, right? ☺

ACKNOWLEDGEMENTS

Thanks to all those who helped make this book happen. First and foremost, thank you Tae. Thank you for all your support, time, and love. Thank you for letting me take the time I needed to complete this book. Thank you for always being in my corner and being unfailingly there when I needed you. You are my rock.

Special thanks to all those critters who read and re-read The Belial Library in its multiple iteration. In particular, thanks to Alan Chaput, Glenda, Ernie, Alex Sheridan, Mark Munroe, and Sarah Zama.

And most of all, thanks to Christine King-Raggio and Dana Griffin, my special critters and writing support squad. You are priceless.

Thanks to Syracuse Martial Arts Academy and the larger martial arts community for their indispensible help not just with this book but with life lessons. I am blessed to have found you.

Thanks to my editorial team. Thank you to Damon and Benjamin at Damonza.com for their cover design and formatting work. You guys are incredible. And thanks to my copy editor Evelyn Duffy.

Special thanks to Elizabeth McCartan for her editing help with the later editions. As well as the million of other little things she does to make my life and the rest of those lucky enough to be around her, better.

And finally, thanks to my little gang of three for their support, love, and hugs.

ABOUT THE AUTHOR

R.D. Brady has a Ph.D. in criminology and lives in upstate New York. When she's not writing, she can be found studying Jeet Kune Do, reading, or trying to find more hours in the day.

The Belial Library is the second book in *The Belial Series*. (Book 1 is *The Belial Stone*.) R.D. is currently working on the third book in the series, *The Belial Ring*.

For more information on R.D., her upcoming publications, or what she's currently reading, check out her blog: http://desperateforagoodbook.com

If you are interested in being notified about upcoming publications by R.D., you can sign up on her webpage (http://desperateforagoodbook.com) or send her an email and ask to be placed on her mailing list: rdbradywriter@gmail.com

33359746R00280

Made in the USA
Lexington, KY
22 June 2014